The Sons of Avrom

Roger Ikor

*Translated by Leonard M. Friedman
and Maxwell Singer*

G. P. Putna

c. 4

© 1958 ROGER IKOR

Second Impression

Originally published in France under the title
Les Eaux Mêlées

Library of Congress Catalog
Card Number: 57-6728

HR

The Sons of Avrom

Yankel and Moishe, sons of the
ultra-religious Russian Jew,
Avrom, strive to become truly
French in their new homeland.

Prologue

THE river flowed majestically toward the sea.

Abruptly the poplar trembled, then fell heavily. Now the Seine seemed somehow broader, grayer, untamed. Rudely exposed beyond where the tree had stood, the plain stretched, anonymous, industrial, between a river and a forest.

An instant later, a cracking of shattered branches, drowning out a muffled thud, came across the water. Baptiste could almost feel the earth quivering. He took his pipe from his mouth, tapped the bowl against his leather legging and swore softly.

Thieves, that's what they are! He had seen those poplars planted thirty years before. Magnificent specimens! Trunks . . . Of course, you have to be fair. Since the trees belong to the city of Paris and not to the commune of Virelay, the city has the right to cut them down, if it feels like it. But just the same . . .

Ever since the city had begun felling the poplars on the other bank, old man Saulnier had nursed an implacable anger. He had discovered a violent inner passion for beautiful landscapes and exploited it to accuse the city of the foulest plots. "It's a disgrace!" he would proclaim daily at Bertault's, the café-tobacconist on the Place de l'Église. "For the few sous they'll make out of it they're ruining the whole countryside! And besides, it's illegal!"

He would look about him, searching for support. Alas! With few exceptions, only the older inhabitants of Virelay-Bord-de-Seine frequented Bertault's. And all of them—the Brus, the Vacquaires, the Dénichés, the Maréchals—whose families, like Saulnier's, had lived here from time immemorial, never failed to applaud their leader. But what did he care for that dreary, zestless approval? He wanted an angry insurrection against the encroachments of the city of Paris— and these clods thought only of swilling their wine. Ah, they damned well deserved their fate.

If only he could have met with a single contradiction! But when an enemy, one of the Parisians from Virelay-Plateau, showed his nose in the café, it was only to buy cigarettes. At most, the enemy would say hello on entering and good-bye when leaving. Then Baptiste would hurl himself even more furiously into the battle against the Plateau. "Who do they think they are, anyhow? What makes them think they're so superior to us? Bourgeois, that's what they are!"

But recently, a third category of Virelaisiens had made its appearance at Bertault's. They didn't shrink from discussions! In fact, they even sought them out, but in a way which troubled Saulnier even more than it stimulated him, although he could not explain the reasons for his uneasiness. These newcomers weren't like the others; they left you with a strange, uneasy feeling.

Yes, all those people who had flooded in since the war, living in rough shanties of cardboard and corrugated iron, all those railroad workers, clerks, factory hands and day laborers, they were really the sweepings of the earth. They had names like Lopez, Verhaegen, Ben Saïd or Jindreziek more often than Dupont, Thevenot or Bouissounas; they came from God-knows-where, were . . . were foreigners, in short, but real ones, not like the Parisians on the Plateau who were also called foreigners. . . . Saulnier bogged down in the different meanings of the word foreigner; and all the more so since his own son-in-law was the son of a foreigner, and a Jew in the bargain, a man with a name long enough to lie down behind. In short, he began to realize that his old enemies of the Plateau were natives compared to these lice of the Avenue Général-de-Gaulle; and that was just too much!

In truth, the old Virelay was dead. Those poplars they were cutting down . . . Still, motionless on the bank, Baptiste heaved a sigh. They would plant others! Of course! In a few months, the gap would be lined with broomsticks topped with thin whisks. And in a few years, they'd have grown tall and full. But by then, he would be under the earth. So?

Baptiste was watching his own death, as well as Virelay's, there across the Seine.

He whistled for his dog and, drawing on his empty pipe, walked heavily down the deserted towpath.

The tree swayed, hesitated, then bowed and flopped gently on the bank. Yankel grimaced in pain. Tchch! What an ugly thing, that hole, right in the middle of all the beautiful foliage that borders the

Seine along its whole length! A queen, the Seine! Majestically, she advances toward the sea between a double file of noblemen, the lordly trees, which salute her as she passes. And now, suddenly, abruptly, death had brutally felled one of them, and confusion and ugliness reigned. Tchch!

And I, too, am going to die. After all, you must make room! Nobody needs me any longer on this earth. So it's just as well I leave, discreetly, without making any trouble. That's life!

And besides, at bottom, I've had enough of it. People are too brazen here. Where I come from, the young people were full of respect for their elders, never had an impolite word for them. But these French are so thoughtless, so noisy, so tumultuous! Real bundles of nerves! They drink too much. . . . Always under pressure, they jostle you, scream in your ears. No regard for anyone! Tchip! Tchip! You don't even have time to turn around! Afterward, of course, they excuse themselves—oh, very politely!—but the harm is done and already they've forgotten it. I don't hold it against them, they're the way they are and I, I'm the way I am. But all the same, I can't help brooding over it all. . . . I'm not happy.

No, I'm not happy. Take my grandchildren for example. What's wrong with them? Nothing, of course! It's just that they're so French! What distinguishes them from the others, eh? Nothing! Simon's son isn't even circumcised! So what can you do? Fernand, yes, Fernand had his sons circumcised. But it isn't really the same. Ah, I just don't know any more!

I'd prefer they didn't forget their origins completely. Oh, I know how life is, and I don't ask much of them! Just so they keep something of my native Russia. . . . If not, what becomes of *me?* Is my whole youth to be wiped out because it wasn't French? Pfeh! What a disgrace! You shouldn't blush because of your grandfather, my children. It's no sin to have been born in Rakwomir; a man is born where he's able.

. . . More than half a century I've been living in France! Fifty-four years, to be exact, fifty-four years in which I've never once left French soil. That's a long time, let me tell you! France is certainly my country now; I speak French almost without an accent. I ought to—I've given more of my flesh and blood to France than many a Frenchmen! I'll die without ever seeing my native Rakwomir again.

In those days, I wore earlocks and hung around in the streets, fighting with the Christian children, or rather, being beaten by them. On

9

the edge of the village was a huge menacing cross. We Jewish children would make a wide detour to avoid it; or else we saved ourselves by spitting over our shoulders. . . .

No, Yankel, you can't say it was a good life. It was good only because you were young. Your native land treated you like a foreigner, Yankel, like a pariah, Yankel! You hated that savage, backward country. You left it, fully conscious of what you were doing, and you chose France as your homeland, France the land of freedom, of human dignity. Do you dare pretend today that you're sorry, Yankel? You know that you're not, that if you had your life to live over you'd do the very same thing again. You know the people here are civilized; you know you love this country with all your heart . . .

This country in which, despite everything, you don't feel at home.

But where your children, your grandchildren, are at home. You, Yankel, who have learned through bitter experience that there is no greater misfortune than to be, and to feel, a foreigner, are you going to reproach your children and grandchildren for being so completely French? You should be filled with joy! . . .

Go, they're lucky, those who are born of my loins. They have a fatherland, a true, good one. How happy they should be! I only ask one thing of them—that they keep at least something of me and mine alive in themselves, that they shouldn't become Catholics.

Aie! Aie! What am I saying! Of course, they'll convert, or their children will, and that will create more anti-Semites. The only hope of preventing that would be for them to remain Jews, to marry French Jews, so that the religion would hold them. . . .

Religion? Ho! Ho! Yankel Mykhanowitzki, what have you just said? Are you defending religion now?

Tchch! When a man's young, he's foolish. Today I understand things better. God and religion are deep questions and worth thinking about.

In *cheder,* the rabbi taught us that God created the world in six days, and that He rested on the seventh; that the world is flat, encircled by Leviathan and held up by two crossbeams. That's stupid! . . . I remember one day, I asked the rabbi what was holding up the two crossbeams. He answered by unbuckling his belt and thrashing me in front of all my classmates. Because you mustn't ask questions, you must believe like an animal; that's what all the religions say.

Well, as for me, I like to ask questions, to learn. When I meet a learned man I always ask questions; and I've never met a truly learned man who refused to answer. Afterwards, of course, I made up my mind for myself. . . . The day I learned the world was round, not flat, I also learned that the religions are lying.

All the same, maybe the Jewish religion lies a little bit less? Let's be reasonable about it; how can any intelligent, educated man believe that the Messiah has come already, when there's still so much misery in the world? So?

And then our religion is pure, more disinterested. The priests get paid for everything, for a Mass, even for a funeral; if you're rich, you're entitled to a fine burial. A rabbi would never dare to behave like that.

A rabbi—but, after all, what's a rabbi? The French Jews think of nothing but aping the Catholics. They dress their rabbis up like priests. But back home, we knew what religion was, and the *reb* kept his place; he didn't mix in family *simchas,* like a busybody. That wasn't his business, but the father's. Or else when, for instance, you wanted to hold a really beautiful circumcision or a fine Yom Kippur for the family, you looked for a *kohen,* a descendant of Aaron, and you asked him to bless the people, you offered him a gift for the first-born son. . . .

What was I thinking about, before? I've forgotten. My mind is tired . . . Oh, yes; God.

Is there really a God? Oh, not the God of the religions! If one eats pork or not, or fasts on Fridays, or covers or uncovers in a house of worship, or kisses the *mezuzah* on the doorframe, or rings the bells in church—if God exists, what do these superstitions mean to Him?

But God? God? Someone had to create the world, no? It was a Frenchman who said: "I can't believe in the existence of the clock without believing in the clock-maker." That's deep, that is! Intelligent!

All the great men have said that God exists, and that He is good. Who else ordained: "Love one another"; and: "Turn the other cheek"? The Jew, Yoshke, no? The one they call Jesus. . . . As for me, I'm a liberal man; I have no hatred for Christianity—when it's pure. And that was truly God's word! And what have they done with their religion? Pogroms and Hitlers! Human wickedness is infinite. . . .

But why, why are men so evil? Why are they so determined to make life horrible when it could be so good?

If I love the Jews, it's not because I'm one of them. No! I haven't such a narrow mind. But I know our Jews well. Basically they aren't evil, and that's why I love them. We have our thieves, our swindlers, and all sorts of blackguards; men are all the same, no? But no murderers! A Jew is too kind to kill, even animals; have you ever seen Jews who go hunting? No, eh? So? The Jew knows the price of suffering, and he knows there's no payment for it. Suffering once endured is endured forever. Irreparable! Then what do you want from' us? Why do you make martyrs of us? We, the gentlest men alive!

His hands in his pockets, Baptiste walked along the abandoned towpath, sucking on his empty pipe. Ploum dashed about madly before him, tail held high.

"It'll be the same way with my Snow Queen. They won't give a damn for it; they'll cut it up for firewood the moment I'm gone! . . ."

Sixty years! His rose tree was sixty years old, but Baptiste still remembered its beginnings. One March day, when he was a little boy, he had found a wild eglantine growing all by itself. Instead of pulling it out, he amused himself by grafting a Snow Queen, a very fashionable rose then, to it. Springtime grafts, as everyone knows, take quickly (when they take!) but are weak. Lest he be laughed at, Baptiste had told no one of his attempt. The plant had been stunted and sickly for a long time; then it began to grow extraordinarily. Now it was a real tree, as tall as an apple tree, and to complete the resemblance, Baptiste kept it pruned round. A visitor would cry out: "What's that? A rose tree? There's no such thing!" And Baptiste would draw himself up proudly and feel that he had created a work of art.

The old truck gardener came to a stop. Halfway up the bluff, a rectangle of raw earth had been laid bare, and a number of masons were nonchalantly plying their trade. "Another house going up," he said to himself. A little farther on, the house begun in the spring was already almost completed. . . . He shook his head, torn between pride and discontent. Certainly, Virelay was becoming important. But it wasn't home any more. Every ten yards you hit your nose against some Parisian's bungalow or shack; those buggers weren't even satisfied with the Plateau any more! Once upon a time—ah, once upon a time . . .

There had been freedom in the air, once upon a time. The lilacs . . . No, that was before the lilacs. When Baptiste had been a boy, the bluff had been the kingdom of the vine. And what marvelous wine you could make!

On the bluff, the vines. Down below, the figs, peaches, and apricots, lovingly tended. Upstream a few meadows for the livestock. And on the Plateau, the fields; real farming, sound farming: wheat, oats, and also, as a luxury, a few fields of asparagus—the Parisians would pay plenty for asparagus. It was the same with cherries, they were crazy about them; they would come back again and again for choice Montmorency cherries in season. . . . The cherry trees did well, up above, at the edge of the Plateau and the bluff. . . . And there it was, old Virelay, a well-balanced village firmly rooted in its soil!

And then came the phylloxera. Baptiste had been only a youngster at the time, but he still remembered it. Overnight the winegrowers were ruined. Most of them had emigrated to Paris, became policemen or factory hands, were lost in the great world. The population of Virelay was cut in half. Those who owned land on the Plateau had borne the blow somewhat better by converting to truck gardening, which paid well. Only . . . How many things had to be sacrificed! For lack of time, for lack of labor, they had abandoned the marginal farms and given up the less profitable crops. The figs and the apricots had almost disappeared; the cherries, left to themselves, had been invaded by the hardier plums and choked out, and the plum trees themselves produced little or nothing. Many of the peasants had been forced to go into debt, and to mortgage their homes. . . . Indeed, it was as if everything happened to facilitate the invasion of that other phylloxera, the Parisians. Oh, they would have come in any case! But the vacuum helped to bring them in. The wastelands? The Parisians bought them. The mortgages? They were ready with their cash. Truck gardening? They had you under their thumbs since they were your only customers. And when Cyprien Bru, Emile's father, had found that lilacs flourished on the bluff and that flower growing was a good business, he had put another shackle on the village—for who bought flowers? The Parisians, always the Parisians! Everyone had planted lilacs on the bluff; they required no care and spread like grass.

But Paris seemed so far away! From the hills above the Plateau, high up, you could dimly make out the silhouette of the brand-new Eiffel Tower on the horizon. Only a fool could have imagined that Virelay's death was being prepared down there. No, we complained about being so far from the city, and about the poor train service.

13

. . . Now, at rush hours, there was a train every fifteen minutes. In the morning you watched a bleary-eyed crowd rush off; in the evening, you saw them come back, exhausted, hurrying home to their stinking shacks. . . .

Baptiste sighed. Oh, those had been the old old days! Like the day when . . . He knotted his brows. The old memories were coming back too often, these last few months! That was a bad sign, it smelled of the coffin!

"Papa, you don't know how to be happy!"

How often my daughter-in-law Jacqueline hurls that reproach in my face. . . . I know, I know, she loves me. But she's French, no? She has a certain contempt for me. And not only because I'm old. . . . What can you do, she can't understand! In this life you have to know how to dream, and the French don't like dreaming.

Shouldn't I be happy? At least, as happy as a widower of seventy-six can be. . . . No illness, no infirmity; I trot along like a young man. No more worries; done with capmaking and the bills falling due!

Tchch! Just the same, it's not nice! I do what old men do in a household, I perform little services, oil the hinges, repair electric plugs or the sewing machine. . . . But you'd think it hurt them to see me working! "Go, Papa, leave it alone!" Jacqueline screams at me. "Go take a walk, the weather's fine." She throws me out! Oh, I'm not in my own house!

I never should have left the Rue des Francs-Bourgeois after my poor Hannah died. I never should have given in to the young people. . . . I know capmaking isn't much of a profession. But that's my business, no? Simon never understood. Simon's like my father, old Avrom. A tradesman right to the bone . . .

. . . Yankel, Yankel, what are you talking about? It's not nice. Your children are good children, after all. Simon has his faults—who hasn't?—but look what he does for you! He takes care of you, clothes you, houses you, and takes you on vacations to the seashore! Everything you want, you get! You want a workbench to play at making caps? You get it right away! You want a book—Tolstoy, Zola, Victor Hugo? Right away, here's the book!

. . . Remember how gently Simon insisted on taking you to his home, his fine house, after your poor Hannah died. What advantage was it to him? None! He wanted to do the right thing, that's all. So what does it matter if his words were clumsy? "At your age, Papa, you shouldn't live alone. Especially in this dark hole, when we have such a fine house in the country. Besides, what will people think of us?"

When I left our apartment for the last time, I had a strange feeling. I said to myself: "So that's it now? Life is over?" And then I realized that Hannah was dead. Strange, isn't it? Up to then, all I could think was that she was freed of her cancer, that she was finished with suffering.

Life is hard! We were just beginning to breathe again, we had just gotten rid of Hitler, that vampire, may he burn in his blood, even if he's already burned! And then the cancer! . . . Poor Jews we are, but then what does everybody want from us? Dirty Jew! says one. Kill the Jews! says another. They steal from us, beat us, massacre us, make martyrs of us! Just like their God, whom they call on while they inflict abominable tortures on a poor defenseless old woman who never hurt anyone. . . . Tchch! The world is badly made, and God, if he exists, is very wicked. . . .

Well, let's get on, let's take our walk, a little old man who takes a walk every day.

Baptiste, scaling the bluff by the winding footpath, paused a moment to draw breath, and looked back over the countryside. Not far from him, somewhere in the lilacs, Ploum was sniffing, scratching, and growling. Across the Seine, to the west, the endless fields of cabbages and beans gave way to meadows where cows and horses were grazing.

"By God, it's still a beautiful country!" Baptiste growled peevishly. He turned away immediately, shamefaced; he had spoken aloud. Fortunately, there was no one there. He resumed his climb.

On the road above, Yankel was trotting along, halting every ten steps to meditate. The sun was gently warming, and the countryside bared itself to his caress. The old man hadn't yet noticed that, for the last ten minutes, he had been happy.

Finally this abnormal state irked him. He drew his watch from its pocket. There! His face brightened; now he had an excuse for an inner twinge of conscience. He was late! Hadn't he promised himself to be at the cemetery early? Hadn't he failed to keep that promise? Hadn't he hatefully enjoyed life while the poor child lay all alone down below, forgotten? Wasn't it a shame that a grandfather could so neglect his dead grandson, his own flesh and blood? Tchch! Man is selfish, human indifference is unending and the world is evil. . . .

The old man hurried, although he had plenty of time and nothing that had to be done.

The cemetery lay at the top of the bluff; great gusts from the west swept it unceasingly. Happy dead! Yankel thought. He knew very well that bones are neither happy nor unhappy. But, remembering that it was "diotic," that religions are born of this sort of superstition, he couldn't help feeling glad that his body would rest here, after his death; as if you were less choked down below when there was clear air above. He was happy that Simon had bought his parents a plot in such a beautiful place, not far from his own family plot.

Tombs in the shape of chapels, broken columns, ogival steles, trifoliate or clasped together, wrought-iron grilles scaly with rust, flattened graves with cracked slabs, green granite, marble yellow with lichen; clematis, viburnum, brambles, wandering vines among the shapeless debris, heaving the stones, twining them together . . . *To my dearest wife, eternal regret* . . . Yankel liked this oldest part of the cemetery with its sentimental symbols, artificial flowers, cherubs, opened books, portraits; he felt that the dead deserved respect.

Marble or imitation marble: white, black, gray, polished, glazed like a mirror, with sharp crests, pretentiously severe curves that ended, strangely, in cornices, Ionic capitals, stylized volutes, names and dates clearly incised. *Regrets. Requiescat.* This was a brevity and bareness which horrified Yankel. "Pfeh! They think they're being modern. . . ." This was the new cemetery.

Suddenly the old man noticed the shadow of a cross seeming to bar the way to him.

"Tchch! That's idiotic!" He forced himself to go past it as if there was nothing there.

But he didn't dare to lift his eyes. All those crosses on all those stones—how they were watching him! "What is this Jew doing here?" they were saying. And Yankel bent his back. A beautiful cemetery, yes. But not for Jews. For Christians, for *Aryans.*

Hitler had taught him that word, and the lesson had not been lost on him. Once—men are all the same, no?—he had perceived nothing but superficial differences between Jews and goys, differences of religion, tradition, and manners; differences even less obvious than those between nations. Thus, the French Jews seemed infinitely closer to French goys than to himself, a Russian Jew. As for the insane custom the Christians had of persecuting Jews, and the Jews of submitting to the Christians' persecutions, that seemed to be expressing nothing but the relationship between the majority and the minority in the population; were the relationship reversed, perhaps the persecution would have changed its direction. In any case, if being persecuted bothered you, you had a perfect right to escape it: a simple conversion to Christianity and the turn was taken, you passed into the other category. Finally, you didn't die in a collective massacre, but through individual choice, because you had freely decided to remain a Jew, thus shutting that door on life that the butchers had left open to you; you died for your faith in man, as a man, and with dignity.

Then along came Hitler, may he wallow in his own blood, that bloodsucker! After all, it wasn't so much the massive dimensions of the massacre which had impressed the old capmaker. Jews had been massacred throughout their history. They were used to it! Hadn't Yankel himself fled from Russia because of the pogroms? Like a hunted beast which sleeps with one eye open, he had hardly had to arouse himself, even after forty years of peace.

Only, this time the persecution had been different. No more choice: the door to the outside is closed. Are you born "non-Aryan"? That's a fact, your destiny is decided, and nothing can ever alter that fact; your death is robbed of all human meaning. You don't die for what you believe, but for what you are, and what you can't help being. In the eyes of the law, you no longer belong to humanity; the law has extracted your soul, and has ranked you with the animals. Argue about whether you wish to go under the knife; a chicken also argues. Revolt, submission, courage, cowardice: words stripped of all meaning to a chicken. Nothing can force respect for your person on your butchers, since you are nothing but a chicken, and a chicken *insists*, as they say, on being roasted on a spit. . . .

The tomb in which Jean-Claude Mykhanowitzki reposed was a sumptuous polished black granite monument in the most modern style; Simon hadn't cared about cost. Yankel knotted his brows; before him stood a man in coarse clothes, his cap pulled down almost to his ears, his legs spread wide, his hands jammed down into his pockets; at his feet a dog was seated. He should have tied him up outside! Yankel thought.

He hesitated to draw near. But, after all, wasn't Jean-Claude as

17

much his as the other's? Abruptly, the man started and turned; in a lightning flash, Yankel noticed a cross-grained, wrinkled face that he hardly recognized; but Baptiste was already greeting him.

"Well, it's old Papa Mica! It's a long time since we saw each other, eh, Grandpa? How's everything going?"

Baptiste held out his hand, and Yankel placed his own in it warily. He was shocked. The dog, the man's gross joviality, that unspeakable cap which Baptiste had barely touched with his finger, the apellations "Papa" and "Grandpa," all these seemed vulgar and indecent to him. And why did the French insist on substituting "Mica" for "Mykhanowitzki?" A name is a name, truth is truth; and a cemetery is a cemetery, where you don't joke in the presence of the dead, and dogs . . .

"Beautiful weather, eh?" Baptiste began, to get the conversation under way.

On the stone in large gold letters was the legend: *Mykhanowitzki-Saulnier.*

"Oh, yes, Monsieur Saulnier!" Yankel agreed.

The dog began to leap about wildly.

"Down, Ploum!" Baptiste growled.

Ploum flattened and wagged his tail imploringly. Why didn't M. Saulnier realize that he should have left Ploum outside? Just because there's no watchman, it doesn't mean that you can take dogs into the cemetery. A dog is a dog; the poor beasts don't understand, they sniff everywhere, relieve themselves on the graves.

He stood there, his arms dangling, nodding his head slightly, pondering how he could make M. Saulnier realize the indecency of a dog's presence in this place without offending him.

Baptiste eyed the little stunted man who stood beside him; then, with an imperceptible shrug, he turned back to the grave. Let him stay where he is! he thought. Simon, well he'll pass. Although I wonder what Jacqueline could have seen in him. But the old man! . . . He was furious. He had wanted to be alone with his memories of Jean-Claude. He had adored his grandson, although he had concealed it carefully; and when the Boches . . .

"Have to take care of the grave!" he growled haughtily. "What you don't do yourself never gets done!"

He crouched, gathered some formless lumps—pieces of glass, or shards of pottery—from the floral border and threw them, raging, on another grave. Then he rose and rubbed his hands together, to

18

brush the dirt off. Behind him Ploum, curled in a ball, was frantically searching for a flea at the root of his tail. Yankel cast a furtive look at the dog and then at the big stout man who was a head taller than he—and who still kept his cap screwed down on his head. Is he going to leave? he wondered. It's my turn to meditate before the poor martyr, no?

But Baptiste seemed not at all disposed to yield his place; and Yankel began to realize that he was deliberately staying there. For no reason except to annoy him, Yankel, the Jewish grandfather! Did he think he had a right of precedence because he was an Aryan? "Jean-Claude is as much my grandson as his," Yankel repeated to himself. "Even more, since it's through the male line! He's a Mykhanowitzki, no?"

Out of the corner of his eye, he continued to watch his neighbor suspiciously. What was the man thinking of? His grandson? Pfeh! What sensitivity could exist in such a *zhlub*? (Yankel expressed the word for "boor" in Yiddish to load it with more scorn.) What had Simon ever found so remarkable in that Jacqueline Saulnier? The finest matches had been proposed to him, the prettiest girls, I tell you, and some with fine dowries; all the *shadchans* of the Rue des Rosiers had been busy with it. No use! He had wanted this one, and no other, even though she was neither beautiful nor rich nor Jewish. . . . Or maybe just because she wasn't Jewish? Simon acts a little bit like an anti-Semite. . . . Well, who can tell human nature? Everything considered, the marriage turned out well, no? So then what are you complaining about, Yankel?

Baptiste's fist reached into his pocket and reappeared gripping a pipe, carried it to his mouth, fixed it there. . . . A wet sound; Baptiste was sucking on his empty pipe and Yankel sensed that his neighbor was about to load it. Oh, no! he thought, revolted. He brings his dog to the grave, he keeps his hat screwed on his head, and now is he going to smoke? No, no!

But how to make the man understand that he should conduct himself properly before the dead, and even that he should go away now, since he had accomplished his mission: to throw away the bits of glass lying in the floral border? Slowly, ostentatiously, Yankel took off his little black hat and held it with both hands against his belly. He would show this boor that he was entering into meditation and so recall him to decency.

He watched to see the result out of the corner of his eye . . .
None: Baptiste remained like a stone.

Tired of the conflict, Yankel tried to forget his neighbor, to commune with himself, and to begin his familiar dialogue with the poor child. But the presence beside him oppressed him.

"He was a hero, you know, M'sieu Saulnier!"

He expected a duet of alternate praises to the glory of the deceased; the only real method of celebrating funeral rites religiously.

The tombstone bore an inscription engraved on a marble plaque:

HERE RESTS JEAN-CLAUDE MYKHANOWITZKI,
MARTYR OF LIBERTY AND HIS NATIVE LAND.
Born May 21, 1926,
Shot by the German Barbarians
At the age of eighteen, June 4, 1944.
WE SHALL NEVER FORGET HIS SUPREME SACRIFICE!

Simon had written the text, and Yankel, for once in agreement with his son, thought it extremely beautiful and yet pathetic.

Beneath the inscription a bronze palm leaf had been affixed; Jean-Claude had been decorated posthumously and the Mayor, M. Touquet, himself had presided at the moving ceremony.

Baptiste slowly turned his head toward his neighbor and lowered his eyes to him. A sudden hatred flared through his whole being; he wanted to smash this foreigner who didn't even know enough to keep quiet, who was mouthing fine phrases in his filthy accent, while the poor boy lay there beneath them. A hero! I don't give a God-damn for your heroes. . . .

"Oh, yes, a hero!" Baptiste grinned mechanically. "Look how well off he is now, the hero! If it had been left to me, I'd have locked the hero up in a closet to keep him quiet, and he'd be here now!"

Stopped in his tracks, Yankel, tears in his eyes, babbled some meaningless words; it wasn't nice to talk like that, the German barbarians.
. . . Baptiste leaned toward him sneeringly:

"Tell me, Papa Mica . . . You think everything that's going on today is so fine? This atomic bomb business, and the collabos coming back out of their holes? You think it was worth the boy's life?"

He nodded violently toward the grave. Then he straightened up and pulled himself together.

"Well . . . we can't bring the dead back, eh? When you're dead, it's forever! . . . Down, Ploum!" he roared, although the dog hadn't moved.

On whom should he vent this anger that was choking him? Yankel was eying him fearfully.

"You've taken off your hat?" Baptiste mocked gutturally. "I thought your religion forbids it?"

Shivering, Yankel drew himself up, and with all the dignity he could summon, undertook to explain to M. Saulnier that he was a freethinker, freed of all religious prejudices, as M. Saulnier knew very well. At the same time, he tried to make him feel that it was he, M. Saulnier, who was at fault for having kept his cap on his head, and not he, Yankel Mykhanowitzki, for having taken his own off. But since he didn't want to hurt M. Saulnier any more, his allusions bogged down in verbiage. Baptiste, his wrath evaporated, wanted to laugh, the old man seemed so comical, fighting his way out of his sentences, making his accusations, swearing that his conscience was clear. Poor old Mica! he thought. It isn't his fault that he's like that! He worshiped his Jean-Claude. . . .

Baptiste Saulnier never realized that he himself had piled up seventy-one years. He thought of himself as a mature man (and sometimes he even felt a little itch below his belly). He treated Jacqueline as a little girl, Simon as a young man, and Papa Mica as a grandfather.

"Come, come, Papa Mica, don't get upset, I was only joking. Keep your hat on, don't keep it on, we're in a free country, aren't we? Only I . . ." He hesitated, and struck the flat of his hand violently against the stone. "I don't like these gestures. Jean-Claude is dead, and that's finished, finished, finished!"

He still had many things to say, but they stuck in his throat. He made a sweeping gesture with his arm.

Shocked by this overly familiar outburst, and at the same time moved by some inner agreement, Yankel searched desperately for something to say. But he had not yet found words for a reply, when Baptiste started to speak again, in a strangely hesitant manner.

"But . . . tell me . . . haven't you noticed, down there . . . ?"

Down there? What was the matter now? These sudden changes of mood tortured Yankel. He liked long discussions, honestly, laboriously, weightily nursed to a conclusion. You chose an interesting question, then you reflected, you supported the pro or the con, you

21

debated like men, not hysterically, like women! But these Frenchmen never stopped moving, hooked onto one idea, dropped it for
another. You saw them here, and immediately, *tchip, tchip,* they
were somewhere else! Superficial minds, there was no way to con-
verse seriously with them.

With his eye, he had followed Baptiste's gesture and felt a pang
seize his heart. Leaning against one of the angles of the stone, half-
hidden behind the flowers, was a little cross. A cross! Yankel opened
his mouth, but Baptiste forestalled him apologetically:

"It's my sister Eugénie. The one who was a nun in Madagascar.
She came back yesterday, and . . ."

He paused for a moment before plunging on.

"Her pupils made that for him, you understand? She had to tell
them about Jean-Claude, she gossips like a magpie. But she'll be
seventy-five soon . . ."

And I'll be seventy-six, Yankel thought.

"Well," Baptiste said, suddenly resolved, "she insisted on putting
it here. You know how women are, eh? She . . ."

He fell silent. How could he admit the truth to this old Jew? That
he, big, bluff Baptiste, had always been fond of his older sister; that
even yesterday, when Eugénie had unwrapped her gift and told him
of her intention, he hadn't said a word. She had placed her trinket—
a horror, besides—right in the middle of the stone, directly below the
palm. You could see nothing else. Fortunately, Baptiste had found
a chance to return later and had shamefacedly hidden the object in
a corner behind some flowers. That was why Yankel hadn't noticed
it immediately.

Yankel stared at the cross and nodded his head—he was smiling
his martyr's smile which ordinarily so annoyed Baptiste.

"So, leave it," Yankel murmured, nodding his head like a man
who has survived everything and can endure one more persecution.
"Since your sister is a believer, well, it's not good to hurt people!"

He stretched his sentence with some plaintive sounds and replaced
his hat on his head. Baptiste felt tenderness sweep over him. Good,
generous old Papa Mica!

"You know, Papa Mica, I know there's nothing inside there. . . .
But women are as headstrong as she-goats." Damned old nanny goat,
he thought of his sister; couldn't you stay where you were? "A lot
the dead care about our affairs! And the living . . . You and I, we

won't be bothered with them for long, either. . . . Look, come over here for a little while!"

He seized Yankel by the arm and pulled him before the neighboring grave. At the head was a double plaque; on one side, an inscription: *Anna Mykhanowitzki, nee Schmirzmann, 1878-1946.* The other side was blank. Yankel thought, This is where I . . . But Baptiste was talking.

"You see, while I was here, I cleaned out everything, there were weeds . . ."

Yankel heard no more. There was a bitterness in his mouth as he stood there before his wife's grave. Poor Hannah! Six years had passed. . . . Yankel was acquainted with Death. It had struck all about him: his parents, two of his brothers, his own daughter Rivka, his grandson Jean-Claude . . . So many blows, so many sorrows. But when it is your own wife who disappears, the being who has been one flesh with you, then . . . For the last six years Yankel had been living in a kind of numbness; he never ceased to feel a sort of emptiness at his side, and sometimes he felt tempted to turn his head, as if Hannah were going to appear, smiling, and say: "Haven't I a beautiful grave? Thank you, Yankel." Absence, emptiness, a constant lack of something impossible to define. She wasn't there, that was all, and in spite of himself he searched for her. . . . He had forgotten Baptiste, forgotten the sun, philosophy, God; fixedly, with empty mind, he stared at the granite square.

"She was so kind," Yankel murmured. "She had such a good heart."

"Do you remember the time when . . ."

And so, in the same tender manner, they alternated their praises like a funeral oration. Then Yankel interrupted the litany by declaring, almost gaily, "Oh yes, it's fine now! Thank you, Monsieur Saulnier, it was kind of you to do it!"

Baptiste's first sentence had just penetrated his understanding.

"It was nothing," Baptiste growled. "All right, Ploum, let's go!"

He broke off brusquely; he wanted to rejoin his friends at Bertault's café. Down there, at least you were among men, and there was no need to beat your breast every time you came to the end of a field!

He's a fine man all the same! thought Yankel, remembering M. Saulnier's words and gestures; he had apologized for the cross, he had taken care of poor Hannah's grave, he . . . Should he, to show his gratitude, offer to accompany him to Mme. Saulnier's grave? But how could he suggest it gracefully? Mechanically he followed Baptiste who, mechanically, was thinking: Hasn't he finished hanging on my rear?

The two of them leaned on their elbows on the low wall marking the cemetery's end at the edge of the bluff.

The sun sank, and the river grew lacquered with rose and fragile blue. Barges and tugs crossed and passed each other as joyously as pleasure craft; two tiny sailboats were tacking about. Ploum set his forepaws up on the wall and stood on his hind legs, seemingly contemplating the landscape with the two men. Everything was peaceful. Squatted at the bottom of the shallow basin, backed up by the hills on the south, the forest stretched away. A fresh breeze sighed past.

"Nature is beautiful," Yankel certified, with assurance.

Baptiste did not reply; perhaps he hadn't heard. Confused ideas and images were thronging in his brain. He felt at peace with the universe; he was home. A happy lassitude enveloped him, and he began to think of Death without distaste, as you think of your bed after a long day.

"It's going to rain tomorrow," he murmured lazily.

The sun had not yet sunk to the horizon, but the light had already grown dim. A white mist rose, turned purple, touched the sun, which changed shape, became red, orange, yellow, seemed to twist and struggle. The colors flamed out suddenly, and then were extinguished; the mist had choked the sun. The Seine took on the pallor of steel, the forest sank back into the earth; opposite, the profile of the hills grew sharper and began to cut into the white sky.

Nothing survived but that which Death could not alter: the straight yet supple line of the horizon, straight as an arrow to the clear widening of the valley; and below, the sovereign arc of the Seine, now all white.

BOOK I

The Springtide Graft

I

VAST Russia lay spread out behind them.

"Will you shut up!" the guide whispered furiously. Every hundred paces he had had to repeat the warning.

A woman's fragile laugh was abruptly stifled in the darkness; a masculine voice droned on, hardly muted.

We Jews! Yankel thought scornfully. No matter how great the danger we've got to go right on chattering!

Unless volubility is only a mask for fear . . .

No! Ignorant, that's what they were, those people! They were flee-ing Czarist Russia, were thinking that in a few minutes, an hour, two hours perhaps, they would be beyond the reach of their execu-tioners. So they believed it was already over, and the dangerous, clan-destine border-crossing was turning into an escapade. The night was so beautiful, so mild! Many of those beings, cooped up till now in fetid ghettos, were discovering the forest for the first time in their lives. So they chattered, they jabbered, they chirped like boarding-school girls. . . . Each time the guide called for silence, the voices would be lowered for a moment, and then would begin again.

Are they really as stupid as all that? Yankel wondered. Naturally, every precaution had been taken to insure that the crossing of the German border would be without incident. The Organization func-tioned like a commercial enterprise: You paid so much and you wor-ried about nothing; the passage was guaranteed, gift-wrapped and delivered. With the money it collected, the Organization could easily close the eyes of every frontier guard in all of Holy Russia and still realize a substantial profit for itself. Thus, since the soldiers as well as the fugitives had an interest in the business, a betrayal was hardly likely; it would have shut down the gold mine.

But nevertheless, Yankel said to himself, when you're doing some-thing illegal it's better to be a little careful, no? What was there to

27

prove that tonight they weren't going to stumble upon some honest fool who had taken it into his head to go out on patrol?

Yankel, for his part, remained silent. He was happy, intensely happy. Every step lessened the distance to the border. He could feel the entire weight of that huge, dark, barbarous land on his back; the steppe, stretching interminably to the Urals and beyond, spread over a sixth of the globe, across the whole of Asia to the fabulous oceans. But ahead it was Light which reigned, it was Liberty, Civilization, Life! He felt like flinging wide his arms, singing at the top of his voice. At the age of twenty-two he was becoming a free man! All those poor people around him, plodding along, jabbering—mediocrities incapable of understanding the exceptional character of that moment! Softly Yankel began humming the *Marseillaise,* marching in cadence with the rhythm. Behind, darkness; ahead, light . . .

The group suddenly drew to a halt, closed in around the guide, who was explaining something. A second voice could be heard now, translating into Yiddish: "Quiet . . . We're almost at the border . . . the guide's going ahead to see if everything is all right. . . . We're to wait here for him."

Even before the interpreter had finished, the guide had disappeared into the night. Everyone fell silent. Anxiety was on the prowl, gnawing at its victims. Yankel smiled and stretched himself luxuriously. All around him, he could hear a confused bustle and could vaguely make out shadows stirring in the darkness.

Someone blew his nose, loudly. Then a murmur rose up, swelled. "Quiet!" ordered an incisive voice which Yankel recognized as the interpreter's. The voices fell silent, and Yankel was sorry it wasn't he who had given the order; he had wanted to but had hesitated a bit too long. True men of action never hesitate; they act, they act at once!

The guide had still not returned. The nervousness of the group was now perceptible: sighs, the cracking of branches, someone who had been lying down stood up, someone who had been standing lay down. A woman began to cough. "Calm down!" commanded the same authoritarian voice. And calm was restored. . . . If the guide doesn't come back that's the one who'll be the leader, Yankel thought, and a pang of envy swept through him. But immediately afterward he began to reason with himself: Yankel, come now, Yankel! That man must be educated, he speaks Russian; so he deserves to command more than you. And besides, he seems to know what he's doing. I'll wager he's a real revolutionary, and at least forty, while a young man like you, only a member of the *Bund,* the illegal union, where do you come off having such pretentions? Ah, but in a few years, when you've had more experience . . .

He crossed his arms, again breathed deeply. The air had the chilly taste of earth, of mold, of death. What if a patrol should happen along? Anxiety, delicious when it served only to give greater value to his approaching freedom, more flavor to the forbidden march, was beginning to sour. What if the guide had sold out? What if the soldier the Organization had bribed had been replaced at the last moment? What if the general, the colonel, the captain had changed their orders? . . . I won't let them take me! Yankel decided. I'd rather die! His imagination began working hard, and in vivid detail: Here comes the patrol. Lanterns, men swearing, women screaming . . . Shots maybe? Barking—they have dogs with them. Turmoil, officers shouting, soldiers running . . . And Yankel? There he goes, slipping away swiftly, silently, into the night! Nobody saw him—yes; a soldier. He's pointing at him, shouting. Well, run then! Run straight ahead, that way, toward the border! They can't run faster than I, can they? With their heavy equipment and all! They fire at me, miss . . . No, I'm hit, only a scratch, and I, the coolheaded hero, I run on without faltering, I run, I run. . . . Here's the border! Crossed! Saved! Free! I faint in the arms of a German soldier, a Social Democrat. . . .

A sudden hubbub swept through the group; the guide had returned. As they set out again, a voice whispered in Yankel's ear: "Everything's all right, but no noise—the patrols." Dried twigs snapped under their feet; in the silent night, the hubbub must have been audible for miles around! No matter—Yankel was happy. And once more he swore not to let himself be taken, come what might. The anti-Semites could say whatever they pleased, but Yankel knew that the Jew is courageous, that the Jew isn't afraid of death, that the Jew will risk his life when he must. . . . An ardor he had never before known welled up in him; not only the joy of approaching freedom, but especially the exciting sensation of hurling himself recklessly into the unknown, of acting, of gambling—all prudence cast to the winds.

He bumped into the man ahead of him, seized hold of him to keep from falling, and blushed in the darkness; it wasn't a man, but a woman. Through her dress, his hand had felt the softness of a breast.

29

She began reviling him in a low voice. "I'm sorry," he whispered contritely. "I didn't do it on purpose. . . . But will you be quiet!" he said louder, impatiently, as *Hushes!* came from here and there.

The group stopped before a path, grayish in the darkness. Yankel could still feel the soft breast he had so involuntarily touched. Hadn't he pressed it a little harder than necessary? Who was that woman? Wasn't she the pretty girl whom all the men had been eying the preceding day? Even Yankel, a married man and a father, hadn't been able to keep himself from sneaking an occasional glance at her. And in doing so, wasn't he being just a little unfaithful to his Hannah? He tried to feel a decent remorse but failed.

Ah, why that halt? In the middle of the path, a man was bending over, placing things on the ground; finally, he straightened up, returned. "Walk on the branches," said a voice. Shadows began flitting across, Indian file. The woman ahead of Yankel moved along in turn. Yankel followed her. She stepped onto the branches, thrown across the path like a bridge. Yankel stopped at the edge. The sand was carefully raked; yes, that was why the branches had to be used—so as not to leave any telltale marks. . . .

"You going or not?" growled the guide, stationed at the entrance to the bridge. He was a tall man, massive as a bear. He had taken charge of the group after nightfall, and in the darkness Yankel was unable to make out his features.

"Is this . . . is this the border?" Yankel asked, his voice hoarse with emotion.

"No, it's your mother's teat!" And with a thump on the back, the man shoved him ahead. Yankel stumbled, almost fell, regained his footing and moved forward unsteadily. Sick with humiliation, he could hear behind him the muffled laughter of those who were still on the Russian side. "Your mother's teat!" Ah, those Russian peasants! They couldn't speak three words without uttering an obscenity. Pfeh! A lot of good it did Yankel to ask his question, out of politeness, in Russian rather than Yiddish! He had been well paid for his trouble! And yet it wasn't a stupid question, was it? Nor insolent? He had a right to know what they were making him do; after all, he wasn't a dog! . . . Hopping from branch to branch, he almost forgot that at that very moment he was crossing the border. The border! Russia ended there, just behind him; he had left it, forever. Ahead lay that land of freedom which for years had held him fascinated;

for years he had dreamed of that moment, a moment he had always imagined would be extraordinarily solemn.

The path was wide, the branches bent under his weight, then at last he sensed the other side of the path before him. With a light bound, he landed on solid ground. The girl he had bumped into a little while before was there facing him, her eyes gleaming in the darkness. She was laughing! Yes, but without a sound. Yankel felt himself being clutched, hugged, kissed all over the face. Savagely, he drew the woman against him, crushed her body . . . No! They were separated now, and she was laughing, convulsively, but still in silence. One of the hysterical kind! Yankel suddenly thought, embarrassed. Without looking at him, she squeezed his arm, her fingers pinching his flesh while at the same time she stammered out incoherent words in Yiddish. Deeply stirred, Yankel turned around. The border had been crossed, Russia had been left behind, once and for all, in another world, a world of darkness. It was over!

Then he thought of Hannah, of Rivka, poor little Rivkele, who were still there, exposed to all sorts of dangers. He, he was already a free man. But his wife, his child, his family? No, he couldn't fully rejoice. He had no right to.

Nor the desire! Beneath the hate he harbored for bloody Russia, even now he felt a vague nostalgia welling up within him; voices were whispering gentle, sad reproaches. Rakwomir, land of my childhood . . . Everything was beginning anew; but nothing had been blotted out. With tears in his eyes, Yankel contemplated the pine forest, blacker than the night, on the other side of the path. Russia, foreign now and forever . . . For he knew he would never return; his way lay toward the cities of the West, toward light and freedom. . . .

Now the last of the emigrants was crossing the bridge. Figures bumped into him. He felt lonely, and utterly wretched.

Finally, heaving a great sigh, he came to himself. The refugees were all on the German side now. Little laughs, little chortles, little sobs, for though they were safe, they nevertheless kept their voices down, out of politeness, out of respect, hardly out of fear. . . . After all, we must let them sleep, these free men who are welcoming us so nobly. We mustn't disturb them, mustn't set them against us. For what *are* we here, anyhow, but dirt?

The guide, alone now in the middle of the path, was engaged in some mysterious task. He would bend over, gather up an armful of branches, withdraw, set them down, return, rake the ground, and repeat the whole process. . . . Of course, how stupid! He's removing the marks we left—niggling pettiness, worthy indeed of Mother Russia! Every fifty yards a soldier, rifle in hand; endless patrols, with police dogs; a broad strip of sand, scrupulously raked in order to reveal the slightest footprint; and behind it a whole bureaucracy in uniform, a huge man-crushing machine. "No one can get through!" the pompous autocrats must be saying to themselves, back there, in St. Petersburg. Yes! And every night, entire populations get through. For the border guards are bought, and they step aside; the officers are bought, and they reroute their patrols; the bureaucrats are bought and they disclose the orders even before they are received by the men who will carry them out. Foolish, bloodthirsty Russia, barbarous country!

A suspicion suddenly entered Yankel's mind. Who knows? Maybe the autocrats themselves are aware of and not only permit but desire the exodus. Maybe they, too, are profiting from it. The ferocious Pobedonostev, the Procurator of the Holy Synod, made no bones about declaring, publicly, the fate he planned for the Russian Jews: "A third will die, a third will emigrate, the rest we will convert." A third will die . . . the Black Hundred, organizers of pogroms, were taking care of that. A third will emigrate, but not without first being bled white. The rest . . .

The guide had finished his raking. Once more, the border strip was flawless, innocent, impassable. The group got under way again and Yankel followed. He wondered whether he had been right to leave Russia. At least he would make every effort to send for Hannah and the little one at the earliest possible moment. As soon as he got settled down in Paris, as soon as he found a job, he would work things out, somehow. And later, he would send for his brothers and sisters too, and his parents. . . .

Paris, had he said?

All at once, it dawned upon him: He was going to Paris!

Paris! City of Light! Yes, he would soon be in Paris! It was true, it wasn't a dream! A wave of happiness rushed over him, obliterating everything else.

"Can't leave today!"

"Not leaving? What's going on?"

The door slammed; the man was gone.

Grumbling, Yankel turned over on his bed of straw, then got up. The Organization operated smoothly, you had to admit that. But its employees treated the emigrants like a herd of cattle. "Up! Down! Stay! Go! Do this! Don't do that!" Always orders, never an explanation. After all, we *are* men, aren't we? Yankel thought, in disgust. They could at least tell us their reasons. Men? No! Not even cattle. Packages! Just so much freight to be handled, delivery guaranteed.

Humiliated, Yankel went outside. They had crossed the border at one in the morning; it was now eight. And during those first seven hours of his new life, only for a fleeting moment had he felt really free and happy. For his initial joy had quickly faded in the tramping of the herd which the guide scathingly drove on toward the resting place. And yet, only a short while before, what wondrous dreams he had had, dreams celebrating his entry into a world that was free. Once through the triumphal arch, his slave's tatters would fall to the ground; and, miraculously made a man, resplendent, he would advance through a shower of golden light. . . . Alas, not even the faintest glimmer of that light! Yankel he was, Yankel he remained, Yankel from Rakwomir. A vague uneasiness was the only feeling he experienced, and now that he was out of danger he even found himself cheated of his hatred of the pogromists, the reactionary, barbaric Russians. Deprived of that prop, he felt obscure regrets rising in his throat; he was ashamed of them and yet was unable to repress them.

He had still seen nothing of Germany. Driven through the night by the guide, the herd of emigrants had suddenly found itself before a dark opening which turned out to be a barn door. "Hurry up and get in there, you . . ." Followed by the customary rain of curses. Jostling, stumbling; vague objects are bumped into, a woman twists her ankle and whimpers, another laughs nervously; voices rise. . . . "Quiet!" The straw and the dust bring on a rash of sneezes. Again, hotly: "Be quiet!" And then: "No one's to leave!" And then: "No fires!" Each order, of course, followed by a torrent of oaths.

The door closes, blotting out the rectangle of gray sky. Pitch-blackness. Vague noises. Smells. Seated on a pile of straw, Yankel meditated at length, but to no avail. Then, stretched out on his back, his hands behind his neck, he tried in vain to feel happy. The only images that passed behind his closed eyelids were those with a taste of melancholy, nostalgia and remorse: Hannah and Rivka, so far away, his brothers and sisters, Rakwomir's birch forest, the stream;

childhood memories, diffused and luminous; cavalcades of white clouds against the blue of the sky, at spring's first blush . . . *I'm free!* And with that thought, all the humiliations of the flight rushed to his mind. Someone was snoring, a man and a woman were whispering. What were they doing, the two of them? Why had Yankel kissed that hysterical woman so passionately, that woman who wasn't his? Pfeh! He had even enjoyed it! A wave of remorse swept through him. He had behaved like a goy, that's what! All goys are unfaithful to their wives—everyone knows it. Would he at least have the courage to confess his lapse to Hannah? And suddenly, all the taboos of his upbringing flew out the window. Since he had begun to sin, had sinned a little, why not go all the way and really enjoy life? His teeth clenched, he bitterly regretted not having the woman at his side. Ah, how he would have caressed her, crushed her against him! For that night only, of course; the next day, everything would be forgotten. He propped himself up on his elbows, trying to make her out in the darkness. . . . And then the shame returned, and to shield himself from it, he attempted once more to rejoice in his status as a free man. . . .

He was certain he hadn't slept a wink all night; after all, what kind of man would find time to sleep on such a solemn occasion? Well, maybe just a few winks. . . . At any rate, when the employee of the Organization had opened the door and shouted out: "Can't leave today!" and a harsh stream of light had flooded the inside of the barn, Yankel had been surprised to find that it was already broad daylight; in July, at eight in the morning, the sun is in full blaze. Pfeh! What a stench in there! Rubbing his eyes, he suddenly realized he was outside.

The fresh air cleared his brain, washed him. He stretched, feeling young and proud. The world was his.

He was in a barnyard. Near the gate a watchdog was barking fiercely, straining at its chain. Yankel repressed a shudder, and then promptly reprimanded himself. Would he never be rid of that morbid terror that big dogs inspired in him? Wasn't the chain strong? Wasn't he himself strong?

He looked around him. A farm! So? So it's a farm, like all other farms! German or Russian, what's the difference? What are borders but imaginary lines drawn by human folly? Tolstoy was right when he said that men are the same everywhere, and only society sets up artificial barriers between them.

34

Nevertheless, the cleanness of the place surprised him. The hard ground was well swept, the manure neatly gathered together, the wooden doors of cowshed, stable and pigsty spotless. And as for the farmer's house, made of red brick and all decked out with pink and yellow flowers, never would Yankel have taken it for a peasant's dwelling. The more he looked at it, the greater his surprise was. Green shutters at the windows, and even—yes, even curtains, snow-white curtains! In Rakwomir, only the doctor's house could compare with this jewel. Was he looking upon the first fruit of freedom? Or was the farmer an important dignitary in the district?

He looked down at his boots, gray with dust, drew a huge handkerchief from his pocket and whipped his boots with it. The dust came off in little puffs. No, it didn't work. The boots seemed even dirtier than before, now that black streaks shone through the gray crust. He bent over and rubbed the high leather tops with his hands; finally, he resigned himself to using his handkerchief as a rag. Luckily, he had waxed the boots only three days before; the grime did not stick to the leather.

He stood up. The boots were black now—although the handkerchief was gray. Yankel shook it out; it didn't help. No matter; what counted was the boots. After all, he had to make a good impression on the civilized people he would be meeting from now on. It would have made Yankel sick with shame if one of them were to characterize him, justifiably, as a "dirty Jew."

He walked over to the pump. Was he permitted to use it? Of course he was! Water is sacred. No one has a right to deprive anyone of water, whether for drinking or for washing.

His jacket buttoned up to his neck, his cap pulled down to his ears, he tugged first at one sleeve, then the other, clearing his wrists a little; next, he gripped the pump handle and began pumping, gently, with discretion, so as not to disturb his hosts. The pump coughed hollowly, hiccuped, gurgled. . . . Nothing! Unprimed. Beneath it, a stone trough lay bone-dry. An old pot beside the trough—dry too. Yankel glanced timidly at the farmer's dwelling. Nobody. Shut tight. Should he go ask for a little water to prime the pump?

All at once, an unreasoning fury took hold of him. They did it on purpose! They don't want Jews to wash! An enormous force swelled his biceps; he seized the handle and pumped it frenziedly, as if he wanted with every stroke to smash the heads of all the pogromists in Russia. The handle beating the air, the pump was jumping so vio-

35

lently it threatened to rip itself from its base and the dog was howling like a demon, when a man suddenly appeared on the threshold of the house and began yelling and waving his arms. Instantly calmed, Yankel halted. The man approached him, still yelling. Yankel couldn't understand a word he was saying, but he faced him bravely. Jew or not, a man has a right to wash himself, hasn't he?

Having drawn beside him, the peasant, his face severe, pointed to a jug hidden behind the pump and made a motion of pouring. A jug! Yes, there was a jug there, a magnificent blue jug, full of water— and practically staring him right in the face! And Yankel—what an idiot!—hadn't seen it! He let out a loud guffaw and slapped his thigh in an effort to unbend the impassive peasant; and then, Germanizing his Yiddish as best he could, he tried to explain his distraction, and how funny it was, and how ridiculous he, Yankel, was. At that moment, he felt at peace with the whole universe, Christian or not. To think that that good man had everything all prepared for him, had even gone out of his way to help Yankel out of his predicament! And what had he, Yankel, been doing? Ay-yi! Full of evil thoughts, forgetting he was in a free, enlightened country, he had been trying his best to break that poor old pump to pieces and thus cause his host a lot of expense! Pfeh, Yankel, pfeh! "Excuse me," he said, full of contrition. And from his mop of tousled hair, he raised his stiff cap, which, despite its cloth-covered peak, looked very much like the cap of a Russian officer. The man looked at him, his face as bleak as ever, his eyes expressionless. Again he pointed to the jug, then the pump, repeated the motion of pouring and resumed his yelling. Yankel could catch only a word here and there in the torrent; resigned, he took the jug and primed the pump. *"Gut, gut!"* the man shouted and went off. What an oaf! thought Yankel. What does he take me for? A fool who doesn't know how to use a pump?

There was a little stubble on his face, but not too much. Thank God Yankel didn't need a shave, for what would he have done without hot water? It could wait a few more days. He wasn't one of those hairy, apelike men, and despite all the veneration, the forced veneration, he held for his father, old Avrom, he couldn't help feeling a physical repugnance for the old man's long orthodox beard and the way it smelled. Jews' beards or moujiks' beards, to Yankel they were all the same: the outward sign of fanaticism and backwardness. Therefore, despite his father's terrible rages, he had been shaving

36

ever since he had reached adulthood. Beard and earlocks, not for him. Yes, he was a free, enlightened man, Yankel Mykhanowitzki!

Pensively, his head thrust forward to keep the water from dripping on his jacket, his hands held out to dry in the sun, Yankel contemplated the pump. It felt good on his face, that fresh water. His hand was just reaching for the pump again when the peasant's gruff voice sounded in his ear. *Now* what does he want? With an abrupt gesture, the man pushed him aside and gripped the pump handle. Good man, so kind to the poor homeless refugee, sacrificing his precious time to work the pump while the poor refugee washes himself! That apparent brusqueness of gesture and voice? Ah, what of it! Thanking him effusively, Yankel cupped his hands under the nozzle of the pump. . . . No, something was still amiss. The man failed to pump the handle; he was yelling again, pointing at Yankel's jacket. And then Yankel suddenly understood: He wants me to get undressed! All his modesty welled up in him and made him rebel violently at the idea. At home, naturally, he used to wash himself every week from head to toe, in a great tub of hot water. But here? Strip naked, just like that, in broad daylight, and in a barnyard, when a woman could come out at any moment? Even in the steam baths, in front of men, Yankel had had difficulty overcoming his modesty.

Suddenly, a perfidious suspicion crossed his mind. Was this a trap? A Jew naked before a Christian—a fine opportunity for the anti-Semites to point an accusing finger at the depravity of the race!

But he was a reasonable man, Yankel Mykhanowitzki, and therefore quickly drove the evil thought from his mind. . . . We mustn't always think we're being persecuted! We're in Germany, aren't we? A free, enlightened country!

Nevertheless, all smiles, he made the peasant understand that no, really, thank you all the same, don't trouble yourself, I don't want to bother you. And to show how meager were his needs, he pinched his index finger against his thumb. Then he cupped his hands again under the nozzle. The man shrugged his shoulders and gave the handle a mighty pump; a powerful gush of water spouted forth, splashing Yankel from head to foot.

Then an extraordinary thing happened. Until that moment, the man had seemed as incapable of changing his expression as a block of wood; through all his yelling and bawling, his face had remained perfectly bleak. But now, with the spectacle of a drenched Yankel before him, he burst out laughing. And before Yankel had time to react, a friendly thump, which could have felled an ox, landed on his back. Then off he went, still laughing.

Annoyed, Yankel contemplated his handsome, water-splotched jacket, his wet boots on which all the Prussian dust would quickly collect. So that's the way free men were, eh? As loutish as the worst moujiks! And Yankel understood that he wasn't yet through with being persecuted. And thinking, he was seized with a strong desire to see his native Russia again. The people there were what they were, but at least he could understand their words. When a Russian called you a dirty Jew, you knew he wasn't saying "my dear friend." And you knew how to react!

I think I'll go say good-bye to my homeland, Yankel said to himself, feeling very sentimental. And he left the farm and set out in the direction of the border.

No sooner did he pass through the gate than his bad humor disappeared. Ay-yi! How pretty that village was! So clean, so pleasant in the sun's light! Village? No, town rather, for the farms soon gave way to houses with bright little shops, and there were sidewalks, and a street along which carts passed from time to time. And all in stone, the houses, the sidewalks, even the street! And everywhere, flowers! And how clean! No rubbish in the streets! No heaps of garbage to skirt. You could sit down on the cobblestones without getting your trousers dirty. Compared to Rakwomir—ay hoo! there was no comparison! In Rakwomir, the streets were dirt and perpetually rutted. As soon as the thaw set in you would wade through pools of mud, and when the sun dried them out a sea of dust was swept up in whirling clouds by the wind. And the housewives, as if it were the most natural thing in the world, would dump their garbage into those streets for the dogs and the chickens and the Christian farmer's pigs to fight over. Even the big neighboring city, to which Yankel had once gone with special permission from the police (for it was forbidden to Jews) seemed squalid by comparison, with its wretched wooden sidewalks. And yet, at the time, it had roused Yankel's enthusiasm.

And the people! The men clean-shaven, neatly clothed; the women scrubbed, combed, dressed up! There was one, for example, who was washing her windows; tied around her hair was a silk scarf, and a pretty one at that, not an old dishcloth. Why, at that time of day, in Rakwomir, even the most coquettish of the young women would

38

still be poking about the house, uncorseted, hair disheveled; and as for the old busybodies, old before their time, *they* went unkempt all day long, breasts hanging, skin flabby, wigs askew. The only time they ever paid a little attention to themselves was during the holidays. I'll tell Hannele all about it, he decided. Hannele would understand. For she was an enlightened young woman, Hannele. She hadn't begun neglecting herself once she got married, like so many others; she was still neat, well-groomed—a pretty young woman, all in all, even though she was a mother. And besides, why did they let themselves go simply because they were married! It was stupid! The wigs, yes, the wigs were the real cause of it. If so many women acted as if they were old from the day of their marriage, it was because of the wigs. Yankel congratulated himself for having a wife who, willingly complying with her husband's wish, had kept her magnificent head of hair even after marrying. What a barbaric superstition, believing that angels, if they exist at all, will come down to earth and carry off married women who keep their hair! Why should they be especially tempted by hair? It's stupid, that's all! A perfect example of the stupidities of religions!

Yankel walked slowly along the sidewalks. Sunk deep in reverie, he nevertheless took care to keep close to the curb, so that he would be able to step into the street instantly if he saw a soldier or bureaucrat coming toward him. For, not knowing the German law, he thought it best to abide by the Russian one: make way for officers! No, that he wouldn't soon forget. . . .

He must have been about sixteen that day when, on the only street in Rakwomir with a sidewalk, he had seen the officer in the distance coming in his direction, walking along with that arrogant strut they all had. An officer in Rakwomir? Rare occurrence! Curious, Yankel paused to behold that pure product of Russian autocracy; here and there, others had stopped too. It was a sight not to be missed. Right down the middle of the deserted sidewalk, ramrod-stiff, his lower lip protruding scornfully, the officer advanced steadily, completely alone in the world. He was very young, his face still boyish, but nevertheless a monocled Junker, a colossus standing more than six feet tall.

Suddenly an old, half-blind Jewish woman left a shop directly in his path. . . . He changed neither his gait nor his bearing in the slightest degree, neither slowed down nor took his eye off the horizon. Just as if there were nothing in his way, he continued straight ahead. Thrown aside by the impact, the old woman fell into the

39

street, rolled in the mud, and lay weeping. . . . As for the officer, he continued on his way, impassive, arrogant, unaffected. It made you wonder whether he had even felt the blow.

Behind the officer's back, people muttered and shook their fists. Not Yankel! He, Yankel, said nothing, did nothing. What good are useless gestures? Do you argue with a wild beast? When you come upon a mad dog, you kill it if you can; if not, you avoid it. That's all.

He sighed. All that was over! In Germany, in France, people weren't savages. . . . Come, it was useless mulling over the past. Now he was a free man.

It suddenly occurred to him that he was hungry. Did he dare buy something to eat in one of those cheerful little shops? In Russia many of the Christian stores had signs reading: "No dogs, Poles or Jews allowed." Of course it's true that the Poles, for their part, posted signs which said only: "No dogs or Jews allowed." But for the Jews it amounted to the same thing, and for the dogs, too. How were the people here? Less barbaric, probably; but you could never tell. Russia wasn't so far away. And hadn't there recently been anti-Semitic stirrings in Germany? Reports had reached Rakwomir. . . . Being in doubt, Yankel preferred not to chance it. So, his mouth watering, he went hungrily past the *Kolonialwaren,* the *Konditorei* and the *Bäckerei,* with their heaps of rolls, cakes, fruits and sausages.

There were few people in the streets. Each time he passed someone in conversation, he would listen attentively, trying to make out what was being said. Not out of any unwholesome curiosity, for he was a most tactful man, Yankel Mykhanowitzki. But he was still annoyed at his encounter with the farmer. Why hadn't he been able to understand a word the man had said? Everyone knows German is a lot like Yiddish! So? Was the difference between the two languages greater than he had thought?

Since his musings proved devoid of results, Yankel decided to attack the problem head-on and undertook to decipher systematically each and every sign he came upon.

They struck him as being quite strange, those signs. He tried to spell them out but was stopped by most of the letters. And yet he *had* learned the Latin alphabet before leaving, hadn't he? Of course he wasn't used to it, but nevertheless . . . To make certain he still remembered, Yankel took an old envelope from his pocket and wrote out all the Latin letters just as he had learned them. Then he began comparing . . . No, they weren't the same! Or rather yes, they were *almost* the same, but contorted, twisted a thousand different ways! What was the reason for it? Is that a *B* there? Funny kind of a *B!* A German-style *B,* possibly? Maybe the Germans prefer having a writing of their own. Who knows?

Tenaciously, Yankel worked out a table of concordance. And in the end his patience was rewarded: He managed, not without difficulty, to read most of the signs. And he beamed, for, once he was able to read them, he understood them; therefore he hadn't been misled about the similarity of German and Yiddish. *Schneider:* tailor, in German as in Yiddish! You see, the world isn't so complicated! Reassured, he stuffed the envelope and pencil in his pocket and continued on his way.

And yet, he reflected, seen from Rakwomir, the question of writing had seemed quite simple. Besides the Hebrew alphabet, there was the Cyrillic for the Russians and the Latin for the rest of the world— except the savages, of course. But already, with the border hardly crossed, there were complications. There existed not one, but several Latin alphabets. Ah, how vast the world is! he thought, and a feeling of anguish gripped him, so violent that it stopped him short. What have you got yourself into, Yankel! Yankel Mykhanowitzki from Rakwomir, blind man that you are, into what unknown are you plunging? What have you done? You leave your home like a carefree schoolboy with nothing on his mind but the hike and the fresh air! To go where? I know, I know, you say, frivolous as a woman. What do you know? Nothing, Yankel! You know Rakwomir, a pinpoint on the vast earth. But as for the rest? You *think* you know, and that's the worst thing of all!

His head lowered, he set out again, slowly now. Yankel Mykhanowitzki—a cautious, thoughtful, methodical man! No hotheaded adventurer he! Not Yankel Mykhanowitzki! . . . Well, if you want to know, he's an idiot! France, France, France—that's all he can think of! But what does he know about France? Nothing! A lot of nonsense! And just where is France, anyhow? At the other end of the world!

Before leaving his homeland, he had taken every possible precaution. He had a little money with him, half his savings, having left the other half with Hannah.

And how long will that money last you there? You don't even know if the cost of living is high, if . . .

I'll find work! A steady, reliable man can always find something. Capmaking is a good trade, isn't it? And I'm a good worker.

Yes! And suppose the French don't wear caps? Or suppose their caps are completely different from Rakwomirian caps? They're civilized people, the French, and all you've ever known are barbarians! And suppose there isn't any work for you there?

I looked into it. They say that . . .

"They" say! Who are "they?" Do you know "they" personally, at least?

Neh, neh, neh! It's no good exaggerating all the time! Let's be reasonable! First of all, I won't be alone in Paris; I have an address—

An address! Whose address? The cousin of the sister-in-law of a friend of Schloyma the shoemaker. You think that's being reasonable?

It seems he's doing quite well, and he's a fine man, and . . .

Come on now, admit you really know nothing about him! And what if he's moved? What if he's dead? Or sick? Or bankrupt? Or . . .

Ay, stop it now, Yankel moaned. I'm young, no? I'm in good health? I speak a little French? No need to worry: I'll get along!

Relieved, he raised his head and continued on at a brisk pace.

. . . Ho, ho! Yankel Mykhanowitzki the capmaker, son of Avrom the grocer, our little Yankele from Rakwomir speaks French! Hats swept low before Yankele the Frenchman! For French is the language of noblemen, and to prove how extraordinary a country France is, old Schloyma, the professional wag, repeats his famous joke a hundred times a year to anyone who'll listen: "France? You don't know about France? Well, let me tell you! In France—listen carefully—the poorest butcher boy speaks French!"

Thus, in Rakwomir, nothing can do more to build up your standing among your friends than to recite a few carefully memorized French sentences: *"Notrrre maison de campagne n'est pas trrrès grrrande, mais elle offrrre de nombrrreuses commodités . . ."*

Yes, very fine in Rakwomir! But in Paris?

Yankel frowned. He no longer had much confidence in his French. He had taken lessons, yes. And his teacher was an intellectual, a scholar, a revolutionary student sought by the police and hiding in Rakwomir. But how much French did he really know? All right, so he knew a great deal. There remained the problem of teach-

42

ing it. For the student didn't know Yiddish and Yankel spoke Russian only poorly.

And as a crowning misfortune, after six weeks the student, rooted out by the police, had been shipped off to Siberia.

Six weeks of lessons—certainly not much. All in all, Yankel knew a hundred words or so and a few stock phrases. Meager baggage indeed for an emigrant!

Staggered by this new revelation, Yankel decided he would have to re-examine the very heart of the problem. Why, yes, why had he chosen France as his adopted land?

Of course, he had debated the question a hundred times before making his decision; and, the decision once made, a hundred times more. But one can never reflect enough before acting.

For the two hundredth and first time, then, he attacked the problem. France, Germany, England or America?

The rest of the world he preferred not to think about; it was all too blurred. Considering only the four classic countries of immigration, the choice was difficult enough. Where would he end up if he began considering China, Africa?

Germany? Definitely not! Yankel re-examined the case for Germany only to satisfy his conscience. Bismarck, Nietzsche, Wagner—the names produced a dull uneasiness in him, almost a fear, though he would have been hard put to say exactly why. They seemed not to compare well with Tolstoy, his god; they conjured up not goodness nor kindness nor benevolence, but a frenzied, mystic, brutal, militaristic energy—a Dark Ages clad in armor; yes, that was it! Of course, they did have their Social Democrats, but they also had a Kaiser and harsh feudal Junkers. . . . No no not Germany!

England then? Ah, there was much to be said for England! But no, not England either. Why not? Well, the English are rich, you see; poor people wouldn't feel at ease among them. And furthermore, they're considered haughty, imperialistic. Liberals, you say? Of course, they're liberals! But full of prejudices, traditions. And why do they have to have a king, even a decorative one? What good is that parasite to them?

Thus Yankel amassed good reasons for avoiding England, ignoring his real one: England was an island, and he could not settle down on an island. For you can't easily flee from an island, and he was determined to keep that possibility in reserve. You never know!

43

There remained the two republics, America and France—America meaning the United States, naturally. Yankel had wavered between the two for a long time, and he was still wavering, or pretending to. The news from New York was good; the immigrants' letters all spoke of money to be made. But Yankel was the sort who cared little about making money; he had modest tastes, and wealth as such failed to attract him. He would have willingly declared, with his beloved Tolstoy, that money is a corrupting influence. And there had also been alarming reports of the brutality with which the American immigration service greeted foreigners. To be sure, the immigration formalities were but a single bad moment to be endured, but nevertheless it seemed a bad omen. Compared to France—ah, France! . . .

When you pronounced that word in Rakwomir, faces would light up. Victor Hugo, Voltaire, the Rights of Man, the Revolution, the barricades, *liberté-égalité-fraternité* . . . How many tyrants the French had overthrown! For how many noble causes had they risen up in fiery wrath! Even their national anthem was that noble *Marseillaise* which democrats, nihilists, socialists and revolutionaries all sing, as a challenge to autocracy, under the Cossacks' whiplashes.

As a child, Yankel had listened while his old great-grandmother dolefully recounted her memories of that bygone war, when the French had come as far as Rakwomir with their Napoleon. "As a rule," she would say, "they were little men with black hair. And so gallant, so gay! Always playing pranks on the women, or doing them little favors. Even the Jewish women, yes, even the Jews—they treated everyone alike. If they saw a woman carrying a bucket of water, hup! they would take the bucket from her and carry it right up to the house! Yes, indeed! And when it came to cooking, ay, what experts. Of course, Papa forbade us to eat their food, because of the dietary laws. But I was just a girl in those days, maybe ten or twelve, and I would taste their dishes secretly, and how good they were, mmmm! If only you knew, Yankele! . . . There was one who was quartered here with us, and he used to bounce me on his knee and sing me songs. . . ."

And the old woman, in her cracked voice, would hum fragments of lively tunes not at all like the Russian or Yiddish ones; they made you think of—of bubbling, sparkling wine! Then she would stop, sigh: "I don't remember any more; I must be getting old. . . ."

All in all, Yankel said to himself, it was probably my great-grandmother's stories that made me decide on France. What childishness!

Even if the French in those days were as she described them, what's to prove they haven't changed? The letters from Paris are good, too, but less enthusiastic than those from New York. So?

So why not go to New York? What's to prevent me? I'm free!

Free . . . *Free?* Suddenly a hot flush burned the nape of his neck, his ears; and then all at once he shivered. He took a deep breath. Free! Stay in Germany, continue on to France, to America—he could do anything! Anything! The decision was his alone. And he could even, if the whim took hold of him, forget all about Hannah and Rivka in the homeland, give them no sign he even was alive for the rest of his days, and lose himself in the vast world. An odious thought, and he promptly drove it from his mind. But not impossible; he had only to want to make it possible in order for it to be so. Frightening, to tell the truth! Whichever way he turned, there were no obstacles. All he had to do was pick himself up and go.

All at once, raising his head, he saw he had arrived at the border. *The border!*

If I want, I can even go back there, to Russia!

Stunned by the thought, his mouth dropped open. Free . . . Free . . . The terrible word once more throbbed inside him, as electrifying as before. Yankel's legs trembled, the blood pounded against his temples. . . . Free . . . Run, jump, a few bounds, never mind the footprints, and plunge into the Russian world, plunge back into my native land! Yes, why not? Freedom was so vast a thing that it even spilled over into slavery, but this time a slavery freely chosen. . . . Hastily, seized with panic, Yankel summoned up all the reasons he had ever had for hating his native land. Go back? No, it was impossible! Freedom, after all, is operative only within certain limits. The word's dazzling brilliance weakened, died out. Relieved, Yankel caught his breath; but from now on he would be on his guard.

The sun radiated a gentle warmth. The sky was blue. A few flies buzzed about, birds were warbling, the barking of a dog somewhere behind Yankel rose and then died away in the untroubled air. On the Russian side, there was only impenetrable silence. Another world began right there. The border. A group of men had ravished it during the night; in the morning, it was once more virginal, innocent.

Suddenly, he spied a soldier, motionless on the other side of the path, observing him. At once all the power of the Russian continent converged in that sentry, petrified in his heavy boots and his long gray overcoat; the whole huge Russian mass focused in that man and con-

45

densed in him. Rifle in hand, he was standing guard at the entrance to his country; under his flat cap, he had a beardless, still childlike face. Was it that very soldier who, only last night, had let the emigrants through? And if not he, then another alike in every way. Fascinated, Yankel stared at him. He felt a desire to speak to him, find out his name, his age, where he came from.

Slowly, Yankel's lips formed a smile. The soldier raised his hand and motioned him back. Yankel continued to smile almost tenderly; he had so many things to share with that youngster before leaving him forever, before forgetting that hated uniform forever. Yankel knew that a Russian soldier had no authority over a man standing on German soil, that Russian power, for all its might, ended there, at the edge of the path. And yet he felt uneasy; slowly, regretfully, he took two steps back. . . . There, it was done with! He had disowned his country; his country had disowned him. Farewell, my native Russia, primitive Russia! Draw back, far back into your dark shadows. . . .

The soldier had set his rifle down. Suddenly animated, he looked about him, then winked at Yankel and, his face greedily tense, rounded his hand in the shape of a glass and brought it to his lips, indicating he wanted a drink. *"Schnapps! Schnapps!"* his lips formed in silence. Abruptly softened, Yankel began to laugh. *"Da! Da!"* he answered with his lips, nodding his head affirmatively. Of course he would go get some *schnapps* for that poor youngster!

But just at that moment, behind him, there was a tumult, shouting: *"Los, Mensch, los, los! Schnell! Weg!"*

Barking, galloping . . . Yankel glanced quickly around just in time to see a patrol of green-clad soldiers bearing down on him, the man in the lead clutching the leashes of two huge mastiffs. Head bent low, spine bristling with terror, Yankel raced off, while on the other side of the border the Russian soldier burst out laughing.

His native Russia had driven him out; strangers were welcoming him to the land of freedom.

So many houses! So many people! So much noise! Deafened, blinded, choked by the dust, crushed by the heat, Yankel walked along happily. He was in Paris!

He had been walking since early morning, and he could no longer think except in exclamations. How wide the streets were! How tall the houses! How gay the people! How gigantic the city!

46

At times he emerged on avenues ten times, even twenty times wider than the widest street in Rakwomir, or on vast squares surrounded by trees. Then, persuaded that those trees announced the suburbs, and afraid to stray too far from his lodgings, he would turn back.

He preferred the wider arteries, but he liked the narrower little streets too, and was astounded to find them all paved and bordered on both sides by stone sidewalks. And so many of the people he passed were speaking Yiddish! And all laughing! And at every intersection men and women were dancing, for there were bands everywhere, with flags, streamers, flowers and multicolored Chinese lanterns. Once he even came upon a square so huge that he could hardly see to the other side; three Rakwomirs would easily have fit in it. And it was jam-packed; the people, crammed one against the other, could hardly move and were barely pretending to dance. The sight was so amazing that Yankel, half frightened, quickly slipped away.

Of course he wasn't so naïve, Yankel Mykhanowitzki; he knew that every day, even in Paris, wasn't like that. "It's the national holiday," M. Kratzmann, his host, had said. "Today France celebrates the storming of the Bastille." But holiday or not, the French certainly were a gay people; his old great-grandmother hadn't exaggerated.

Occasionally he wondered where that famous Eiffel Tower could possibly be hiding; he still hadn't seen it. And the Seine? It did flow through Paris, after all, didn't it? He had hoped to discover those two symbols of the city by himself, but he was beginning to fear that he would not succeed in his quest. So be it! He would accept the help M. Kratzmann had so kindly offered him.

A fine man, M. Kratzmann! What luck for Yankel to have happened on such a contact! Old Schloyma had certainly made a happy choice. . . . Educated, enlightened, completely French, he seemed in the bargain to be quite well off. He was a tailor by trade—and a self-employed tailor at that! And he lived in a vast, opulent apartment (Rue Sainte-Croix-de-la-Bretonnerie, fifth floor) consisting of a bedroom which he and his wife used, a dining room in which his daughter slept, and a workroom where he sewed during the day and in which his two sons slept at night. In addition, a kitchen, a foyer, a large storage closet . . . and a toilet right in the apartment! And running water! No need to go out to a pump; you turn a faucet and water flows, just like that, all you want. In fact, M. Kratzmann had hinted with modest pride that soon he would even have running water installed in the kitchen! As for the lighting, a luxurious hanging oil lamp made do "while they were waiting for gaslight," as M. Kratzmann had added with a satisfied smile. Gaslight? What was that gaslight, Yankel wondered in his ignorance. But since, apparently, it was superior to the oil lamp, it must be something truly magnificent.

Having arrived in the middle of the night, Yankel, half dazed from the interminable trip, had fallen into the arms of M. Kratzmann, who had been waiting for him at the station. How had M. Kratzmann been able to pick him out in that throng of travelers? A mystery! Whatever the solution, the fact remained that Yankel had suddenly felt his arm being gripped. "You are Herr Yankel Mykhanowitzki?" a voice had whispered in Yiddish. As easy as that! Greeted like a son, loaded into a hackney, a few minutes later he had found himself in the midst of the Kratzmann family, his head swimming with words of welcome. A good, hot meal had been awaiting him, and he had gulped it down while answering as best he could a flood of questions about the homeland, about the shoemaker Schloyma and all his relatives, about the pogroms and the horrible fate of the Jews in the Territory. After which, they had bundled him off to bed—a mattress on the kitchen floor. In the morning he had been awakened, very late, by whispering and muffled laughter. A good cup of coffee, bread, butter, jam . . . Right off, M. Kratzmann had offered to take him in as a boarder; by coincidence, he happened to know someone who wanted to sell a folding bed, as good as new. Yankel had protested that he didn't want to put him to any trouble; but in the end, politeness having been satisfied, he had accepted enthusiastically.

Thereupon, M. Kratzmann—what a lively little man he was—had offered to show him around Paris. . . . "No? You don't want me to? But why not?" Seeing his host's face cloud over, Yankel had undertaken to explain that the first day—"Yes, it's stupid, but that's the way I am!"—the first day, he wanted to taste by himself, in his own way, the surprises which Paris, the City of Light, held in store for him.

And hearing Yankel speak thus, M. Kratzmann had exclaimed in delight: "So! We have an intellectual with us! What do you think of that!" The whole Kratzmann family had cried out in admiration, and Yankel, a little embarrassed, had thanked them all politely, had then left the apartment, gone down the five flights of stairs and had let himself be submerged by the "human sea." For hours now, he had been wandering about, from the Place des Vosges to the Rue du

48

Renard, from the Rue de Rivoli to the Rue Rambuteau. And finally, he realized he had had enough. Besides, it was dinnertime.

Let's see now, where in that immense city was Rue Sainte-Croix-de-la-Bretonnerie?

He had, or believed he had, a good sense of direction; in his mind, the city had already begun to arrange itself around its principal arteries. As a matter of pride, therefore, he abstained from asking his way and set out bravely into the labyrinth.

What struck him now was the absence of sky. It was midafternoon of a lovely, warm summer day; in the country the sun must be shining resplendently against a bright blue sky. But here the sky was reduced to narrow bands above the city's man-made canyons, and it wasn't even blue, but white or reddish brown. Yankel felt as if he were suffocating. Dust was everywhere, blanketing the houses, the sidewalks, the people; the air was saturated with it.

He stopped a moment to read a street sign: RUE DU ROI-DE-SICILE. Good! He remembered having passed there before. But in which direction was Rue Sainte-Croix-de-la-Bretonnerie?

Not that he was anxious to get back to the pleasant, noisy Kratzmann household, but he felt certain obligations toward his hosts. In fact, what he really wanted was to go someplace where he could breathe some fresh air and clear his lungs a little; he dreamed longingly of that wondrous Place des Vosges, lined with trees. This way! he finally decided. And he set out again.

Streets following streets, streets crossing streets. The crowd, everywhere teeming, boisterous. Children squealing, chasing each other, fighting; men calling out to their friends. Vulgar women, hatless; several of them—the sluts!—went so far as to speak to him, in Yiddish, to tempt him into vice. Jewish prostitutes, pfeh!

And many of the Jewish men he saw weren't much better. In every cabaret he passed (and God knows, Paris was full of them!), he noticed drunken Jews—drunk, yes sir!—arguing and fighting just like Christians! Ah, in Rakwomir you'd never have seen such scandalous behavior!

Troublesome questions began cropping up in Yankel's mind; prudently, he decided to set them aside for later, but nevertheless they continued throbbing somewhere in the deep recesses of his soul. To begin with, why so many Jews? After all, Paris isn't a Jewish city, is it? Where do the Christians live? It seemed to Yankel that he hadn't seen a real Frenchman since he had arrived in France, except perhaps

49

on the train that had brought him to Paris. In a way, it was comforting; but on the other hand . . . And yet, the names of the streets were certainly French, and often even Christian. Rue Saint this, Rue Sainte that; M. Kratzmann lived on a Rue Sainte-Croix, if you please! And moreover, it didn't seem to bother him in the least!

Two men were coming toward Yankel, and from afar he could hear their shrill Yiddish. I'll ask them the way, he thought. But he said nothing; from their accent, he could tell as they passed that they were Polish Jews. Polacks, riffraff! Yankel despised the Polish Jews almost as much as he hated the Russian pogromists. They spent their lives bawling obscene songs, drinking, playing cards, running after loose women; their only goal was to make money, in any way possible, but preferably dishonestly. On top of that they were cowardly, lying, treacherous, slippery and hysterical. With all that, was it any wonder there were so many anti-Semites on earth! The Polacks almost justified them.

In particular, Yankel reproached those contemptible beings for the way they had of pronouncing Yiddish—flabby, slobbering, as if they were always about to spit or throw up. For example, to ask "What is that?" Yankel would say simply, *"Vuss iss duss?"* It was natural, correct, human! And do you know what that became in the mouth of a Polack? *"Voo-es iz doo-es?"* Yes, just like that, disgusting!

Yankel classed only the Romanian Jews lower than the Polish. Except for the Algerian whom he didn't even bother to classify— they were hardly Jews any more, bloodthirsty as they were, like the Arabs, and wielding knives with the same facility.

Not for anything in the world would Yankel have asked such disreputable beings the way. What he was looking for was an honest compatriot, a *landsman* like M. Kratzmann. Or a French Jew, maybe? But how do you tell a French Jew from a non-Jewish Frenchman?

In the end, Yankel gathered all his courage together and, attracted by the debonnaire countenance and the heavy mustaches of a policeman who was standing on a street corner, his hands behind his back, Yankel went up to him, his heart pounding, politely raised his cap and handed him the slip of paper on which M. Kratzmann's address was written. The policeman took the slip of paper and studied it a long while at arm's length; then, bending over Yankel, he began to speak. Naturally, Yankel was unable to distinguish a single familiar word in that monotone buzz. But out of politeness he smiled and nodded, as if the explanation were perfectly clear to him.

The police officer finally drew himself erect. He had finished, and the discourse had been long. Was Rue Sainte-Croix-de-la-Bretonnerie that distant? Yankel had caught only one word, the last: ". . . understand?" He turned both his palms up, drew in his head between his shoulders and broadened his conciliatory smile: no, he hadn't understood! The officer pushed up the peak of his kepi with his index finger and patiently began his explanation all over again, speaking very loudly and with the aid of broad gestures: that way, to the right, two (Two what? Two streets, probably), then to your left . . . Yankel nodded assent: yes, this time he had understood. A feeling of gratitude welled up in him for that fine, worthy policeman. In Russia, of course, the police were all stupid oafs.

The officer continued speaking, stopping every ten words to ask: "Understand?" Yes, yes, Yankel indicated that he understood, though actually he wasn't quite sure whether the man was going on with his explanation or repeating it. He felt like thanking him and leaving; he knew the beginning of the way, at least, and he would manage the rest. But he didn't dare interrupt before the policeman had finished. So he kept nodding in agreement.

In the meantime, a man had stopped and was listening to the officer's monologue. A second man joined him, then others, then women, children. Yankel was beginning to feel uneasy. The crowd of celebrants streamed around the group, fastened onto it, swelled it. In the center, the first man had got into a discussion with the policeman, both of them employing a great array of gestures, fingers pointing to the right, to the left, hands raised to the heavens, taking them to witness. . . . They seemed very angry to Yankel. Whatever is the matter with them? he wondered, growing more apprehensive by the minute. Other men, and even women, intervened. All at once the policeman turned crimson, dug violently in the inside pocket of his tunic, drew out a little book, brandished it menacingly and began thumbing the pages, stopping from time to time to lash out with a furious word or two. It appeared to Yankel as if he were defending himself against the entire crowd. A false impression, of course; a police officer, in uniform, doesn't have to defend himself. And why should he have to defend himself to begin with? Why should anyone want to attack him? Yankel decided the moment had come to slip quietly away. But just as he was preparing to leave, the first man caught him by the arm and said in Yiddish:

"Ay, don't listen to that idiot! Come, I'll show you where it is."

51

But Yankel was determined to thank the kindly policeman before leaving. He raised his cap, searched his memory for the few French phrases he knew and finally, carefully spacing out the words, pronounced in a firm voice:

"Beaucoup . . . merci . . . monsieur!"

Without looking at him, still absorbed in his discussion, the policeman raised two fingers to his kepi in a salute. And that little mechanical gesture sufficed to fill Yankel with love for all Frenchmen, uniformed or not.

"Come! This way!" said his guide, whisking him off.

Yankel was floating in a sea of happiness. For the first time in his life, he had spoken French with a real Frenchman, a polite, accommodating, intelligent man! Civilized, in short! And in uniform! He turned around, wanting to give him one last affectionate smile . . . Ay-yi! What was going on back there? The policeman was angrily berating the protesting crowd.

"But what's got into them?"

"Oy, it's nothing! Don't worry about those idiots. They're only arguing!"

"But what for?"

After all, there had to be a reason for such a kindly man to be transformed into a ranting demon!

His guide explained then that the policeman was an idiot who, not knowing the neighborhood, had indicated a long, roundabout way. The people had wanted to correct him, and so there you were—everyone began arguing.

"Just for that?"

"What else?"

Yankel, nevertheless, was skeptical. And he became even more so when he realized that his benevolent guide was a Polish Jew. For a Polack, it's well known, never does anything, never says anything without some ulterior motive in the back of his head. And who had given him permission to address Yankel in the familiar form? Why, the man had never so much as set eyes on him before!

Yankel glanced quickly at his companion. Well-dressed, clean-shaven—rather likable all in all, despite that deplorable accent . . . But he remained on his guard; the man was trying too hard to be of service. Too much is too much! There, what did I tell you! Now he's beginning to ask questions! All Yankel could think of was getting away from that shady character.

But the shady character insisted upon accompanying him right to the house; with the least encouragement he would have gone upstairs and invited himself in. If you imagine you've found yourself some naïve child, Yankel thought, you're very wrong, my friend! And he took leave of the man almost coldly, barely thanking him for his trouble.

Yankel had long known that Paris wasn't just the City of Light, but was also, as Tolstoy had said, the modern Babylon. He was nobody's fool, Yankel Mykhanowitzki!

Yankel was unable to sleep. All the excitement, added to his fatigue, had pushed him beyond the bounds of slumber. His first night in Paris, it was wonderful! Brilliant ideas sprang up in his mind, glittered, faded, were replaced by others which they spontaneously evoked. What would remain of them the next morning? Probably nothing but dull, empty shells. But meanwhile, the wheels were turning, turning, tirelessly with a smooth, regular motion.

He was soaring to dizzying heights, the whole earth spread out beneath him. And to his utter astonishment he felt not the slightest dizziness, he who grew faint whenever he looked down at the street too intensely from a second-story window. But . . . but what was happening? The earth was racing away, was now only a dot, a speck, a pinpoint! Ah, a feeling of anguish knotted his stomach, he suddenly lost heart. Tumbling, tumbling, like a rock . . . A violent flip and, despondently, he fell flat on his mattress. How stupid! He had been dreaming; but now he was wide-awake, his heart pounding heavily.

All at once, precise, concrete thoughts began striking him like bullets. He was positive they were somehow connected, but exactly how he couldn't say.

I'm going to dress like everyone else.

Monsieur Kratzmann isn't a true Frenchman. At home, he speaks Yiddish with his family. He's a foreigner, and he'll stay a foreigner all his life.

I must learn French, and learn it well.

I've got to find a job.

I'll wait a little before sending for Hannah and the baby. You can never tell.

I'm thirsty.

His throat was parched, his tongue glued to his palate. Even at night and on the fifth floor, the air was stagnant, sticky. City air held captive in that jungle of stone. Yankel felt lost, an imperceptible atom somewhere in the vast universe. He got up, noiselessly opened the front door and went out into the hall. "You see," Kratzmann had learnedly explained, "you turn the faucet, like that!" There it was, a handsome copper faucet gleaming in the darkness. Yankel shrugged his shoulders. A fine man, Kratzmann, but why did he always have to explain the simplest things in such detail, as if his guest were a savage or a four-year-old child? Yankel knew what a faucet was, no? In Rakwomir, they didn't have running water, but they certainly did have faucets. There was one on every cistern!

He turned the faucet and water gushed forth; he doused his face with it, drank thirstily from his cupped hands. Pfeh! What flat, warm, sickly-tasting stuff! In Rakwomir, you could always get good fresh water from the wells.

He returned quietly to the apartment, closed the door and went back to the kitchen. Suddenly he felt very sleepy, but he walked over to the window, leaned out and looked up at the sky—*the Paris sky!* Was he dreaming? No, it was really Paris, Paris, Paris! A surge of joy swept through him, fresh, youthful, free, ineffable! He stretched himself voluptuously, smiled. He was in Paris. Yes!

"Yes!" he said aloud, in the language of his adopted country.

He ran back to his mattress and curled up under the sheet. The air had abruptly freshened.

You're always a foreigner to someone, he thought oddly, just before falling off into a dreamless sleep.

II

THEN, all at once, time began rushing past with such dizzying swiftness that Yankel lost his footing. Borne along by the tide, he could no longer find a moment to spare for his treasured meditations, his beloved introspections. The moment he jumped out of bed in the morning he would begin rushing; no sooner did he lie down at night than sleep would overtake him. He was constantly beset by emotions, violently contradictory, always irresistible, and always forgotten the instant they had passed. As if in a dream, he forged ahead doggedly, teeth clenched, nerves vibrant, eyes constantly on the watch.

That, at least, was how he saw himself. For to others, he was simply a nice young man, quiet, polite, content with his lot and easily provoked to sententious discourse; he was considered dull—and very slow. In the street, heading to work at his even gait, he seemed always to be taking a stroll, as if he were a man who had his entire life ahead of him, a man to whom nothing ever happens and who goes his peaceful way without fuss or bother. He, on the contrary, in the rare moments when he stopped to catch his breath, had the impression that a torrent had swept him up and was bearing him along in its raging current.

Rakwomir? His gentle, slow, primitive homeland? Whenever he happened to think of it, it was with a derisive yet vaguely affectionate smile—the smile of a mature man at a child's playthings, of an old man at the memories of his own youth.

But he never looked back upon himself. He disliked the picture of that strange, ridiculous, childish individual, that unenlightened youth who used to trot along the main street of the village. He was even ashamed of him. What did he still have in common with that stranger —that foreigner?

He received letters from the homeland. His father's, inevitably full of dogmatic assertions, commands, prohibitions, with Jehovah's thunderbolts constantly brandished. Poor old despot! How harmless his

55

toy weapons seemed now! They didn't even anger Yankel any more. Does a reasonable adult let himself be angered by a petulant child? Neither his mother nor his sisters knew how to write; women had no need of that luxury. It was his father who wrote for them: "Your poor mother says that . . . Sarah sends you . . ." But old Avrom never imagined that thoughts other than his own could exist. And besides, do women think at all? Thus, whether in the name of mother or of sisters, it was always he who spoke.

As for Hannah, rather than ask her terrible father-in-law, or even her own father, she preferred dictating her letters to a stranger, to Schloyma the shoemaker. But how was she to express herself freely with that screen placed between her and her husband? All her letters were alike—discreet, vaguely troubled. Disappointing, all in all. Yankel would run through them distractedly. Always the same thing! "Nothing new . . ." No, nothing new ever happened in Rakwomir; a year there counted for less than a day in Paris; time simply didn't flow at the same speed.

Sometimes, however, unexpectedly, a tiny detail would go straight to his heart. Rivka is walking now? But she was only six months old when I left! What? Little Itcha (Yankel's youngest brother) got a whipping for saying the *reb* smelled bad? He's going to school already? But . . . In a flash, the swift passage of time would burst upon Yankel: He had been in Paris six months, fifteen months! Full of remorse, he would pick up his pen. Poor Hannah! How long has it been since I last wrote to her? But I'll make up for it, I'll write her a ten-page letter and tell her all about everything! After all, why shouldn't she have a little happiness, too?

And then, his writing paper before him, he would find himself completely empty. Yes, he was feeling fine. Yes, France was a wonderful country. Yes, he had a job, but it still wasn't permanent. She would have to wait a little while. He would send for her soon. Soon. It wouldn't be much longer, he hoped, he was sure. Love . . . With a great effort he would manage to fill up a page or two, and he would heave a sigh of relief when at last he was able to sign his name. It eventually reached the point where he answered only one letter in three, four, five; in the end, he let months go by without giving her any sign he was alive.

First of all, he had had to report to the police.

He wasn't the least bit anxious to do so. Police, bureaucrats, governments, authorities of all sorts had but one objective, as Yankel well knew: to crush the lowly and make them even humbler than they were. Now, what could be more humble than a foreigner, if not a Jewish foreigner? Having fled illegally from Russia, he possessed no passport; and no one had asked him to produce one upon entering France. Thank God, civilized countries scorned red tape and welcomed people just as they were. At the border, the customs official had pushed aside the piles of Russian documents—unintelligible to him, in any case—with which the emigrants had provided themselves, just in case.

Good! But why, now that he had both feet in France, now that the hardest part was over, why go to the police? It was like sticking one's head in the lion's mouth!

Patiently, M. Kratzmann explained that ever since the anarchist disorders the French police had been keeping a close eye on foreigners; if Yankel didn't want to be deported, he would have to report to the police.

"But what are they going to do to me?"

"Ah, don't worry so much, it's nothing!" Kratzmann replied in annoyance. "It's a formality, that's all. They enter you in a register and give you your *préfecture*. Come, you'll see for yourself."

Always amiable, Kratzmann would have gone through fire and water for his compatriot, would tell him about French customs, offer to help him in every way possible; in fact, he was so amiable that it put Yankel on his guard and tended to make him quibble.

"My *préfecture*, my *préfecture*, what's that? There aren't any internal passports in France, are there?"

"Of course not! This isn't Russia! You can go where you like, without asking anyone's permission!"

"Jews too?"

"Absolutely, absolutely! Jews, *goyim*, it's all the same here!"

Yankel meditated a moment. What a wonderful country, France! Then he once more took up the thread of his reasoning, which lacked neither logic nor tenacity.

"So what's the use of going to the police?"

And M. Kratzmann began explaining again, and there seemed no end to it as Yankel kept putting off his visit to the police.

He put it off until the moment when he felt M. Kratzmann would throw him out if he continued procrastinating. And after all, Yankel could understand him. He had a wife and children; he wasn't anxious to get into any trouble. Nevertheless, Yankel held it against him. Having acquired a taste for the illegal from his adventure, he asked nothing better than to continue his little game of hide-and-seek with the authorities. It gave him the feeling he was defending his dignity.

When he finally made up his mind to go, M. Kratzmann's affability immediately returned and, chattering contentedly, he accompanied Yankel to the police. They passed beneath a huge portico where people were scurrying about in every direction while a policeman stood there, idly dreaming. Yankel glanced at him. What good was he doing there, that lazy lout? He stopped no one, asked no questions; you simply went right inside, as if you were entering a railroad station! In Russia, the police at least earned their pay. They would loom gigantic, brutal, stubborn in front of every official building. And you didn't go inside just like that, oh, no! "What are you doing here, Jew? Step up! Let's see your papers!" And you would have to show them a pile of documents full of official seals, for most of them didn't know how to read. They would even search you, run their hands over your most intimate parts: And all the while, of course, they would heap foul insults on you, inquire after your prepuce, call you kike, son of a whore, or, at best, when they were polite, Jew every other word. It was shameful, but . . .

Yankel blushed; he had just realized that he was actually on the verge of admiring the methods of the Russian police. Pfeh! Is man such a vile animal that he enjoys being mistreated and humiliated? And therewith his love for France became almost adoration. Noble land in which even the police are humane! For after all—you might as well admit it—a state has to have police. But why brutal, loutish police? There are other methods of governing people besides terror.

A smile on his face, Yankel walked boldly into the lair of the police, close on M. Kratzmann's heels. Behind a table a uniformed figure with a handsome metal chain across his waist was intently reading a newspaper. Politely, M. Kratzmann removed his hat and addressed a question to him; and after a long moment, without raising his nose, the attendant grumbled something. M. Kratzmann thanked him effusively and then, his hat still in his hand, headed for one of the windows. Yankel hesitated. Did he or did he not have to uncover his head in that place? Most of the people were covered. Pfeh! Why leave yourself open for humiliations? Why take a chance of having some bureaucrat knock your cap off with the back of his hand? What does it cost to take it off yourself? Yankel took it off.

There was a crowd at the window, a mangy, vulgar, bad-smelling lot; shabby foreigners, wailing, whining, jabbering in all languages. Yankel felt humiliated mingling with them, being taken for one of them. He was a foreigner, yes, but a respectable foreigner; he didn't belong among these dregs of all nations! So he ignored them, and even to jovial M. Kratzmann he replied only in monosyllables. In truth, he was ashamed to speak Yiddish here; the Paris Police, can you imagine! And all the more ashamed since M. Kratzmann didn't speak, but screeched. As a matter of fact, everyone in that place was screeching, and it raised such an ear-splitting din that every five minutes a police officer would come over and begin roaring furiously. No doubt he was telling them to be quiet, for the shouting would die down a bit, only to pick up again once he had left. But what really astonished Yankel was seeing one of the foreigners, and one of the shabbiest at that, fearlessly arguing with the policeman. Argue with a uniform? But . . . but he would get himself beaten up. . . . No Nothing happened. The policeman suddenly laughed, raised his arms to the heavens and went off. What anarchy! Yankel couldn't help thinking.

Finally he reached the window and was even more astonished. The man on the other side, a wizened old bald-headed fellow with a drooping mustache, wasn't even wearing a uniform! Yes, a simple civilian, clad in a plain black shiny jacket. In Russia, each and every bureaucrat was privileged to wear a uniform complete with gilded buttons, epaulets and various insignia; and not for anything in the world would any of them have declined that privilege. And here, right in the main police station, there were people without uniforms? And in Paris yet, in the capital? Hmm! Now that's what you call civilized, Yankel said to himself with somewhat artificial fervor. For actually he missed the uniforms. It makes a man a man, a uniform; say what you will, it gives the wearer a sense of responsibility, of importance. And it inspires respect, too, while that little old man there —why, he's a picture of shabbiness, of poverty! Almost of degradation.

Yankel deposited his innumerable Russian papers on the counter and M. Kratzmann presented them one by one to the little old man, accompanying each with a flood of gracious prattle and equally gracious hand-waving. Yankel was unable to understand a single word. Sullen, passive, he waited; it was all he could do. A package, that's what he was, waiting there while others were settling his fate. And M. Kratzmann jabbered, jabbered, desperately . . .

Jabbered alone. On the other side of the window, the bureaucrat didn't open his mouth or raise his eyes, or touch or even look at the papers that Kratzmann smilingly waved at him and placed on the counter. He wrote in a register, dabbed what he wrote with a blotter, banged down a rubber stamp; then he turned to his neighbor behind the next window and, as Kratzmann sank into silence, laughingly exchanged a few words with him; after which, he returned to his register, and Kratzmann, whose lively little eyes had never left the man for a single instant, began again.

"But . . . but he isn't even listening to us!" Yankel said to him in disgust. So why did M. Kratzmann have to jabber away like that, for nothing? Had the man no dignity?

At last the bureaucrat, still without looking, reached for the papers, picked them up, glanced through them and heaved a weary sigh which raised the ends of his mustache; apparently he had no use for Russian script. There were translators at his disposal, no doubt, but he would have had to summon them and that of course meant considerable bother. . . . In the meantime, Kratzmann went on prattling ever more vigorously, and it occurred to Yankel that while French was a melodious language, all the same it was not as melodious or as forceful as Russian.

Abruptly, familiar sounds rose above the French prattle.

"What name would you like?" M. Kratzmann asked in Yiddish.

"What?"

Yankel failed to grasp the meaning of the question. And Kratzmann explained that due to the transcription from Russian into French, he could, if he wished, Frenchify his name a little. It might be useful later on; you could never tell. . . .

"I'd like my real name," Yankel replied firmly.

"Aiyee, take advantage of the opportunity, why don't you?"

At that moment, the bureaucrat began shouting and French ceased to be a jabbering, babbling language.

"He says he has no time to waste," M. Kratzmann mumbled as he scratched something on a printed form. The man took the paper and, holding it at arm's length as if he were afraid of dirtying himself (perhaps he was simply farsighted), read something aloud that Yankel couldn't quite catch, then raised his eyes.

"He asked you if that's your right name," M. Kratzmann stammered nervously.

Yankel held out his hand, motioning that he wanted to see the paper. The man scowled, but Yankel remained undaunted and it was the bureaucrat who gave in.

Yankel was still unable to speak French, but he had learned to read a bit of the language and he carefully examined what M. Kratzmann had written:

Family name: *Miranoviski.* First name: *Jacques.*

Furious, he seized the pen, crossed out the two words and wrote instead *Mykhanowitzki* and *Yankel.* Mykhanowitzki, the only honest way to transcribe his name! His teacher had taught him that the *kha* and the hard *i,* Russian letters pronounced in the back of the throat, had no equivalent in French, but that they were written *kh* and *y;* thus his name in French was Mykha and not Mira. A name's a name! And why *viski* when it was obviously *witzki, Jacques* when it was *Yankel?* He didn't know, fortunately for Kratzmann, that the latter had considered Frenchifying the name completely while he was at it. With the *witzki* dropped outright, the name would have become *Mirano.* Jacques Mirano—that's a name Kratzmann considered truly French! He was a man full of good intentions, M. Kratzmann.

His corrections finished, Yankel handed back the paper and, at peace with himself, patiently awaited the next move.

"Ah, la la!"

The crushing scorn with which the Frenchman had pronounced these sounds spoke for itself. And there followed a flood of words, unintelligible to Yankel, but obviously ill-tempered.

Happy as a king, Yankel allowed himself the luxury of flashing the bureaucrat a patronizing smile. He was more than a little pleased with himself; he had stood up to the police.

A few days later, he went to pick up his celebrated prefecture. They handed him a document which bore on top in large letters: PREFECTURE of POLICE. And beneath: REGISTRATION CERTIFICATE. And then what did he read? *Mykhanowitzki,* to be sure, and spelled the way he desired; but also *Jacob!* Jacob for Yankel! The bureaucrat had yielded only partially.

Yankel felt a terrible anger well up within him. What should he do? Ah, he was going to do something, let me tell you!

He did nothing. For he suddenly found a good excuse for keeping his new name. A family name, of course, is sacred; you don't give it up without demeaning yourself. But since first names are the same the world over, why not translate them from one language into another? He was hoping to establish himself permanently in France, wasn't he? So? So he had to adopt French customs, the French language. Then why not a good French first name as well?

Carried forward by the momentum of that beginning, and despite all his scruples, he almost regretted that the bureaucrat hadn't renamed him completely—Dupont or Durand, for example, since all Frenchmen, it seemed, were either Duponts or Durands.

Next, he set about making himself look like everyone else.

Not without misgivings, but what had to be had to be, he got rid of his boots, his long jacket and his Russian-style cap. For a very reasonable price, M. Kratzmann got him a French suit which was still in good condition; but when Yankel put it on for the first time, he felt almost naked with that limp cloth floating lifelessly about him. His boss (Kratzmann had found him a job with a compatriot the very first week) sold him a French-style cap produced in his own workshop, and Yankel tried it on before a mirror. At first he didn't like himself in it, pulled the crown up high and even released the snap-button on the peak—in short, did everything possible to lend some military snap to the thing. In vain: It wasn't made for that; the cloth tumbled either to the right or to the left.

His boss laughed. "Not like that, Yankel! This isn't Russia!"

He took off the cap, reset the snap-button and set it back on Yankel's head—rakishly aslant. Yankel contemplated himself, frowned, straightened the cap and in the end pulled it forward so that it lay perfectly horizontal.

When, for the first time, he went out into the street dressed as a Frenchman, he nervously hugged the walls. But no, nobody stopped to stare at him now; he was lost in the crowd, protected by it, anonymous; he looked like everyone else, Jew or Christian. Though that was exactly what he had wanted, nevertheless, in the beginning, he felt a vague uneasiness as if he had lost something. His conscience, too, troubled him, accused him of being a hypocrite. Wasn't he trying to pass himself off as something other than what he really was? Actually, he had become so used to seeing the eyes of passers-by come to rest on him a moment that being invisible disturbed him; he missed his foreignness. But that didn't prevent him from almost bursting with joy the day someone, taking him for a Frenchman, asked him a direction—in French! From that moment on, he stopped hugging the walls and dared to look boldly around him.

He grew a mustache, the currently fashionable type, and learned to twirl the ends with a studied offhandedness.

He cultivated himself.

The little Yiddish newspaper to which M. Kratzmann subscribed was quite adequate for him in the beginning. Every evening after dinner, M. Kratzmann, his hat on his head, would read aloud to the entire family. He read conscientiously, underscoring the end of each sentence with a nod of his head, bursting out laughing or waxing indignant as the case required, taking Yankel to witness, then his wife, then the rest of the family in hierarchical order. Then he would begin the story over again, not reading it this time, but explaining and annotating the essential passages. If necessary, he would repeat it several times to make sure that everyone thoroughly understood it. Then, a lump of sugar between his teeth, he would take a gulp of steaming tea and swish it around in his mouth, in the Russian manner. It was the pause, the respite necessary for a perfect assimilation of the article. Yankel, elbows on the table and chin in hand, would muse over it distractedly, lethargic and content in the warm intimacy of that family life. He felt at home, was no longer a foreigner struggling to make his way in a new world. At times, his eyes would wander over to Esther, M. Kratzmann's daughter; she was going on nineteen and had a calm, gentle face. Ah, how good it felt, that complete relaxation after a hard day's work! In the meantime, Kratzmann would pick up the paper again and begin another article.

And the things that were in that paper! From gruesome accounts of the Russian pogroms to humorous anecdotes about the rabbi besting the priest, along with statements in praise of the Jewish people made by important Jews or Christians around the world. From time to time Herzl would contribute an article on Zionism, or a scholar would write about the latest scientific discoveries, or a world traveler would present a study on the living conditions of Jewish workers in various countries; there was even religious news. In short, the whole vast world breathed in those pages. And with absolutely no censuring, without the slightest intervention by the police! In complete freedom, high-minded intellectuals expressed the most audacious, the most liberal ideas, cried out the Truth! So much so, that it made Yankel dizzy. He would think of the miserable Russian papers which the ignorant police emptied of all substance, reduced to insipid non-sense fit only for housewives. How could a vast people like the Russians tolerate being kept in such darkness?

Every evening, as M. Kratzmann's voice droned on, thrashing out at the powerful and defending the oppressed, Yankel felt himself growing and blossoming under the sun of freedom; and every evening, too, he acquired more knowledge, learned new things, bared his mind to the bracing winds of science. Poor Yankel! In Rakwomir, because he had read a few pages of Tolstoy and knew that the earth was round, he had thought of himself as being practically an intellectual; but here, everyone knew Tolstoy, Victor Hugo, and Zola, and many others! Children of ten had already learned that the earth is round, that it circles the sun, that the sun itself is only a speck in the immensity of space. Oh, the blessings of freedom! At times, sudden, almost unbearable flashes would disclose to Yankel the abyss of ignorance in which he was still engulfed, he who so fiercely scorned the darkness in which his compatriots walked. Then, dazzled, he would reel back from the blinding light.

Was his critical judgment growing keener with time? Or was M. Kratzmann's voice beginning to grate on his nerves? Or was it the monotony of the evening rite? Whatever the reason, he eventually reached the point where he found the newspaper boring. It was always the same story, in the same plaintive tone. His suspicions were aroused and, once aroused, probed relentlessly. First of all, why did that paper, whose readers were all immigrants, speak so little about France? It was all very fine courageously to proclaim the truth about America, Africa or Russia! But we're in France, aren't we? So why so much timidity when it comes to French matters, the Dreyfus affair, the anti-Semitic stirrings in the country itself? For those ugly things did exist, as Yankel well knew, though he lived in almost complete isolation. Were they afraid of the police? So was that what the newspaper's independence amounted to?

Yankel didn't dare give expression to other, less honorable, grievances. The accounts of the pogroms were interesting, of course, but . . . Well, out with it, pogroms, more pogroms, always pogroms! In the end, it got to be a nuisance! You shouldn't bore people with the same thing all the time. Thus, take Yankel for example, an honest, sensitive, reasonable man. He fled Russia precisely to have a little peace; and you, you seem actually to take pleasure in upsetting that peace! There's nothing *he* can do about the pogroms, is there? So?

64

So leave him alone a little. Those who aren't content in Russia can do as he has done: leave. The whole world is open to them. . . . Yankel avoided thinking too much about his wife, his daughter and all his family who were still under the yoke of Russian autocracy.

As for the paper's humorous anecdotes, they now seemed intolerably inane, and all the more so because of the ritual surrounding their reading. Old Father Kratzmann (Yankel no longer thought of him as Monsieur Kratzmann) would first tap on the table to get the undivided attention of his audience and would then begin to laugh in advance to show that something amusing was coming. "Listen to this! Oy-yoy, how witty these writers can be, *ken ein hurra!*" Then he would adjust his spectacles and clear his throat.

"Then the priest said: You don't eat ham, my good rabbi? It's quite good, you know! But the rabbi smiled and replied: You aren't married, my worthy father? It's quite good, you know!"

Immediately side-splitting laughter would break out.

At such moments, Yankel would find it difficult to keep from yawning. He felt so superior to the Kratzmanns!

At least to the two elder Kratzmanns. For he soon noticed that the children, both the girl and the boys, had their minds on other things while their father was reading aloud. The boys played dominoes and were interested solely in their game. As for Esther, one had only to observe her as she mended her stockings to realize that she was lost in her own private dreams.

Yankel found the young woman quite appealing. So gentle, so calm, so reserved, always even-tempered . . . Poor girl! She could not be very happy with such primitive parents, she who had learned French in a French school, who spoke the language to perfection. She must be anxious to get married, he thought with fatherly affection.

The only thing in the newspaper that interested him now was the want ads. In fact, they interested him very much; he had come to the realization that his boss was exploiting him.

In the beginning, he had been overjoyed to find work so quickly, and with a *landsman,* a man who spoke Yiddish, who understood things, who was doing him a favor, in a way. Twelve hours of work a day, and a salary of thirteen francs every week; it was reasonable, you could live on it. You could even save a little, since room and board at the Kratzmanns', everything included, cost only forty francs a month.

Yes, Yankel considered himself privileged, and not without reason. For numberless immigrants, stripped of all resources, helpless, lost, were forced to carry on a constant struggle against poverty. They would eat at the Rothschild lunch counter, on the Rue des Juifs. For ten centimes they were given a bowl of soup, some meat and a vegetable. This with another ten centimes' worth of bread had to suffice until the next day. Yes, very fine, but what it amounted to was depending on public charity! Like going to the Jewish shelter to sleep, without paying a single sou, and getting yourself fed there, moreover, and even clothed. Or further, attending synagogue Friday evening to seek out a pious man who would take you to his home and put you up for the night, as a good deed, a *mitzvah*. Others, hardly better off, lived five and six to a room, men and women all together. Naturally, the women were scrupulously respected; it would have been ignoble indeed for a man to take advantage of the situation. In fact, Yankel even knew a young man who shared a bed with a young woman—and had never laid a hand to her. They both slept fully clothed! For purity sometimes springs from extreme poverty. Which didn't prevent Yankel from rejoicing at having escaped such purity. He, Yankel, earned his own living, paid his board, could even contribute to the collections constantly being taken up for the less fortunate. He was a man, Yankel Mykhanowitzki, independent, respectable! Yes, that was the advantage of knowing a good trade; you had no trouble finding a boss who recognized your worth, who respected you.

Nevertheless, he soon noticed with surprise that the workers generally stayed only a very short time in the employ of that philanthropic boss. One after another, they would disappear, to be replaced by more recent immigrants. With each resignation, the boss, taking the heavens to witness, would rail at human ingratitude, would then give Yankel, who had become one of his veterans, a slap on the shoulder, would treat him as a comrade, joke with him, and, in the end, would ask him as a special favor to stay a few more seconds to finish up a rush job. Every evening, he would thus squeeze out an extra ten minutes, a quarter-hour, which he paid for with a cup of tea accompanied by a few jests. And when it wasn't the evening, it was noontime. Yankel found that sort of thing annoying, but he didn't dare protest. The atmosphere was so familylike, the boss so friendly, so cheerful, and so progressive too, with nothing but words of justice and socialism on his lips. But justice or not, Yankel flatly refused the day the boss asked him to come in the following Saturday —Saturday, of course, being the day of rest for Jews.

"But this is exceptional!" moaned the goodhearted man. "And I'll pay you for it! You aren't religious, are you? So? You've got to make money, Yankele," he added sententiously. "You've got to save to bring your wife here. You mustn't be lazy."

All his arguments fell on deaf ears as Yankel stoutly held his ground. He wasn't religious, to be sure, but his day of rest he considered sacred. If you became a slave to work, what was the use of living at all? And he needed his Saturdays to get acquainted with his new land. Not that he went outside the Jewish quarter very often (he didn't feel at ease in places that were too luxurious, too French), but still he wanted to reserve for himself the *possibility* of venturing out, if the desire overtook him. Wasn't that precisely what freedom was?

At bottom, the passion Yankel put into his indignation at human wickedness was born of an ineradicable faith in human goodness. It always required a great deal of time and innumerable disillusionments to convince him that a man with whom he was dealing was in fact evil. But the conviction once fastened upon, then . . . then Yankel became truly terrible. Just a few additional weeks of reflection was all he required for the decision to ripen. After that he would never again go back on it. . . . By the time he decided to leave his philanthropic boss, he was the dean of the workshop; the only one who had been there longer was a simple-minded individual obviously rooted forever to the place. His employer almost tore his own hair out, beat his breast, gave his word of honor, swore by his children that he was bleeding himself white for his compatriots, that Yankel would never be happy anyplace else. Finally even offered him a raise of a franc a week. "No? Then a franc and a half, but that's my last word! I've got a family to feed. . . ." He could have offered him the moon and Yankel wouldn't have budged; besides, at his new job he would earn eighteen francs a week.

He had stayed fifteen months on his first job. He didn't stay five weeks on the second. Nor did the third last any longer, nor the others that followed. It was always the same story: a philanthropic boss, a *landsman* who spoke Yiddish, treated you as a comrade, offered you cups of tea—and exploited you. In less than a year, Yankel had had a half-dozen employers and was discouraged. What was going on in France? In the homeland, you didn't change jobs the way you

67

changed your shirt; you stayed at the same one for years and years. Having started at the age of eleven with old Gribowitzki, a decent sort of man who made caps for the entire population of Rakwomir, Jew as well as Christian, Yankel had stayed with him until he left for France. In the interval, he had graduated from apprentice to second journeyman and then, when Samuel had gone into business for himself in another town, to first journeyman. That's how a reasonable man does things! Why all this galloping from shop to shop? What's the matter with these lunatics here, these *meshugener*? Yankel never dreamed that he, too, was becoming a bit of a *meshugener*.

He was beginning to be known in capmaking circles. Finally he found a promising job. A cutter at Sokolowitz', after all, isn't anything to sneeze at! A well-established business, Sokolowitz', not one of those little philanthropic sweatshops! There were nineteen workers, four of them French, and all specialists—cutters, basters, padders, finishers, sewing-machine operators. You never saw the boss; a foreman ran the shop. No favors, no stories. You began work on time, you finished on time. Yes, a clean operation!

There were, of course, some bad features, as there are to anything in this world. First of all, the shop was located in the Sentier arrondissement and thus was rather far from the Kratzmanns', so Yankel lost quite a bit of time coming and going. But it did give him a chance to get to know Paris a little. And besides, he had no intention of staying with the Kratzmanns forever.

One day—he had been working at Sokolowitz' about a month—his neighbor slipped him a note written in both French and Yiddish which, after attacking Sokolowitz violently as an exploiter of proletarian misery, invited his workers to a meeting in a nearby café. It was signed: United Jewish Capmakers' Union. "Pass it along," whispered his neighbor. Yankel passed it along, but he hadn't the slightest intention of going to the meeting. All things considered, he was quite satisfied working at Sokolowitz'. Moreover, he didn't feel that he, a foreigner, had the right to get mixed up in politics. But as he was leaving that evening, one of his fellow workers collared him.

"A foreigner? The police? But unions are legal in France! And if the workers don't look out for themselves, who's going to look out for them? You belonged to the union in Russia, didn't you, Yankele? So?"

Yankel was unable to resist that kind of argument. He went to the meeting.

About ten of them had gathered in the back room of the café—ten, of whom three were union delegates. It was one of the latter who began speaking, in Yiddish naturally. He was a Romanian Jew who posed as an intellectual, quoting Marx, Guesde, Millerand, Zola and Victor Hugo at every opportunity, but never Tolstoy, which displeased Yankel almost as much as his being Romanian. He spoke stirringly, describing the atrocious misery of Sokolowitz' workers, exposing the infamy of the burden of fines which that vampire inflicted upon his employees for nothing, fines which were really camouflaged wage cuts. "He's sucking the very blood out of you!" shouted the Romanian, who seemed to have a far better knowledge of his audience's living conditions than they themselves had.

Yankel was worried; the speaker was going too far. If the police knew . . . Fortunately, the assemblage consisted entirely of Jews, and, of course, no Jew would ever become a police informer. Nevertheless, Yankel promised himself not to breathe a word of the meeting and to slip away as soon as he could do so without casting shame upon himself. He was genuinely shocked; he had a strong distaste for excesses of any sort. France, after all, was a free country, a hospitable country; you shouldn't speak of France the way you spoke of Russia. They don't massacre people in France, do they? So? That Romanian knows how to talk, all right, but he's too quick to take people for idiots! Anyone who isn't satisfied here can just pack up and go somewhere else. There's nothing to stop him; the police aren't forcing him to stay, are they?

The speaker went on, seemingly inexhaustible. He had the eloquence and the passion of a prophet; from beginning to end, he kept his speech at a fever pitch without the least apparent difficulty. Yankel admired his facility with words, but it seemed to him rather extravagant for seven listeners. What he, Yankel, would have liked was a good discussion, simple, human, among comrades!

Finally, with an appeal for contributions to the union, the Romanian ended his talk, and one of the delegates passed the plate around. Yankel didn't dare refuse him his sou and, at bottom, even contributed it with pleasure.

Now the floor was turned over to the audience, but no one claimed it, despite the Romanian's solicitations. Then—what demon had pushed him to it?—Yankel, timid Yankel, heard himself speaking. Oh, it was just a little question, a tiny point of absolutely no importance which he hadn't understood. But it always annoyed him not to understand something. The speaker had mentioned "scale wages" and had upbraided Sokolowitz' employees for working beneath scale, for breaking the workers' solidarity, for being "scabs." Well, Yankel simply wanted to know the meaning of all that. Patiently, the Romanian explained it to him. Yankel agreed. They discussed, reasoned, argued. There was nothing Yankel loved more. An hour later, when he came to himself, he realized that he was the only one of Sokolowitz' workers who had spoken up. And if he experienced a quite natural pride, it was tempered by a slight uneasiness.

For he had allowed himself to become more deeply involved than he had wanted. Yes, he had promised "to lay the workers' grievances" before the boss. He, Yankel Mykhanowitzki from Rakwomir! Yankel, Yankel, what have you got yourself into now? he said to himself. Well, when you break a plate, you pay for it, no? He eased his mind a little with the thought that Sokolowitz was a *landsman*, or practically one, and thus a humane, reasonable man. We can have a few words together, can't we? Just like that, a little chat, nothing binding, you understand . . . You won't give us the raise, Monsieur Sokolowitz? All right, good, let it go at that, no reason not to shake hands and part on good terms. . . .

When Yankel made a promise, he stuck to it. The very next day, his heart pounding, he went in to see his employer. The latter listened to him, waited till he had finished stammering out his little speech and then said: "No."

Yankel replied, "So! Well, that's that. . . . It was nice talking to you, Monsieur Sokolowitz."

"Yes, certainly. Anything else on your mind?"

And Yankel, relieved, went back to work. You see, Yankele, it wasn't so bad after all! Sokolowitz seemed to find the whole thing quite natural; he didn't even get angry. . . . Saturday evening (at Sokolowitz', Sunday was the day off, the same as the French), Yankel got his pay, as usual—and his notice. He was only moderately surprised and made no attempt to appeal to the workers' solidarity. The approbation of his own conscience was enough for him.

Except that from now on, no more nonsense, no more acting like a child! No more letting himself be carried away by circumstances! The time had come to do some serious thinking, and to stake out a clear course. He was beginning to adapt himself to French life, to know the customs, the wage scales; he could make himself understood and more or less understand what others were saying. Sou by sou, he had accumulated a little savings—125 francs in all. In short, he wasn't just a poor defenseless immigrant any more. So watch out, world! Yankel Mykhanowitzki is going to buckle down now, and you'll see, you'll see!

He returned to the Kratzmanns', told them nothing, went to bed right after dinner, slept badly and got up bright and early the next morning when all the Kratzmanns were still sound asleep. Fresh and alert, he left without breakfast, walked to the Seine and sat on one of the quays, his legs dangling over the water.

It was a sparkling morning. A warm sun drenched the clear blue sky with light. It's too nice out, Yankel thought. When it's so nice this early in the morning, it's a bad sign. It's going to cloud over by noon. He sighed; he was beginning to know the treacheries of the Parisian sky. In Rakwomir, when you had nice weather in the morning, you knew it would be nice the whole day.

At his feet, the water lapped gently against the quay. Yankel raised his head. There, on the other side of the river, in the wine-market district and the Jardin des Plantes, the treetops stood out against the sky with the precision of engravings. Yankel tried not to look at the houses; if, when he had set out that morning, he had gone as far as the Quai Henri IV instead of choosing the closer Quai de l'Hôtel-de-Ville, it was precisely to find a more rustic view. He had had more than his fill of the Big City; now he longed only for water and greenery.

From the first moment he had set eyes on the Seine, everything else in Paris had ceased to matter to him. The monuments? They were beautiful, but, after all, they were nothing but stone! While that vast liquid artery stretching before him, always the same and yet always different . . . Ah, how he wished he were a poet so that he could fully express his feelings! Even Tolstoy seemed somehow inadequate.

What he liked above all was the confluence of the river and the Saint Martin Canal. Why that spot especially? He had no idea. On the quays, there was constant movement—cranes unloading sand, coal, stones, sacks swollen with mysterious products, as exotic as your imagination wished to make them. On the other side of the river, casks were piled high in pyramids. To the right, the tip of the Île Saint Louis jutted out, and whenever Yankel looked at it he would always liken it to the prow of a ship. Paris: seaport. He had once heard that expression somewhere, and now he rolled it over in his mouth with immense relish, he who had never seen the sea.

Yes, it was the confluence of the canal and the river that he liked best. And at times, vague images would form in his mind and drift off with the current, and then they too would vanish. Streams flow into rivers which flow into the sea, and are lost. Yes, rivers flow into the sea and, no matter how different their waters, they always end up by mixing and mingling, for water mingles with water, water combines drop by drop with water. Thus, human rivers.

Around one o'clock, his stomach tortured by cramps, Yankel decided to have lunch. Return to the Kratzmanns'? Pfeh! It smelled bad there! He discovered a little restaurant with a view of the Seine and sat down at a table on the terrace. It was the first time he had ever gone to a restaurant, but he felt born to it. A quick glance around: no Jews, neither among the diners nor among the personnel. Good! He would finally have a chance to try out his French.

He studied the menu, especially the prices. Pfeh! It's a special occasion today, so forget the cost, Yankele! He had difficulty making out the handwritten letters, which only remotely resembled those with which he was familiar. But since the waitress was beginning to grow impatient, his timidity jostled him into action. Haphazardly, he stuck his finger on the menu.

"That! . . . And that!"

The waitress said something he didn't understand, leaned over his shoulder to read the menu, and then let out some more sounds, in a questioning tone. He reflected a moment, trying to piece together what he had heard. No, honestly, he couldn't make it out! He gave the woman his warmest smile and said to her, as if it were a pleasant, obvious fact:

"I . . . foreigner . . . not understand French!"

At the same time he held out both his hands, palms turned up, to indicate his helplessness and his good will. He had a totally disarming smile; he was youthful, slender and fine-featured. Conquered on the spot, the waitress, a vast middle-aged woman, became maternal.

"Well, well! You don't say! English?"

"No," he replied with a laugh, bursting with pride at being taken for an upper-class foreigner. He hesitated. "Russian!" he finally specified, not without a pang of conscience. But could he have said "Jewish"? After all, "Jewish" wasn't a nationality, was it?

72

At the word Russian, the waitress literally went into raptures.

She clasped her hands together. The Franco-Russian alliance was still fresh in all minds, and the whole of France swore only by the Russians. Embarrassed, Yankel smiled and nodded approval. The waitress wasn't at all in a hurry any more; her other customers had ceased to exist.

Happy as a true Russian prince, noble Yankel Mykhanowitzki from Rakwomir leaned back in his chair. What a wonderful country, France! Wonderful people! All his cares evaporated; he pushed his cap back and waited to be served.

He was totally unfamiliar with French cooking. The hors d'oeuvres disappointed him a little; they weren't up to the *zakuski* of his homeland. The herring, for example, despite the little onion rings, seemed definitely inferior to good Russian herring, chopped up with hard-boiled eggs and heavily spiced. Nevertheless, he rated the tomatoes, a luxury in Rakwomir, very highly. But when he tasted the "Lapin Sauté Chasseur" (the waitress pointed out the names of the dishes on the menu, to help him improve his French), then, ay yi! he felt his whole life taking on new meaning. The taste of it! The full-bodied unctuousness of the sauce, the crusty yet succulent meat which literally melted in your mouth, the firmness of the mushrooms!

"Well, how do you like it?" asked the waitress, beaming.

"Good! Good!" Yankel mumbled, his mouth full.

"But you must have some wine with that! You won't get wine like ours in Russia! A little Beaujolais?"

She filled his glass; he emptied it. Yes, it was good! It was very good! Most of all, he couldn't get over the fact that meat could be so succulent. Until then, meat to him meant a sort of tasteless, stringy substance. You ate it because you had to, but it was certainly no pleasure. The trouble with Rakwomirian culinary arts, which Mme. Kratzmann practiced exclusively, was that they knew only one method of cooking: boiling in water. Everything cooked was boiled. Chicken, veal, beef, goose—into a pot of boiling water with it! And the longer it boiled, the better. Roasting, frying, grilling? Unknown practices. One single exception: Sometimes an old hen, first boiled, would then be roasted, because a golden-brown skin was more appetizing to look at. But roasting raw flesh? Pfeh! They weren't savages!

In the end, stuffed, gorged, blissful, he sat back in his chair as the owner of the restaurant, his white chef's cap on his head, came over in person to offer him a "little digestive." And then the owner raised his glass in a toast to the Czar, to Russia, and to the Franco-Russian alliance; and Yankel—oh, the shame of it!—actually drank to the health of his persecutors. He didn't even experience any remorse. He felt light—light and completely immoral, and delighted to be so. Not since the night he crossed the border had he known such happiness. He regretted one thing only, unashamedly—not having a pretty girl beside him. Esther Kratzmann, for example, no need to look any further! How he would have caressed her, ah, la, la! . . . *Ah, la, la!* he repeated like a true Frenchman, laughing and enormously pleased with that feeling of complete freedom.

The check came to one franc, fifteen centimes, in itself a huge sum but not at all excessive considering the copiousness and the excellence of the meal. And besides, it's a special occasion! he declared as he set out again, not too steadily, for his beloved Seine.

He knew now what he had to do: become French, that's what! French from head to foot. First of all, learn the language. Not like a beggar cadging scraps of knowledge left and right from any Frenchmen he might happen upon. No! In earnest, like a man, with a textbook and a teacher! And then, leave the Kratzmanns, who were very nice, but who spoke nothing but Yiddish from morning to night. Except that—how everything seemed to tie together—in order to leave the Kratzmanns' and take a room of his own, he would have to earn more money, therefore work at scale wages, therefore work for a Frenchman, like the French. For those Jewish bosses—oy-yoy, how stupid he had been!—those Jewish bosses he had sought out believing they would be more humane, more brotherly to a compatriot, why they were the worst exploiters of all! They took advantage of the wretchedness and ignorance of the poor immigrants to pay them starvation wages. So it was no surprise that the few French workers he had met, even those at Sokolowitz', were all good-for-nothings, alcoholics, unreliable, incapable; they were satisfied with low salaries because they weren't able to do any better, that's all there was to it!

But there must be good French workers, he said to himself, and he blushed for having generalized so hastily upon his meager experience. Yes, of course there were good French workers, but only where they paid honest salaries—that is, among French employers. Learning French, that was the key. Once he knew the language, he would stop wandering blindly through an unintelligible world. He

74

would do as the French, would pick out an employer. And he would get his scale wages, and that was how you had to do things!

Suddenly he began to laugh. Scale wages! Why it would be a fortune! He had some nerve, that Romanian, claiming that even scale wages weren't enough! Not enough perhaps for those insatiable Frenchmen who required so many things—huge quantities of meats, wines, cognac. Naturally, it cost a lot to live like that! Yankel, however, had modest tastes. He ate little, drank only water and tea, and never went out at night. He hadn't even needed an overcoat the previous winter. What for? You call that a winter? Ha! Compared to the Russian winters, your French winters are like springtime. Yankel had gone about in a suit all winter, astonished at the sight of those poor Frenchmen shivering in their overcoats. Yes, if he got scale wages, he'd be a king!

Therefore, learn French.

For five whole minutes, he had completely forgotten the Seine, flowing placidly before him. Yankel's tipsiness had worn off; slowly, skirting the bank, he began walking back toward the Hôtel de Ville.

Suddenly, a disagreeable thought crossed his mind: All through his long meditation, not once had he thought of Hannah and the little one. Not once! Yankel, Yankel, what's happening to you? He quickened his pace. Poor Hannah! Poor Rivka! If he were beginning to forget them already . . . I'll write as soon as I get back to the Kratzmanns', he thought, to ease his remorse.

And after all, why remorse? Wasn't he thinking of them as well when he considered how to go about earning a decent living? As long as he stayed with the Kratzmanns, he'd never be able to send for them. That at least was clear! To send for them, he had to have an apartment. To pay the rent, he had to earn a good salary. To earn a good salary, he had to learn French. Everything ties together; you always end up in the same place.

Would it take much longer? Ho! We have our entire lives ahead of us, he thought breezily. Besides, what was he to do? After all, he couldn't tell Hannah to come only to have her thrown into terrible hardships right at the start. When she arrived, he wanted to have everything ready for her. For he was a good husband, Yankel Mykhanowitzki! She'd have enough trouble as it was, adapting herself to French life. After all, he did send her a little money from time to time, didn't he? So, there you are!

Somewhat less relieved than he would have liked, he took the shortest way back to the house. He wanted to write to Hannah immediately. Besides, the weather was turning bad.

Passing a newspaper stand, he recalled that he had decided to learn French. He placed his finger on the first paper that caught his eye, said "That!"; paid, and prudently stuffed it deep in his pocket. It was the first time he had ever risked such an audacious act. Who knows? A policeman, lying in wait near the stand, might suddenly have put his hand on Yankel's shoulder. "You, foreigner, what's the idea of sticking your nose in French politics? Let's see that paper a moment! Anarchist, of course! Come along, off to prison with you! Deported! Back where you came from!" Yankel, whose imagination could be fertile when it came to catastrophes, had often dwelled on that theme.

"Where have you been all day?" M. Kratzmann asked severely the moment Yankel opened the door. For some time now, the old man had been treating him more or less as a son. It was just the sort of thing Yankel didn't like, but, ever respectful of the prerogatives of age, he abstained from protesting. Without answering, he sat down at the table and spread out the paper, completely forgetting he had wanted to write to Hannah.

"What? You read French newspapers, Yankele?" exclaimed the old man, dumfounded.

Yankel shrugged. "Of course. I've decided to learn French."

"You?"

Father Kratzmann couldn't get over it. What a waste of time! Hadn't he got along fine without making such a big fuss about it? French had sunk into his head all by itself, little by little. And what he knew of the language was more than enough for him! So why did he, Yankel, have to make such a show of being an intellectual?

Esther was seated off in a corner, sewing. She rose, walked over to the table and leaned over Yankel's shoulder.

"Have you become an anti-Semite, Yankel?" she asked in her deep, beautiful voice. A voice that came from down inside, thought Yankel, who was always a little disturbed by it.

"Why?"

She smiled. "That's the *Libre Parole* you have there. It's the paper all the anti-Semites read."

"But . . . but I didn't know!" Yankel stammered. "I . . ."

She laughed, a calm, throaty laugh, heard so rarely in the Kratzmann household.

"Really, you didn't know? Now see here, Yankel, if you want to

76

learn French, why don't you simply ask me? I'd be glad to help you!"

She was standing next to him, her smile still on her lips. Her dark eyes looked down unblinking upon Yankel's. Embarrassed, he squirmed, managed finally to free himself from her gaze. Almost touching his cheek, her heavy bosom slowly rose and fell as she breathed. The sweet fragrance of a young woman's breath—Yankel had almost forgotten what it was like—drifted past him. She always seemed to be waiting for something, wanting to say more than she had said.

"Thank you, Esther!" Yankel mumbled. "I didn't want to trouble you, you understand. I . . ."

He was convinced he had done wrong to accept.

"Would you like to begin tomorrow evening?" she proposed, her voice as steady as ever. "Or right now, if you're free?"

"Tomorrow, I think," Yankel decided, regaining his wits. "I have to buy a grammar; and besides, I don't want to begin with this filthy paper."

"What difference does it make?" she flung back disdainfully. Her dark eyes once more settled on Yankel's. Then, all at once, Esther pivoted on her high-button shoes; a silky sleeve brushed the young man's arm.

Overnight, a new Yankel was born, a Yankel unknown even to himself, a Yankel who regarded himself with satisfaction.

The nice young man, the good young man, honest, tractable, smiling, respectful of his elders, racked with Tolstoyan scruples and enamored of nebulous ideas, withdrew all at once into the Rakwomirian past where he rejoined his Hannah and his Rivka, his bearded, thundering father, his plaintive mother, his exalted brothers and sisters, Schloyma the shoemaker with all his inane pleasantries—and the two elder Kratzmanns as well. In his place, a sharp, hard, tenacious Jewish worker rose up. Darkness and light, victors and vanquished, merciless combat—that's what civilization was! And Yankel sallied forth.

He knew his goal: to speak, to look, to become French. And when Yankel wanted something, he set out to get it with bulldog tenacity. All his will power concentrated on the goal, he pitilessly drove from his mind everything that disturbed him. Hannah, Rivka—later, all that, later.

To begin with, earn a living. For the moment he grabbed the first job that was offered him. Scale wages? A joke! Later, later! Once he knew French, he'd have a right to do anything and everything. Unprotestingly, he even accepted a slightly lower wage than he had at Sokolowitz'. But he gave them exactly what they paid for. No more, no less. Gone was the loving care he had taken with his caps, treating them as objects of art; especially since the bosses themselves would tell him, "Come, Yankel, that's good enough! We're not asking for a jewel!" Now he knew only dull, competent work, capmaking without joy. Later there would be time for joy, later . . .

In the meantime, Yankel went about his work mechanically, no longer joked, no longer smiled at the jokes of others. His fellow workers regarded him as being in a constant fog.

And in truth, he was. Esther, having taken his tutelage in hand, had had him purchase a few secondhand texts from the bookstalls along the quays. He learned them by heart, down to the last comma. At night he dreamed of them; during the day, as he put the finishing touches to his caps with a hot iron, he would see the pages dancing in the blasts of steam which rose hissing from the damp cloth— rules of agreement, conjugations of irregular verbs, unconnected words.

She was a good teacher, Esther Kratzmann, and Yankel made giant strides. Every evening now, after dinner, the two young people would draw their chairs together; the oil lamp hanging above would cast a yellow light on the book set between them on the table. Softly, Yankel would recite the day's lessons; then Esther would go over the next day's lesson with him. On the other side of the table, the boys would be playing dominoes while Mme. Kratzmann mended socks. Father Kratzmann had agreed, in deference to the Intellect, to stop reading the entire paper aloud; he would pick out only the really interesting articles, which, for that matter, were still rather numerous. Esther's shoulder, close to Yankel's, radiated a gentle warmth; at times their knees would touch, and Yankel would draw quickly away, apologizing profusely. When they grew weary of grammar, Esther would take her youngest brother's reader and Yankel would stumble through it, trying his best to put the emphasis on the last syllable and not to roll the *r*'s. Or else, to make the lesson doubly profitable, they would choose a history of France, or a geography. And since Yankel had an excellent memory, he soon knew entire sentences by heart. But there were times when Yankel would lose contact with his book for a moment, having noticed the light down which shaded—oh, so slightly!—the corners of his companion's mouth (or it would be the full curves of her lips, or the white skin of her hand stretched out on the table). But quickly, he would take hold of himself, thoroughly ashamed. Fortunately, Esther seemed never to notice anything. At times, too, he would catch Father Kratzmann looking tenderly at him over his steel-rimmed glasses, and then Yankel would give him a pleasant smile, as if to say: "You see, it's going well; I'm making progress!" For after all, Father Kratzmann did know, though he never spoke of it, that Yankel was married, and a father. How, at first, could Yankel have been so evil-minded as to have dared interpret that look as the look of a good papa brooding a pair of lovebirds!

As for Mme. Kratzmann, Yankel had almost forgotten she existed. It was as if that great hulk of a woman were transparent; it would take him completely by surprise, at times, to hear one of her heavy sighs.

At precisely ten-fifteen each night, Father Kratzmann would yawn, carefully fold his newspaper, and say, "Well, intellectuals?" And everyone would go off to bed.

One Sunday morning, when Yankel and Esther found themselves alone for a moment in the dining room, the girl asked him point-blank:

"What are you doing today, Yankel?"

She had asked the question in Yiddish, which was unusual. For the sake of practice, they had agreed to speak only French. Surprised, Yankel managed to stammer that he hadn't planned anything. Esther, meanwhile, had gone over to the window. It was a lovely spring morning, clear and pleasantly warm. The young woman folded her hands behind her head and stretched herself voluptuously, her face raised toward the blue sky high above; then, her body still arched, she turned to Yankel.

"It must be nice out in the country, don't you think?"

Not once in the nearly two years he had been living in Paris had Yankel gone outside that "ocean of houses," as he called it; his only contact with nature had been along the quays of the Seine. Now the young woman's words abruptly unleashed a torrent of images; he felt an irresistible need for trees, grass, water. It's really a crime, Yankel thought, never to tear yourself away from their human anthill! You live only once, no?

He looked up at the young woman, who, for her part, was looking at him. She was hoping he'd invite her, that was clear enough! He had realized that right off; after all, he wasn't an idiot! But would it be proper for him, a married man, a father, to go out alone with that lovely girl?

For a long moment, he weighed the pros and cons, argued with himself, quibbled. On the one hand, his relations with Esther had been completely innocent. And how could they have been otherwise? He, a married man, a father—an adult, in short, not a callow youth! And she, an innocent virgin, and the daughter of his host! Pfeh! Yankel respected morality.

But on the other hand, Esther was a Parisian. Paris, the modern Babylon, Sodom and Gomorrah! There was no telling, was there? Women, those weak creatures, yielded so easily to temptation!

Yes! But wasn't Yankel under obligation to Esther? She had been so good about offering to teach him French—and without payment! Certainly Yankel owed her *something* in return, didn't he?

In fact, he had racked his brains many an hour trying to find a way to show the young woman his gratitude. Once, in the beginning, he had bought her some pastries. Or rather, in order not to create any jealousy, he had bought pastries for the entire Kratzmann brood. There had been only one thing wrong. She, Esther, didn't care for pastry at all and had given her share to her brothers. So after that, Yankel didn't buy any more pastry. He wasn't going to fatten the whole Kratzmann family!

Offer her a little trinket? A broach, a bracelet, a ring? But those were engagement presents! Or the presents of a philanderer trying to seduce a loose woman. Yankel didn't want his gesture to be taken wrongly.

What could he give her then? Scarves, gloves, perfume? They were the same as jewelry—suspect. Flowers? He hadn't even given them a thought; he preferred durable gifts. So time slipped by, and he found no solution. In the end, he decided he would give Esther a handsome wedding present, later, when she married. Something solid and useful, a good set of pots and pans, for example. Oh, she'd have nothing to complain about!

Good! But since the opportunity had arisen to return her kindness, why not say yes? Poor girl! All week long, every day, she works in her drygoods store; and in the evening she sacrifices herself for Yankel! No, she isn't getting very much enjoyment out of her youth. Just once, someone could very well . . .

Yankel was on the point of accepting, and enthusiastically, when a new thought sprang into his mind: After so many months, what made her ask me today? Yes, why? What has she been doing on Sundays till now? There was something fishy there! Oh, Yankel had no evil thoughts! But anyhow, this young woman seemed to have neither boy nor girl friends; at least, she never brought any home. Always close-mouthed, shut in on herself; Sundays she simply wasn't there, that's all. Yankel had no idea where she went, and, to tell the truth, he had never worried about it, either. But obviously, she must have had friends where she worked, no? Young women, and young men, too! She was very pretty, with her magnificent bosom and her huge dark eyes. How was he to believe that some young fellow or other wasn't paying her court? Did she prefer to keep her parents ignorant of her actions? Then that indicated vice.

Even when he pronounced the word to himself, it literally shook Yankel from head to foot.

Impossible! The drygoods store where Esther worked belonged to a *landsman,* and no doubt the young woman's friends were *landsmen* too, and therefore decent, honest people incapable of thinking or doing ugly things. But what if there were Frenchmen in the lot? A shudder ran through Yankel's entire being. The French have no morality, as everyone well knows. A lone Frenchman in the barrel is enough to turn everyone else rotten. . . . So Esther is going out with a Frenchman? Pfeh! So that's why she doesn't dare bring him home to meet her parents. She's ashamed to face them. Or maybe she's ashamed *of* them. Who knows? Children are ungrateful, and the Kratzmanns, it's true, would seem primitive indeed to a real Frenchman. At any rate, thought Yankel, Esther's true life is unfolding somewhere else, far away from her family. But . . .

"Is it the spring air that's making you so morose, Yankel?"

Tchch! How coquettish, how perverse, how French that young woman showed herself! In the homeland, the girls were shy, retiring, simple. You could understand them immediately, no need to rack your brains. But what was Esther up to? Had she been jilted (Yankel stumbled over the unfamiliar word)? And was she turning to Yankel to replace him? No! Pfeh! He, a married man, a father . . .

All at once, the new Yankel, the Parisian Yankel, reared his head. Husband, father—bah, what of it? You live only once, no? When you stop to think of it, what's to prevent a married man, even a Jew, from going out with another woman if it gives him pleasure?

It had been almost two years since Yankel had left Hannah and

81

for all that time he had been good, ah, la, la, good! And she, far off in the depths of Russia, what had she been doing in the meantime, huh? Living in her little corner, quiet and peaceful, contented, no worries! Yankel began reproaching her bitterly for it. He was a man, after all! An intelligent woman doesn't leave a man alone all his life. A man's a man; he can't go on living like a bachelor forever, pushing away all the beautiful women who offer themselves to him. That might be all right in Rakwomir, but this was Paris.

And at the very moment when that unthinkable act—sharing the bed of another woman—became possible, easy, Yankel suddenly realized that he was burning with desire for every pretty girl he had laid eyes on in Paris. And for Esther first of all, so near and apparently so available. He thrust out his chest and, all puffed up, asked in French:

"Would you like to take a walk with me, *ma'moiselle?*"

She took him boating in the Bois de Vincennes and even taught him how to use the oars. They spent a wondrous morning together on the lake. Yankel had taken off his jacket but, out of decency, had kept on his vest, his tie and the straw hat that he had recently purchased in deference to the sun. Unhurriedly he pulled at the oars, swelling his biceps under his shirt. His eyes never left his companion. She, lolling in the bottom of the boat, her high-button shoes jutting out from under her skirt, let the tips of her fingers glide lazily through the water. Her huge sunbonnet, tilted jauntily over one ear, gave her a saucy look. Yankel was more than a little proud to be escorting a true Parisienne like Esther.

They spoke hardly at all. But Esther, who never sang at home, hummed popular tunes one after another—slow waltzes, sentimental and languorous, the pauses of which set Yankel's heart rapturously aglow in expectation:

> *J'ai tant pleuré . . . pour toi . . .*
> *C'est la val . . . se brune . . .*

They had lunch in a restaurant and returned home in the evening intoxicated with air, light, greenery and music, and thoroughly enchanted with themselves.

Before setting out that morning, Yankel had secretly taken off his wedding band. He had felt it would be more tactful with Esther, for certainly he didn't want to compromise her. Nor did he put the ring on again until just before climbing the stairs to the apartment.

He did the same the following Sunday, then the next, until the day he forgot the ring once and for all.

For now, the ice having been broken, they went out every Sunday together. She took him to the Bois de Vincennes, to La Varenne, to Nogent, to little inns along the river where they would eat mussels and fish and chips while listening to soft music. She had a way all her own—oblique and seemingly indifferent—of suggesting what she wanted; and Yankel could never resist. She dragged him to carnivals which he didn't like because he thought them vulgar, and to café-concerts, where he was in heaven, feeling very Parisian. When she felt like riding in a hackney, she was remarkably adept at getting him to hail one, despite the cost. Still, if she sensed a real opposition in him, even a budding one, she wouldn't insist. For example, take the time she wanted to make him dance: He balked, finally consented, but found that dancing, decidedly, was stupid. She didn't repeat the experiment and even refused to dance with others, though he gallantly urged her to. Several times she brought along some friends. On each of these occasions Yankel wore a long face, declared them superficial and brainless. The fact is, their quickness of mind put his own slowness to shame. Esther didn't insist.

On the other hand, he learned to swim easily—that too she knew how to do—and they enjoyed several good afternoons together on the Marne.

Yes, he was happy. Of course, his French lessons suffered a little because of all that carousing, but after all, you live only once! It's true that, in compensation, he did acquire a great deal of practical experience in the language.

His pocketbook also suffered. You know how young women are—they've always got to have trinkets, baubles, all kinds of nonsense! Esther, to be sure, was a modest, chaste young woman, with simple tastes, well brought up; why, she would never have thought of asking for anything, had in fact offered to share expenses with him! But Yankel had refused indignantly; no one was going to accuse *him* of not knowing how to do things right! Thus, the outings ended up by costing him quite a lot, for when Yankel was in the company of a handsome young woman he paid absolutely no heed to what he spent. He wouldn't hesitate to suggest a coffee, an ice cream, a frappé, or even another course to supplement the regular fixed-price dinner. His thriftiness he reserved for weekdays. It wasn't long before he ceased totaling up the week's expenditures, as he had been in the habit of doing Sunday nights; it was too complicated, he always forgot something. But he did note, with some surprise, that his savings account had stopped growing and that his entire salary always managed to disappear without any trouble. He blamed the high cost of living; he'd have to earn more, that's all!

It took him a good month of reflecting, of vacillating, of deliberating, before he dared offer Esther his arm. As a matter of fact, one day as they were stepping from a public coach into a crowded street, it was Esther who took Yankel's arm, with a perfectly natural gesture. From that time on, they walked no other way but arm in arm, a respectable young couple. They were about the same height; it was perfect. The moment they went outside, they would lock arms.

Hands too, while they were at it, and their fingers would intertwine by themselves. Yankel hadn't even remarked the birth of that new habit.

Then one evening, as they were returning from the Bois de Vincennes, without reflecting, without deliberating, without even knowing what he was doing, Yankel kissed Esther on the cheek. Her soft skin made his lips tingle, completely enraptured him; against his chest he felt the swell of two opulent breasts. Calmly, she let herself be embraced for a few seconds, as if indifferent to it; then she drew away unhurriedly.

"Why did you do that, Yankel?" she asked simply, but in Yiddish. "You're married!"

He swallowed hard, and didn't know what to answer. Yes, it's true, he was married; he even had a child. Pfeh, Yankel, pfeh! They returned home without exchanging a word.

The following evenings, Esther went on with the French lessons as usual; she seemed to have forgotten the kiss. But as for Yankel, his heart just wasn't in it any more. At night, in his bed, he would once more feel Esther's downy cheek against his lips; he would reproach himself vehemently and yet be unable to keep himself from thinking of the young woman lying there, so close to him, on the other side of a simple dividing wall. He forgot to go over his grammar and vocabulary. He became ceremonious again with her and succeeded only in accentuating the uneasiness, at least his own uneasiness, for Esther seemed totally unaware that anything was wrong.

Apprehensively, he awaited the coming Sunday. They had grown so used to going out together that neither of them felt it necessary any more to ask if the other was free. "Where are we going today?"

That was enough. Would Esther call it off this time? But wasn't it up to him to take the initiative? Yankel was at a loss; dejectedly, he waited for events to take their course.

For a long time now, he hadn't paid any attention to the rest of the Kratzmann family, which stirred vaguely around him. But that Friday evening, a surprising thing occurred: Father Kratzmann once more became visible. Abruptly, he set his paper down, took a sip of tea, swished it over the lump of sugar clamped between his teeth, crunched the sugar and asked:

"Well, children?"

The children were Esther and Yankel.

Surprised and slightly uneasy, Yankel looked up at Kratzmann, then at Esther, then at Kratzmann again. As usual, Esther's face was expressionless and her father's creased with mischievous wrinkles. Friday evening's a holiday for him, thought Yankel, since he doesn't work on Saturday. Has he got a good story to tell, maybe? He asked himself the question only for reassurance. Thereupon, Mme. Kratzmann heaved one of her enormous sighs and, without warning, began to weep in great, silent gushes. Esther told them, Yankel said to himself, horror-stricken.

"Now, now, Merkele, what's this all about?" asked Father Kratzmann, seemingly genuinely stupefied. "There, there, now . . ."

The heavy woman got up and fled to her room, followed immediately by Esther. As for the boys, it would have taken far more than this to tear them from their dominoes.

"Tutt, tutt, tutt!" exploded M. Kratzmann. "They get upset so easy, women . . . especially at her age!" he added confidentially, puckering his lips in a knowing look.

And he immersed himself once more in his newspaper, only to raise his nose a second later to explain, in case Yankel hadn't understood:

"Change of life, Yankele!"

And back to the newspaper. Yes, decidedly, something was on his mind that evening, for he looked up at Yankel yet again, this time to affirm with great conviction:

"Esther, ah, now there's a good child for you! A jewel!"

He smacked his lips and, wagging his head to further emphasize the statement, resumed his reading, this time for good.

Sunday, Esther calmly suggested to Yankel that they go to the Bois de Boulogne for a change. They took the passenger boat at the

Hôtel de Ville and went down the Seine to Auteuil; and all along the way, she pointed out the historic monuments to him. The day was so radiant, the boat ride so pleasant, the young woman's temper so even that Yankel, little by little, relaxed. Come now, everything's been forgotten! . . . They walked along arm in arm, but discreetly, without holding hands. And, Yankel noticed, too, that Esther failed to hum; he was most observant.

The following Friday, Father Kratzmann, in an unusually jovial mood, proposed a game of checkers.

"Come, come, leave your books for once, intellectual! And besides, Esther's going to get married some day, no? She has to work on her trousseau a little, too!"

As he laid the checkers out on the board, he began chattering; and not once the whole evening did he stop. He congratulated himself on his brilliant coups: "Huh, Yankele, what do you say about that jump?" And pitilessly jeered at his adversary's errors: "Yankele, Yankele, where did you ever learn to play?" And told stories, stories, stories. . . . Numbed, Yankel felt an obscure uneasiness welling in him. What was the old man trying to get at with his chattering?

"A good boy and a good girl, that's all that counts in life! . . . No, look here, Yankele, if you do that, you're going to lose!" (Kratzmann played a very honest game.) "Ah, Paris, Paris, now there's a city for you! In the homeland, they don't know what life is, they're primitives. . . . Merkele, what are you dreaming about? Give us a little schnapps, the good schnapps! Tonight's a holiday!"

And suddenly he began relating the story of a boy he knew, a very fine boy, a *landsman,* a real intellectual.

"He worked in the fur business and he made a good living, let me tell you! And then he met a nice Jewish girl and he married her— that's life, no?—and what a fine couple they made! Mmmm! Pure sugar!" Powerless to express his delight in words, Kratzmann joined his fingers in front of his lips, then spread them out like a rapidly blossoming flower as he kissed the air. "But one day . . . Oy-yoyoy!" His face screwed up in pain, he rolled his head from right to left and back again. "Oy, men are such pigs, Yankele! One day it came out that the young man was already married back in the homeland. Can you imagine such a thing, Yankele! Oy, what a fuss it stirred up! The whole Rue des Rosiers was talking about it! But what could we do, huh? What's done is done!" Sadly, M. Kratzmann nodded his head, and the corners of his mouth, sagging almost to the bottom of his chin, expressed both the blackest dejection and complete resignation to inexorable fate.

"What would *you* have said, Yankele, if you had been the father of that young woman? Hmm?"

M. Kratzmann's sharp little eyes settled on Yankel's. Without awaiting an answer, the old man continued on, distressed:

"Well, things stayed just as they were! There was nothing anyone could do, hmm? So?"

Hands spread out on a level with his ears, head tilted over on his shoulder, neck drawn into his body, M. Kratzmann was the living image of human helplessness. Yankel glanced over at Esther. Her face expressionless, the young woman was sewing, as if the conversation in no way concerned her.

A lump of sugar between his teeth, M. Kratzmann took a sip of tea and swished it around in his mouth.

"Mmmm! Good!" he declared with satisfaction, smacking his lips. "So that's how it is, the first wife stayed in the homeland. I heard she found someone else and she isn't unhappy. . . . You know, Yankele, the French don't recognize marriages from back there. They have to have papers, statements before the mayor—oy, a lot of red tape with the government! There you don't need any papers, so it doesn't count for the French."

He leaned toward the young man and his nose crinkled confidentially:

"To tell the truth, it was the best thing for the both of them. Yes, yes! The first wife, I knew her, she was a good woman, yes, but too primitive for him. It never would have worked. No, he became a real Parisian, a gentleman, a—"

He slapped his brow, as if he had had a sudden revelation:

"But you know him! How could I be so stupid! Schmuel! You know—Schmuel, the furrier on Rue Réaumur. He's the one! Ah, he's gone a long way since then! . . . Come, Yankel, frankly, don't you think it was better that way? A divorce, that's all it amounts to! Hmm? You, an enlightened man, a real Frenchman now, can you see her—the good housewife from Russia, with her wig on her head and her old-fashioned ways—can you see her in a high-class store on Rue Réaumur? Pfeh! Yes, Schmuel was right; he has a nice little wife for himself, enlightened, a real Parisian, a jewel! That's what brings in the customers, Yankele! You have to be modern . . ."

Despite himself, Yankel nodded his head in agreement, a forced

87

smile pasted on his face. For you mustn't contradict elderly people, you've got to respect gray hair. But his ears were burning. Rather oddly, it was Esther toward whom he felt resentful, the Kratzmann girl, as he had begun to call her. So is that what she had in the back of her head? Pfeh! A Jezebel! As for himself, he felt pure as a dove —he was the victim.

Saturday passed slowly, and Yankel had still found no solution; a single day doesn't give you very much time for reflecting. And Sunday arrived. And once again, since Yankel didn't know how to get out of the ritual, the Bois de Vincennes welcomed the two young people. All day they loitered among the trees, silent, dragging their cankered friendship.

Toward evening, as they were crossing a solitary thicket, Esther stopped short and turned to face her companion.

"Yankel, Yankel, where is all this going to lead us?" she murmured in Yiddish with a sob. "What do you want of me?"

The attack was so sudden that Yankel was paralyzed by it. Being near that even-tempered young woman for so many months had made him forget that she was a living being with possibly passionate reactions; he looked upon her as a pleasant piece of furniture that could be handled without great care. And now, a flesh-and-blood woman loomed before him, a woman who seemed to be suffering! *Because of him!* His mind in a state of chaos, he tried desperately to think. But there was no time, and that tenderness welling up in him, and that feeling of guilt . . . guilt, yes! But for what?

Her lips trembling, the young woman waited. All at once, she seized Yankel's hands, squeezed them nervously.

"Speak, for God's sake, say something! For months . . . Can't you see what's going on at home? Just yesterday, Papa carried on something awful again! He said that—oh, I don't care! I'll do whatever you say, Yankel, but tell me at least what you want!"

She wrung his hands. Abruptly she dropped them, clutched his shoulders:

"Listen, Yankel," she whispered hoarsely, "give me one last kiss, if you want to, and then . . . and then go away, leave us, or it's going to end up badly!"

How beautiful she was in her pathetic bewilderment! A breeze rustled through the treetops, but here all was silent, motionless, drenched in shadow and anguish. . . . Not knowing what he was doing, Yankel fervently clasped his companion, pressed his lips

88

against that cheek he so much desired. Impatient, the young woman shook her head and kissed him full on the mouth, greedily, the way French lovers did. The surprise and the rapture of it cut his breath, stopped his heart.

She drew away a little and began laughing, a nervous, grating, gasping laugh. He couldn't bear it, and without thinking, the way one dives, eyes shut, into a very dark river, he mumbled:

"Don't cry, don't cry. We'll get married soon and—"

"Get married?" The young woman's laugh rose to a shrill pitch. "Get married? We?"

"But your father said . . ."

She stepped back.

"Oh, Yankel, Yankel!" she said reproachfully. "And what about your little girl, your pretty little Rivkele?"

Stunned, Yankel bowed his head. She drew near to him again, took his cheeks between her hands, forced him to endure her scrutiny.

"You'd go as far as that for me, my Yankel? You're that fond of me? Oh!"

Her eyes gleaming, she studied him. All at once she pressed her lips against his, then tore herself away an instant later and ran off into the dark woods. Quickly he caught up with her and put his arm around her waist; she stopped running, fell into step with him. They walked in silence, her head on his shoulder as she abandoned herself against him. After a few moments, he noticed she was weeping.

His own calm now finally restored, he undertook to read her a lecture. He could never agree to her becoming his mistress. . . . "Oh, no, that's no good, Esther! A chaste young woman doesn't become a tramp, you've got to keep yourself pure until you marry. I who have had a great deal of experience in life . . ."

The more he spoke, the more noble, generous and reasonable he felt. At the same time, within him the conviction that he had just escaped a grave peril grew ever stronger. They had laid a *trap* for him, that's what! First of all, that young lady was a little too good at French-style kissing; she seemed much too used to it. A Jezebel, he concluded to himself. And besides, she's one of those hysterical types! He was rather satisfied with his psychological acumen. And a schemer, too. Father and daughter had hatched a plot to ensnare the naïve immigrant. But not as naïve as all that, our Yankel Myk-hanowitzki! He couldn't be taken in so easily, oh, no!

89

She had stopped snuggling against him, had removed his arm from around her waist. Yankel noticed nothing; he was talking. When the first lights of the city began glowing through the trees, Esther stopped to fix her face. He stood in front of her, still chattering. But all the while, his subconscience was hard at work, and the mood of that woodland scene changed radically; for Yankel now knew that the Kratzmann girl had tried to seduce him—a married man, a father! And he had almost given in—tchch, the flesh is weak! —but, thank God, he had held firm.

Yankel hadn't been put on his guard in vain. When they got back to the apartment, he intercepted a glance from Kratzmann to his daughter and a shrug of the shoulders from daughter to father. He interpreted those two signs with his usual perspicacity and was strengthened in his conviction that father was in league with daughter. But they weren't going to catch *him,* oh, no! I'll start looking for a room, yes, right away! And afterward, they can say whatever they want. What you don't know doesn't hurt!

The following days, the atmosphere in the Kratzmann household became more and more unbearable. And it was the old man especially who changed. To Yankel's civilities he replied only with grunts, or not at all; in short, he was in a vile mood. Esther, for her part, remained just the same; she did seem a bit absent-minded during the French lessons, but it was hardly noticeable. The old lady existed neither more nor less than before, and the boys played dominoes.

There were any number of furnished rooms to choose from, and Yankel soon found exactly what he wanted, on the Quai de la Tournelle. He was in heaven. To think that every morning, every evening, every time he looked out the window, he would have a view of the Seine! That, that was living!

He returned to the Kratzmanns' in high spirits and pinched his nose in disgust upon opening the door. Pfeh! Why had he stayed so long in that smelly hole when all Paris lay open before him? But now, all that would change!

The Kratzmanns were already at table. Joyously, he greeted them as a group, not singling each one out as usual, snapped open his napkin and rubbed his hands together at the thought of the good meal to come. Tchch! How sinister those people looked! No one was speaking.

"Well . . ." he began jovially, and fell silent. He wanted to announce, without hurting anyone's feelings, that he had found a room and was leaving. Nothing simpler, is there? But the words refused to come. He could feel Esther's huge black eyes fastening upon him. And yet he hadn't said a word, hadn't even begun, and the old man, for his part, suspected nothing; nose in his plate, he was wearing his now customary long face. But Esther suspected, Esther knew. . . . Ill at ease, Yankel fidgeted in his chair. He cleared his throat.

"M. Kratzmann!" he said at last, gathering all his courage.

"Huh?" The old man finally gave in and raised his nose.

And Yankel began stumbling through a host of explanations, excuses, precautions. The old man's face grew brighter the more Yankel spoke, and his nods of approval became less mechanical. As for Esther, Yankel didn't even have to look at her to feel the silent weight of her eyes upon him.

When at last M. Kratzmann was certain that Yankel was going to leave, had made his decision, rented the room, paid the deposit even, he then became extremely talkative and extremely friendly. "No, no, Yankele, see here, you're not inconveniencing us at all, you're like a son to us! Stay or go, whatever you like, there's no hurry! You'll always be welcome here." Mme. Kratzmann began weeping, but no one paid her any attention. That was the way she was—births, marriages, deaths, leave-takings, any event, happy or unhappy, that broke life's humdrum routine would bring on floods of heavy tears that flowed effortlessly. The atmosphere had now become very gay; old Kratzmann yelped and thumped the table, and Yankel laughed very loudly, and amid her tears Mme. Kratzmann choked with mirth, so droll were her husband's jokes.

Esther rose and, without a word, went to the kitchen, presumably to bring out the next dish. Everyone was careful not to remark her departure, but when it became apparent that Esther wasn't going to return, Mme. Kratzmann, as if driven by some unconscious duty, rose in turn and, her heavy bosom shaking with laughter and damp with tears, went to the kitchen, remained absent awhile, then finally reappeared, still laughing and weeping, a plate of lentils in her hands.

Esther's place remained empty, and no one asked any questions, for they were well-mannered in the Kratzmann household.

And Yankel took wing.

Judging himself sufficiently polished, sure in particular of speaking French rather fluently, he decided that the moment had come to leave his Jewish employers, his *landsmen,* to their philanthropies. From now on, he would live as a Frenchman.

The first French employer he chose respected the "scale" no more than the previous Jewish ones; but at least he was French, and so were most of his employees. Delighted at the honor of working among Frenchmen, Yankel, in return, acted as docile, amiable and humble as he could; as a result, before long he became the whipping boy for his fellow workers. Not that they were basically mean, you understand, but there was one mischief-maker who kept egging them on, an anti-Semite by the name of Klopfenberg who claimed he was from Alsace-Lorraine, no doubt because he was afraid to admit he was a German. Thus, every day, interminably, Klopfenberg and the others made fun of Yankel's accent; and there were constant pranks, in the worst possible taste: They would hide his tools, they would sew up the sleeves of his jacket; once, as he opened the door to come inside, a pot of water tumbled down on his head. In the beginning, he forced himself to laugh along with his persecutors; then he grew angry. The pranks became still nastier. He had a fight with Klopfenberg and finally left.

Many years later, he bumped into Klopfenberg on the street; the man flung his arms around Yankel, asked about his health, and offered to buy him a drink. And, little by little, it dawned upon Yankel that Klopfenberg, the anti-Semite, was a Jew from Nancy. But the revelation had come too late. All he could do now was laugh along with him at the joyous memories of bygone days. And incidentally, Yankel learned that his former comrades had actually liked him, that all they had held against him was the fact that he was too meek with the boss, too much of a moralizer, and that he couldn't take a joke.

Deeply disappointed by his first experience with French life, Yankel wondered if he shouldn't wash his hands of all those churlish Frenchmen and go back to his *landsmen.* But one robin doesn't make springtime, no? If at first you don't succeed . . . In short, having thought it over, he realized that he had been too easygoing, that life was a hard battle. He forged himself a shield of iron, firmly decided to keep everyone at a distance. After all, what did he need with people! After a few weeks with his new boss, he had succeeded completely in his objective: He hadn't a single friend, but his superiors were quite pleased with him. In the end, however, Yankel became disgusted with the whole thing; for him, work meant laughter, warmth, companionship. Once more, he left.

Then he found a job in a truly fabulous factory. It belonged to a young blueblood named Legay who, wanting to rebuild his fortune (much dented by high living), had had an inspired whim—manufacturing caps by mass-production methods, the American way. He must have picked up his information in a night club. At any rate, in getting his business started, he had paid no attention to expenses. He loved to spend money, that man! Interviews in the press: "M. Legay, the charming, man-about-town capmaker, informs us that . . ." A magnificent factory, all brick and steel! The last word in equipment, capable of inundating half of Europe with caps—that, to cut down on costs. Finally, M. Legay, always up-to-the-minute, was particularly interested in labor relations. Everywhere flowers. The cafeteria was like the dining room of a luxury hotel; the cook had been selected by virtue of his laurels. Gymnasium, billiard room, library— nothing had been overlooked to improve the lot of the workingman. Naturally, Legay made it a policy to pay high wages; he wanted to attract the best workers in the Paris labor market.

When Yankel walked into the Legay factory for the first time, he gaped in wonder, rubbed his hands together, took the smiling workers as proof of his good fortune and resolved to work doubly hard in order to pay back such a kind, such a socialist boss. The foreman began by returning the same piece to him once, twice, three times, for various reasons; then he explained that, due to a lack of outlets, the factory was still working at half-speed. Finally, he gave it to Yankel straight: Yankel worked too hard, too well and too fast; he was ruining things for the others, and his fellow workers weren't at all happy about it. Yankel got the point, worked less hard, less well and less fast, and spent his numerous breaks devouring Zola's *Rougon-Macquart* series, which he borrowed from the factory library. His fellow workers, for their part, preferred playing cards.

The liquidation of the Legay enterprise soon cast him out into the street again. Then he was offered a promising job in Lyon and took it, happy at the prospect of being able to see a little of the country. But Lyon was not to his liking; he stayed there only a short while, went on to Tours, then Angers, Limoges. He liked the provinces with their less frantic way of life. And yet, something always prevented him from staying in one place; something kept pushing him to leave; the more he traveled, the more he felt like traveling. He could no longer look at a hill without wondering what lay behind it; whenever he stayed too long in a city, a sort of feverishness would overtake him.

Nevers at last held him. Why that city rather than the others? He couldn't say. When he arrived there, on a dismal February day, he was in a glum mood. It had been raining all morning, he had been cold in the train and, through the window, he had seen nothing but a flat, drenched, hopelessly bleak countryside. Shivering, he walked up the deserted main street. The rain was coming down harder than ever, an icy-cold rain mixed with melting snow. Never had Yankel felt so miserable, so alone—a stranger in a hostile land.

The next day, happily, the sun came out, and the main street looked all spick and span. Yankel corrected his first impression; then, little by little, he made discoveries. It was as if the city had placed its charms so that they would be revealed only gradually, day by day. Yankel savored one nuance after another and soon found that Nevers was completely to his taste. He liked its animated little streets, busy but without the shrill Kratzmannian shouting of Paris' Jewish quarter. He would dream, would go into raptures before the staid old houses; and when he grew weary of houses, a few steps would lead him to the Place du Palais-Ducal, where he could contemplate to his heart's content the panorama of the Loire and the vast plain stretching beyond it. And if, by chance, he grew tired of looking out upon broad horizons, he would walk over to the old stone bridge and watch the river flowing between its sandy banks. The sand would make him think of the sea, and on days when it was covered over by the rushing water Yankel would conjure up images of raging oceans. At other times, he longed for the gentleness, the intimacy of trees and meadows; then he had only to go just beyond the limits of the city, a short walk, and his wish would be fulfilled. And when he began to miss the sight of people, he would return to Nevers and—there you are!—would stroll along clean, bright streets, past smart little shops. It was impossible to be bored in Nevers; whatever your mood, the city could accommodate you. Take, for example, the taste for luxury —and even the most modest of people have a craving for luxury at times. Well, Nevers had a sumptuous, brand-new café, a café of indescribable richness, with its glazed ceramic decorations and all. Only—and this is where the city's true charm lies—that splendid café didn't sit enthroned on the main square; no, one had to go looking for it in little back streets, one had to *know!* Even more perhaps than its variety, it was the city's discreetness which pleased Yankel.

The people too were to Yankel's liking. Calm but not phlegmatic, ironical without being unkind, they answered precisely to his human ideal. Even their physical appearance made him feel at home—there were few tall men among them. Yankel, who always felt humiliated when a voice came from a foot above his head, and who retained from Russia an awed horror of tall men, had at last found a people built to his own scale. Finally, when he heard it said that the region was one of the least clerical in France and traditionally one of the most republican, he knew he had gained port. In the little sitting room in the boardinghouse where he lived, a map of France was pinned to the wall. Often Yankel would plant himself before it; Nevers was precisely in the center, and he could feel, almost palpably, that he had at last reached the heart of his new country.

His boss was a decent sort by the name of Guyot. Simple and friendly, he made a go of his little business without overtiring himself. Three workers, one apprentice. Yankel felt as if he were back in familiar territory. Nevers, at bottom, was merely a French Rakwomir, only much better. He struck up acquaintance with some young men of the town and was soon accepted into their group. After work, they would play billiards or bowl, depending upon the weather. Sundays, they would all go out to the country, have lunch on the grass, swim in the Loire or the canal, kick a soccer ball around or, if there were girls along, play blindman's buff. A few of the girls were rather pretty and Yankel longed to flirt with them; but he held himself in check. And when his companions scoffed at him for his abstinence, he would answer them with dignity. Once, the two or three troublemakers in the group tried to drag him to a brothel, but he turned them down quickly and they didn't press him. In the end, everyone accepted him for what he was: the good, obliging friend who puts the wine to chill and who takes charge of the homelier girls; the serious, likable fellow who can nevertheless, when the occasion demands, add a verse to the drinking song or do gymnastics in the trees. They called him Quéquel, because it was easier for them to pronounce than Yankel; and since, after a few months, he had lost practically all trace of an accent, the newcomers to the group took him for a Frenchman, or perhaps a Belgian. Then it was Quéquel here, Quéquel there; and the barber, the waiter in the café, the shop-keepers even began addressing him exclusively as "Monsieur Qué-quel."

He joined the Nevers Athletic Club and tried his hand at weight lifting, Greco-Roman wrestling, gymnastics, swimming. He learned to ride a bicycle and bought a superb Saint-Étienne. And he developed a taste for the excellent local wines. Without even realizing it, he adapted himself little by little to French customs and celebrated Easter and All Saints' Day with his friends just as he did Bastille Day.

Finally—the supreme happiness—he made a friend. Louis was a photographer, an intellectual, that is, and very cultured. Of austere disposition, like Yankel, he had no more taste than he for lusty pleas-antries which, Louis held, transformed men into animals; he enjoyed only serious conversations, on the most stimulating subjects. He was Protestant, and that too pleased Yankel, though he wasn't quite sure why. The two young men soon became inseparable; when they began a discussion it would often last till three in the morning. Louis pro-fessed anti-Semitism and was fond of developing it into lofty theo-ries, which Yankel would attack fiercely.

"Look here, Quéquel," Louis would say, "you've got to be objec-tive about it. The big Jewish banks . . ."

"Am *I* a banker?" Yankel would protest.

"Ah, if all Jews were like you, there wouldn't be any Jewish prob-lem!"

"How many Jews have you known?"

They would part thoroughly enraptured with each other, and Louis, whenever he could, would invite Yankel to his mother's for dinner.

Meanwhile, Yankel's savings gradually swelled. At times, he would tell himself that the moment was drawing near when he could send for Hannah and the little one. But for one reason or another, he would always put off that momentous decision. He feared . . . Ah, he didn't know what he feared! If only Hannah could speak a little French! But she hadn't even tried to learn the language. So what would become of her, here, in Nevers? How would she ever manage? And besides . . . Perfidious images loomed up before him and he tried as best he could to drive them off. He could see a poor panic-stricken woman, in Rakwomir garb, speaking Yiddish, Yiddish, Yiddish. True, she didn't wear a wig, but . . . And people would whisper to each other: "That, that's Quéquel's wife!" "What? He's married? Quéquel? He certainly kept it well hidden!" "Ah, those kikes, they're all the same!" And Louis, what would Louis have to say about it? Yankel couldn't remember whether he had even told Louis he was married. Certainly his wedding band had remained hidden in his watch pocket ever since . . .

M. Guyot had a daughter. She was about twenty, not very pretty, but refined. Yankel would greet her politely, without the slightest ulterior motive. Then one day in September, M. Guyot took him aside and asked him quite bluntly what he thought of Marguerite. Yankel stammered out that he thought very highly of her. Then M. Guyot came out with his little proposition. In seven months, you can get to know someone pretty well, isn't that so? Yankel was a serious, hard-working lad, not a woman-chaser or a drinker. And Marguerite was a fine girl, a good housekeeper, and had a little dowry, a few plots of ground here and there. And later, in ten or twelve years, well, a man can't go on forever, eh? Well? What did he say to it?

He felt like saying a great deal, poor Yankel! All at once, however, he recalled Kratzmann's obnoxious allusions. But Marguerite, ah, Marguerite wasn't the Kratzmann girl! Less voluptuous perhaps, less richly endowed in the bust and rump departments, but . . . Well, to speak plainly, alongside that delicate, that distinguished-looking French girl, Esther seemed as thick and heavy as a cow. One doesn't regret giving up an Esther Kratzmann, but a Marguerite Guyot, from Nevers, ah! . . . Deep down in the farthest reaches of Yankel's consciousness, an image struggled to appear, flickered, so pale, so weak, so easy to snuff out: a young woman who, with a thin smile, was cradling a baby in her arms. . . . In a sudden burst of honesty, Yankel brought himself to admit to M. Guyot that he was married, that he even had a child back in the homeland.

Good M. Guyot frowned, scratched his head. "Of course, of course. But what are you waiting for, then? Why don't you send for them?"

Heartsick, realizing that Nevers was now closed to him forever, Yankel returned to Paris.

Then he lived through his darkest hours. Convinced he had ruined his chances for a good life, he turned his bitterness on Hannah and wandered aimlessly, numbly through the city. He began looking women squarely in the eyes. On several occasions he almost let himself be tempted by prostitutes; the thing that stopped him, more even than distaste for a paid pleasure and the fear of loathsome diseases, was the possible anguish of happening upon an anti-Semite. He trembled at the mere thought of one of those hideous women casting slurs, at the last moment, on his circumcised organ. But his flesh was torturing him. Until now, he had been able to accommodate himself to chastity without too much difficulty. The first months, aside from loving his wife, that terrible word *adulterer* had still held all the force of a religious interdiction; later, inurement came into play, supported by those obscure fears deposited over the centuries in the hearts of slaves facing their masters' untouchable women. But his stay in Nevers had changed everything. While the other young men and women would be frolicking and making love, unashamedly, healthily, Yankel, alone, kept a tight rein on himself. Then along came Marguerite, and the desire which, despite himself, had been welling in him suddenly appeared simple, indeed easy to satisfy. What? No one would be shocked by his alliance with a French girl? No one saw the least harm in it? No one cared about his being a Jew? But then . . . then . . . where was the obstacle? In his own conscience? Yes, but his conscience as a human being, not as a Jew!

It's a heavy load to bear, a conscience, when there's nothing external to support it. Yankel wondered briefly whether he shouldn't perhaps quit France completely, leaving no trace behind, and thus break his last ties with Rakwomir. Go anywhere, as far away as possible, where no one knew him, and build a completely new life. What was holding him back? For one thing, the thought of poor little Rivkele despicably abandoned by her papa; but also, perhaps above all, inertia. After all, he had been living in France for so many long months, had become used to the country, to the people, had grown roots in its earth. Tear himself away once more, find himself lost again in a strange land, begin anew? The very thought of it made him want to lie down on the ground and die. A man can't change countries twice in one lifetime, he told himself. And France is my country now. Confusedly, he felt that if he left, nowhere would he be able to grow new roots; and without roots, he knew, he would be unable to go on living.

His old room on the Quai de la Tournelle was taken, but he found another one, in a so-so neighborhood, the Grenelle section; it wasn't at all to his liking, but what difference did it make? You've got to live somewhere, no? Now again he gave serious thought to sending for Hannah, so fed up was he with being alone. But in the end he continued to vacillate, wondering what he still had in common with his wife. The longer he waited, the greater the chasm between them seemed to grow. So? No way out. As for everything else, he felt completely indifferent, and profoundly sad.

He had no friends, for those he had he had left in Nevers. Should he renew contact with his Parisian acquaintances, with whom he had been out of touch since his departure for the provinces? What good would it do? He felt he would no longer fit in with them. So he lived as a hermit. When the weather permitted, he would take his bicycle and spend his entire Sunday riding aimlessly about, mulling over unhealthy thoughts. When the weather was bad, he stayed in his room, reading whatever fell into his hands.

All Saints' Day came, and he had the day off. It was gray outside, winter was in the air, and Yankel wondered how he would spend the long, gloomy days ahead. Eat in restaurants, always and forever in restaurants, and then back once more to his cold, lonely, anonymous room. . . . Morose, utterly dejected, he went downstairs and began walking the interminable streets. Reaching the Seine, he strolled awhile along the quays, unable to recapture any of his former joys. The hostile river thrust its dirty waters against the banks. Abruptly, Yankel wondered why he shouldn't go say hello to the Kratzmanns; and with that thought, a great surge of homesickness welled up in him. Ah, just once to eat some good kosher cooking! He quickened his pace. At last he had a goal.

The Kratzmanns welcomed him with open arms. The old woman wept for joy, the old man called him Yankele, and the elder of the two boys, Solomon, a regular little man, asked him very intelligent questions about Nevers and its monuments, the ironworks of Fourchambault, and the shipping on the Loire. And Yankel went into raptures over such a display of knowledge, while old Kratzmann puffed himself up and Mme. Kratzmann wept all the more, repeating: *"Ken ein hurra,* he's so smart, that boy!" No, except for Solomon, nothing had really changed here. What fine people, Yankel thought affectionately. Now that he had become a Frenchman, he took a somewhat aloof view of the Kratzmanns and could therefore judge them, he believed, more objectively: good, simple beings, that's all, a little primitive, still very close to the homeland. And what could be less surprising? In all the twenty years he had been living in France, Father Kratzmann had never budged from the Jewish section; having

99

left Rakwomir, he had hastened to bury himself again, this time in those narrow little streets grouped around the Rue des Rosiers. Was he right, wrong? Who can say? That's life!

Esther wasn't there. Yes, she was fine, thank God, *ken ein hurra!* . . . Yankel smiled. He had forgotten that his compatriots never mentioned a blessing, no matter how small, without warding off the Evil Eye with a *ken ein hurra,* nor a misfortune without moaning *oy, veh iss mir.* There was a time when those interjections would escape his ear. Now he could hear nothing else. Ah, what a wonderful feeling, he thought, to be able to speak Yiddish freely again! . . . And just then, he realized he had been at the limit of his endurance. Ever since he had left the Kratzmanns'—an eternity ago, it seemed, but in fact barely a year and a half—he had not once spoken his mother tongue. Not once! Oh, he could express himself easily enough in French, of course. But it wasn't the same as Yiddish.

Being a well-mannered man, he had gone to the Kratzmanns' after lunch, and not before. He stayed until evening, politely insisted upon leaving at six-thirty, and finally let himself be coaxed into staying for dinner. As they were about to take their places at table, the doorbell rang.

"That must be Esther!" exclaimed old Kratzmann and, sprightly as a youth, he ran to open the door. Yankel heard the old man's shrill voice: "A surprise, Esther! We have a visitor!" The sound of rapid steps, the clicking of high heels; Esther appeared in the dining room.

"Yankel!" she exclaimed joyously, running over to him. A clean, frank kiss on either cheek. She exchanged a few words with him, in French, while her father rubbed his hands together delightedly. She seemed happy, and not the least bit embarrassed. Yankel found her changed, more alive, as if that neutral sheath which used to envelop her had melted away.

"Come, tell us everything, Yankel! What have you been doing all this time?"

"Oy!" exclaimed old Kratzmann with a sour look. "Stop already with your French, the two of you!"

Yankel smiled. The older he grew, the more difficulty Father Kratzmann had expressing himself in his adopted tongue. But the one thing that surprised Yankel was that Esther herself now seemed to speak French with an odd, vaguely nasal, intonation.

Mme. Kratzmann had taken special pains with her meal. Suddenly Nathan, the younger boy, shoved his plate away, a few stringy pieces of boiled chicken still on it. He was a sullen youngster who, now that his brother had become a regular little man, seemed decidedly unhappy. Yankel couldn't understand it; by his recollection, Solomon and Nathan were both very well-behaved children, forever playing dominoes. But time passes, yes, it certainly does.

Tearfully, Mme. Kratzmann began scolding him until the youngster burst out: "It's no good, this chicken! I don't want any!"

He had spoken in French, as he no doubt did whenever he wanted to demonstrate his superiority over his parents. Furious, trembling, Mme. Kratzmann shouted: "Finishtoeat, I'm giving you dessert!"

And Yankel recognized a phrase he had often heard before in the mouth of that ponderous woman without ever having been able to decipher its meaning. Led on by her son, Mme. Kratzmann had simply spoken in French. But it's completely wrong, that sentence! thought Yankel. He was so proud of his discovery that he almost announced it to the others. Alas, he had no chance, for father, mother, brother and sister, all had fallen upon the youngster and were heaping reproaches upon him. His lower lip thrust forward and an obstinate look in his eyes, the boy faced the onslaught boldly, waiting for it to pass.

It passed. "Oy, that boy! He's digging my grave for me!" whined Mme. Kratzmann as she removed the plate of boiled chicken and served her son his dessert.

"Say thank you, Nathan, or you're going to get it!" roared M. Kratzmann, red with anger. Oh, he was fearsome, his hand raised and his eyes sparking beneath his heavy eyebrows!

Nathan again drew his head between his shoulders and gave his father a defiant look. Fiercely, M. Kratzmann slammed his fist down on the table; the dishes and the women all jumped as the old man shouted:

"The reformatory, that's what you need! Wait, wait, you'll see when you're a soldier!"

The youngster stood fast, and the father mopped his brow, took Yankel to witness that the child would send them to their graves, yes, to their graves just as surely as he was sitting there!

"You're too easy with him!" shouted Mme. Kratzmann.

"You're the one to talk!" shouted M. Kratzmann.

And they began squabbling while Nathan, victorious, wolfed his cake and surreptitiously served himself another slice.

Yankel glanced over at Esther. A vacant smile on her lips, she was plainly thinking of something else. This is all perfectly natural to her, thought Yankel, part of the daily routine. Ah, Jews don't know how to raise their children! They shout, and then they give in. The French never shout; no, they speak calmly, softly, and their children obey them. That's the right way! He dreamed of Nevers, of Marguerite; he vaguely regretted that . . .

Old Kratzmann was still yapping away. Old, old? Not more than fifty or so, Yankel thought. And you certainly can't call that old! But as soon as they marry, our Jews somehow become old. And in the bargain, Kratzmann doesn't even wear a beard! Monsieur Guyot is older than he, and yet no one would ever think of referring to him as "old Guyot."

Ah, why don't they shut up awhile! he thought, suddenly annoyed. Talk, talk, talk, endlessly, like a machine. And to say what? A lot of nonsense! The French talk a great deal, too, but not as much as all this, and they shout less, wave their hands less. Why in the world did I come here, anyhow? My place is among Frenchmen, not with these . . . these primitives!

"And there's something you don't know yet." The old man was now addressing Yankel. No doubt a good piece of news was on the way, for his whole face was slyly crinkled up.

"Esther's getting married!" he finally announced.

"No!" Yankel exclaimed, trying to sound as joyously astounded as possible; with great effort, he tuned himself to the Kratzmann pitch. "Congratulations, Esther! *Mazeltov!*"

God, how she looked like her father at that moment! Her mother, too, for that matter. She was going to get married? Good! Well, get married, my girl, get married! Yankel had other things to worry about.

"Ay-yiyi! And if you only knew the fiancé!" continued Father Kratzmann. "An angel, that boy, pure sugar! Mmmm!"

And for a good quarter-hour he sang the praises of Esther's fiancé, whom Yankel didn't know.

Then all at once M. Kratzmann leaned forward and fixed his crafty little eyes on Yankel's.

"And you, Yankele?"

"Me? What about me?"

"Your wife. Have you made up your mind yet to send for her?"

And when Yankel, sickened, failed to answer, the old man promptly went on, his head wagging.

102

"Oyyy, it's no good, Yankele! You've got to send for her right away! A man shouldn't be alone too long. It's unhealthy!"

For a full hour by the clock, Yankel hung his head and pretended to listen to Kratzmann's discourse. Later, back in his room, he wondered why in God's name he had ever gone to Rue Sainte-Croix-de-la-Bretonnerie, and firmly promised himself never to set foot there again.

He not only returned, but soon had made a habit of it.

He didn't know which way to turn any more. Wherever he happened to be, a feeling of uneasiness would soon take hold of him, and all he would wish for was to be somewhere else. Among the French, he missed the straightforward, unadorned simplicity of his compatriots; among the latter, he soon grew annoyed and desired only to return to the French, with their broader outlook on the world and on life.

Torn apart, he wandered about the city, morosely, aimlessly. At times, in a French mood, he would settle down in a café and have a beer; or he would take a ride on his bicycle. At other times, craving Jewish cooking and Yiddish hair-splitting, he would return to the Kratzmanns', and utter boredom.

Obscurely, he felt that chance alone, at the stage he had now reached, would determine his life for him. And all he hoped for was an incident of any sort, a push from without, that would at last tumble him to one side or the other.

But to remain like that, between two worlds . . . No, it just couldn't go on much longer!

One evening the concierge, seeing Yankel go past on his way home from work, stepped out of her cubbyhole.

"Monsieur Mica!" she called out to him.

All the French now called him Mica. And if he tried to correct them: "Russian names, you know. You aren't angry, are you?" Angry or not, Yankel had resigned himself to it.

"There's a lady waiting for you upstairs," the concierge went on.

"A lady? Upstairs? So who is she?"

She shrugged her shoulders; she seemed troubled, almost hostile.

"How should I know? I told her you weren't in. I even asked her if she wanted to wait in my apartment. Because of the little girl, you know—we aren't barbarians here! But do you think she understood a word I was saying? Not a word—"

"Has she been here long?" Yankel cut in, and without waiting for an answer he began climbing the stairs. *A foreigner, a little girl . . .*

"No scandals in this house!" the woman shouted after him, and she returned to her cubbyhole.

No scandals? What did she mean? *A foreigner, a little girl . . .*

He didn't want to understand. But his heart was beating wildly.

Third, fourth, fifth . . . He lived on the seventh floor, just beneath the roof.

"Is that you, Yankel?" a calm voice asked in Yiddish.

He stopped short, breathless, and his words caught in his throat.

"Hannele, is it you?" he finally murmured.

Above, all was blackness; the gas lamps on the landings had been installed only up to the sixth floor. A shadowy form stirred. A rustling of cloth, a creaking of wood. A sigh. Then a child's voice.

"Mamele, is that Tatele?"

His legs heavy as lead, Yankel climbed the last few steps as if in a dream. Vaguely, he wondered if he would kiss his wife.

"I was beginning to get frightened," Hannah murmured as he reached the landing.

"Frightened of what?" he asked in a trembling voice. He didn't know what he was saying; he had only one desire—to put an end to that absurd stirring of shadows in the darkness. But his key clinked against the lock without finding the hole.

"What would I have done if you hadn't come back this evening?"

Ah, at last! The key found its way into the lock, was turning.

"Why did you think I wouldn't come back? Did I have any reason for not coming back?" he replied stupidly. "Wait, I'll light the lamp for you."

In the blackness, the window framed a square of gray sky, tinged with pink by the glow of the city. Yankel groped about for the oil lamp, found it, lit it. The reassuring yellow light quickly swelled, filled the room as he turned around. Hannah was still outside on the dark landing, her heavy valise hanging from one hand, Rivka clutching the other. Yankel, his vision fogged by emotion, could see nothing but those humble human forms which appeared to be waiting. Waiting for what? An invitation to come in? But it was *their* home, too!

"Hannele, why are you standing there like that? Come in!"

He rushed to her, seized the valise, set it down in a corner, scarcely noticing his wife's astonishment at his gesture. He had forgotten that attentiveness and gallantry were unknown in Rakwomir.

Standing in the middle of the room, Hannah and Rivka, still hand in hand, looked about. Yankel closed the door. There, now they were at home! All three of them. Reunited. Saved. At long last! A wave of happiness flooded his heart, but he didn't dare look his wife in the face. Instead he crouched before the child with tears in his eyes.

"Rivkela!" he moaned, holding out his arms to her. "Come give your papa a kiss!"

Frightened, the child hid her face in her mother's dress.

"Rivka, do as your father says," Hannah ordered.

When at last Yankel had his daughter in his arms, he hugged her fervently, kissed her cheeks a thousand times, cradled her, tossed her in the air to hear her laugh; all the old customs that had surrounded his own childhood returned to him in a flash.

Finally he set the child down and raised his clouded eyes to his wife. They had so much to say to each other, and Yankel felt so guilty! He didn't dare meet Hannah's eyes, looked rather at some point or other behind her head.

"Did you have a nice trip, Hannele?"

Oy, what a stupid question! But what else could he ask? Later, perhaps. Not in front of the child, in any case.

Hannah continued looking around her.

"You have a nice room here, Yankel!" she remarked at last.

She doesn't dare speak, either, Yankel thought, and a cowardly feeling of relief swept through him. Bah, it's better that way, after all! What's past is past, that's all, and now we have the whole future ahead of us.

"But why are you standing there like that, Hannele?" he exclaimed. "Sit down, sit down! You must be tired!"

It was as if she were waiting for an invitation to sit.

"Are you hungry?" he asked, full of solicitude, after she had sat down on the narrow iron bed that occupied a whole side of the room. Meanwhile he wondered how they would manage for the night. With three of them in that little room, it wouldn't be easy. Well, one night passes quickly. And tomorrow he'd see about doing something.

"I have something to eat in my valise," she murmured in a voice so infinitely weary that for the first time Yankel dared look her in the eyes. My God, how she's aged! he thought, and he felt a sudden wrench in his heart. She was twenty-four, still a young woman, but not the girl-woman he used to know. In four short years . . .

He jumped to his feet.

"No, Hannele, we'll go eat in a restaurant, all three of us, eh? After all, we must celebrate the—"

"Oh, no! No, no!" she murmured, as if frightened by the prospect.

"But why not?"

"Because!"

She hesitated, and then, deliberately:

"Go alone, if that's what you usually do. I . . . I'll wait for you here."

"Now, Hannele, think a little, you're being silly."

"I can't go," she murmured. "I'll make you ashamed!"

He turned his head away, fidgeted.

"Ah, how can you say a thing like that! You don't really want to go? . . . All right, good, I have a little stove here," he continued, trying to give new life to his good humor, which was rapidly fading. "I'm going to cook you a little dinner, mmmm!—you'll lick your fingers, the both of you!"

"No, I'll do it," she said in her weary voice, and she rose, shoulders sagging, and started toward the stove.

"Will you sit down and rest!" he exclaimed, seizing his wife by the wrists; it was the first time he had touched her. He forced her to take her place again on the bed, hesitated a moment, then, awkwardly, smoothed her hair, her lovely, dark-auburn hair of which he had always been so fond. Under his caress, she bowed her head; finally, she raised a pair of tear-filled eyes to him.

"You know how to cook now?" she murmured with effort, and a moment later: "You've become so French, Yankel!" She sighed, drew Rivka against her and began humming a melancholy tune.

"Did you have trouble finding the place?" Yankel asked, simply to say something. Anything! At all cost, silence had to be prevented from setting in.

"No," she replied softly. She reflected a moment. "Herr Kratzmann showed me the way."

"Kratzmann? How did—"

Yankel cut himself off sharply. Careful! Dangerous, that question! "How did Kratzmann get into this?" could elicit only one answer: "Whom else could I go to?" And then, then all the rest . . . For-

106

tunately, at that very moment Yankel was breaking eggs into a bowl, an occupation which demanded all his attention, for bits of eggshell, as everyone knows, can cause appendicitis. Finally he saw an opportunity to vent his indignation:

"So Kratzmann left you here all alone with the little one! The least he could have done was . . ."

Sheepish, ashamed, full of repentance and feeling like a little boy, Yankel didn't for a moment imagine that Hannah dreaded to touch upon the essentials even more than he. He, he wanted only to avoid all unpleasantness and to be pardoned without having to ask to be. But she, she was afraid, truly afraid. What would become of her if he should leave her, all alone, in that huge, foreign city, with the little one on her hands, and without relatives, almost without money? And he *could* leave her, yes, she knew very well that at any moment the idea might occur to him!

In Rakwomir, she had made her decision in a split second and, once it was made, had lost no time in setting out upon the journey. And what had she found upon arriving? A dandified, mustached Yankel, a real Parisian! And in her confusion, she had only one thought: not to break that frayed bond which still held her to her husband. She must approach him gently, win him over, like an animal whose leash is broken and who still isn't aware of it.

"I asked Herr Kratzmann not to wait," she said, her voice still weary. "I told him that . . . Oh, let's not talk about it, Yankel. What difference does it make? You're here, that's all that counts!"

He didn't press the point.

They had a pleasant little dinner together. Yankel acted the fool to win over his daughter, spoke French to impress his wife. They decided that Hannah and Rivka would sleep together in the bed, and Yankel on the mattress which they set on the floor. The critical moment arrived when, the little one in bed but still awake, husband and wife found themselves face to face and were forced to make conversation. Fortunately, Rivka soon fell asleep, and Hannah and Yankel were able to undress and come together in silence. Then Hannah lay down beside her daughter and promptly sank into sleep.

The next day brought a host of tasks, one more urgent than the other. They didn't complete them that day, nor the day after, nor for many days more. But little by little, time began flowing again, weaving new ties between husband and wife. They never made any attempt to rehash the past. Hannah raised no questions, uttered no retrospective reproaches and as soon as she stopped fearing her husband she also stopped bearing a grudge against him. Good, gentle, passive, she preferred turning her eyes away from disagreeable things.

Just once, years later, she inadvertently revealed to Yankel that old Kratzmann had written to her in Rakwomir. Yes, it was that very letter which had made her decide to come. Oh, no, she didn't have the letter any more, she had torn it up right away! What had he written? Well, that if she wanted to keep her husband, she had better hurry up and come to Paris, and without any warning! Hannah said no more, for already Yankel was storming, raging, calling old Kratzmann a scoundrel, a *paskudnyak,* swearing by his children that he, Yankel, was just about to write Hannah to come when the old man had to stick his nose into it, and that he had even announced his decision to Kratzmann, yes, yes, he clearly remembered it, but all that no-good *paskudnyak* could think of was to break up marriages, and Hannah knew it perfectly well, didn't she? If she wanted proof . . . No, Hannah took her husband at his word. And besides, what was past was past.

They broke with the Kratzmanns, and from time to time, when a spat erupted in the Mykhanowitzki household, Yankel would vehemently berate his wife for having given credence to the words of a slanderer, a liar, a *paskudnyak.* It became his favorite weapon against his wife.

They began by moving into two small rooms and a kitchen in the same neighborhood. All of Yankel's old exuberance returned to him, and, overflowing with energy, he worked hard and his savings grew steadily even though he had two more mouths to feed. A nice little household, all in all!

But Hannah wasn't happy. Often, when he came home from work, he would find her sitting dolefully at the window.

"What's the matter, Hannele?" he would ask.

"Nothing, nothing . . ."

"Why don't you take a little walk with Rivka when I'm away? I showed you the Seine, didn't I? It's beautiful! Don't you like all that?"

Yes, she liked it. But she was afraid, all alone. "Afraid of what?" he would ask, dumfounded. She was afraid, that's all—of the noise, the people, the houses. When he was with her, it was different.

So he devoted all his free time to taking his wife walking. At times, just before going out, he would look longingly at his beautiful Saint-Étienne bicycle, hanging by a nail on a wall of the apartment; his legs were itching to ride it. He began singing the praises of cycling.

"Why don't you learn, Hannele? I'll buy you a bicycle and we'll go out riding together."

"Yes, but what about the little one?"

"Well, we can ask a neighbor to mind her."

"Oh, no! No, never!"

In truth, it was the contraption itself which frightened Hannah. So Yankel rebelled, took down his Saint-Étienne, and went out riding by himself. But upon returning home he would find his wife so terrified that he gave it up and eventually even sold the bicycle. Every Sunday now, the three of them would roam the streets, Rivka clutching Hannah, and Hannah clutching her husband, as if she were afraid of losing him. She was afraid of crossing the streets, afraid of going to a café, and she admired her protector with such childlike fervor, went into such raptures at hearing him speak French, that he began dreading those promenades and soon put an end to them. Their Sundays, thereafter, were spent at home, and Yankel became a little embittered over it all. He didn't understand his wife, having forgotten his own difficulties in adapting himself to a new land.

He got in touch again with some of his old acquaintances, Jews and otherwise, a few of whom were married, hoping that Hannah would make friends. But in the presence of the French, walled in by her ignorance of the language, it was as if she were deaf and dumb— an idiot! She would come to life only among their compatriots. And just as he had given up his bicycle, Yankel, little by little, gave up his French friends.

Right from the beginning, he had tried to teach Hannah the language. But after a few lessons she burst into tears.

"My head is too thick," she moaned.

"But you've only just begun! You've got to try at least!"

Yankel didn't bother to consider that there was an essential difference between Hannah and himself. For he had gone to the Jewish parochial school in Rakwomir, had learned to read and write Yiddish. Thus when he attacked French he had encountered only the difficulties inherent in the approach to all foreign languages. But Hannah had never gone to school; she barely knew how to read. How could she learn a foreign language when she didn't even know her own well?

So they gave up any systematic approach to French, although in the long run Hannah laboriously acquired sufficient knowledge of the language to divine what was being said to her and to make herself understood. After all, she did have to go shopping, didn't she?

One day Yankel came home to find her in tears. At first she refused to say why until he pressed her for an explanation, pleaded with her, became angry, was divided between panic and exasperation.

"Come, Hannele, tell me what's wrong! You mustn't let yourself get into such a state, it might be bad for the boy."

For Hannah was four months pregnant. Pregnant of course with a boy; Yankel never doubted it for a second. In contact with the French his prejudices about the inferiority of girls had receded a bit, but now they were flooding back.

In the end, Hannah admitted that she was simply bored to death—no one to talk to, no friends, and all those people making fun of her because she didn't know French very well.

Yankel clenched his fists. Who could have dared make fun of a pregnant woman? Whoever it was, Yankel would give it to him good. . . .

"Oh, it's nothing, it's nothing, Yankele!" stammered Hannah.

In the municipal washhouse she had found herself next to a woman who seemed very nice, but who was also very talkative and very stupid. Hannah had kept trying to tell her she didn't understand French, but the woman went right on talking, talking, talking. In the end, Hannah, unnerved, had shouted in Yiddish:

"Vasch! Vasch!"

Actually it meant simply "Do your wash!" But the woman flared up (Hannah wasn't aware that in French the word was an insult). Oh, there was a big fuss. Yankel couldn't help laughing.

"Hannele, Hannele . . ."

He translated the French word *vache* into Yiddish, thinking that Hannah would laugh along with him at the misunderstanding. Alas! A new flood of tears.

Yankel raised his arms to the heavens. How could you get out of that imbroglio? *Vasch,* the Yiddish word for wash, and *vache,* the French word for cow, both pronounced the same; but cow also used to describe a nasty person in French and a whore or an idiot in Yiddish. He tried hard to explain it to Hannah but she refused to understand and went on weeping, weeping. No, she hadn't refused to understand; she actually *hadn't* understood, truly! Crushed, Yankel had to face that unhappy fact, and only then did he begin to glimpse the distance between himself and his wife. Hannah couldn't understand, not because she was stupid, but because—there it was again—she didn't know any foreign language!

Yankel raised his cap, scratched his head. . . . Not long afterward, they moved to the Rue des Écouffes, a few steps from the Rue des Rosiers, in the heart of the Jewish section. Hannah would be happy there; at least she would have people to talk to.

Now Hannah was happy. From one day to the next Yankel saw her blossom out. All her old cheerfulness returned, she ruffled her husband's hair, snuggled up to him, enticed him to caress her a little; then she would run off to her kitchen and prepare him a good meal while humming old Yiddish tunes. Yankel had taught her the arts of frying and roasting; she quickly put these new discoveries to good use, and her Jewish cuisine became enriched with a number of French recipes. And the Lord blessed them: Amid a chorus of admiring housewives, Hannah brought a big healthy son into the world. Yankel named him Simon; at once French and Jewish, the name seemed a perfect choice to him. Hannah squeezed every last drop from her happiness, never wearying of repeating: "Ah, it's so nice here, Yankele! We don't belong with goys, Yankele!" And Yankel would nod in agreement, although in his heart he didn't agree. Not at all! He felt he had somehow sacrificed himself, and he became morose and irritable.

Each time he returned from work and found himself again on the Rue des Écouffes, he would screw up his nose in disgust. Pfeh! How narrow, dirty and noisy it was! He who had once known the good life, the French life, now felt as if he were being dragged down. No, never would he be able to adapt himself!

He would literally run up the squalid stairway, with its rickety steps, its sweating walls. Hovel, hovel! He had read the word in the newspapers and it never failed to return to him at that moment. But his apartment itself was no hovel. Hannah always kept it spotlessly clean, enlivened it with her youth and her cheerfulness; and occasionally a ray of sunlight even managed to slip through the window. When Yankel was home, together with his wife and children, he almost felt happy again. With the windows shut, the noises from the street and the neighbors barely penetrated the apartment; it was quite possible to believe himself elsewhere. Then Hannah would ask him to take down the garbage, he would pick up the pail, open the door—and again that stale, putrid odor would fill his nostrils! Descending the five flights of stairs, he would breathe as little as possible. The garbage cans were in the courtyard. Naturally, there were always two or three big rats lurking in the vicinity. And the arrogance of them! Impossible to chase them away; they would barely retreat before you. Seated on their backsides, they would look you fearlessly in the face with their mean little red eyes. You hardly dared approach them, so great was your fear of their leaping at you, clinging to your clothes, scratching your eyes out. There were stories of children half devoured, women attacked; they could hold their own against cats, laughed at poison. His garbage pail emptied, Yankel would go back upstairs, thinking of all the vermin the house was crawling with— rats, mice, fleas, cockroaches, and especially bedbugs. Simon had little red swellings all over his body; there was no mistaking what they came from. But whenever Yankel confided his anxieties to Hannah she would simply shrug her shoulders; to her, it was all part of life, you had to resign yourself to it.

Yankel refused to resign himself. No, decidedly, Rue des Écouffes wouldn't do. Why shouldn't Hannah make a few concessions, after all? He spent a few weeks thinking it over, then, his decision made, set out in search of a real apartment. And he found exactly what he wanted: four rooms on the fourth floor, Rue des Francs-Bourgeois. The street was completely to his liking—quiet, uncommercial, in short, bourgeois, as its name indicated. Yankel would be happy there; as for Hannah, a few steps and she was back on her beloved Rue des Rosiers, where she could talk to whomever she pleased. He signed the lease, then broke the news to Hannah. Dutiful wife that she was, she raised no objections. She asked only if it were far away; her husband assured her it wasn't. "And why such a big apartment? The rent must be very high."

In a single gush, Yankel spilled out all his plans for the future. They might have more children, no? So they had to have enough space. And Yankel wouldn't see his children grow up among rats and bedbugs, in a "hovel" (he explained the meaning of the word, which he had inserted as such in the stream of Yiddish).

"We're civilized people, Hannele, not primitives from Rakwomir or the Rue des Écouffes!" And besides, he was hoping to go into business for himself, wasn't he? He'd had enough of working for others; in the new apartment, he'd be able to set up a nice little workroom. Of course, he wouldn't leave his job right away, but with the connections he had already made he'd have no trouble getting a few subcontracts, and little by little he'd build up his own clientele. And he would let it grow—oh, he had plenty of time, he was in no hurry! And when it was going well, then good-bye bosses!

They moved a few days later. Hannah was truly enchanted and at last felt herself mistress of the house. Rivka rushed through the rooms, jumping and clapping her hands with glee. In his cradle, the baby howled. And Yankel realized that he had now become a man, a gentleman. He had a wife, two children, a large apartment, responsibilities. Yes, that was something to think about, all right! He began at once to set up his workroom. And he went out in search of orders.

Then one Sunday he was at the window, savoring his new life and the wonderful future that was opening before him, when he heard a vague rumble in the distance. What was going on? Down in the street, people were running. Yankel leaned out the window. Over on the Rue des Blancs-Manteaux, near the heart of the Jewish section, the shopkeepers were hastily taking in their stands, putting up their shutters. In the wink of an eye, the street was empty, the houses dead. Usually so animated Sunday mornings, the neighborhood had become sinister. Behind every locked and barricaded door, behind every tightly shuttered window, one could feel almost palpably the presence of human beings, waiting, waiting. . . . Oy, could it by any chance be . . . ? Yankel strained his ears, feeling his mouth parched. The rumble swelled, and now he began to make out shouts. Yes, it was indeed a mob, and it was coming closer . . . over there somewhere, behind the National Archives Building . . .

Suddenly they appeared, turned the corner, entered that very street; in the lead, young men armed with sticks . . .

"Down with the Jews! Down with the Jews!"

The cry had burst out, was taken up by hundreds of throats. Yankel felt himself go pale. *A pogrom!* With trembling hands, he shut the window. Hannah was in the kitchen; she hadn't heard; she would hear soon enough. A weapon, a weapon! Wild-eyed, he looked about him. His thick capmaker's scissors? But would he be able to use them? A modeling block? Too heavy. So long as at least one dies before I do! The hammer, yes, that's it! He seized the tool, clutched it convulsively. Ah, to have fled Russia, to have crossed all of Europe in order to escape the pogroms, and then to find one here, in France, in the land of Freedom and the Rights of Man. What a mockery!

But what do they want of me? What did I ever do to them? The shouts were now coming from directly below. Yankel raced to the window. No, the mob was passing by; no group had detached itself to enter the building. Could it be they weren't going to stop here? And at that instant, Yankel remembered that the door to the apartment wasn't even locked. He hesitated—should he erect a barricade? Hannah would get panicky, possibly for nothing. No, rather wait, see how the situation develops . . .

"Down with the Jews! Down with the Jews!"

The rioters were marching down the deserted street, behind every window of which a young Jew was watching, an improvised weapon in his hand, while the old men and women were beseeching the Lord.

Suddenly Yankel caught sight of an old woman who had suddenly appeared out of nowhere and was running for all she was worth. A Jew, certainly; otherwise she wouldn't be running. . . . Yankel's heart stopped beating. In three steps, they'd catch up with her. What could he do? How could he stop them from . . . The woman stumbled, fell. Three or four of the young men swooped down upon her, and Yankel's eyes opened wide in horror. Oh, God, that's it! They'll tear her to pieces . . . And suddenly, a nervous laugh shook him from head to foot. My God, what was this! They had helped the woman up, were dusting her off, speaking to her. Apparently she was thanking them, for one of the young men raised his cap and then, together with his companions, rejoined the mob and again the cry went up: "Down with the Jews!" Idiots! Yankel repeated to himself softly. The woman stood there, dumfounded, watching the anti-Semites pass. They were singing now, their sticks striking the ground in cadence:

The Jews take all we got, one, two!
The French want no more of the Jew!

The Jews take all we got. . . . What did *I* ever take from you? Idiots, idiots! Yankel set his hammer down on the workbench. Louis might very possibly have been one of those young men, and there's nothing of the murderer in Louis. Louis would have been incapable of killing a poor defenseless woman. Louis might fight another man, perhaps, but even then it would be man to man, not fifty against one.

France wasn't Russia, ah, no, far from it! So why, you idiots, why are you doing this?

That afternoon Yankel went down to find out what had happened. To be sure, there had been a few shop windows broken, a few Jews beaten, one of them was in serious condition as a result of a bludgeoning. But in actual fact, the young men had mostly fought with the police. It had been a pogrom, yes, but a French-style pogrom. Even so Yankel enlisted in an organization for Jewish self-defense, and every Sunday morning he went out to join a troop of tough young *landsmen* who would stroll nonchalantly between the Rue des Rosiers and the Rue des Blancs-Manteaux past the knots of unperturbed policemen stationed at strategic positions along the way. Then, after a few weeks, the policemen disappeared except for an isolated specimen or so at the street corners. And Yankel stopped going out to join his young toughs, whom he disliked because of their vulgarity.

Soon he was able to leave his job and devote himself entirely to his own business. He had a faithful clientele which was steadily increasing, and he even considered taking on a worker—the room was big enough for it.

Absorbed in his work, he rarely went out. Hannah was happy, the children were growing up. Yes, life was good!

He was to remain almost half a century in the apartment on the Rue des Francs-Bourgeois, turning more and more in upon himself, isolated from the world. Kratzmannized.

III

YANKEL took a lump of sugar, clamped it between his teeth and swished a sip of tea over it. He smacked his lips with satisfaction. Then, sovereignly, he let his eyes wander from face to face.

He had reserved one whole side of the square table for himself. Opposite him, their backs to the room, he had placed his younger brother Peretz and his sister Rachel, as at a trial. His second brother, Moishe, hadn't waited for an invitation to occupy the third side, on the left of the master of the house. That rascal certainly knew how to make himself at home. As for the fourth side, no one challenged Hannah's claim to it. Little Simon was feeding at his mother's breast, which for a moment made her forget the tea, and she was constantly getting up, going to the kitchen and returning.

Only a few days before, Peretz, Moishe and Rachel had arrived from the homeland. Naturally, they were staying with Yankel (you can always make room, no?), and in fact he rejoiced at the thought that soon, perhaps, the whole family would be gathered round him. Already they were four, which left only his father and mother, his older sister Sarah and the youngest of the lot, little Itcha, who was no more than nine or ten. (For though old Avrom had sired thirteen children, seven had died in childhood.) So why not complete the transplanting of the whole Mykhanowitzki brood? A family isn't meant to be scattered over the four corners of the earth, but to provide warmth in a hostile world. Pridefully Yankel pictured his aged parents coming to seek refuge beside their eldest son. As for Sarah, who was married, why shouldn't she come, too, together with her husband and children? He had a good strong back, didn't he?

But even as he was fondling that beautiful dream, Peretz, stammering with emotion, announced that he and Rachel had definitely made up their minds to seek their fortune in America, no less, out there, beyond the seas! The other end of the world! Rachel, that child of seventeen! And Peretz, that . . . Pfeh!

116

Yankel had never felt much affection for his younger brother. He had always tyrannized him, perhaps for the simple reason that Peretz followed him among the Mykhanowitzki sons. Now, as he looked at his brother sitting opposite him, with his corkscrew earlocks, his hat pulled down to his eyebrows, old already at twenty-four, as he listened to him mechanically thanking the Lord every three words, or warding off the Evil Eye, he felt an overpowering desire to let him go wherever he pleased, straight to the devil, if he liked. Except that Yankel was very conscious of his family obligations; and besides, there was Rachel, that child. After all, she couldn't be left in the care of a Peretz, could she? So he had brought together all the Parisian members of the family in solemn council. Wasn't he the eldest, a married man, a father, in business for himself? Established as master in his own apartment, in his own home, he was beginning to taste the joys of power and to enjoy it.

Now he studied the two defendants, first seedy-looking Peretz, then Rachel. Almost absently he noticed that Rachel had grown into quite a beautiful girl. Actually, Yankel reflected, it isn't good when there are too many children in a family; they stop being purely fraternal and become either friends or enemies, or simply indifferent. Little Itcha was as dear to Yankel as if he were his own son, and as for Moishe, though Yankel's feelings toward him were rather confused they did at least exist. The others? Well, to tell the truth, he really couldn't say. What, for example, did he know about Rachel? Practically nothing. . . . He returned to Peretz.

"But what are you going to do in America?" he asked severely.

Peretz opened his mouth to reply, but Moishe beat him to it.

"Rivkela!" he called out affectionately. "Aren't you going to come sit on my lap tonight?"

Moishe adored children, his niece in particular, and ever since his arrival he had been stuffing her with candies. With a shriek of glee, the child ran over to him. Ignoring the furious glare Yankel had turned on him, the young man caught the little girl up, set her on his knee and began bouncing her up and down while humming a song. The child shook with laughter, her braids flying in every direction.

"Don't get her all excited!" Hannah moaned. "For hours she won't fall asleep!"

So Moishe took the child in his arms, held her against him and, gently, began cradling her, humming a chant of his own composition.

Burning with impatience, Yankel slammed his fist on the table. "Moishe, that's enough now! We have serious things to talk about!" Regretfully, Moishe set the child down.

"All right, all right!" he said nonchalantly. "But you know, Yankele, I haven't the least desire to go to America. Paris suits me fine."

Too bad! Yankel thought, despite himself. A scoundrel like that . . .

A scoundrel, perhaps; at any rate, a man. Six feet tall, with the build of a stevedore. And he wore a beard. Not, to be sure, the shaggy beard of the orthodox Jews, but the beard of a bourgeois Christian, shaped into a point and carefully trimmed. And red as a devil—so much so that Yankel accused him of smelling of sulfur. He had the ways of a devil, too, and he had had them at a tender age. When Yankel left Rakwomir Moishe was just going on sixteen, but his reputation was already well established. He had gathered a few good-for-nothings, of the same stripe as himself, and whenever someone warned, "Here comes Moishe's gang!" the older Jews would barricade themselves behind their doors and invoke the aid of the Lord, while the merchants would station themselves in their doorways, sticks in hand. Battles with the goys; tricks played on the most respected members of the community. In truth, Moishe had an incomparable talent for providing grist for the town's gossip mill. Most of all, he had it in for the *reb,* God only knows why! He was an old man, a little simple-minded, the *reb,* whose name was Avrom, like Yankel's own father. One night he was sleeping peacefully in his bed when a voice as cavernous as it was imperious reverberated from above, a voice calling him by name:

"Avrohom! Avroho-o-o-m!"

Awakening with a start, the poor man began stammering in terror.

"Avrohom! Avro-o-o-hom!"

Even more imperious than before, the voice repeated its call, in the exact tone of the Sabbath invocations. Then, panic-stricken, certain it was the Lord in person who was calling to him, as in the Bible, the old man leaped out of bed and, his two hands raised aloft, bleated out:

"Lord, I am here! What dost Thou wish of Thy servant?"

Silence. In the attic, Moishe was suppressing an overwhelming urge to burst out laughing. Finally, in the same tone in which Jehovah had no doubt voiced the Ten Commandments, he ordered:

"Wipe your mustache and kiss my backside!"

The poor old *reb* was sick over the thing for an entire week. As for Father Mykhanowitzki, he took off his belt yet again and gave the boy a sound thrashing. Which didn't make Moishe any the less his favorite son. Ah, yes! He would whip him regularly every week, but at the same time he showed a disgraceful, scandalous preference for him, which used to fill Yankel with righteous indignation.

Of course, the girls also adored Moishe, and the gossipmongers even claimed that certain married women . . . But, well, why go into that! In spite of everything, he was the finest fellow in the world, willing to bend over backwards even for total strangers and to offer them his purse, when it wasn't empty. Yankel could never quite bring himself to believe that that cynical rascal belonged to the same race as he. Naturally, he tried his best to love his brother, because, after all, one had to love one's own brother; but he always regarded him askance, constantly on his guard. And Moishe, who was far from stupid, was keenly aware of this, chuckled over it, and displayed a completely sincere, almost admiring affection for Yankel. Yes, it was beyond all comprehension—Moishe respected Yankel! In fact, Yankel was the only being on earth for whom he had such a surprising feeling.

Rivka asleep, Simon fed, Yankel was at last able to open the debate. Patiently he explained to Peretz that his project was unreasonable. Why go running so far away, when he could just as easily settle down and make a nice life for himself right here?

"In America, you'll be all alone among complete strangers. What will you do if things don't go well? Suppose you get sick? It can happen, no? In Paris, you have nothing to worry about, you can always turn to me. After all, I make a good living, I . . ."

He was addressing himself exclusively to Peretz, for Rachel, that child, didn't count. Yet it was she who spoke up, cutting him off into the bargain, the insolent thing!

"If he gets sick, I'll look after him!" she declared forcefully.

"You!" Yankel said with that wave of the hand which dampens all hope and imposes silence.

"My God, but you can be backward, Yankel!" exclaimed Rachel exaltedly. "Just because I'm a woman, you—"

"A woman? A child, you mean!"

She jumped to her feet, her eyes glittering.

"If you think I got away from Papa's tyranny to take yours, you're badly mistaken!"

The shameless brat! To speak that way about her father—and to her older brother, a married man, a father, a man in business for himself! Yankel was speechless.

"Rachel," Moishe broke in, in a mock-serious bass voice, "Rachel, you're being ill-mannered."

He meant to create a diversion, for he didn't like family quarrels. But Rachel was much too wrought up to pay any heed to such nonsense.

"If I have to, I'll go alone!" she shouted, on the verge of hysterics now.

"Shah! Shah!" exploded Yankel, Hannah and Peretz in unison, their six hands flaying the air to drive down the volume of the voices. No point in letting the neighbors in on the discussion!

Still standing, the young woman placed both hands on the table, leaned forward a little and in a shrill but nevertheless subdued voice said:

"You're a tyrant, Yankel! A tyrant! And I'm going, do you hear? Even if that one stays!"

"That one" was Peretz, who, under the onslaught, drew his head down between his shoulders.

"And where are you going to get the money?" Yankel asked calmly, confident of his power.

"The money? I . . . I . . ." Her whole face turned crimson. "I'll find myself an old man and let him take me! There!"

And she spun around and ran from the room.

"Ay yiyi," murmured Yankel pensively. He felt a heavy responsibility weighing on his shoulders.

Until now, he had thought it was Peretz who was dragging his sister along, perhaps because he wanted a slave at his disposal. Rachel's explosion had suddenly opened his eyes for him. How could he have been so mistaken? Peretz? Why, he's nothing but a mole! Set him down wherever you please and right away he digs his little hole, that's all he knows! Alone, he'd stay here, or in Berlin, or he wouldn't even have left the homeland. But that hothead of a Rachel leads him around by the nose. That's what you call a man? Pfeh! Yankel's eyes met Moishe's. The latter smiled; his brother smiled back—they had understood each other. Peretz' head swung from one to the other, troubled, his corkscrew earlocks jumping with each turn.

"Listen, Yankele," he began soothingly, "if I go to Nev York, I'll . . ."

"It isn't *Nev* York," Yankel cut in sharply. "It's *Nu* York! I already taught you that, didn't I?"

"Ah, Nev York, Nu York, what's the difference? I . . ."

"Peretz!" Moishe called out affectionately.

"What! You too now! What do you want from me?"

"Oy! Peretz! Why don't you take your hat off?" groaned Moishe plaintively. "Your poor lice, they need some air!"

"All right, enough of this nonsense, the both of you!" enjoined the head of the family, severely. "We're not children any more. Hannah, go get that hothead, so we can talk a little."

Hannah obeyed, only to return an instant later, alone, leave the room again and finally come back with her sister-in-law.

The discussion was resumed, but this time Yankel addressed himself only to Rachel; in fact, by a supreme effort of the will he even exaggerated the consideration he gave her. It went on until Moishe yawningly announced that he was going to bed, began again the next day, and the day after, and a good many more days after that.

In the end, it was Hannah who decided she had had enough, and one night she let it be known to her husband: The discussions were upsetting the children, the presence of three extra people in the house was too heavy a burden; and besides, a decision had to be reached sooner or later! Yankel agreed readily, even added that, all things considered, Peretz and Rachel had a perfect right to do whatever they pleased with their own lives, no? And if they were heading for a catastrophe, well, too bad for them! He, Yankel, had performed his duty.

And so, the very next day, he flew into an awesome rage, gave Peretz a terrible tongue-lashing (for this once, he ignored Rachel), predicted dreadful calamities for the two deserters—in fact, *wished* the calamities upon them—and finally gave them the money for the trip.

Yankel wept the day he took them to the train, and Hannah wept, too, and Peretz; and Rachel wept more than the three others put together. As for Moishe, he wasn't there; Moishe, it just so happened, had something to attend to that day.

Since he first began working, Moishe had tried his hand at almost every conceivable trade. Just before leaving Rakwomir, he passed for a watchmaker; that is, he repaired watches, sewing machines and everything that, directly or remotely, had anything to do with precision instruments. But upon arriving in Paris, he abruptly decided he was a photographer.

When Yankel began to tire of seeing his brother leading an idle life, he went out and tried to find a job for him, without, of course, letting Moishe know about it. He soon found one, and a good one at that! Ah, if only *he* had had such an opportunity when he had first arrived! It was with a photographer on the Rue de Rivoli! Rubbing his hands together, he announced the good news to his brother, causing Moishe's eyes to pop open.

"A photographer! But why do you want me to spend my life taking pictures, Yankele?"

Well, there you are, he was no longer a photographer, that good-for-nothing! So what was he now? Yankel cleared his throat and began one of his moralizing, big-brother speeches:

"Listen, Moishe, you're not going to go on like this forever? You've got to start earning a living; I can't support you forever. After all, I have a wife, children . . ."

"Ay, is that all that's bothering you? You want some money?"

And with a princely gesture, Moishe tossed several gold louis d'or on the table. Yankel's mouth fell open.

"Where did you get all that? Are you working?"

"Oh, I manage!" he replied evasively.

"But . . . but . . . but . . ."

Moishe never got up before nine; then, in no particular hurry, he would proceed to wash and dress.

When he was through, he would go for a stroll, or so it seemed. He would return for lunch, take a nap, then play with Rivka or read a book (he read a great deal); at times a sudden whim would take hold of him and he would lend his brother a hand, or help his sister-in-law wipe the dishes—a gesture inconceivable for a Jew. He would stay till four or five, then disappear, occasionally reappearing for dinner, but not always. There were times he didn't get back till eleven, midnight, perhaps even later, who knows?—by that time, the whole household would long since have been asleep. And on top of that, always dressed to perfection, in the latest style. Ah, no, it hadn't taken him long to adapt himself to Parisian life! The moment he arrived, he had set to work on it. And already he was beginning to speak a little French, without Yankel having anything to do with it.

"I'm a diamond dealer," he said at last, as if to be left in peace.

"A diamond dealer? You?"

"Yes, a broker in diamonds."

"In diamonds?"

"In diamonds. Certainly!" And then, an inane smile on his face, he drawled: "You know what diamonds are, don't you, Yankele?"

And Yankel gave up.

He did nevertheless establish a price for lodging his brother, a very reasonable price, naturally, calculated as close as possible. "Good, good!" Moishe promptly agreed, adding only: "Are you sure that's enough?"

The only trouble was that Moishe never paid his board voluntarily. When he got too far behind and Yankel ventured to ask for a little money, oh, Moishe wouldn't plead for more time, no indeed! Worse than that, he would dig into his pocket, saying graciously:

"You need some money, Yankele? Why, you should have spoken up!"

And without counting them out, he would toss a fistful of coins on the table, gold, silver and copper, all mixed together.

"Is that enough?" he would ask. "If you want more, Yankele, don't be bashful."

As a rule, the coins added up to two or three times the amount actually due. So Yankel, after counting them, would protest that it was too much, and Moishe would give him a hearty slap on the back, saying: "Don't let it trouble you, Yankele!"

Very fine, those lordly ways of his! But Moishe wasn't doing Yankel any favor by staying with him, and it became humiliating, in the end, to have money practically thrown in his face, like charity! And from the debtor, moreover! Scrupulous Yankel, who wanted only his due, no more, no less, was forced, in order to cheat neither his brother nor himself, to involve himself in complicated calculations. It would have been so simple to receive a fixed amount every week or every month! But no, instead he had to figure out how many days Moishe's money would cover, and he would have to jot down numbers in a notebook, on slips of paper, on calendars, which would get lost, then turn up again in unexpected places. And with it all went doubts, pangs of conscience, fits of anger. Every night, in bed, he would hold endless, whispered conferences with Hannah; he slept badly, and his wife complained of his violent tossing.

Since things were still too simple for Moishe, he complicated them further with loans.

"Yankele, listen, I'm broke today. You wouldn't have a louis to spare, would you? I'll pay you back tomorrow."

Yankel would hand over the louis, but not without asking in astonishment: "Do you mean to say you're down to where you have to ask for *one* louis? Moishele, really, you should save a little!"

Moishe would only laugh.

Sometimes the loans were much more considerable. And it was useless asking what they were for; the answer never varied: "Don't let it worry you, Yankele! Business, you know!"

And that was that! Yankel would write down the debt on a slip of paper, and then there would be the adding, the subtracting, the dividing to determine the number of days. . . .

And then there were the presents. Presents are nice, aren't they? Inoffensive—yes? Well, just listen a moment . . .

When Moishe had money, he was generosity itself—his own money or borrowed money, it mattered little to him.

"Here's a little something for you!" he would say offhandedly, tossing a package on the table—a toy for Rivka, a set of blankets for Simon's crib, a brooch for Hannah, a tie for Yankel. Just like that, for no apparent reason. Expensive presents, let me tell you! And if you wanted to thank him? Protest that it was much too nice? Refuse it, even?

"Don't be a *schlemiel!*" he would reply jovially.

Poor Yankel floundered helplessly in that sea of gifts. Racked with scruples, he wondered if he shouldn't deduct their approximate price from Moishe's board. But his dignity immediately rebelled. For after all, if you pay for a present, even indirectly, it isn't a present any more, is it? What it would amount to is an improper utilization by someone else of your money, and Yankel wasn't going to allow anyone to force his hand. Nevertheless, he felt ashamed whenever, despite the opulent gifts, he decided to ask his brother for his board.

He did see one solution: return present for present, as one returns blow for blow. But that, too, had its drawbacks. Moishe, he well knew, received with as much indifference as he gave.

But more than that, Yankel became indignant at the thought of plunging into stupid expenditures. Not that he was miserly, but . . . Well, after all, if he didn't feel like bombarding people with presents, he was perfectly free not to, wasn't he? Entering into the game of presents, at bottom, meant accepting Moishe's way of life, and that Yankel firmly refused to do. He was a Yankel, not a Moishe!

In the end, Yankel became fed up. First of all, he asked himself, where does Moishe get all that money that runs through his fingers like water? Diamond dealer, diamond dealer—you don't become a diamond dealer just like that, from one day to the next! Dealing in diamonds is a trade! I learned capmaking, so I'm a capmaker; but he, he never learned diamonds, did he? Yankel had great respect for education, and he venerated titles.

So he decided to find out what Moishe was up to. Wasn't he the elder brother? Didn't he have certain obligations? He picked his day, took his hat and cane, and followed Moishe through the streets, at a safe distance.

Completely unsuspecting, the younger man walked on ahead, arms swinging, taking up the whole width of the sidewalk. His rolling, almost swaggering gait irritated Yankel, whose walk was stiff and precise. But the thing that surprised him was the number of hats that were tipped to his younger brother in passing. Ah, that devil of a Moishe! he thought. Such a short time in Paris and already everyone knows him! It made Yankel feel rather proud, but at the same time it troubled him too; dangerous, men who are too charming!

Then he saw a woman approach his brother and speak to him. Without stopping, Moishe patted her cheek with a protective, paternal air; the woman remained behind, motionless, at the edge of the sidewalk, following him with her eyes.

Aha! thought Yankel, knitting his brows. Something wrong there! They know each other. Now what could Moishe have to do with that big-bellied old whore? Because she *is* a whore, it's as plain as day . . . A whore, perhaps; big-bellied, certainly, for she was pregnant, as Yankel noted when he passed her; but not old. Not at all! If she was eighteen, she was a lot. What kind of stupid thing has that rascal got himself into now? Tchch, tchch! Incorrigible Moishe, tchch! It's going to end up badly, all this!

And suddenly a monstrous thought gripped him, stopped him short. Could it be that Moishe was living off women? Instantly, Yankel stopped fretting, stopped quibbling with himself. A cold rage, such as he had known only once or twice before in his entire life, took hold of him. He clenched his fists, gritted his teeth. If it's true, big or not, I'll give you a thrashing you'll never forget! And the door! . . . He set out again, quickened his pace. Moishe, as majestic and untroubled as ever, had turned the corner. Yankel reached it just in time to see him go into a café halfway down the street.

125

He hesitated, waited, turned back, stopped again. A café! Moishe in a café. So what does it prove? Probably he spends his days there playing cards. Maybe he makes a little money that way? Ay, the whole thing smells bad, but after all . . . How to be certain? Go back home, wait for the good-for-nothing to return, question him, try to catch him in an out-and-out lie? Even now Yankel could hear him drawling: "What did I do this afternoon? A little game of cards, yes! And I won, too! Yes! Money's nothing but manure!" And there you are, you'd know no more than before.

So Yankel set off again, passed slowly in front of the café, glanced inside. Marble tables; men standing or sitting, conversing, playing cards, checkers, chess; some seemed to be waiting, little packages wrapped in brown paper placed carefully in front of them. Not a woman. At one of the tables, Moishe was engaged in conversation with three other men. Oy! More and more fishy, all this!

No, no, see here now! Yankel, Yankel, what's got into you today? Why, it's simply the diamond dealers' café, that's all! Their market place, so to speak, where they discuss all their deals! Yankel heaved a great sigh. What a load off his mind! The diamond dealers' café! Of course! He felt like laughing out loud. Naturally, everyone knows you'll find a few disreputable characters in the bunch. But they *are* diamond dealers, aren't they? Not pimps! Pfeh, Yankel, pfeh! How could you ever suspect your own brother of such a filthy thing?

Yes. Yes, yes! All the same, the whole business did have a fishy odor. They're distrustful, diamond dealers, distrustful! So how had Moishe managed to get himself accepted by them? Even Yankel would have encountered serious obstacles. So Moishe, hardly off the train from Russia, had found every door open to him, just like that, because of his good looks? Come, now! Furthermore, he didn't at all like that lordly, imperious air his brother so easily assumed in the streets of the Jewish section. And known, greeted, respectfully accosted by prostitutes! *By pregnant prostitutes,* who weren't seeking, therefore, to entice him, but . . . *but to talk business with him, maybe?*

Yankel was pure, but not naïve; he had learned quite a lot in traveling about France. The more he thought about it, the stronger his suspicions grew, and as soon as he got home he shared them with Hannah. She raised her arms to the heavens but in the end, at her husband's request, agreed to conduct a little investigation of her own; at the market, in the shops, she would try to find out whatever she could. It was a promise.

That very evening, Yankel launched his attack immediately upon Moishe's return. Rubbing his hands together, he took a jovial approach—a sly fox, Yankel Mykhanowitzki!

"So, Moishele, how's business?"

Moishe stroked his handsome, flame-red beard, looked at Yankel and smiled:

"You need some money, Yankele?"

"No, no!" Yankel raised his arms in protestation. And he launched into a detailed accounting, from which it developed that Moishe was paid up for a good two more weeks.

"Good," said Moishe calmly, "but if you're broke, don't be bashful, eh?"

"Tchch! I don't like to borrow!" Yankel screwed up his nose in distaste. "I . . ."

He had hoped to draw his brother into a serious conversation on the art of living; he got from him only a "Don't be a *schlemiel!*" And since dinner wasn't yet ready, Moishe picked up a book and began reading—in French, if you please!

For her part, Hannah was able to gather only meager information from the gossips at the market. Moishe Mykhanowitzki? No, I don't know him . . . Oh, you mean the one everybody calls the Big One? The one the French call Monsieur Maurice? So naturally, I know him! Ay-yiyi, what a fine-looking man! Your brother-in-law? Congratulations! He looks like he's doing very well. . . .

Yankel winced at the mention of that name, M. Maurice. But he didn't dare speak to his brother about it. After all, Moishe was free to do as he pleased, no? And he himself, hadn't the French christened him M. Mica? Moishe, Maurice . . . Well, why not, if that's the way the French like it?

And the matter rested there. Yankel stopped making inquiries, even though he was unable to stop worrying.

Some time later, Moishe announced to his brother that he was going on a trip.

"On a trip?"

Moishe seemed annoyed, which was rare with him; but in the end he explained he was going to London.

"To London?"

"To London, yes!" Moishe repeated without batting an eye. "To London, in England. You know where England is, Yankele, don't you?" he asked gently, with that inane smile he reserved for just such questions.

"You mean . . . you mean permanently?"

"*Schlemiel!*" Moishe replied, and burst out laughing. "I'll be back next week. It's business!"

"Business?"

"You know what business is, don't you, Yankele?" he mumbled, this time without a trace of a smile.

Yankel reflected a moment.

"So you're rolling in money, eh, Moishe?"

"Oh, I'm doing all right!" came the vague reply.

It's true, thought Yankel, that diamond dealers often have to go to London, to Amsterdam . . .

But Moishe went only to London. Every three or four months, as it turned out.

It was Moishe who took the initiative in the separation.

"Yankele, the time has come to change hotels!" he announced one day with his customary tact. Naturally Yankel protested, out of politeness. Moishe then consented to offer a few good reasons for his decision, and Yankel in turn consented to give in to them. And so the younger brother set out on his own into the vast world, and once more peace returned to the Rue des Francs-Bourgeois.

Among the good reasons Moishe advanced to justify his departure, one had brought a smile to Yankel's face. "And now that I speak French, I . . ." Yes, Moishe spoke French! But with what an accent, oy, God have mercy on us! You knew immediately you were dealing with a foreigner. For Moishe, like Hannah, had no ear. So naturally, their accents were awful. Simply a question of having a good ear, languages, no?

Yankel, for his part, had an excellent ear, and his French accent was all but perfect. He was well aware that since Hannah's arrival he had let himself get a bit rusty; but it didn't trouble him, for he knew that a few minutes of conversation with a Frenchman would bring back all his old facility. French, after all, was his second mother tongue!

Nevertheless, and not without annoyance, he began to notice the invasion, in that second mother tongue, of grunts, mumbles and various expressions from the first. For example, "Nu!" for "Well!" And he found himself unable to drive them back. Yes, a good dose of French, that's what he needed!

With Moishe gone, Yankel became thoroughly bored, and Hannah, too, for that matter, though less visibly. No more troublesome questions to torture himself with, no more arguments pro and con to debate to his heart's content, no more diverting, unexpected gifts— the gray life, in all its bareness. To be sure, Yankel now slept more peacefully, but his tossings weren't entirely eliminated: you can always find something to fret about when you want to, and that natural talent he had for worrying he perfected more and more with age. When Hannah, as full of good sense as ever, would urge him to stop worrying so much about his brother and think of his own children a little, he would promptly take up the challenge:

"Can't you see that Rivka isn't well? She's thin as a rail, that child, and she doesn't eat. And just look how her teeth are growing in all crooked! And Simon? Twelve months old before he walked! At nine months already, I was walking! I tell you that baby's got rickets!"

Hannah felt it useless to protest; at most, she permitted herself a few tears when her husband went beyond the limit. She was pregnant again. Out of sorts, because that's the way pregnant women are, the fact was she carried her huge body quite bravely. She busied herself about the house, wagging her head and heaving great sighs, and the apartment was just as well kept as ever, their dinner always ready on time.

Occasionally, Moishe came to see them, always without giving any advance notice. "I didn't want you to prepare anything special for me," he would say to his sister-in-law. In reality, he loathed all obligations. At seven o'clock, then, even later sometimes, the doorbell would ring unexpectedly. "Uncle Moishe! Uncle Moishe!" Rivka would shout, jumping for joy. And in he would come, more imposing than ever behind his red beard, straight as a colonel of the guard, his pockets stuffed with presents for both children and grownups. And he never failed to bring his contribution to the dinner. In the beginning, he would set on the table a simple cake, a *kugel* with icing; later, a tart or a Saint-Honoré, and a bottle of red or white wine—but vintage, not ordinary wine. With his increasing sophistication came oysters and, finally, foie gras and champagne, usually Mumm Cordon Rouge. He would unwrap it all with extreme solemnity and then, suddenly, would begin acting the clown, seizing Rivka and leading her off in a cakewalk while singing full-throated, in his fine bass voice, with his Russian accent. He would bounce little Simon on his knee and finally would sit down, out of breath but happy, and drawl out:

"Nu, Yankele, how's business?"

With Hannah, he was extremely courteous, displaying a gallantry toward her that was totally un-Rakwomirian. One evening, in fact, like a nobleman or a Pole, he even kissed her hand upon arriving, no doubt as a joke, but Yankel wondered a moment, though the idea seemed insane to him, whether he hadn't done it inadvertently.

At table, the young man hardly spoke; and yet, God knows why, his mere presence would transform you, put you in a sparkling mood, make you feel gay and light. The effects of the cure, moreover, would last long after Moishe had left. For several days, Yankel would remain in high spirits, would play jokes on his wife or the children, and Hannah would catch herself humming as she went about her chores. Then, little by little, the gray mood would return, and the questions, and the endless inner debates.

Moishe's visits were highly irregular. Once, he invited himself four times in a single week, and the word "sponger" began gnawing at Yankel's subconscious. At other times, for no apparent reason, he would disappear for weeks on end, and then Yankel would become worried, would wonder if he weren't ill, or if he had left the country without letting them know, or even . . . Yes—why not arrested by the police? Why not? He was quite capable of doing something stupid enough to get himself arrested, that scoundrel! And the French police weren't like the Russian police, always for sale.

Once, Moishe stayed away so long that Yankel, truly disturbed this time, decided to go find out what was wrong. He took his hat, his cane, and presented himself at the address his brother had given him—a hotel on the Rue Montmartre. He hesitated a moment at the door. What name should he ask for? M. Mykhanowitzki? Surely, Moishe had adopted a French name. M. Mica, then? His heart full of shame, he settled upon M. Maurice, certain that that was it.

"Monsieur Maurice?" repeated the clerk at the desk. "Which one? Ah, you mean the . . ."

He didn't complete the sentence. Had he intended to say the Redhead? the Big One? the Kike? the . . . hmmm! the diamond dealer, maybe?

The clerk bent over the register.

"Checked out."

"Checked out? Where did he go? Didn't he leave any forwarding address?"

The man gave him an inscrutable look, shrugged his shoulders, and stuck his nose back in his register.

Should I explain that he's my brother? Yankel wondered. But, after giving the matter due consideration, he ended up by saying only good-bye and thank you, received no reply, put his hat back on his head, turned around and walked out, as aggravated over the clerk's rudeness as he was worried about what had become of his brother.

Not long after, Moishe reappeared in the apartment on the Rue des Francs-Bourgeois, ever smiling, ever at ease, ever himself. Yankel, not without misgivings, told him about his inquiries at the hotel. Moishe laughed heartily but offered no explanation, other than that he was now living in a bachelor's flat on the Rue Godot-de-Maurcy, over toward the Madeleine, the Opéra. "Like to see the place, Yankele?" But before his brother could answer, he invited the whole family for lunch. In a restaurant, of course, a poor bachelor like him . . .

"So what are you waiting for to get married, Moishele?" interrupted Yankel, overjoyed at being able to seize an opportunity for which he had long been watching; he was convinced that marriage would make a completely new man of Moishe.

"Married? Me?" exclaimed the young man, startled. "I don't want to be tied down!"

"But you like children so much, Moishele."

"Ah, don't be a *schlemiel!*" Moishe drawled out affectionately.

And once again, Yankel failed to engage his brother in a serious discussion. However, Moishe did show a little more animation that evening than usual; he told funny stories and let drop a few remarks which, upon consideration, seemed rather strange, especially coming from Moishe's lips.

"Did you ever think of becoming naturalized, Yankele?"

131

"Naturalized? What for?"

"Well, you never know, it might come in handy some day!"

That Moishe! Naturalization, come in handy? How? First of all, you are what you are, no? And Yankel wasn't French, was he? Nu? Of course, when he had registered Simon's birth with the authorities and they had told him a lot of obscure things concerning the child's nationality, the possible options, and so forth, he had said to himself, Good! My son will be French! Since Simon had been born in France, there was no doubt he ought to be French—as French as he, Yankel, was Russian. But in truth, that whole complicated business, he felt, belonged to another, unreal world, the world of administrations, police, governments—of red tape, in short.

"And you?" he asked at last. "Do you intend to become naturalized?"

"Me? Oh, there's plenty of time yet! You've got to be here six, ten years. But you, Yankele, you've been in France a long time, you're married, you have children, a good reputation! If you wanted to . . ."

Just then—for what earthly reason, he didn't know—a bizarre thought crossed Yankel's mind. He wondered what possible pleasure a man like Moishe could derive from his company. Yes, why did Moishe come so willingly to the house? No one, certainly, was forcing him, and family sentiment was all but completely alien to him. His whole life unfolded elsewhere, in a universe unknown to Yankel, where people worried about naturalization without worrying about acquiring a real trade—a universe, Yankel thought, where people like me must be looked upon as poor fools, as tenderhearted simpletons.

Tenderhearted . . . Yes, maybe, at bottom, what Moishe came looking for here was a little tenderness, a little honesty, a little humanity, a little purity?

When Hannah brought a second daughter into the world, whom they named Clara, Moishe rushed right over, bearing a princely gift: a gold-plated spoon-and-fork set with a bowl to match.

At last, old Avrom, the head of the clan, the patriarch who had sired thirteen children, set out in turn for France.

For months, years, Yankel had been pleading with him to seek refuge in Paris. In vain. Persecutions, pogroms, massacres could rage in every corner of the czar's vast empire, but the old man would only find in them another opportunity to give thanks to the Lord. "By

God's grace," he would write in his letters, "we, we were spared. Praise be to God!"

We was Rakwomir and the surrounding territory.

What finally made him decide to leave he never said; perhaps he himself didn't know. There was the monstrous slaughter at Kishinev, which surpassed in horror all previously known horrors. And there was, in Rakwomir itself, a change of climate which decidedly didn't augur well. First, troops of Cossacks appeared, to maintain an order which nothing had been disturbing, and the whips began lashing out at innocent passers-by. Then, the peasants took on a shifty look, stopped returning your hellos, or, if they did, would turn their eyes away; some even spat on the ground as they went by. The Jewish self-defense organizations held meeting upon meeting, in the greatest secrecy, but of course everyone knew what went on at them.

Old Avrom didn't lack a nose for trouble. Nor was he lacking in good sense. The war against the little Japanese had begun, and since big, burly Russians were getting themselves soundly beaten, it was a foregone conclusion that they would take it out on their Jews. He gave Yankel notice he was coming, in less than two weeks sold his grocery, his house and his furniture, and took the train with his wife and child.

Yankel had got all dressed up to go meet them at the station. Standing on tiptoe, he finally spotted in the crowd a little old Jew in a black overcoat, loaded down with packages. It's . . . it's he! he said to himself after hesitating an instant, too surprised to be moved. He hadn't recognized his father at first glance. And yet, the old man hadn't changed. The same pepper-and-salt beard covered his whole face, the same quick, imperious walk; the only thing different about him was the round, wide-brimmed hat instead of the customary black serge *yarmulke*. No, it wasn't old Avrom who had changed, but Yankel; Yankel who, unconsciously, had expected to find a French father, not that fugitive from an East European ghetto. Ah, what a long way I've come since I arrived in France! he suddenly thought.

He looked around for his mother, finally caught sight of her. A black kerchief around her head, she was jogging along behind her husband, even more loaded down with packages than he; a boy of ten or twelve was holding fast to her skirt—little Itcha, no doubt. With tears in his eyes, Yankel made his way over to them and kissed his father on both cheeks.

133

"Well, Papa, did you have a good trip?"

But before the old man could answer, his wife threw herself into her son's arms, sobbing pathetically:

"Yankele, my little Yankele! My sweet little baby!"

Her packages had fallen to the ground, but she paid no attention. Clinging to her son's shoulders, she kissed him unashamedly, released him a moment to press his cheeks between her hands, then hugged him tightly again. The day Yankel left the homeland, his mother had felt sure she would never see him again. And now they were reunited, and Yankel, full of remorse, suddenly realized that at bottom he had rather easily got used to the idea of a definitive separation. Pfeh! Human ingratitude!

Breina's packages were lying on the ground; happily, old Avrom was there—oh, he kept his eyes open, the old man, and potential thieves had to slink off empty-handed! Very fine, those sentimental outpourings, but there's time enough later. Whereas if some scoundrel should steal the baggage, it's gone for good, no?

"Na, na, na, Breina!" he grumbled. "So now let's get started! Where's Moishe?" he added quickly.

Yankel was his mother's son, Moishe his father's.

Without replying, Yankel picked up as many packages as he could carry; then, since his father repeated the question in an insistent tone, he explained grudgingly that Moishe had some business to tend to, and that . . .

"Good, good!" said Avrom, all pleased. "Business is business!"

As a matter of fact, Yankel didn't know why his brother hadn't come; perhaps he simply didn't feel like it. Yankel had written to let him know about his father's arrival. Moishe hadn't even taken the trouble to answer. But Yankel couldn't very well tell the truth and put his brother to shame, could he? After all, he wasn't a savage, Yankel Mykhanowitzki!

"He makes a good living, Moishe?"

It was hardly a question; rather, the statement of a fact. Yankel pretended not to hear, and the old man repeated the question louder. When Avrom asked a question, he was determined to get an answer.

"Yes," Yankel replied, resigned.

"Mmmm! That's a head for you, Moishe!" declared the old man with conviction, puckering his lips and wagging his head; had his hands been free, he would have tapped his temple to illustrate his words.

Not a word about Hannah and the children, not a word about how his eldest son was making out. Yankel's heart was bitter; Moishe was the only one who counted! And yet, when his father needed something, it was he, Yankel, to whom he always came—not Moishe! While looking for an apartment of his own, it was Yankel with whom he would stay—not Moishe! So? Couldn't he make just a little effort to be nice, then? It suddenly occurred to Yankel that, in all the excitement, he himself had neglected to give his little brother Itcha a kiss. He turned to the child, smiled at him—too late, now, encumbered as he was with all those packages.

"Not too tired, Itchele?" he asked tenderly.

He had left a four-year-old child; now, before him, was a little man. To think that frenzied pogromists might have crushed that innocent head, laughingly split open that belly with knives! Now, now you're safe, little Itcha!

"Oy, *Gott!*" exclaimed his mother timorously. "So many lights!"

They were standing on the sidewalk. With the falling night, shop fronts and apartment windows had begun lighting up one after the other. A lamplighter passed, carrying a long iron staff on his shoulder; he thrust the staff inside the globe of a lamppost, poked about a moment, and a yellow light swelled up, filled the globe, spilled over into the street.

"Oy, *Gott!* repeated Breina, who had followed the maneuver with intense interest.

"It's nothing, Mama. He's just lighting up the street," explained Yankel affectionately.

"There are so many lamps in Paris, in the streets?"

A fine rain had just dampened the sidewalks, on which the lights of the city were shimmering. The autumn air was still warm, but from time to time a slight chill could be felt. In the street all manner of vehicles passed by in an unending stream. With her eyes, the old woman devoured that extraordinary world into which life had suddenly cast her, and Yankel respected her contemplation.

"Na, na! Which way do we go?"

Avrom contemplated nothing, remarked nothing, looked at nothing. It was the Christian world, all that! Those people passing by, jabbering an incomprehensible language—*goyim!* Those houses, that city—a Christian city. It might just as well have been nonexistent, for old Avrom spoke as loudly, was as much at ease in that crowd as if he were in a deserted field.

135

"Nu?" he repeated impatiently, anxious to set out in the direction his son indicated. On foot, of course.

Yankel reflected. What means of transportation should he choose to take his parents home with him? The brand-new subway? No, better to reserve that surprise for later. The streetcar? The omnibus? With all the baggage, and in the rush hour, it would be difficult, to say the least. And besides, though he didn't dare admit it to himself, Yankel was a little ashamed to place this strangely garbed tribe yapping away in Yiddish on exhibition, before a crowd of snickering Frenchmen.

"We can't walk there with all this baggage, Papa," he said, smiling. "It's too far."

"Too far, too far—I have no legs? I'm not a cripple yet!"

Yankel was distressed. If we get into an argument now, we'll end up sleeping here! he thought.

"Mama and Itcha are tired, Papa. And besides," he added, raising his voice and drowning out his father's for the first time in his life, "and besides, I don't want you to worry about this! Today, I'm giving the orders!"

He had spoken in a jesting tone, and, to cut the matter short, he rushed off and hailed a passing fiacre. Submissively, the carriage pulled up alongside the curb, directly in front of them.

"A carriage!" murmured his mother, frightened; even his father seemed troubled.

"Get in, get in!"

Yankel had become so French that he had forgotten the innumerable prohibitions to which Jews in the homeland were subject. He gave the coachman his address and climbed aboard in turn.

"You speak French so well, my sweet Yankele!" his mother murmured adoringly, clasping her hands together.

His father said nothing. Slumped far back in his seat, old Avrom was mumbling into his beard—a prayer, no doubt. The ride through the streets didn't interest him; it was a Christian ride.

"So high up you live, Yankele!" His mother was out of breath.

Laboriously, they climbed the stairs, Yankel happily looking forward to hearing his parents go into raptures over the beauty of the apartment, the furniture, the running water, the inside toilet, the gaslights. Gas, can you imagine! Not everyone in Paris has gas!

Alas! No sooner did they step inside the apartment than his mother threw herself upon her daughter-in-law and her grandchildren, and began weeping—for joy, naturally. As for his father, he inspected the door jamb, then gave his son a severe look:

"Where's the *mezuzah*?"

When it came to things religious, old Avrom would stand for no nonsense.

Brokenly, Yankel shook his head.

"Listen, Papa, you know very well that . . ."

"Yes, yes, I know that you're an impious sinner, a goy! But that, that you could have respected! Is your son circumcised, at least?"

It was surprising he didn't ask to see.

"But I wrote you right away that he was, Papa!" Yankel groaned. "Am I in the habit of lying?"

To that stubborn, fanatical old man, an uncircumcised grandson would have meant less than a total stranger; and as for a son guilty of such an outrage to God, he would have considered him dead. Yankel wasn't unaware of this. But as a matter of fact, if he had had Simon circumcised, it was, he believed, purely for hygienic reasons; he wasn't a savage, was he?

"No, you're not a liar," the old man grudgingly conceded. "But you're too quick to take your father for a *schlemiel!* And what kind of a name is that—Simon, Simon?" He spat out the syllables contemptuously. "A goy name, that's what it is, not a Jewish name!"

Is this going to go on much longer? Yankel thought, his patience sorely taxed. He translated Simon into Yiddish; then, while he was at it, also gave the nearest Yiddish equivalent to Clara. But his father wasn't interested in Clara—she was merely a girl.

Driven by a vague feeling of guilt, Yankel tried to explain to the old man the advantage of choosing French names for the children, names which, at the same time, were still Jewish, because . . . He gave it up. How could he ever make his father feel the gulf which separated a Russia partitioned into ethnic minorities all tightly shut in upon themselves, and a unified, equalitarian France? Brows knitted, old Avrom remained silent, firmly resolved to understand nothing—stories for *goyim,* all that!

"You," he suddenly cut in, pointing an accusing finger between his son's eyes, "you, you're ashamed to be a Jew!"

Yankel felt his face turning crimson; maybe it was true, in part, or at one time had been . . .

All right, what now? Squatting on the floor, the old man was un-

137

wrapping one of his packages, while everyone stood there watching him, not daring to say a word. He had traveled hundreds upon hundreds of miles, entered an astonishing new world, rejoined his children, from whom he might very well have believed himself separated forever, and his first act wasn't to embrace his daughter-in-law, his grandchildren (he hadn't so much as glanced at them, hadn't so much as looked about him, except to remark the absence of a *mezuzah*). No, his first act was to unwrap a package. Exactly as if he were returning to his own home after a day's shopping! His own home, yes, for no matter where Avrom happened to find himself, he would always be at home. Like the snail, which carries its shell with it wherever it goes.

"Listen, Papa," began Yankel in extreme annoyance, "you can unpack your things later. There's no fire!"

What on earth could he have in there? A present for the children, maybe?

The old man raised his head:

"I won't stay in a house," he replied emphatically, "even the house of my eldest son, in which God is not present!"

And he took from the package a *mezuzah* of his own, demanded a hammer and nail, pushed aside his son, who had offered to attach the little box to the door jamb, attached it himself, kissed it devoutly and said a prayer. Then, with crushing contempt, he looked Yankel up and down, called his daughter-in-law to him, inquired as to whether the food in that impious house was kosher at least, went to the kitchen to make sure there were the prescribed two sets of dishes, one for dairy products, the other for meats, asked the young woman a number of probing questions, and only then, his misgivings slightly allayed, consented to sit down.

"Come, Hannele!" he said to his daughter-in-law with a warm smile. "Mmmm! Prettier than ever! You're looking fine, fine!"

In the wink of an eye, he had once more become the lovable old grandfather.

Finally, he set the children down, looked all around, nodded his head approvingly, and fixed Yankel with his little eyes—eyes set too close but sparkling with mischievousness.

"A nice little place you've got, Yankel!" he said, as if acknowledging an established fact.

Too late! thought Yankel. The pleasure had already been spoiled. Well, at least the intention was good.

"Nu! Do we eat?"

Old Avrom rubbed his hands together, and Yankel smiled, a torrent of memories racing through his head. Yes, he liked to eat, Papa did; huge meals had never frightened him! Nor the ritualistic fasts, either, for that matter; his stomach was equal to any ordeal.

"Let's wait a few more minutes," Yankel suggested. "Maybe Moishe will come."

"Na, na, na! If he comes, he'll eat what's left! So, ladies, is it ready?" he called out happily.

Breina bounded from the kitchen, replied, "A few minutes!" and disappeared again.

"Mama, see here now, Mama!" Yankel shouted. Then, "Hannele!"

Now it was Hannah's turn to spring forth. It was like a scene from a comic opera, that opening to the kitchen.

"Aren't you ashamed to let Mama help you? Why, she must be exhausted!"

"But she won't listen to me!" Hannah moaned. "After all, I can't *throw* her out of the kitchen, can I?"

She disappeared.

"Nu, let the women work it out between themselves!" said the old man with a sly wink.

Yankel thought of his mother. What a woman! Never tired, never inactive! Ah, she was certainly a wife worthy of old Avrom! And furthermore . . . And furthermore what? he suddenly wondered. For he was unable to find anything else to say about his mother—he simply didn't know her. She was the invisible housewife, thanks to whom everything functioned smoothly in the house. Nothing more! Disappointed, he sat down and glanced at his father, foraging happily among the hors d'oeuvres. What should he say to him? What topic should he bring up for discussion? Talk to him about France? The old man couldn't care less about France!

Off in a corner of the room, Itcha and Rivka were talking softly together, while little Simon listened gravely, a finger in his mouth, half asleep.

"Uncle and niece!" murmured Yankel with a smile.

It seemed strange that the uncle was only four years older than the niece. "Uncle Itcha"—it made you think of an old man, not a boy of ten.

"Uh-huh!" grunted Yankel's father, his mouth full.

That was all he could find to say. So, for lack of a father, Yankel decided to chat with his brother.

"Itchele!" he called out. "Come and sit here with me awhile, so we can get to know each other. Do you still remember me?"

Timidly, the boy shook his head from side to side. In his thin, triangular face, all one could see were a pair of huge black eyes. Of course, Yankel thought. How could he remember? He was too little. Ah, time flies!

"Na, na, na!" let out the old man in his grating voice. A few moments before, he hadn't found it necessary to respond to his son's overtures, but now that the latter had found someone else to talk to he had to intervene. He could not tolerate being left out, no matter where he happened to be. Now he pulled up a chair opposite Yankel's and sat looking his son squarely in the eyes.

He still had on his good black frock coat with its cloth-covered buttons, the same coat he had worn ever since Yankel was a child, as clean and as new-looking as always; but he had replaced the round hat with his famous *yarmulke*. Ah, that *yarmulke!* No matter how much Yankel searched his memory, he could not recall ever having seen the top of his father's head. Even when old Avrom took his weekly foot bath, a rite that invariably took place before the whole family, the *yarmulke* never left his skull.

"So what kind of a life do you have here? So how's business? How . . ."

The interrogation had begun, and to Yankel it was as if he were a little boy again, as if he were facing his Judge. Submissively, he answered him; or rather he started to answer, for new questions constantly cut him off before he could finish. Meanwhile, the Judge, with an involuntary, absent-minded, mechanical gesture, would reach behind him from time to time and snatch another olive. The dish was rapidly emptying, and Yankel, worried, wondered whether Hannah had any more olives left in the kitchen. Why, he too was very fond of olives, and his mother as well, and Hannah, not to mention the children!

At last old Avrom leaned back; the interrogation was over.

"Na, na, Yankele, you're a good boy, even so. If only you weren't such an impious— Mmmm! Do you smell that?" he asked, interrupting himself, his nose palpitating with gluttony.

Mouth-watering odors were drifting in from the kitchen.

"Nu, do we eat or not?" he called out to the women, and with that he rose and trotted off to the kitchen. He knew nothing at all about the art of cooking, yet he loved to poke about the stove, sniff the odors, lift the pot covers, guess the surprises that were being prepared; occasionally he would manage to filch a choice morsel, and would scamper off, delighted, his prize in his hand.

After a moment, the sound of a playful dispute rose up: Breina was trying to get her thief of a husband out of the kitchen.

"Will you leave me in peace, old man! Out with you now, old fool!"

And a grotesque couple bounded forth. The old father, his *yarmulke* glued to his head, had grabbed hold of his old bewigged wife and was pulling her into the dining room. She struggled awkwardly, made herself limp, clung to him—and she laughed, yes, laughed so hard that tears came to her eyes, old Breina, her face suffused with happiness as she gurgled ecstatically:

"Ah, old man, you! Aren't you ashamed of yourself, at your age! Enough now, old man!"

But he, without speaking a word, a fierce look on his face, tugged and pulled all the more. When he reached an open space, he began to waltz, forcing the old woman, now all limp in his arms, to follow him. And as he danced, he sang, in a voice that was only slightly tremulous, one of those popular Yiddish tunes, punctuated with joyous *Ay, ay, ays!* It was so contagious, that explosion of naked joy, that Yankel too joined in, as did Hannah, who appeared in turn at the door; and they clapped their hands and tapped their feet on the floor, while Rivka, off in the corner, preened herself, while poor little Simon, terrified, howled at the top of his lungs, and Itcha, his mouth open, pensively contemplated the grownups' madness.

Ah, yes, that's the way he was, old Avrom! When he felt like laughing, the whole household must enter into the gaiety, willingly or by force. But usually it was willingly, for he had a rare gift for injecting life into parties and had always been in great demand at all sorts of joyous celebrations—marriages, circumcisions, *bar mitzvahs*. Why had Yankel's memory retained only the image of a sullen, pious old despot? Scolding he was, to be sure! But when his joy was unleashed, it was irresistible.

Abruptly the sound of the doorbell interrupted the sport.

"Na! What's that?" grunted the old man, stopping short. Breina, gasping for breath, her face dripping with perspiration, leaned heavily on her husband for support.

"Uncle Moishe! Uncle Moishe!" shouted Rivka in her shrill voice, and, jumping with glee, she ran to open the door.

Yes, it was he, very tall, very straight, very imposing, very much the gentleman in his handsome tailor-made suit and holding his hat in his hand, like an aristocratic Christian.

"Oy, *veh iss mir!*" moaned old Breina, bursting into tears and throwing herself into her son's arms. Before that prodigious being born of her own womb, she could find no better words than the classic Yiddish exclamation of woe to express the intensity of her happiness.

"So, you finally made it!" said the old man severely. "Where were you?"

"Oh, business, business . . ."

"You couldn't find a few minutes to come to the station and welcome your old father and your poor mother?"

"Here, Papa, here's a little something for you." Moishe's voice was nonchalant as he spread out a superb prayer shawl.

"Yes, yes, an unbeliever like you . . ." The old man was grumbling, but he had been touched—it was as plain as day.

But already Moishe had begun unwrapping his other gifts—until his father held up his hand for him to stop:

"Come, eat, eat! We can see the rest later. So there's no fire, is there?"

He had got his present; the others could wait.

Hannah had prepared a feast—chicken broth with matzoth balls, gefilte fish, stuffed cabbage—and though the old man worried constantly about whether the food was kosher, whether the silverware came from a Christian shop, whether the baker was a pious Jew, the dinner was very gay. Yankel's mother erupted into tears half a dozen times; now she would go into raptures over the beauty of her grandchildren (Thank God, little angels, *ken ein hurra!*); now she would weep over the fact that Sarah, her eldest daughter, who had married one of the Feinschneider boys (May the Lord protect them!), had stubbornly refused to leave the homeland, where the wretched pogromists (May the Lord strike them dead!) were committing such abominations . . . Yankel didn't remember his mother invoking the Lord so often. Was it age? Or was it that he, Yankel, had simply forgotten? He was surprised also to see her weep so easily; it reminded him, disturbingly, of Mother Kratzmann.

The old man, for his part, was stuffing himself ecstatically. In fact, it was only because his jaws were so occupied that the others were able to speak. From time to time, however, he would interject a terse comment:

"Fine girl, Hannah! Good cook!"

That compliment represented in his eyes the second highest honor a woman could attain, ranking just below bringing a healthy son into the world.

And if Sarah's or Peretz' name happened to crop up in the conversation?

"Sarah, that idiot!" he would spit out. "Peretz, pfeh!" And turning to his wife: "That one takes after your side, Breina! Your brother Chaim, exactly!"

"Peretz is a very pious boy," Moishe slipped in once, innocently.

The old man's lively little eyes turned swiftly to his son.

"Don't take your father for an idiot, you!"

And back to the gefilte fish.

But when Hannah, who hadn't noticed her mother-in-law's warning signals, began to speak of Rachel, the old man set his fork on the tablecloth, straightened up, stonily eyed each member of the family in turn, and declared:

"Rachel is a wicked girl."

It was an irrevocable condemnation, beyond all possibility of appeal. But still Breina attempted to put in a little plea for the defense, only to have the old man fly into a rage and slam his fist on the table.

"A wicked girl, I say! She . . ."

He almost choked, coughed once or twice, and picked up his fork: "Never speak to me again of Rachel. She's dead."

And he resumed eating.

When a pious man says of one of his living children, "She's dead," he utters an ineradicable malediction. Yankel glanced at Moishe, who raised his eyebrows and spread his hands a little. Breina was whimpering, but softly so as not to vex her terrible husband. Hannah made herself small, the children hardly dared stir.

What crime did the girl commit? Yankel wondered. Moishe had indeed let drop a few allusions to the storms Rachel had caused by her decision to leave home. But with Moishe, it was impossible to know the real truth; things always seemed stripped of importance when he told about them. Until now, Yankel had thought there had been nothing but a little, insignificant squabble between his father and Rachel.

And now the child was at the other end of the world, and no doubt up to some pretty things there! Actually, Yankel had no idea what she *was* up to. On her arrival in America, she had sent him a post card with a picture of the Statue of Liberty. Printed in three languages were all sorts of details about the statue: height of the right index finger, weight of the big toe of the left foot, number of steps in the winding stairway; but of Rachel herself, nothing but a signature. A few months later came a money order, repayment for the money he had loaned her for the voyage. Since then, nothing more, and Peretz, who from time to time would write a letter, spoke only of himself, of the good "job" (Job, job? So what does he mean, job? That's not Yiddish, that!) he had found in "Nev York," but not a word about his sister.

Yankel awakened from his reverie. Since executing Rachel, old Avrom hadn't opened his mouth except to shovel food into it. Thus the two women, little by little, had got over their apprehensions and were treating themselves to a good portion of gossip—although not too much, so the men permitted them that luxury. At table, as everyone knows, when the men speak, the women remain silent. But now the entire Meltchik family passed in review (Breina had been born a Meltchik), and the Schmirzmanns (Hannah was a Schmirzmann); and since the Meltchiks and the Schmirzmanns were every bit as prolific as the Mykhanowitzkis, since their alliances with the Feinschneiders, the Lipschitzes, the Weisbergs and others were myriad, there was matter indeed for conversation. Yankel listened with only one ear, for those distant relationships held no interest for him; like his father, he limited the family to the Mykhanowitzkis. That was enough; if you dragged in Schmirzmanns, Meltchiks and all the others, there would be no end to it. When a girl gets married, well, she enters her husband's family, no? So she gives up her own. Of course, a sister is still a sister, an aunt an aunt; but when you get to second and third cousins by marriage . . . Pfeh, only women can take an interest in relationships that remote! In fact, they have a passion for it. Hannah could place for you, instantly and infallibly, any person in any family to which her father, her mother, her sisters and brothers, or any of her corresponding in-laws were related, however remotely. And she did it with such ease that it didn't seem like much of a feat, although actually it represented a mental file of some several hundred names.

"Na!" interrupted old Avrom in his grating voice. Having satisfied

144

his hunger, he was ready to talk. He folded his hands and glanced from face to face.

"Nu, what if we have a little talk, now?"

Everything said thus far—drivel. His wife had been explaining how, during a pogrom, the Poles of Bialystok had demonstrated they were even fiercer and more inventive in the art of torture than the Russians, as if being persecuted themselves only gave them more of a taste for persecuting others. She stopped right in the middle of a sentence; the master had spoken.

"It's stuffy in here!" said the master to Yankel after a moment.

And hup!—off came his jacket, which he hung on the back of the chair.

"Nu, take your jacket off!" he said with a solicitous gesture, and Yankel wondered how close his father came to adding, "Make yourself at home!"

Finally, the old man was ready to broach the subject. He knitted his brow, thrust his head forward.

"So, it's good for the Jews here in France?" he asked in a confidential tone.

He had addressed himself to Moishe, but Yankel, displeased that the hierarchical order had not been respected, attempted to answer. He was brushed aside by an irritated gesture.

"Tss! Tss! I'm speaking to your brother. You, you're an idealist. Nu, Moishe?"

"Yes," Moishe replied in that ambiguous way of his; Moishe could never say yes without it sounding like "Who knows?" or "Why not?"

"What yes, what yes?" grumbled the old man crossly. "God gave you a tongue to explain yourself, no? . . . Hannah, some tea!" And without looking at his daughter-in-law he held out his glass.

The sound of running water.

The old man's grating voice:

"Breina! Hurry already, I'm hungry!"

His eyelids sticky with sleep, Yankel groaned, turned over in his bed, and tried to doze off again. What a life! In the middle of the night, as usual, Clara had begun howling at the top of her lungs. Teething! But teething or not, Hannah had got up, and Yankel had got up, and they had both become irritable and had quarreled, while the baby howled all the louder. And it had gone on and on. Had gone on until they had finally taken the baby into their bed with them. Then, instantly calmed, she had fallen asleep.

Yankel had been having a wonderful dream when the old man began to raise a racket. Couldn't he have a little consideration for the others and lower his voice? What time was it, anyhow? Yankel reached a leaden arm toward his vest, draped over the back of a chair beside the bed, fumbled about a moment, and finally found his watch. Five after six! And they had gone to bed at midnight! He's out of his mind, the old man!

. . . What? . . . Oy, veh, that's too much! Now he's singing!

Angrily, Yankel shook his sleeping wife; he had to have someone with whom to share his indignation.

"Hannah, are you sleeping? Do you hear him?"

"Oh, let me sleep, Yankele!" Hannah whined and turned over heavily.

At that moment, the door burst open.

"Nu, nu, children, still in bed?"

There he stood, bright and fresh beneath his black *yarmulke;* which meant he had been up a good hour already, since he had had the time to say his prayers.

"Papa," protested Yankel, furious, "at least you could have knocked."

The old man's eyes were sparkling mischievously.

"Nu, I heard you talking! And besides, it's Wednesday morning, not Friday night!"

Painfully, Yankel sat up. Friday night, Wednesday morning . . . Suddenly he remembered. In Rakwomir husbands shared their wives' beds only on Friday night; the other nights the father slept with his sons, the mother with her daughters. Yankel crimsoned. His own father, that Puritan of Judaism . . . No, impossible! Never would his father joke about a thing like that! Deeply ashamed of having supposed old Avrom capable of such Christian thoughts, Yankel looked up at him, guiltily. But . . . but the old man was chuckling, yes, he was actually chuckling!

"Nu, Yankele, so old-fashioned! You've got to be modern, Yankele! Look at me—am *I* backward?"

Yankel's eyes blinked in disbelief. Old Avrom considered himself *enlightened!* Will wonders never . . .

"Nu, up, up!"

In vain Yankel tried to argue his way out of it; the old man was

146

intractable. He had errands to perform that morning, it seemed, and naturally, Yankel had to guide him about the city.

"But Papa, everything's closed this early!"

"And by the time you're dressed? Washed?" (He, Yankel, had formed in France the habit, unheard of in Russia, of washing before dressing.) "Say your prayers? Eat? Na-a?"

"All right, I'm getting up," Yankel said, resigned.

Old Avrom did not budge. He caught two or three hairs of his mustache with his lower lip, drew them into his mouth, and pensively began chewing on them, like a rabbit.

Old Avrom was not one to let things drag. He had errands to perform that morning—that is, visits to one and another of his *landsmen*. He had made up a list in Rakwomir, following a precise order which was no doubt strictly in accordance with protocol, for he categorically refused to modify it as a concession to Parisian geography. Thus he and Yankel spent the day jumping all over the city. At first, of course, by foot—"I've got good legs, no?" In the end, however, the old man consented to take the omnibus.

Yankel had been looking forward to showing Papa his beloved Paris. But all that the city drew from Avrom was a contemptuous "Pfeh!" because of the long distances and the time lost in traversing them. The truth was he looked at nothing, thought only of attaining his objective.

Naturally, those visits were completely disinterested. What else! Oh, he was an obliging man, Avrom Mykhanowitzki! Leib and Chaim of Rakwomir had entrusted their regards to him to give to Benjamin and Samuel of Paris? The day after his arrival, the message was delivered. How else could it be?

But being obliging doesn't necessarily prevent you from thinking a little of yourself, too, does it? You chat, you pick up bits of information; and how's business? and is it good for the Jews here? In short, since the old man was most observant, in no time at all he knew exactly what he had set out to learn, had located the Jewish quarter, had pinpointed the best business streets within it and, in the bargain, had earned a lot of good will for himself. Ah, yes, it was obvious whom Moishe took after!

The groundwork laid, he stopped using Yankel for his business reconnaissances—"You, you're an idealist!" Nor did he call upon Moishe, knowing only too well that that shiftless one would be of no help to him. Instead, it was a distant cousin on his mother's side to whom he went, a certain Schwarz, a butcher on the Rue des Blancs-Manteaux; Yankel hadn't even known they were related. Avrom had chosen him on the basis of his qualities; pious, solid, of good repute, M. Schwarz was a *Kohen,* a descendant of Aaron, and therefore a religious personage of the highest importance in the synagogue. In addition, he was solemnly stupid. In the wink of an eye, the old man had him eating out of his hand, and the word began to spread through the whole neighborhood that a very pious, very orthodox Jew—a sort of saint, in short—would soon honor the Rue des Rosiers by opening a grocery, a very fine one, and the people who shopped there would surely receive the blessings of the Lord. Even now, in the street, they respectfully accosted M. Mykhanowitzki the *Chassid,* greeted him, and asked him if the news was true. In a matter of days, he had become a notable, an authority on Jewish law.

The painting of the store, which he supervised closely from morning to night, permitted him to make the acquaintance of anyone who cared to drop in, and thus multiply his relations. And since he was a congenial man, a good many people, delighted to find that that saintly *Chassid* knew how to smile, soon took to roaring with laughter at his slightest jest and going into raptures over his intelligence. Those, if he wanted to, he could swindle a thousand different ways and they would still remain his devoted customers.

When the big day arrived, the shop unveiled its wonders to a veritable mob. All the busybodies in the neighborhood were there, jostling each other to offer their congratulations to M. and Mme. Mykhanowitzki. Then M. Schwarz appeared, no longer just the plain, everyday butcher, but the *Kohen* in all his priestly nobility. A *Kohen* and a *Chassid,* imagine! The crowd opened respectfully, silence fell over the store for a few seconds; the presence of the Lord could be felt almost palpably.

Best-quality pickles, prunes at a sacrifice, herring on sale, homemade sauerkraut, a gift with every purchase. And to leave no space empty, signs in chalk covered every window. All in Yiddish, naturally, and in Hebrew characters. The ritualistic purity of the foods went without saying, but, to make doubly certain, M. Mykhanowitzki guaranteed them kosher at every turn. Here and there were a few French translations, for the convenience of such Christian customers as might happen in; they were Yankel's only contribution to the paternal establishment.

Around eleven, as Yankel was tranquilly putting the finishing touches to a cap, and Wolf, his worker (for he had recently taken on a worker), was preparing a pattern, the door to the workshop suddenly flew open. It was Hannah, her eyes starting out of her head and so agitated that for a moment Yankel thought something dreadful had happened. But no, just the contrary! She had been shopping and had passed by her father-in-law's store . . .

"Yankel, you've got to go and see!" she exclaimed for the third time. "It's a madhouse! A madhouse!"

He was a dutiful son, Yankel Mykhanowitzki. So, despite his father's disdain for him, he had decided that a visit to the grocery on its opening was an inescapable obligation. Nevertheless, to impress his displeasure upon the old man, he had made up his mind not to go before evening. But Hannah's account had aroused his curiosity.

In front of his father's store he ran into the mob, a mob so great that it spilled over onto the street; in fact, a policeman even considered it necessary to station himself on the opposite sidewalk, to keep an eye on things. And the shouting, the yapping, the jabbering! They can't all be customers, thought Yankel. With considerable difficulty, he forced his way through the crowd, picking up bits of conversation on the way—the Russo-Japanese War, the Kiev pogrom, the high cost of living, troubles in the fur business, a ten-per-cent profit, Mme. Goldenberg's varicose veins. At first, probably, the *Chassid*'s brand-new shop had served as a point of congregation; then, people had begun massing there simply because there were others before them. And since the crowd kept replenishing itself, the place had become a sort of forum where you discussed your business affairs, where you stopped to gossip awhile. Life is short, no? So enjoy it while you can!

The old pirate must be tickled to death! Yankel thought irreverently. So will it last?

And yet he knew it would last. His father had always had a talent for drawing people about him; back in the homeland, the store had been a meeting place where one went to chat as much as to buy. And here it was beginning again.

Inside the store, the crowd was even denser than out on the street. Yankel finally found his father and mother, smiling, holding court, their hands folded across their blue aprons. They weren't selling anything; no, there would be time enough for selling! Besides, no one was buying; everyone was helping himself. Men and women both, in a holiday mood, their tongues wagging and their heads nodding, were dipping freely into the pickle barrels, into the sacks of walnuts and hazelnuts, the cases of prunes and Corinthian raisins. Oh, one thing at a time, of course! After all, they weren't thieves! The gesture was simply automatic: hup, a prune; hup, a walnut! Just to occupy the mouth, you understand, while the other person had the floor. And besides, among friends, do you stand on ceremony? M. and Mme. Mykhanowitzki are such friendly people! Right away, they make you feel at ease!

"Well, Papa, so business is good!" Yankel remarked, not without irony.

"Nu!"

The old man winked his eye, slyly. He bent over toward his son and whispered in his ear:

"Did you see my competitor, around the corner? What a face he's making? Oy, he's going to have an apoplexy, that one!"

And he began chortling with delight.

"Oy, *veh iss mir!* Is this your son, Monsieur Mykhanowitzki?" yapped a fat, waxen-faced woman. And to show her admiration, she clasped her hands together on her bosom. "So big he is! And so handsome, so strong, oy, *ken ein hurra!*"

Yankel was every bit of five feet, five inches tall and was a full twenty-nine years old. She spoke of him as if she were looking down at a little boy.

"Yes," replied old Avrom, "but if you could see my other son, Moishe, now there—"

"Moishe? The Big One? Hooooo! I didn't know he was your son! Hoooo, *ken ein hurra,* that's a man for you!"

"You know him?"

"Do I know him? Oy, *veh iss mir!*"

And she threw back her head, so great was her hilarity, and with a loud shout screamed to one of her friends, a good yard away:

"Dvoshka! Dvoshka! He asked me if I knew the Big One!" She doubled over with laughter at such a childish question. "He's Monsieur Mykhanowitzki's son!" she explained.

"No! *Ken ein . . .*"

Now the other woman went into raptures, clasped her hands together on her bosom, invoked the Lord and warded off the Evil Eye, the same as the first. Yankel would have had as much trouble telling them apart as two Chinese. But there must have been something wrong in their performance, for Avrom's sharp little eyes darted from one to the other as if to ask, "Na? Na? So what have you got in the back of your heads?"

"Not too tired, Mama?"

A permanent smile was fixed on Breina Mykhanowitzki's face.

"Oh, I am!" she replied almost gleefully. "But that's business! . . . Can I help you, Madame Gourkine?"

Like her husband, she already knew many of her future customers by name and never failed to mention them loudly.

The clock struck noon. All at once a sort of electric charge ran through the store, and the ponderous housewives, until now gossipy, good-humored and dawdling, quickly came to life, began scurrying about.

"Hurry, Madame Mykhanowitzki! So do I have all day? It's you, maybe, who's going to cook lunch for me?"

So the two Mykhanowitzkis set to work, darting about the store, the pack close on their heels. The honeymoon was over! Now they were dealing with real customers, customers who bought, even if they didn't pay till the next day, and who, consequently, had rights and could demand, command, insult, who weren't going to let themselves be fooled just like that. For they continued sampling everything in the store that could possibly be sampled. But it was no longer a question of good fellowship; it was a question now of plain suspicion.

Prudently, Yankel had got out of the way of the whirlwind, and as he stood there a host of childhood memories suddenly returned, and he was surprised to find himself so deeply moved. His father's grocery, a wondrous universe in which he used to lose himself amid the smells and colors, in which the breath of adventure hung restlessly in every corner, in which the most ordinary objects were transformed into exotic treasures from the far ends of the earth!

"Nu! So what are you thinking about now, dreamer?"

His hands folded under his apron, old Avrom was getting restless in his now empty shop. Yes, back in his element! Yankel thought, almost affectionately. If he had never truly loved his father, the older he grew the better he understood him; and he was even beginning to feel a sort of indulgence.

"So take a prune? An almond, maybe! They're good with raisins!"

The old man cracked a shell between his teeth. (He still had all his teeth, good, strong teeth, and even hard-shelled nuts didn't frighten him. He boasted of never having been to a dentist.) Generously, he offered the shelled almond to his son. A child! thought Yankel. Yes, a child, an old child, and, like a child, selfish, tyrannical and truculent, yet at times childishly sweet. And that good woman who was his wife led him about by the nose, just like a child.

"Take, take, help yourself! Have a herring? A pickle?"

"Thank you, Papa," replied Yankel, smiling. "But it would spoil my appetite."

"Na, na, na! You French people, always you've got to eat at regular hours! Your religion, maybe? Ah, la la!" he added with a disgusted look, parodying the French intonation.

Then, jumping to another thought, he inquired as to what Moishe was doing.

Port Arthur, Mukden, Tsushima Strait . . . "The hand of the Lord is upon our enemies!" old Avrom would repeat to anyone who cared to listen. "Ah, the brave soldiers of the Czar! Ah, our fine pogromists! You know, I saw them leave, Madame Axenbaum! . . . A pound of prunes? Delicious! Pure sugar! Go, go, taste one! (Mme. Axenbaum hadn't awaited the invitation.) Yes, waving their caps! The little Japanese, they were saying, we'll finish them off in one bite. So, but what about the Lord, eh? They forgot about the Lord! But the Lord, the Lord never forgets, and those who persecute His people . . ."

Yankel didn't entirely share his father's joy, though he did rub his hands together in public over every Russian disaster. To be sure, he was happy that the pogromists were getting themselves soundly thrashed by the little Japanese. Nevertheless, something stirred in Yankel's tender heart. After all, it *was* the homeland, wasn't it? He made careful distinctions between the scoundrelly instigators of pogroms and the mass of the population. The moujik, at bottom, isn't mean, you know. A decent sort of man, if you don't push him, peaceful, simple, good. Only there are some filthy scoundrels on earth—oy, may they stew in their own blood! And they spread horrible lies—the Jews practice ritual murder, they need the blood of a Christian child for their holidays, and so on. And the poor moujiks believe what they're told, and there you are—a pogrom! But they aren't responsible. . . . Yankel's tender heart bled at the thought of their being cut

152

to pieces, horribly, by the shells and bayonets of the little Japanese. The little Japanese, pfeh! Yellow people! So do you really believe that they're civilized, the yellow people? With the tortures they invent, their famous Chinese tortures, you know? Whereas the Russian peasants, after all, only peasants they are, like all other peasants! If only they could be delivered from their autocratic masters. Well, what could you expect? Less than forty years since serfdom was abolished there, and in fact it still exists in a lot of places. Can you ask serfs to behave like men? The hairy moujik with his drooping jaw and his dull look—why, he's just a poor, dumb animal! Do you hold it against a watchdog because he bites you? But change the masters, and you'll see if the moujik doesn't become exactly like the French peasant, who goes to school, who can read and write—in short, who's educated, civilized! Education, yes, it's all a matter of education.

Nevertheless, Yankel was unable to prevent himself from feeling embarrassed by those sentiments. Giving one's enemies their due, trying to understand them, what a strange idea! But he just couldn't help himself. One day it finally dawned upon him—and he was filled with a sudden pride—that what was happening was simply that he was reasoning like a Frenchman. Ah, yes, the lessons of France were bearing fruit; without realizing it, he had learned to shade, to question, to humanize his judgments. He had begun to look upon the world from a certain elevation, and not just from ground level any more. No matter what the future might hold for him, he was certain that that at least would remain; once acquired, the stamp of civilization can never be entirely rubbed out. I have a new pair of eyes! he thought proudly.

Had Moishe, too, acquired a new pair of eyes? One evening, shortly after that notorious Red Sunday on which the Czar had ordered a pleading, defenseless mob brutally slaughtered, the two brothers were discussing the latest events when Moishe suddenly turned away, stroked his beard and finally asked:

"Tell me, Yankele, do you ever get homesick?"

Flabbergasted, Yankel searched his mind for an answer as Moishe went on, in his drawling voice:

"You know, me, I feel almost sorry about not being there, alongside the ones who are trying to throw that bunch of no-goods out."

"You . . . you want to go back?" mumbled Yankel, his heart pounding. He knew that before leaving Russia his brother had taken an active part in the revolutionary struggles; in fact it was precisely to escape being sent to Siberia that he had come to France, or at least so Peretz had said, for the hero himself remained silent about his exploits.

"No, of course not!" Moishe protested weakly.

Which means yes, thought Yankel.

"Don't do anything stupid!" he burst out, deeply troubled, for he knew his brother only too well. With Moishe, debates of conscience never dragged on but were quickly broken off by action.

"You know, I went to the Russian Embassy the other day," Moishe admitted abruptly.

"So? And they encouraged you to go throw the Czar out, no?"

"Don't be a *schlemiel!*" Moishe muttered absent-mindedly. He seemed to be reflecting, but suddenly he looked his brother straight in the eye.

"I'm going to tell you something, Yankele—ah, it's stupid! But what I'd like most of all—ah, if only you knew how it's itching me—what I'd like most of all is to lay my hands on those little Japanese! Doesn't it make your blood boil, Yankele, those yellow monkeys playing at being soldiers?"

Moishe, a volunteer of the Czar! Yankel had never thought he would live to see the day!

"Moishe, you're an idiot!" he shouted, growing angrier by the second. "Save a few tears for the Jewish women of Odessa who were raped and gutted, for the innocent little children who were caught by the feet and *crack!* ripped in two by the Russian beasts! Moishe, if you enlist, I . . . I . . ."

Moishe gave him a quick glance and stroked his beard.

But he spoke no more of enlisting. For his part, Yankel trembled with rage for several days after. Not for a moment did he imagine that Moishe had come purposely to consult him. Moishe, consult someone? Don't make me laugh! That rascal needed no one to help him plan his idiocies.

Modest Yankel had no idea of the influence he exerted upon the people around him. Moishe in particular, with his lordly mien and his free and easy ways, seemed to him completely impervious. And yet it was a fact that on several occasions the young man, in his customarily oblique way, sought the advice of his elder brother and, moreover, adhered to it. Yankel was his conscience. But Yankel himself was quite unaware of it, for Moishe consulted his conscience only when, in his eyes, the thing seemed worth the trouble; and Moishe's eyes weren't Yankel's, they didn't look upon the world from the same viewpoint. What mattered to Yankel, for example, were affairs of the heart and of money; it was in these realms that he felt his advice should have been sought, in these that he felt he could give good counsel. But Moishe didn't care a rap for the heart and for money. On the other hand (and Yankel was completely unconscious of this), if Moishe had emigrated to France, it was because Yankel had settled in Paris. When all was said and done, he had an admiration and an affection for his elder brother that no rebuff could ever shake; and, even as he joked about the "idealists," he bowed before an intellectual superiority acknowledged without discussion.

The doorbell rang.

"Uncle Moishe! Uncle Moishe! Rivka shouted, clapping her hands. She ran to the door, opened it.

It wasn't Uncle Moishe. It was Grandpa—and in ceremonial attire: black overcoat, black wide-brimmed hat and black umbrella. He bent over the frightened little girl, gave her cheek a hasty tickle with his mustache, then hurried into the dining room.

"Yankel! Yankel! Na, so where is he? Hannah!" he grumbled, catching sight of his daughter-in-law.

Whatever it was all about, it certainly sounded urgent. Yankel appeared from his workroom in his vest and with the sleeves of his shirt rolled up.

"Aren't you ashamed of yourself, Yankel?" scolded the old man without even taking the time to sit down. Yankel's eyes popped open.

"Ashamed of what, Papa? Sit down, for God's sake! What's happened?"

Yankel himself sat down, but the old man remained standing, gesticulating and waving his umbrella.

"Ashamed of what, ashamed of what!" he repeated sarcastically, with frightful grimaces meant to imitate his son's expression. "Hannah, a schnapps!" he ordered. "Outside, children, outside!"

Rivka didn't have to be told twice; she fled to her room, taking Simon with her. Yankel exchanged a glance with Hannah; the latter shrugged her shoulders and began cradling little Clara in her arms.

The old man finally sat down, tossed off the schnapps in one gulp, smacked his lips, and wiped his mustache with the back of his hand.

"Nu? You see where it leads to, your impiety? That one," he said contemptuously, pointing to Hannah, "who goes around showing her hair to the whole world, like a prostitute . . ."

"Papa!" shouted Yankel, half rising from his chair. "I forbid you—"

"Sit down! . . . Nu, nu, Hannele," he grumbled in a surly, but nevertheless softened, tone, "that isn't what I meant to say! I know you're a good girl, yes, yes!"

Coming from old Avrom, words such as those were equivalent to an apology. Nevertheless, he couldn't restrain himself from calling attention to the fact that he wasn't entirely wrong.

"All the same, it's not decent for a woman to show her hair like that, for everyone to see! You're not a young girl any more, no? And you, Yankel . . ."

With an angry gesture, Yankel sat down. All right! He would submit to the tongue-lashing until the bitter end, but afterward . . . Hannah looked across at him and smiled to calm him; she knew her husband's repressed furies. He turned his eyes away. Finally, when he had had enough of hearing his father repeat in every possible way that he was an impious sinner, he coldly interrupted him in the middle of the tirade:

"Papa, I have work to do today, so hurry, please!" And as the old man grew red, then white, Yankel calmly sent his wife to brew some tea for them, then turned back to his father.

"I'm almost thirty, Papa. A father, with my own business. I owe nothing to no one, I—"

"Wicked son!" thundered the old man. "I don't know what's stopping me from—"

"You'd like to whip me? Is it the Lord who commands you to torment your children by beating them with a belt?"

The old man stood up so abruptly that his chair almost fell over; he caught it just in time, carefully set it in place again. Yankel was unable to repress a smile, and his anger melted away as he too rose. He was a little taller than his father, or perhaps the old man was beginning to shrink. A sort of tenderness, or pity, overcame him, and a feeling almost of shame. A poor old man, at bottom . . .

"Yankel," the old man murmured. "I'm an enlightened man, you know! In life, you have to be able to adapt yourself . . ."

Old Avrom, champion of modernism!

"Listen to this, for example: I do as the Frenchmen now—I sleep in the same bed with my wife all week long, not just on Fridays. So

156

you see! But your grandfather, you should have known your grandfather! Now there was a real . . ."

He stopped, as if checking himself before a too-harsh word. Which word? Savage? Primitive? Barbarian?

". . . a really pious Jew, the old style," he continued after an instant. "Years ago, I too rebelled. You didn't invent anything new, you know! But when I got old, I realized . . ."

All at once, he did indeed seem very old, very tired.

"Ah, sit down, Papa," said Yankel affectionately, "and let's stop arguing. What was it you wanted to talk to me about?"

"Yes, yes, yes . . ." The old man shook his head. "Never would I have allowed myself to speak to my father the way you just did. Never, you hear?"

Mechanically, he sat down, his head still wagging, picked up the glass of tea, took a sip and swished it around in his mouth, sadly. In the silence, the ticking of the clock on the mantelpiece sounded like a drumbeat. Hannah was cradling Clara in her arms; whenever she put her to bed, the baby would immediately begin bawling. Teething.

"Listen, Papa . . ."

Though he had taken pains to speak very softly, Yankel's voice seemed to have exploded; it gave the old man a start.

". . . it's been a long time that we haven't agreed about religion," Yankel continued, "and . . ."

All at once, the old man came to life; he pointed a menacing finger at his son and spoke in the tone of Jehovah reprimanding His people:

"Yankel, you're a bad brother!"

Yankel raised his arms to the heavens and sank back in his chair.

"Yankel!" (The finger was shaking now.) "Yankel, what have you made of your brother?"

"Brother? Which brother?" asked the accused, stupidly.

"Which brother, which brother!" spat out the old man, returning momentarily to earth. "So who but Moishe!"

"Well, what about Moishe?"

Jehovah again:

"You, the eldest son, failed to watch over your younger brother! You left him to sink into the filth of Babylon . . . Be quiet and listen!"

Now at last the old man went back to his normal tone of voice; he had concrete things to relate.

It seemed that in the neighborhood, there existed a gang of good-for-nothings, toughs—hoodlums, in short!—who engaged in white slavery. Jews, yes! And with Jewish girls! They would ship them to England . . .

"To England?" Yankel echoed.

"Tss, tss!" hissed the old man, displeased at losing the thread of his discourse. But he quickly picked it up again and minutely exposed the whole mechanism of the operation. At its head was a jeweler on the Rue des Archives whose shop served as a front. Poor unfortunate girls who had been seduced would be brought to him and from there shipped off to London. Oh, to be sure, those scoundrels didn't lack a certain integrity! Or rather, they were smart enough to know that integrity paid off. Abandon one of their herd of women over there in England? Never! On the contrary, they kept a close watch on them to make sure that everything went well—while collecting their percentage, of course. And if one of the girls became pregnant? Did they throw her out in the street, did they force her to undergo an abortion? Of course not! They brought her back to France, found her a job—as a dishwasher, for example. (So that was why so many dishwashers were pregnant!) And once she had given birth, all that remained was to turn the child over to the State Foundling Home and ship the girl back to England . . .

Yankel was champing the bit. What did he care about all those details? Was his father enumerating them only to put off the moment when he would have to accuse his beloved son of being a hoodlum? He hadn't even spoken Moishe's name yet!

"In short," Yankel cut in, "Moishe is mixed up in this?"

"You, you're a bad brother!" thundered the old man. "You're—"

"I'm not the white slaver, Papa; he is!"

"Yes, but you should have . . ."

Indignant, Yankel got up and began pacing the floor. Stubborn old mule! Your favorite son can commit the worst sins and you haven't a word of blame for him; no, you take it out on me! The eldest son, the eldest son—well, what of it? After all, I couldn't tie him to me with a string, your Moishe, could I? . . . Abruptly Yankel remembered certain tales the *goyim* recounted in their holy books: the prodigal son and the good son, Martha and Magdalene. Ah, yes, Christ knew them well, His fanatical Jews! That Yoshka who was no more of a goy than . . .

"What do you want from me?" he flung out savagely. "You've come

158

to my home and carried on. And I've got nothing to do with this whole business! So?"

How could he have suspected that the old man, in his shame and confusion, had come simply to consult him? Avrom would have let himself be chopped to pieces rather than admit, even to himself, to such a humiliating act.

And then a seemingly harmless little thing occurred, and yet it was equivalent to a scandal. During a momentary silence, Hannah's voice spoke up, softly, timidly; yes, Hannah, that well-mannered wife, who was so adept at effacing herself that you would continually forget she was present—the glasses seemed to fill up with tea all by themselves.

"And what now, Papa?" she asked. "What are you going to do about Moishe?"

The question was so reasonable it left the two men speechless. Going to do, going to do? But there was nothing they could do. Enjoin Moishe to put an end to that dirty business? He would laugh in their faces, or would say yes, yes, and go right on with it. Curse him? Consider him dead? Of course, but . . .

It was Yankel who found his tongue first. He noticed that his wife had remained surprisingly calm in the face of that terrible revelation of family dishonor. Now he looked her in the eye, like a judge.

"Hannah! You knew! And you've known for a long time! Is that right?"

The young woman's face slowly reddened.

"What?" shouted Yankel, thoroughly enraged. "You knew and you didn't tell me? You—"

"Scha, scha! You'll wake Clara!" warned the old man, putting his hand on his son's arm.

Hannah raised grateful eyes to her father-in-law.

"But why, tell me why!" stormed Yankel in a lowered voice. "I have a right to—"

"Enough, idiot!" grumbled the old man. "Don't you understand that she didn't want to hurt you?"

Avrom defending his daughter-in-law now? The whole world had turned upside down! Yankel was at a loss for words.

"I spoke to him about it!" Hannah suddenly blurted out, courageously.

"You spoke to him? When did you speak to him? So! When I wasn't home, then?

A hideous suspicion crossed Yankel's mind; he felt himself go pale.

"So you spoke to him in my absence, did you? And maybe he got a little friendly with you?"

Hannah started, then burst into tears.

"That's enough!" Avrom cut in sharply. "Hannah is a good girl, an honest girl! She never lies, do you hear?" He paused a moment and then added, very softly: "Enough dirt we've got in the family as it is. Lord, what have we . . ."

Painfully, he stood up and began debating aloud with the Lord, all the while thumping his breast (no mere taps, those blows—they boomed out). Yankel looked at his wife; she was sobbing softly. He hesitated, then went to her and tenderly squeezed her shoulder. She raised her swollen eyes to him, smiled through her tears.

"Na! And what did that good-for-nothing tell you, Hannele?" asked the old man, heartened by his conversation with the Lord.

"Not much," mumbled Hannah fearfully. "You know how he is. First he laughed, and then he said it wasn't true, and then that it was exaggerated, and then that he was all through with it now, because . . ."

She lowered her head.

"I spoke to him only once, and after that he stayed away a long time. You remember, Yankel, when . . ."

"Yes, yes!" Yankel replied impatiently. "So he's all through with it now, you say? And why, tell me, should he be all through with it?"

"Because . . . well, he said he realized it was bad!" She saw Yankel shrug his shoulders and quickly added, "And dangerous!"

Actually, Moishe had told her quite frankly that he now had enough money so that he could turn to something less distasteful. But what was the use of telling that to his brother and his father?

"And you, do you really believe he's through with it?" Yankel demanded skeptically.

Hannah shrugged her shoulders.

"Ah, if only it's true!" sighed the old man, full of hope. "At bottom, Moishe isn't a bad boy, but he lets himself get dragged into things."

Yankel opened his mouth, closed it. What was the use? Whether Moishe was through with it or not, it was plain as day that his father would clutch at the flimsiest pretext to forgive him. Ah, if it had been he instead of Moishe . . . !

Finally they decided to summon Moishe—without letting him know why, naturally. And on the appointed day Yankel went to his father's to participate in the family tribunal. But Moishe didn't come. It wasn't until two days later that he presented himself, as ever, smiling, affable and laden with gifts. The old man was alone. Moishe let the storm pass, then smiled warmly and explained that it was a thing of the past, all that; people were stupid, they gossiped, they got things all mixed up, they made mountains out of molehills; jealousy, that's what it was! And thereupon, he took the old man to see the fine jewelry shop he had just purchased near the Madeleine. Result: The next time Yankel saw his father, he found a happy man, and he left in disgust.

And yet if Avrom, the father, could bury the hatchet, why should the eldest son make a show of righteousness? For a while, Yankel treated Moishe coldly, without the latter seeming to notice it. Then, like everything else, it blew over.

It was warm that morning when Yankel, yawning, stuck his head out the window to view a silken sky. "At last, spring!" he said to himself, suddenly wide-awake, happy and full of energy. Ah, how good it was to be able to stretch himself with that playful breeze tickling the hairs of his chest! After the interminable winter months, it made him feel reborn. My thirtieth springtime! he thought, not knowing whether to consider himself young or old.

He leaned out the window. The sidewalk beckoned him, invited him to carefree, adventurous promenades. Yankel drew in his head and spun around:

"Hannele! Hannele! Hurry and get dressed! Dress the children! We're going for a walk!"

Hannah appeared, pushing her swollen belly before her; she was pregnant again.

"What's got into you, Yankele?" she moaned.

"It's springtime and it's Sunday!" her husband exclaimed joyously. "Come, come! And we'll have lunch in a restaurant!"

"Sunday, Sunday . . . Oy, leave me alone with your Sundays! We're Jews, don't forget; our Sunday is Saturday."

All his joy evaporated, Yankel looked at his wife. Poor Hannah, so deformed by her pregnancy, with her breasts hanging like goatskin bottles on her stomach, and her sallow complexion . . . Enough children! he decided suddenly. This one will be the last! From now on, he would take care. Yes, the French were right to be considerate of their wives. They didn't grow old so fast, Frenchwomen, they could enjoy life a little. Yankel didn't want his poor Hannele to be, at thirty, one of those old, broken-down Jewish women who spend their lives dragging about the house—and all because their pious husbands refuse to commit the sin of Onan and thus inflict child after child upon them, right up to the change of life.

But would Hannah agree to such an arrangement? Yankel had noted recently that she still believed in certain religious nonsense and, in fact, was beginning to believe in it more and more.

"Hannele, come now, take a little walk with me!" he pleaded humbly. "It's so nice out, you'll get a little air!"

"Oy, leave me alone already, I've got work to do. Go with the children if you like!"

And she returned to her kitchen. Crestfallen, Yankel washed and dressed in silence. Ordinarily, while shaving, he sang at the top of his voice, but today his heart just wasn't in it. Listlessly, he finished dressing, called to Rivka and Simon, picked Clara up, forced himself to give his wife a cheerful good-bye, and left.

"Don't come home too late!" Hannah called out after him.

And that was that!

Once outside, he set Clara down to let her walk a little; then, since the pace was much too slow for him, he picked her up again, gave his free hand to Simon—flanked on the other side by his big sister Rivka—and off they went.

"Simon, come now, walk nicely, will you!"

The child tugged and strained, hung by his arms between father and sister. Ah, it was something, that promenade from which he had expected so much pleasure! A real torture!

Where should they go? It was impossible to cover much ground, what with the baby in one arm and Simon wriggling at the end of the other.

"I'll stop off and get Itchele," he decided. "Poor child, he never goes out; he needs to breathe a little, too."

He hesitated. At the moment, he was on bad terms with his father, as often happened, and he had been avoiding the Rue des Rosiers. But for his little brother, whom he idolized, he would have suffered the worst affronts.

"Hello, hello! I've no time now!" grunted old Avrom when Yankel walked into the store, and he quickly turned away; obviously he was in a vile mood. Breina motioned to her son and led him into the back room.

"Don't get him excited," she murmured. "He's got troubles. Here, look what they sent him this morning."

Yankel couldn't believe his eyes. A package of pork!

"His enemies!" sighed the old woman.

"His enemies?"

Yankel, who spurned all contact with the Jewish neighborhood, suspected nothing of the secret intrigues, feuds and hates of that microcosm.

"Nu, what can you do? It's politics!" continued his mother, dejectedly.

Yankel laughed. Old Avrom, a politician? And with whom? what party? Ah, don't be stupid! Yankel said to himself. He's never had but one worry in his head—whether the food he handles is strictly kosher or not.

"You know how he is," his mother explained. "Always he's got to argue; he's never satisfied unless everybody thinks the way he does. So he broke with Schwarz, the *Kohen,* and . . ."

It finally dawned on Yankel that it was a matter of Jewish politics, not French. The old man didn't care a straw about the affairs of the world, but when it came to the local congregation Avrom would rise up in fiery wrath at the slightest breach of the law, denouncing this one or that for his religious slackness, clamoring that it was a disgrace, that people were constantly violating the rites, offending the Lord, but the Lord will take vengeance, you'll see, you'll see!

One day he had even launched an attack on the *Kohen*'s own sister, violently accusing her of being an impious sinner. Yes, with his own eyes, he had seen her working the previous Saturday! Working on a Saturday? Scandal, uproar! Summoned to explain himself, the *Chassid* presented a straightforward argument, set forth with great clarity and precision. "To carry something is to work, everyone agrees?" Yes, everyone agreed, even the accused. "Well, last Saturday you were carrying something!" "I was carrying something?" "Yes, you were carrying a handkerchief!" And when the lukewarm protested that a wretched little handkerchief wasn't really very much, an angry dispute erupted. "Carrying is carrying!" cried the fiery *Chassid*. "You can't play tricks with the Lord!" "But I had a cold!" "So you couldn't put the handkerchief in your pocket, maybe? In your pocket, it's part of your clothing, it's not carrying!"

163

Fed by personal grudges, the quarrel had become bitter; it was still very much alive, and its end was nowhere in sight. Sides were taken and two opposing camps emerged, fierce enemies, constantly riddling each other with insults. Of course, Avrom's competitor had jumped at the opportunity . . .

No, that was another story, but related to the first. During the Passover, the food one eats must be especially pure. And thus it is more expensive, due to the precautions that must be taken in its preparation. Before the arrival of the Mykhanowitzkis, the competitor, a man of few scruples, simply put a "Kosher for Passover" tag on all his merchandise and raised his prices. But the honest *Chassid* would never have thought of doing such a thing. So he had got in touch with the rabbinate of Marseille (it was from Marseille that most of the foodstuffs came) and they agreed to see to it personally that all the ritualistic laws were respected—that, for example, no morsel of leavened bread came into contact with the Passover foods, thus contaminating them. After which, a stamp would be applied: "Rabbinate of Marseille—Kosher for Passover." And that was that; the merchandise was guaranteed pure. Naturally, old Avrom's initiative had dealt a terrible blow to his competitor, who swore revenge.

Thus the affair of the sauerkraut . . . No, that was a third story, but related to the two others . . . "Patience, Yankele, it will all be clear in a minute!"

If a worm should be found in the sauerkraut, the sauerkraut is impure. His father, therefore, chopped his own cabbage, constantly on the alert for the tiniest worm. And it had quite a reputation, his sauerkraut, for he had his own special way of preparing it. In short, he kept selling more and more of it; and the more he sold, the more trouble he had chopping sufficient quantities. So, since he had never in his life encountered a worm in a head of cabbage, he decided, in a moment of weakness, to buy his cabbage already chopped. And when the customers went into raptures over it ("Hoooo! Monsieur Mykhanowitzki, how fine it's chopped, your sauerkraut!"), to be left in peace, he told them that he had bought a mechanical chopper.

At that time, he was still on the best of terms with the *Kohen* Schwarz, who knew the mystery of the sauerkraut and found nothing particularly wrong with it. But then—then Avrom had to go and offend Schwarz's sister! So Schwarz let out the secret of the sauerkraut. Result: The *Chassid's* enemies were now spreading the rumor that the old man ate pork! "He, eat pork! Can you imagine, Yankele!

And they have the nerve to send him a package of pork! Oy, *veh iss mir!*"

The old woman leaned toward her son, hesitated a moment, turned crimson.

"And do you know what else they made up? They say he goes to prostitutes! How can anybody believe such a thing? But the competitor swears by his children that he saw him, with his own eyes, going to a prostitute! They say . . ."

Suddenly a flood of tears.

"They say like father like son, and they tell such awful things about Moishe!"

"Now, now, Mama . . ."

Yankel was more embarrassed than touched. He realized, a little late, that he didn't know whether or not his father had told his mother about Moishe's business. In his place, Yankel thought, I'd have said nothing. But Avrom wasn't Yankel, and the son was forced to admit to himself that he hadn't the slightest notion of what his father did or didn't confide to his mother. He tried to find something to say that wouldn't compromise the old man.

"Look, Mama, there are a lot of mean people in the world . . ."

Nor was it compromising to give her a reassuring little pat on the shoulder. Luckily, she quickly regained her composure, sniffled a little, and dried her tears.

"Don't tell your father I was crying. There, Yankele, go take a walk now with the children. Your mother's a fool to tell you all these stories. It's not for you, all that!"

And, not waiting to hear another word, she pushed him outside.

It's not for you, all that! What did she mean by that? Still carrying Clara, Yankel headed for the Seine, delivered of Simon, who was now flanked by Itcha and Rivka. He crossed the Pont Louis-Philippe, then the Pont Saint-Louis, without even realizing it, so absorbed was he in his reflections. Finally, he found himself in the little park on the Place de l'Archevêché, set Clara down and, unburdened, began thinking in earnest. From time to time, to satisfy his conscience, he glanced absently at the children, who were gamboling about happily. Regular little Frenchmen! Among themselves, they never spoke Yiddish. Itcha was going to school; in a few short months he had caught up to his French classmates just as Rivka had done a few years before. Children are so pliable . . . not like old people!

Not like old people. Yankel sighed. When his parents had first arrived in Paris, he had wanted to show them the wonders of the city and had offered several times to guide them about. To no avail. Each time the old man had sent him packing, and once, in fact, he had even got angry. "Enough now! I have no need of that!" No need of that, no need of that—what stupidity! thought Yankel. Why close your eyes to the world? Age doesn't rule out curiosity, does it? Well, apparently it did, for the old man remained firmly embedded in the Jewish quarter; his Saturdays he spent at home, at the synagogues and with his neighborhood friends.

Once, however, Yankel had persuaded his mother to go out with him. He had taken her to the Jardin des Tuileries. It was one of those mild, end-of-autumn mornings when golden leaves were clicking in the trees. People were strolling idly, children were chasing each other amid birdlike squeals, a cloud of sparrows swooped down on a clump of bushes and then flew off again, cheeping. Fearfully clutching her son, as if she somehow felt herself at fault, the old woman went into raptures over everything she saw—oy-yi! such clean, beautiful paths, such beautiful lawns, and the beautiful statues, oy, *Gott!* just like real people! "And that baby, did you see, Yankele? Such a pretty child, *ken ein hurra!*" Yankel had wanted to show his mother the Louvre; he had gone there once or twice himself. But she had refused: "No, no, Yankele, not in there, not today!" It had been almost as if she were frightened. And yet she knew that France wasn't Russia, that no one had the right to chase her out, or even to insult her. "In France, Mama, you're free!" Yankel had told her. "Do you understand what it means, to be free?" Yes, she had seemed to understand, and even to understand too well, for Yankel had noticed that she was suffering. But why? Why? Freedom is good!

Too old! The thought had struck him like a bullet. Her whole life was behind her, gone, fled, irretrievable. And it was now—but too late, too late!—that the world's splendors were opening before her. No! No! Better to close her eyes, like her husband, shrink into a dark corner. . . . With respect, with love, Yankel had guided the stumbling, dazzled old woman through the lovely park. The children, the trees, the grass—all that she had been able to look upon without too much pain, for it was only the beauty of the sight that astonished her, not its newness. What had been forbidden her was the new, the too new—the too new that excites perfidious curiosities.

All at once, her face had screwed up in anguish.

"Let's go home now, Yankele," she had said in a supplicating tone, tugging his arm. Without another word, he had taken her back to the Jewish district, and it wasn't until they had arrived there that he had felt her relax.

Too old! Not for her, all that! He rose from his bench, went over to the stone parapet, leaned his elbows on it and absently contemplated the Seine. Then he turned around. The children had made friends with some other youngsters, French youngsters. Their fresh voices filled the air. Rivka, all excited, was prancing up and down, her pigtails flying in every direction.

Regular little Frenchmen! Yankel said to himself once more. With the children, he spoke only French; with Hannah and his parents, only Yiddish. A Yiddish studded with French words, a French twisted out of shape by Yiddish constructions. Two worlds! And Yankel astride the two.

Not for you, all that! his mother had said a little while ago. No, of course not! The world of the Rue des Rosiers is no longer mine; it's the world of my father, my mother—of Hannah too, alas!—of all those old unadaptable, unyielding, nationalistic Jews. Yes, nationalistic, for the ghetto is their nation, their country, wherever it may be —in Warsaw or New York, London or Paris! One day, it seems, a goy had called old Avrom a dirty Jew. And what had the old man replied in his halting French? "I Jew, yes! Good to be Jew!" rubbing his stomach to indicate just how good it was. Then, contemptuously: "You, you not Jew!" For he was a Jew by nationality, as others are English or French or Russian. And he didn't feel himself the least bit a foreigner; they, the others, were the foreigners.

I, I'm a foreigner, Yankel said to himself sadly. A foreigner everywhere! I'm no longer completely Jewish, and I'm not entirely French. Stuck in between somewhere. Could I have gone all the way? Maybe. But wasn't I already too old when I came to France?

Moishe, too . . . No, Moishe is even more lost than I. Moishe, even in Rakwomir, had ceased to be a Jew, had become half Russian. And then, a second time, he had torn up his roots to transplant himself in France. What is he now? Jewish, Russian, French? All three— that is, nothing! Whereas I, at least, I try to live like a Frenchman, and I . . .

His mind became entangled. Then, all at once, he thought of Rachel and Peretz, over there in America, a new land, a land where everyone, in a sense, was a foreigner. It must be easier for the latecomer to take root there than in old, timeworn France. Peretz sprinkled his letters with such words as job, business and money; but that proved nothing, actually.

Rachel's case seemed more indicative. After years of silence, a letter had just come. It had been in English, and Yankel had had no little trouble finding a translator. And it was Rachel herself who had written it, in her own hand, yes! Completely changed, Rachel, transformed! Not a trace left in her of the hysterical idealist. Here were only the simpering affectations of a spurious great lady, the purr of false common sense, and declarations of affection that were unbearably mannered. Though Yankel was aware of possible distortions due to the translation, he couldn't help feeling a certain uneasiness. Had Rachel become *that* American? In the letter, she had announced her forthcoming marriage to a Mr. Silverstone, a very English name, it seemed. . . . Seed in the wind, seed in the wind, sprout where the wind sets you down, Yankel suddenly said to himself, and he stopped thinking of his brothers, his sisters, his family.

Yes, I *could* have become French! I *could* have gone all the way! He felt a wrench in his heart. In a flash, he relived all his French experiences—Nevers the beautiful, Marguerite, Louis, billiards, cycling . . . Ah, I could have, I could have! he said to himself bitterly, angrily, painfully. I could have, but at the price of a crime. The memories quickly faded, and all that was left was a great weariness. Come, it's ended now. Ended! Your life is laid out for you. What's the good of useless rebellions? Better a drowsy happiness. I, I began; my children will finish.

A vacant look in his eyes, he watched the children. Then, abruptly, he came to a decision. Hannah's expecting a child? Well, the new baby will have a first name that's truly French. No more Simons, Solomons, Samuels! And the old man can rant and rage all he pleases!

What name? He searched his mind a moment. Georges? No, Georges sounds as Russian as Serge. Paul? Paul is Saul. Pierre, Jacques, Antoine? Louis, maybe, after his friend? No, not Louis, no more than Marguerite if it's a girl. He ended by choosing Fernand. Why, he had no idea; the name simply appealed to him. And if it happened to be a girl, Fernande, of course.

Will you have him circumcised, your little Fernand?

He reflected a long while upon the problem and was tempted to answer in the negative. But Hannah would surely be sick over it, not to mention his father and mother; and besides, he didn't want Simon to feel too different from his brother; and besides . . . Hygiene?

Yankel made an immense effort at impartiality. No, it wasn't for the sake of hygiene that he would have Fernand circumcised. Not *only* for the sake of hygiene. But as a reminder. So that the child would never be tempted to forget his origins, to reject his own people. French by nationality, yes; but also a Jew. No, not Jew like Frenchman, but Jewish like Christian.

A Jew by religion, then?

No, ah no, not that either! When a Frenchman says he's Catholic or Protestant, it doesn't necessarily mean that he goes to church, that he obeys the priest or the pastor. It means . . . Well, what's the difference what it means! Fernand will be not a French Jew, but a Jewish Frenchman, as there are Protestant Frenchmen. There you have it, that's all!

And thereupon, for the first time in his life, Yankel began to hope the baby would be a girl. That way, there'd be no problem.

BOOK II

Mingled Waters

I

ALTHOUGH he had been living in France for an even sixteen years now, Yankel had never attempted to become a citizen. He obeyed the laws of the country that had given him shelter, he kept himself on the right side of the authorities, and he didn't mix into political matters—politics was no business of foreigners. Naturally, like any other human being, a foreigner had the right to his own opinions; but he kept them to himself, he remained quiet in his corner. A foreigner shouldn't let himself be heard from.

So Yankel limited himself faithfully to manufacturing caps, to bringing up his family without asking anything of anyone—to living, what else! Not a penny in debt, for Yankel Mykhanowitzki was an honest man, solvent, sober, a man of his word, respected by everyone. Over the years, through great self-denial, he had accumulated a small reserve. His louis d'or, in bundles of ten wrapped in twists of newspaper, rested in a small padlocked steel box, hidden under some sheets at the bottom of a closet. From time to time, he would detach a few coins to increase his account at the savings bank, or to swell those of Rivka and Clara, since it was time to think of their dowries. But no stocks, no bonds; he didn't trust those capitalist swindlers.

Especially no Russian bonds; he wasn't going to underwrite that Jew-killing czarism. Sometimes he wondered whether he shouldn't buy some French government bonds; that was a sure thing, government bonds, state paper. Think! Backed by the Republic! Well, when the time came to retire, he would see.

Each of his four children had his own coin bank to teach him thrift; and the four little banks—pig, rabbit, pear, and doll's house—were proudly displayed on the buffet, in the midst of the amusing trinkets on which, in their turn, Father and Mother doted.

When the war broke out, Yankel was greatly disturbed. The Fatherland was in danger! Hordes of savage enemies, frothing at the mouth, were rushing upon that noble Republic—the land of Voltaire, Hugo,

Zola—which had taken him to her bosom. What could he do to show his gratitude?

He began by running around in every direction, buying newspapers madly. The assassination of Jaurès threw him into a fit of apprehension; he was afraid of pogroms, knowing only too well that when things are not going well for the *goyim* they take it out on their Jews. But the articles of Gustave Hervé in his *Guerre Sociale*—now *La Victoire*—first reassured him, and then drove him to patriotic frenzy. He forgot that legally he was a Russian citizen, therefore an ally; he acted without thinking. As soon as the newspapers announced the opening of offices for the enlistment of foreign volunteers, he took his hat and his cane and, without saying a word of his intentions to Hannah, went straight to the nearest Bureau.

His heart beat loudly as he marched, head high, through the buzzing streets. Yankel Mykhanowitzki, soldier of France, soldier of Liberty! He felt queer, as though he had risen to a higher plane, that of a fellow citizen, an equal. Until now, he had lived on sufferance; now at last he would acquire rights. After receiving for so long, he would give. He stamped his heels on the pavement arrogantly, like a soldier, head high, eying the passers-by challengingly. What's that you say? What do you want of me? I'm going to risk my life for France! I'm a volunteer!

He thought of the French friends he had once known at Nevers—especially Louis . . . How wonderful it would be to find himself face to face with Louis one day, both of them in uniform! And why not? There was nothing impossible about such a meeting! Yankel was already living the scene; how he would save his friend from death in the midst of battle, carrying him off on his back while all about them the bullets went whistling past. Without hitting them, of course . . . Yes, maybe they would be hit. Why shouldn't the bullets pierce his chest—gently? He would be decorated, and the newspapers would sing the praises of the Jewish capmaker, Yankel Mykhanowitzki, the volunteer.

Then again, his peace-loving temperament would gain the upper hand. To get yourself killed at thirty-eight, with four children to support—that's crazy! But perhaps he wouldn't be put in the front line? The front line—that's where they put the young ones. The young ones liked fighting. Besides, everyone who knew said the war would be short. The army wouldn't have time enough to teach Private Mykhanowitzki, Yankel, even the manual of arms before they would return him to his fireside. Really, wasn't the gesture the important thing? Yankel would make the gesture—and there you were!

Before the doorway of the Bureau, a large crowd was milling about. Being a reasonable man—discipline *is* necessary—Yankel took his place among the latecomers, without trying to force his way to the front. He waited a long time; for some unknown reason, the door stayed shut. All the while people kept coming and piling up; unshaven, ragged, dirty, sweaty, and swearing—Not nice people, thought Yankel—but all uplifted with patriotic fervor. Still the door stayed shut. What, hadn't the authorities foreseen this? The crowd began to yell. The police came running. At that precise moment the door opened. Shouts, kicks, and pushing to be first . . . The police, without being too gentle about it, undertook to restore order and to form a line. Yankel, who found tumult distasteful, had withdrawn somewhat from the center of the mob and, slightly shocked, if not ashamed, watched the show while waiting for it to settle down. Suddenly, a blow on the back knocked him three steps forward. He spun about, furious; an enormous gendarme—a brute!—advanced on him ferociously.

"Come on, get in line or get out!"

"But, Officer, I'm here to defend our country!" the outraged Yankel protested.

"To defend *our* country? When did *you* get a country?" The policeman slapped his thigh and roared with laughter, calling his partner to hear his wit. "Tell the truth, you came for a handout! Go on, admit it."

Yankel Mykhanowitzki was a gentleman—a father of four children, a boss, scrupulously paying his taxes. He was a volunteer, not a compulsory volunteer, still less one to be insulted. And this *zhlub* (Yankel chose the more scornful Yiddish word instead of "boor") dared to get familiar. He turned on his heel and without a word, without a backward look, with firm and measured step, he went back home.

Hannah wept a good deal when he told her the story—not because of the humiliation he had undergone (these moral nuances eluded her), but in retrospective terror. What would have become of her, left with four children, if her husband had gone to war? Who would have fed the five of them? Her father-in-law, old Avrom? Moishe? Public charity?

"Yankel, have you gone crazy, or what?" she sobbed. "You think

175

they need you to protect them? A father of children—at your age, too?"

She wanted him to promise not to go again. He refused to promise, but he agreed to wait.

Furthermore, he heard stories which were disturbing. The rumors had it that the French were turning up their noses at the volunteers; that they were rejecting those who were a little on the puny side; and as for those whom they did condescend to accept, they were placed, not in the Regular Army, but in the Foreign Legion. The Legion—everyone knew it was a gang of thugs, of pimps, even of perverts. And do you know what the veterans do to the rookies? They rape them; yes, every one of them . . . Suddenly the Rue des Rosiers, although it lost none of its patriotic fervor, stopped sending its sons to the Recruiting Office. And there were many who, although they had already signed, sighed with relief when they learned that the first enrollment was not official, that you had to go to other offices for the real enlistment; they took the opportunity to dive back into their burrows.

Thus it was that Yankel did not enlist in the French Army. Inwardly, he was uneasy and hurt, torn between remorse and fear. He avoided leaving his home, seeing suspicious stares everywhere. Holed up in his workshop, he made police helmets all day long now instead of caps. Actually he had the subcontract of a large manufacturer, Champeaux-Bussier, a real Frenchman, who was making a fortune. Although Yankel knew this, he arranged matters so that he took only what was due him, no more and no less. And, at Poincaré's first appeal, Yankel exchanged all his gold for war bonds and a beautiful certificate to his civic virtue; he kept only one louis, as a souvenir, and turned it into a watch charm.

When the war began, he was on the outs with Moishe. But the quarrels between the two men, though frequent, never lasted long. Moishe soon dropped in, calm and smiling as usual.

"So, Yankel, you wanted to enlist?" he drawled, and he pensively stroked his beautiful flaming beard.

Now Yankel had already cooled a good deal toward volunteering. So he told of his scruples, spoke of the atrocities attributed to the Foreign Legion. Moishe listened with half an ear.

Some weeks later, the bell rang at Yankel's house. Yankel went to open the door; there stood a superb French soldier in red breeches, gaiters, cloak, and kepi. Moishe! Yes, it was he, and one would have thought he had never done anything but wear the uniform.

Oh, yes, he had enlisted. . . . "Yes, of course, in the Legion, *schmuck,* where do you want me to go? . . . What's the matter? Is it those stories about eating rookies alive?"

He waited until his sister-in-law had withdrawn to the kitchen. Then, leaning toward his brother, he whispered:

"Tell me, Yankel, between you and me—haven't you had enough of wife and children and business? Me, I want to get out! I need action, Yankel!"

"Need action . . . no strings attached"—these were his habitual catchwords. How they fitted his position in society Yankel preferred not to know. For Moishe owned a fine jewelry shop near the Madeleine, and he had even married, some years earlier, a rich young girl on whom he begot child after child. Now the string was snapped, and the wanderlust was going to be satisfied!

Sprawling in the chair, Moishe smiled and chatted, completely at ease; and before this handsome soldier Yankel felt upset, and even a little ashamed.

Foolishly, just to say something, he asked:

"Nu, how's business, Moishele?"

"Ah, business is finished!" The other laughed brightly. "It's Rose's turn to amuse herself with the shop!"

He grinned at the thought of playing such a good trick on his wife.

And now Hannah, sniveling and shaking her head, warding off the Evil Eye, and repeating, *"Veh iss mir,"* served cookies and poured tea. "Go, go, Moishele, enjoy it while you can!"

The children, wide-eyed in wonder, were circling about their uncle. Not Clara, you may be sure of that! Clara was all contrariness and stayed in her corner. She was the only one of the four who did not idolize Moishe; she even felt a sort of physical repulsion toward him. But the other three, ah! the other three . . . Yankel almost felt a little jealous. Open-mouthed, little Fernand was staring at the soldier without daring to go near; Simon was touching him everywhere and kept interrupting the grownups.

"Tell me, Uncle, tell me, will you show me your bayonet?"

Moishe obediently showed him the bayonet.

"Oh, look, how sharp it is!"

Moishe sheathed the bayonet, then unbuckled his cartridge belt and buckled it about his nephew, the bayonet dangling; then, to keep Fernand from being jealous, he called him over and perched the kepi on his head. The two boys went marching away in step, Simon giving the orders, as usual—not only because he was three years older than his brother, but because, wherever he was, he was the leader. The spitting image of his grandfather, Yankel thought, watching him out of the corner of his eye.

As for the adolescent Rivka, she was gaping at her uncle until her adoration became almost indecent. The little fool didn't realize that she was going on her sixteenth birthday, that she was a young lady, in fact, and a young lady should be circumspect in her behavior. Oy! Daughters give you plenty to worry about! This one behaved as if she were still a child. You should see her playing hide-and-seek with her brothers (Clara didn't like violent games); she threw herself into it spiritedly, running around the apartment with piercing shrieks and making the floor shake under her weight, while her newly formed breasts jumped in her blouse. And if you scolded her? Immediately there would be sobs, or a hysterical fit, or, even worse, she would oppose you with silence for hours at a time. Yankel didn't dare to meddle with Rivka; he didn't know how to behave toward her. He left that to his wife. Besides, he had another reason for surprise, if not fright, in his wife, for Hannah, sweet Hannah, became a real shrew the moment she spoke to her daughters. All day long she was yelling at them. She didn't slap them, oh, no! She pulled their hair, by handfuls. Mostly Clara caught it, because she dared to oppose her. As for Rivka, so much softer, her mother restrained herself to the point of treating her like an idiot. All this made for scenes, and more scenes, in which Yankel dared not intervene because Hannah would reproach him for partiality toward his daughters and he would reproach Hannah for her partiality to Simon, and there would be no end to it. Day would follow day in bitterness and wrangling.

"Oh, let her alone!" soothed Moishe. "Don't you see that she's in love with me? Perhaps it's her age."

The girl flushed suddenly and hid herself at the other end of the kitchen, while Moishe guffawed. Yankel was shocked. This was no way to talk to a young lady—especially an uncle to his niece. He looked around for someone on whom he could vent his spleen.

"Simon! Can't you yell any louder than that? I can't hear myself think!"

The boy stopped himself in the middle of sounding the Charge, stared at his father for a moment with a look like a slap, and then went to caress Moishe. The child's face assumed so tender an expression, so innocently admiring, that Yankel felt himself grow pale.

"When are you leaving, Moishe?" he asked, only to say something.

"Oh, tomorrow," drawled the other, with his habitual nonchalance. His dragging speech always seemed to convey a note of fatalist acceptance.

"Tomorrow? Already? To the front?"

"Oh, you *putz!*" Moishe joyfully insulted his brother. "First they have to teach me how to use a gun, don't they? Yankele, you still think you're in Russia, where anything can happen, and soldiers are sent with sticks against machine guns. Here, everything is organized, planned, and according to the rules. And I'm going to tell you something else, Yankele. Me, I'm a private. The officers make the plans, they direct, they command. That's none of my business; I'll be free to live!"

"And Papa—how did he take this?"

Moishe began to laugh. "Oh, he hasn't taken it at all, because I haven't told him yet! I'm going there right away."

"I'll go with you," Yankel said and he rose.

Unexpectedly, Hannah burst into tears, real tears. She alone realized that soldiers are killed in war, that her brother-in-law . . . that this was perhaps the last time she would see him alive.

In the street, Yankel felt very paternal about his brother. He felt proud to walk beside a soldier, a Jewish soldier, a volunteer—and so handsome—who bore his name. He felt relieved of his feelings of guilt.

While they followed the Rue des Francs-Bourgeois, they received only respectful stares from the passers-by, hat-tippings from the neighbors. But when they had penetrated into the real Jewish quarter, Rue des Hospitalières-Saint-Gervais, Rue des Rosiers, it became a triumphal procession. The Mykhanowitzkis, father and son, were celebrities in the quarter. Standing on their thresholds, the market women and the shopkeepers watched M. Mykhanowitzki, the capmaker, the son of a *Chassid,* approaching, accompanied by a soldier. Who was that soldier? Suddenly:

"Oy! Its the Big One! What? Has he become a soldier now? Houououou! Oy, *veh iss mir,* may no Evil Eye befall him, how beautiful he is! Ay, ay, ay, ay, ay! A real Frenchman!"

And the Big One, a genial prince, saluted left and right—not soldier-style, but with both arms—and shook the hands that were stretched so eagerly toward him.

Old Avrom was in his grocery store, in a gray apron, with a black *yarmulke* on his head. As soon as he saw his son in uniform he began to storm:

"Na, na, what's happened to you, you good-for-nothing? What kind of foolishness have you been chasing after? A soldier, a soldier, at your age, married, with children, a businessman—aren't you ashamed? You think the French were waiting for you? Pfeh!"

And he shook his head, grumbling, as he turned, round-shouldered, back into the store. Obviously, it wasn't the thought of danger that disturbed him; he didn't even seem aware of the danger. He was furious because his son had acted stupidly. The father of a family doesn't go off like that, soldier or no, abandoning everything; anyone with any brains knows that. As for old Mother Breina, the sight of her son as a French soldier drove everything else out of her mind.

"Tell me, Moishele," said the old man, lowering his voice, "aren't you able to . . . fix things up a little? Maybe it isn't too late yet?"

Moishe swayed heavily from one foot to the other and smiled blankly. His great height always seemed to embarrass him before his father. Absent-mindedly, he took a pickle from a barrel and began to crunch it.

"Can't you answer your father when he talks to you, instead of cramming your stomach?" cried the old man furiously.

"Oh, what do you want me to tell you, Papa? I'm leaving tomorrow. That's all there is to it."

Suddenly the old man's eyes sparkled with anger; he drew himself up.

"And what do you think you'll be eating there, eh? Tell me that! Nothing but *treif*. Pfeh! You're a real goy, you are!"

Moishe dropped a quick wink at his brother.

"Oh," he sighed, "why do you want to yell like that before you know what for? We're all Jews—the whole regiment is Jewish."

The old man grumbled, still not convinced. Moishe seemed to sense that this was the time to strike home.

"Even the colonel is a Jew," he remarked casually.

He goes too far, thought Yankel. He takes our father for an imbecile! In Russia, no Jew had the right to be an officer; and in France, the one time that there had been a Jewish officer, his name was Dreyfus. . . . Nevertheless, Yankel felt he had to back up his brother.

"Listen, Papa," he interrupted, gently, "France isn't Russia, you know. In France, everyone is respected, all beliefs, and . . ." He paused. "Did you know that there are rabbis in all the regiments?"

"Pfeh!" the old man spat. "French rabbis are worse than *goyim!*"

"Listen, Papa . . ."

"Well, if it's so good, why don't you go too?"

He turned his back on them angrily and went to serve a customer.

"Don't take it so hard," Moishe soothed. But he found nothing with which to console his brother. At this moment, suddenly, old Breina seemed to wake up.

"Moishele, my treasure, flesh of my flesh!" She sobbed pitifully.

"Don't worry about me, Mama!" Moishe murmured, more soothingly than ever. He sought something else to say and found nothing, so he grinned through his beard, waved his hands the better to reduce things to their minimum proportions.

"Breinele!" The old man called over his shoulder. "Why don't you take them upstairs and pour them some schnapps?"

For the customer was already saying, "Oy! *Veh iss mir,* the Big One has become a soldier? Ooooh, how beautiful he is!" and was trying to work her way into the conversation.

But Yankel refused to go upstairs; pleading an urgent appointment, he left and turned moodily homeward.

Two weeks later, it was his youngest brother, Itcha, whom he accompanied to the station. Twenty years old, a boy! Yankel thought sadly, surveying the frail body of the young man. He had thought that Moishe's act was natural enough for that colossus who dreamed only of bruises and scars; besides, Moishe, at thirty-two, had had the time to get some fun out of life. While poor little Itchele, so fresh, so young, a baby! what was going to become of him in the midst of soldiers, brutes, coarse men? And suppose something happened to him? For it was dangerous, what with the bullets, the shells and all that! Yankel, who had begun by thinking only of the good side, was now haunted by the picture of his brother's tender flesh torn, bruised, bleeding.

He had always thought of Itcha almost as his own son. The youth often came to the Rue des Francs-Bourgeois, where he would settle into a corner and stay for hours, hands on knees, staring slowly about him, following the movements of everyone else with his large liquid eyes. Never a word, never a laugh; at most, a truly irresistible joke would bring a misty smile. After a while, that silent presence would become burdensome.

"Do you want something, Itchele?" Hannah or Yankel would ask when they met his clinging look. "Tea? A little schnapps? Cookies?"

Then Itcha's mouth would take on a wry twist, indifferent and tired; his hands would move as if to say, If you want to. If you have some. But I'm all right as it is.

Yankel had tried to lend him some French books. Itcha said "Thanks," took the books away, brought them back two weeks later, and didn't ask for any more.

"Well, did you like them?"

"Yes." In an unenthusiastic manner.

Did the "Yes" mean "Yes," or "No," or "To hell with it"?

"Well, what do you think of it?"

In reply, that eternal grimace. "Do you really have to think anything about it? It's so tiresome!"

Did he find living tiresome, too?

Yankel began to doubt his brother's intelligence. But then he remembered Itcha's scholastic prowess some ten years earlier, when he had arrived from Russia. Yankel, who had followed his progress closely, wondered whether a genius had been born into the family. Hadn't the schoolmaster assured him that Isaac would surely receive his Primary Studies Certificate? And then the young prodigy fell ill on the eve of his final examination. Oh, nothing serious, you know how it is with children, a swelling of the glands, growing pains, who knows what! Unfortunately, his father had taken advantage of it to withdraw him from school and place him in the store at once. And when Yankel had tried to show him the benefits of education, the old man sent him packing. Science, Science, a lot you needed Science to make a living and praise the Lord!

His head tilted sideways, as though it were too heavy to hold upright—that was Itcha's usual attitude. Heartbroken, Yankel contemplated his little brother. All around them people were yelling, calling questions, jostling.

"Well, then, why did you sign up?"

Itcha spread his hands and made his grimace. Yankel gave up. He couldn't understand how this boy, apparently stripped of all will power, had been able to make such a serious decision. What had passed through his mind? Not a word to anyone; and then, one fine evening, he had announced to his parents that he had enlisted. Old Avrom had stormed, his mother had wept; it was all in vain, everything had been settled. Besides, nothing could break into Itcha's silences. Then his father had ended by crying: "Wait, you'll see! You'll be sorry!" which wasn't quite a curse; but, to punish his son, he had refused to accompany him to the station. Itcha himself had persuaded his mother not to come; he preferred to have Yankel there alone. And now he waited there, his valise at the end of his arm, his head tilted sideways on his thin neck, standing in front of his brother, who had no more to say and was overcome with shame at wishing the train would leave. They were the same height, but Itcha, who always was bent over, looked smaller in spite of his leanness. He was in civilian clothes; he was going to a training camp in the country. The clothes were too small for him, making him look wretched; his hat, pulled down on the back of his head, pushed down his ears, which were large and flat. How young he looked, with his pale cheeks and the scattered long hairs on his upper lip! Poor boy, Yankel repeated to himself; he felt more pity than love for his brother.

"Itchele! You won't be reckless? Nothing foolish? You promise?"

"Yes," said Itcha.

So went another five minutes. . . . Suddenly, Itcha opened his mouth.

"I'm going to ask you a favor, Yankel."

"Certainly, of course!"

The youngster took from his pocket a piece of paper on which he had scribbled something.

"Look, here's her address," he murmured, and his cheeks turned pink. "Will you go to see her?"

"Whose address?" said Yankel, disconcerted; and then he understood. "What? A girl? You're engaged?"

He hadn't dreamed of it. He had never imagined that the poor child, so timid, so tender, so puny, would have been able to go out with girls. But it was true, and Itcha was making his usual grimace, with a tiny smile added, to mean: You understand! What else can you do . . .

"Ho!" laughed Yankel, forcing the smile. "*Mazelto* to you, Itchele! Have you spoken to Papa about this?"

"No."

Why not? he wondered. Was she a bad girl? Anyway, it was too late to drag the business out into the open.

"You'll go to see her, then?" Itcha repeated anxiously.

"Yes, yes, you can depend on me."

Yankel looked at the paper and read aloud:

"Renée Genty, Rue . . . A *goya?*" he exclaimed, stupefied.

That explained everything! If their father had known . . . Ah!
Yankel preferred not to think of what would have happened. Even
he was disturbed, but, for lack of time, he wouldn't make too much
of it. He held back his reproaches, searched for something affectionate to say, and found nothing.

"Well, good-bye," Itcha murmured gently. "You know, she couldn't
come to the station, or I'd have introduced her to you."

They embraced. With a full heart, Yankel watched his brother go
toward his compartment, his ears pushed down by his hat, his feet
turned out and dragging; from the rear, the boy seemed even more
pitiful. Itcha a soldier! A soldier who would risk his life, who would
attack through the bullets that would cleave his flesh, the shells that
would smash him; who would stick his bayonet in someone's belly,
or have his own guts ripped, who would kill or be killed . . .

And engaged, what an idea! And to a *goya,* too!

Pensively, he went home. There you were! Of the six Mykhanowitzki children, three were in France, two of them soldiers; two in
America, across the immense ocean; and one, Sarah, the oldest
daughter, still in Russia, separated from the others by the enormous
German alliance, by the Enemy. . . . Yankel, who thought confusedly that he was the head of the family (since old Avrom lived in
another world), had the feeling that his flesh had extended invisible
feelers throughout the vast world—quivering, painful feelers.

As he had promised Itcha, he paid a visit to Mlle. Renée Genty. It
was a formal visit; he expected to meet a staid young woman, probably sad and quiet like his brother. Instead he encountered a lively,
petulant girl who switched from tears to smiles in two seconds, and
who chirped endlessly. A strange companion for Itcha! he thought.
Anyway, she seemed very much in love with her absent lover, and
she didn't hesitate to say so, which shocked the modest Yankel.

Another thing surprised him—the new image of his brother which
emerged from the girl's talk. For it seemed that Isaac was such a
witty, gay, lively young man, and played the piano so well. Itcha play
the piano? But where could he have learned how? He hadn't
learned, explained the young lady; he played by ear.

"But he was just beginning to take lessons, see, on the piano over there which I inherited from my Aunt Pauline, who . . ." Yankel understood no more of all this. Finally, he recalled some stories he had heard at his father's house: Itcha, without anyone knowing why, had intended to buy a piano with his savings some day; his father opposed it because the young man wouldn't have the time to play it, and moreover, he would play it on Saturday, which was forbidden; in short, the matter ended right there. . . . So, Itcha, who still lived with his parents, came here to play the piano? Actually, he made his home here?

Without seeming to, Yankel questioned the young lady. She told him that her mother was dead, that her father, now called up, before the war lived with some woman in the Eighteenth Arrondissement, so she, Renée, had the whole apartment to herself, and so on and so on, and that she worked as a salesgirl at Felix Potin's, which was where Isaac had met her.

All in all, she made rather a good impression on Yankel. Nevertheless, he kept his guard up; for you never knew with the *goyim*—there was always a little anti-Semitism sleeping somewhere in them. Still, the marriage hadn't taken place yet, and when Itcha came home they would see . . .

Three or four weeks later, Yankel noticed that Mlle. Renée was pregnant. By Isaac, naturally, who else?

A small crowd had already formed before the door of the school, almost all women. The longer the war lasted, the more he hated to show himself publicly—the only man among so many women. Of course, he was nearing his fortieth birthday, he had four children to support. Still . . .

Simon tugged at him.

"Well, Papa, you stuck in the mud?"

Tchch! How badly brought up and vulgar that child is! He collects coarse expressions in school and everywhere else. . . . Yankel, who spoke a very precise French, was always being shocked by his son's language. He halted and began to scold the boy:

"Simon! I've told you a hundred times not to talk like that to your father! I . . ."

The child fidgeted impatiently. The father, at heart just as anxious as the boy, nevertheless forced himself to continue to the end of the reprimand; and when he finally decided to move on into the crowd, he still reined himself in, trying to appear dignified, serious.

But his heart beat heavily. It was no use saying that the Primary Studies Certificate meant nothing. It was a diploma from the state, which certified officially that you were a cultured man, not a savage, that you had studied history, geography, the departments, the Gauls —everything, in fact, which made civilization. It hurt Yankel to hear this youngster speak irreverently of the "certif."

. . . I tell you, my son, the rascal, doesn't know his own good luck. Oh, how happy I would have been, once, if I could have had an education, studied science! I've tried hard to study by myself, in books. But what can you do, it isn't the same thing, and besides, now I'm old, I have my work, my worries, life! So I do all I can for my son, insist that everyone be quiet when he does his homework, I . . . Perhaps I have even too much respect for his work! And do you think it matters to him? Tchch! He doesn't even consider how lucky he is to live in France, to be born in France, to be a true Frenchman. Free school for everyone, and no one cares whether you're a Jew or a foreigner, whether your father is a gentleman or a plain workman, ah! Only look: Simon thinks his good fortune is natural, takes it as due him, and even dares to complain. He doesn't like school, he does his work badly, and soon I'll be humiliated to learn that my eldest son has failed (pfeh!) his Certificate of Primary Studies. . . . Yankel, shamed, horrified, saw that he was beginning to detest his son for not appreciating his good fortune.

The list of graduates had not yet been put up. Father and son mingled with the crowd. All round them the women were chattering—in Yiddish, naturally, which reassured Yankel. Since the school was in the center of the Jewish neighborhood, it was the occasional Frenchman who seemed foreign. But the children spoke only French, pure French streaked with slang, which Yankel followed with difficulty. How quickly Simon changed when he was with his friends! His father no longer knew him; he saw a real little man who spoke of serious matters, settled, decided, commanded, contradicted. With tears in his eyes, Yankel watched his French son. Ah! If only the boy had worked harder in school . . .

Actually, his father couldn't understand the scholastic troubles of his worthless son. Once the whole world had gone into ecstasies over Simon's precocity. At three he could reel off the Hebrew prayers that his grandfather had taught him, and the old man would laugh through his tears at his faults in pronunciation. He would also faultlessly recite the French alphabet, which his father had taught him.

And he never had to be asked; he would willingly offer samples of his talents and was happiest when a large audience applauded him. The whole family boasted of his intelligence to strangers.

At that point Yankel was hugging the hope that he had given a genius to the world.

Unfortunately, school changed all this. Oh, Simon wasn't the last in his class, oh no! But he wasn't the first either, far from it! Each year the same story would be repeated. At the beginning, the boy, who was lively, enterprising, wide-awake and quick-witted, would make a great impression on his teacher. "The pupil is intelligent, understanding, well-mannered, alert"; something of this sort would always appear on the October report. On the subsequent reports, the teacher would say, "A great deal was expected from Simon," then he would be surprised at the boy's "accidents" in composition, then he would show how he had been misled, then would speak of the good resolutions Simon should make, and finally would begin to complain of the boy's conduct. In short, the black dot would grow larger and by the end of the year was a cloud. And when his father would scold the culprit, a reply was always ready:

"The teacher doesn't know what he's talking about."

"Simon!" Yankel would cry, outraged. "Don't talk like that about your teacher, who is learned, an intellectual . . ."

"That one—learned?"

And in a flood of words Simon would explain that the teacher had got lost in the Rule of Three and that he, Simon, had straightened him out, so the teacher was envious of him now. He swore it was true. Yankel believed none of this, but, ignorant himself of the Rule of Three, he would be very much impressed.

Or else Simon would pretend that the teacher taught them nothing but foolishness.

"The Gauls, what do I care about the Gauls!"

And the father would rage, and the son would cry and would swamp him with technical details:

"He gave me a zero because I was wrong in one year on the date of the battle of Crécy! Do you know the date of the battle of Crécy?"

"But, Simon, that's the science of it!"

"Besides, I wasn't wrong, he doesn't hear well, he's deaf!"

"He's what?"

Finally, one day Simon went beyond all limits and touched on grave matters. He swore the teacher was unfair.

"What's that you say, Simon?"

"Yes, he has *chouchoux!*"

"What are they?"

Not without perfidy, Simon liked to baffle his father with school slang. He didn't deign to explain that a *chouchou* was a teacher's pet, and said only:

"He dislikes me!"

"Oh? He dislikes you? Well, I'll tell you why—because you do your work badly, that's why!"

"No, he envies me!"

"Pfeh! Don't speak foolishly, Simon!" Yankel exclaimed, with a gesture wiping out such stupidities; he had heard that argument more than once. So the child sought a better one; he lowered his head and threw a sly look at his father.

"He doesn't like us, I tell you! He doesn't like the Yids!"

Simon had deliberately used "Yid" instead of "Jew" to produce a greater effect; the word dropped like a piece of lead. Yankel lifted his head, opened his mouth, and stayed thus for a good minute to digest the news.

"What's that you say, Simon? Your teacher is an anti-Semite? What are you looking for, you scoundrel? Are you the only Jew in your class? How about your pal Gourkine, and Zimmelberg, that you talk about all the time . . ."

"That's right!" the boy declared, with new assurance. "He doesn't like them either. He doesn't like any of us. Yes, yes, I swear it! One day he even called us kikes. It's true, I swear it, Papa!"

Simon had a fertile imagination. Yankel, who was aware of this, had learned to distrust it. But this time he was shaken. How could the child have invented such a thing? The father put his hand on his son's shoulder.

"Listen, Simon," he said gravely. "I'm going to talk to you man to man. Tell me the truth, I won't scold you. Is your teacher really a Jew-hater?"

"Papa, I swear—"

"You swear as easily as you belch! I want to know the truth, that's all!"

But the more Simon talked, the more did the truth get lost in the fog. His father gave up and began to think about it. On the one hand, it seemed odd that an anti-Semite should have been sent to a school in the Jewish section. On the other hand, it wasn't impossible, because the Republic wasn't going to ask the teachers their political opinions. However, if the teacher was anti-Semitic, it would be known soon enough. Perhaps Simon had been lying again. But there was no smoke without fire, and . . . In short, having weighed the pros and cons and thought about it a great deal, Yankel decided to go see him. This happened shortly before the war, and he hadn't yet acquired an inferiority complex where Frenchmen were concerned. He took his hat and cane and set out, determined to demand an explanation of the teacher's behavior from the school's director.

When he came home, he said not a word. He hung up his hat and his cane, seized Simon, turned him over on his knees, took down his breeches and without saying a single word gave him the soundest thrashing of his life. He didn't answer Hannah when she asked whether he had gone crazy; it was only when she had thrown herself, all claws, at him to snatch away the victim, that he interrupted the execution, raised a face gone white and cried:

"Hannah! This boy is wicked! I'm going to beat the evil out of him!"

"But I've done nothing!" puled the boy.

"What's your teacher's name, Simon?"

"I don't know!"

A rain of slaps on the naked buttocks.

Screams. With a gesture, Yankel halted his wife.

"What's your teacher's name, Simon?"

"But he tells you he doesn't know!" cried Hannah, desperate.

"Oh, yes? He tells lies about his teachers, he causes his father to make a fool of himself before strangers. Nothing is sacred to him!"

And the slaps rained down again, and the boy kept yelling.

"What's your teacher's name, Simon?"

"Levy!" the boy admitted, sobbing.

"Ah! And Monsieur Levy is an anti-Semite? Answer me!"

"N-no!"

Yankel stood his son upright.

"Go to bed! This minute. Without dinner! . . . Hannah!" he roared when the mother wanted to console the child. She felt such a fury in him that she didn't dare to cross the room.

All that evening, Yankel didn't open his mouth. He didn't know which weighed heaviest on his heart, to be made to look foolish to the director, or to have a son who was vicious, a liar, without respect for Learning, Science or Intellectuals. . . .

The school door opened suddenly. The janitor emerged, tacked a sheet of paper to the door and went back in. The crowd surged forward, piling up in front of the door. Yankel also tried to get near it, but he hated these stampedes where everyone selfishly tried to carve a road with his elbows. So he waited his turn, sidling forward all the time between the thighs and the bosoms. What annoyed him most was that the women who had seen the list, instead of moving out to make way for others—be reasonable, eh? See what you come to see, and think of the rest!—well, they stayed there, hugging their offspring passionately to them, boasting of his brains if he had passed, calling heaven to witness that he would be the death of her if he had failed. And while waiting, they blocked the passage. Only Jews could be so stupid, Yankel thought. Slowly he grew angrier.

"Pardon, madam!" he said as coldly as he could, with, hup! a nudge with his shoulder to get by. "Pardon! . . . Pardon!" . . . He was almost there. Then a solid wall of backs blocked him; these women had not yet read the list. He stopped, tried again to make out the list over their heads; still too far. His heart was pounding. He wanted to know, he had the right to know, he was the father! Push here, push there; the elastic mass bounced him back.

"Nu! let me out! What's the use of pushing like a roughneck! Pfeh!" one of the good women was bawling at him.

"But, madam," he cried, indignantly, "I also want to see!"

They began to argue in the midst of the crowd.

"Papa. Papa! I made it!"

Simon's piercing voice. Yankel's heart leaped. Passed! Tenderness overwhelmed him.

"What kind of talk is that, 'I made it'?" he asked reprovingly. "Made what? Can't you speak correctly?"

The boy's sensitive face showed his disappointment and anger, and Yankel felt a pang at having hurt his son at such a moment.

"Oh, you," the boy fretted. "I passed, so there!"

The crowd began to disperse. Yankel went over to the list and slowly began to look for his name. He had a twinge at not finding it immediately. Then it leaped to his eyes: *Mykhanowitzki (Simon)*. He began to savor his pleasure. Now Simon was a real Frenchman. And he had received his diploma even younger than the average; eleven and a half instead of the customary twelve, especially for a foreigner's son, was a brilliant success. Now, perhaps, he would show a taste for study, now that he had grown up a bit.

Mykhanowitzki, Simon, a Frenchman, with the future of a French-man before him . . . Without admitting it to himself, Yankel regretted vaguely not having Gallicized his name when the opportunity offered. Because of the father's self-love, was it fair to force the son to drag through his whole life, like a lead ball, a name which would point him out to everyone as a foreigner, almost as a pariah? And after him, his sons, and the sons of his sons, and ten generations later they would still be asking M. Pierre or M. Paul, "Are you a foreigner?" And M. Paul or M. Pierre, if he presented himself to the election board, would be treated as a dirty foreigner who came to eat our bread. . . . "Oh, well, so much the worse," he said in conclusion, "he will succeed by strength alone and that will only make it worth more. You have to work in this life."

The future seemed rosy and Yankel had just prepared himself to feel happy, when remorse assailed him. A few years earlier, his oldest daughter Rivka had also received her Certificate of Primary Studies, but he hadn't made such a fuss about it then. He hadn't even gone to see the results; Hannah had taken care of it. And why hadn't he gone? Because he had said he had some work to do. Work, work, there's always time to work, and work didn't stop me from moving myself down here today. So then, Yankel Mykhanowitzki, two weights and two measures for the children of your flesh? Less honor for the Certificate of Primary Studies of Mykhanowitzki, Rebecca, than for that of Mykhanowitzki, Simon? Because Simon is a son, eh, Yankel, and according to the ancient prejudices a son is worth more than a daughter? Pfeh, Yankel Mykhanowitzki, what a poor little man you have become, and how easily man gives himself up to these stupidities.

Just the same, just the same, he had given Rivka some beautiful earrings for her Certificate of Primary Studies. It was not a gift to be scorned, and besides the girl had been delighted with it.

Yes, but he had immediately put her out as an apprentice with a furrier friend of his, while as for Simon, he intended to make him pursue his studies, so?

His nose still in the sheet of paper that he no longer saw, Yankel decided that when Clara received her Certificate of Primary Studies, for good or ill, he would bleed himself dry, but she could go to school as long as she wanted.

This was the moment that Simon chose to reappear.

191

"Hey, Papa! Are you learning it by heart?" he screeched in his errand boy's voice.

Tchch, how disagreeable that child is, how badly brought up, and how badly things have worked out. Earlier, instead of being able to enjoy the news that his son's name was on the list, Yankel had been distracted by the boy's "I made it"; then, standing in front of the list, he had been poisoned by bad thoughts; and now that he was about to taste pure happiness, see, Simon had managed to spoil everything. And of course there was no question of scolding him at such a moment. Besides, Yankel realized that the virtue of the list in which Mykhanowitzki (Simon) strutted in the midst of other names was exhausted. Once again, it was too late.

"I haven't congratulated you yet, Simon," he said ceremoniously, without asking himself why he was speaking in Yiddish. Ordinarily the father and son spoke to each other in French. "It was very good, my son. Your father is proud of you and . . ." And while the boy pawed impatiently, he made a long, moral speech on the virtues of work. Then, having finished, and feeling vaguely disappointed, he leaned toward Simon and kissed him on both cheeks.

The next morning he went out with an air of great mystery. On his return, he set himself up nobly in his habitual place in the dining room, his back to the fireplace, and called the family together.

"Come here, Simon," he ordered benevolently when they were all lined up before him.

The child obeyed and stood there before his father, his hands behind his back, as was the custom at school. In the background, in a semicircle, the rest of the family was grouped: Hannah in her housedress, an apron tied around her waist; big Rivka, what a big gawk she was, a head taller than her mother, and didn't know how to carry herself; Fernand, huddled against his sister; and Clara, as sullen and uncaring as ever. Even Wolf, the workman—almost part of the family after so long!—had left his work and stationed himself in the background, leaning against the door of the workroom with a cigarette dangling from his lips. The head of the family proudly swept his glance across everyone; automatically he straightened his hat, which he had forgotten to take off on his return. He coughed and at last began a speech to his elder son, a beautiful congratulatory discourse, stuffed with moral advice. At last the orator paused, thrust his hand into his pocket, withdrew a white cardboard box wrapped in tissue paper, and offered it to his son, saying, "Here you are, my son. You have worked hard and well. Your father is pleased with you."

Blushing with pleasure, Simon took the package, turned it over and over, and began to unwrap it.

"Watch out, it will break!" his father cried, and he stretched out his hand as if to prevent its falling.

"Simon, you bad boy!" cried Hannah. "What are you waiting for? Why don't you say thank you to your father, who bleeds himself white for you?"

The boy looked up. "Thanks, Papa!"

"Nu, nu! First look before you say thanks!" said Yankel, winking his eye and rubbing his hands together joyfully. "Who knows? Maybe you won't like it?"

It was a watch, a beautiful silver watch, with its own chain, and a key to wind it.

"Oh! Thanks, Papa! Honest, I never expected . . ."

And the boy leaped to hug his father.

"Good, good, good, that's enough, that's enough!" grunted Yankel in Yiddish, in the very tone of his own father. "Nu, stop wetting my cheeks, and go kiss your mother, who has suffered so much for . . ."

"Simon, let me see your watch!" exclaimed big Rivka, bouncing. "Look, what a beauty!"

Among themselves, the children always spoke in French. It was in French, therefore, that Yankel interrupted. Having restored order, he began by reminding Rivka that her father was a just man. When she had received her Certificate of Primary Studies, he had given her a present of the same value, beautiful earrings. Did she remember? Then, turning toward Clara-the-sullen, and Fernand-the-timid, he invited them first to rejoice in the family's glory, and then to follow in the footsteps of the older children, so that they, too, would earn handsome rewards and be happy.

"Oh, Papa, you always say there's plenty of time!" Choking with anger, Simon pushed back his chair and went to the window to sulk. Once again, his father had just told him that he had plenty of time to make a living, and that he should first finish school, but Simon had had enough, and more than enough, of school and profs. After getting his Certificate, he had been forcibly placed in the Lycée Charlemagne—and the same stories that had begun in the elementary school were continued here. On the one hand, "He should do better," "Disappointing results"; on the other, "The prof hates me." Every Thursday Simon was kept in for laziness or insolence. His father had tried other schools, in vain.

Behind him now, at the table, there rose a heartbroken little "Tchch," like a collapsing balloon. Simon wanted to smash something. As far back as he could remember, his father had always begun a sermon with that exasperating "Tchch." For instance:

"Tchch! Children are so ungrateful . . ."

Or else:

"Tchch! Hannele, that boy is so badly brought up . . ."

It made no difference; the "Tchch" was obligatory, and Simon had no need to turn to know that Papa at this moment was sadly shaking his head with an aggrieved air, puckering his nose and his eyelids, and screwing up his lips—in short, getting his spirit ready for complaint. The boy didn't wait for it, pivoted on his heels, and, in his finest Parisian accent:

"What's the matter, are you having a baby?" he snapped.

Then he pulled his head between his shoulders, waiting for the heavens to crash down on him. Out of the corner of his eye he watched his parents: Papa, with eyes and mouth wide open, Mama, terrified, her hand to her mouth.

"Simon, be nice," Hannah begged. "Apologize right away!"

She was shamefully weak about her son; he could have set fire to the house, and she would have said nothing but "Oooy, Simon! Oooy, Simon! It isn't nice, what you're doing!" In return, instead of being grateful, Simon looked down on her and respected his father, who, without being hard, let no one step on his feet. But this time, for some unknown reason, Papa chose the jeremiad. Ignoring his son, he turned toward Hannah, and, in sad magnanimity, he said:

"Oh, let him go!" He sighed and made his fly-swatting gesture. "He's a wicked son."

Outraged, Simon defied his father with a look. Why doesn't he give me a good slap, the way the other fathers do, and have everything over with? But no—sad, persecuted airs, and there's nothing you can do. You feel sick all over, for a long time, with your crime heavy on your chest. Papa's always like that. He always arranges it so that you're in the wrong! And when he isn't playing the martyr, suddenly he flies into a terrible rage, without anyone knowing why; insults you, wrings your nose, and imposes his will on you. You can't live with that kind of man! Do you think he'll discuss something with you, man to man, talk things over with you? What the hell, I'm thirteen years old already, Simon thought indignantly. I'm not a baby any more! Who does he think he is, and why doesn't he go to the front, like the others? Slacker! Tyrant!

Yankel pensively studied that little face so arrogantly poised. Sadly he shook his head.

"My poor child!"

And that was all; he rose and, with head bent, walked toward the workroom; slowly the door closed behind him.

"Simon, listen; do you have a stone in your chest? Don't you love your father any more? He's so good to you! Oh, it's a sin!"

Sin or not, Simon didn't care. Of course he loved his father, but how could you get along with a man like that? Simon wanted things to gallop along, he was always under pressure, always running away, always moving; his father's pontifical slowness maddened him. When the old man began to "Tchch!" or else "Aie!" or when he put his hands about his glass of tea to warm them, put down the glass, took a lump of sugar in his teeth, took up the glass again and gurgled, poor Simon would shake with rage, on the verge of a nervous outbreak. What could he do? He was built that way! And he couldn't keep from following his father's slightest gestures with his eyes, as though he were hypnotized. Naturally, the exasperation of one resulted in affecting the other, who, furious at having his way of life undermined, would shake his head, scowl, and roar:

"Na! Na! Na! What's wrong with you, you bundle of nerves?"

And off they would go again, and the eternal quarrel would begin.

". . . Simon, listen, Simon, you aren't nice, you should . . ."

Had it not been for his mother's pleading, Simon would have gone to kiss his father within five minutes after the outburst; he didn't hold a grudge, but, because of her pleadings, he waited for fifteen minutes. Finally, he silently opened the door of the workroom. Papa, in his shirt sleeves, was bent over his bench; Simon saw his round shoulders and the nape of his neck, covered with curls (Yankel never agreed to go to the barber until after some weeks of discussion with his wife). Without knowing why, the boy felt moved by the scene. Sheepishly he stood at the door. In a moment, Wolf the workman noticed him and murmured some words to Papa. But Papa didn't turn and continued to work as if nothing was the matter; when he had finished, he walked aimlessly about the workroom, dragging his feet. Only Jews could be like that, Simon said to himself; but his heart was heavy in him.

Finally he could stand it no longer, and, with lowered head, he buried himself without a word against his father's chest.

"Nu? You have something to say to me?" his father asked after a moment.

Simon said nothing; his throat wouldn't let a sound pass through. After all, you couldn't ask too much of him. . . . Actually, he had forgotten his offense and kept only a feeling of guilt. His father, as usual, gave in.

"You're ashamed of what you said?"

The brown head nodded. Yankel was satisfied with the gesture.

"Good! Go, it's ended now," he murmured.

And Simon felt a hand caressing his hair. He almost burst into sobs but managed to hold back and hugged his father even harder. The rough material of the waistcoat and the softer, smoother material of the shirt caressed his cheek. Papa always was in the habit of working in his shirt sleeves, with the sleeves rolled up, and his collar off.

"Neh! You're always overdoing it! You'll choke me, you idiot."

A sharp, stale odor irritated Simon's nostrils. Papa was clean, if anyone was clean! But he didn't smell good, and for the last year or two Simon had noticed that Papa had been taking less care of himself. He's becoming an old man! Simon drew away.

"Nu! Now that you're quieter, we can have a talk," his father said, and he sat down astride a cane chair. He's beginning again, Simon thought, outraged.

Wolf had stopped working and was blandly watching. It was to him that Yankel spoke—in Yiddish, naturally, since, although he had been in France for ten years, Wolf hadn't found the time to learn French.

"Do you know what's wrong with this youngster? He doesn't want to go to school any more. Do you realize that, Wolf? How lucky he is! Aie, if I had been able . . ."

"Aie, and if I had been able!" Wolf repeated faithfully. "Simon, you aren't using your head, you should . . ."

Good old Wolf! He was Yankel's *landsman,* who had been working for him for several years. Yankel didn't exploit him, of course, he knew them too well himself, those exploiting bosses. He paid him a little under the union scale, because he wasn't rich; but he was always nice to him in every way, he would offer him a cup of tea, he would treat him like a human being, like one of the family.

Simon thought Wolf was opinionated and stupid, and he accused him of always mixing in what wasn't his business; the good, placid workman's face got on his nerves. Besides, when Papa started sermonizing, he didn't need an echo! The boy picked a moment when his father was speaking to reply in French; he had noticed that Yankel automatically continued speaking in the language in which he was addressed; a good way to send Wolf back to his caps.

"I want to go to work!" he insisted in French.

Papa raised his arms to heaven.

"Work! Don't you work in school?"

"I want to make money right away."

"Make money?"

Although it was the hundredth time that Simon had brought out the argument, Yankel still wasn't used to it. Now, I ask you, making money? Who could have stuffed that idea into the boy's head? Maybe his grandfather?

"Well, aren't you always complaining about being poor?"

"But . . . but . . . but, Simon, if you become an educated man, you'll make more money than—"

"Fooey!"

"Fooey? So what kind of talk is that?"

Every time his son slipped into slang, Yankel lost his footing. At the same moment, he saw Wolf's bewildered face desperately trying to understand what was going on; and, without knowing why, Yankel felt worn out by the discussion. It had been going on now for months and months . . .

"Listen, Simon, I've done what I could for you . . ."

The boy stamped with impatience. Yankel felt his anger envelop him. An evil, evil child!

"Well, so much the worse for you! Some day you'll be sorry, but . . . If I take you out of school, what do you want to do for a living?"

There it is! Yankel thought. I've said it, it's too late to take it back. He looked at his son with hatred. The guttersnipe was bouncing from one foot to the other, knocked off balance by his sudden victory.

"Solomon is a salesman in . . ."

"To hell with Solomon," Yankel cried furiously. "What are you interested in?"

"Business," the child said, and his eyes glittered.

"Business, pfeh! A trade of bluffers! First of all, what kind of business?"

"Solomon, he . . ."

"No more about that good-for-nothing or I'll give you a slap," Yankel thundered, and he lifted his hand. Then, in a calmer voice:

"I won't let you go into the world without a trade. And a trade has to be learned. So, what do you want? Capmaker? Tailor? Cabinetmaker? Watchmaker? Speak! Or do you want to be a ditchdigger?"

"I want to be a businessman," the boy groaned stubbornly.

Yankel's eyes narrowed, his lips tightened, and Simon realized he would have to give way.

"Since it's like that, you idiot," his father said scornfully, "you'll work here with me. Get out!"

Simon went out, crestfallen, while his father, lips and hands shaking, went back to work without hearing Wolf's condolences.

Then, for several weeks, the Mykhanowitzki household was a real hell. There were fits of anger on the father's side, an impatient teacher; fits of weeping on the son's side, an intractable pupil. To tell the truth, Yankel didn't forgive himself or Simon for the ruin of his hopes; to think that the idiot had been offered the world and would become, pfeh! a simple capmaker like his father. On his side, Simon was sick of the detailed work that was forced on him; after five minutes of attention, he would always make some clumsy movement which would release his father's anger.

Hannah finally had enough of it, took matters in hand, and without too much trouble persuaded her husband to apprentice their son to a trustworthy fellow capmaker. It didn't work out. "He doesn't like me!" said Simon. A second capmaker made the mistake of slapping him; a third treated him like a servant. This was enough. Yankel, sick to his soul, realized that his son was not born to make caps and would never be a craftsman. There was a final painful scene:

"So you want to be a businessman? You'll be sorry; you'll see!"

"Who cares?"

Yankel was struck dumb; Simon had just spoken in Moishe's very intonation. He thought: My father is a tradesman, my brother

Moishe and my American brother Peretz are both tradesmen. Perhaps Simon should be one, too? Have I the right to force him to be something else?"

The next day, vanquished, he took his son to M. Champeaux-Bussier, who, in addition to his police-helmet factory, owned a retail store near the Place de la République.

M. Champeaux-Bussier was gross in every sense, and a scoundrel too, as Yankel was well aware; but he was everything on a large scale. He received the Mykhanowitzkis with open arms in his thickly carpeted office; rose to shake M. Mykhanowitzki's hand, treated him with protective joviality— "How's the family?"—forced him into an overly comfortable armchair, and looked at his watch. Yankel for his part overdid his salaams and kowtows—that's the way he was, he couldn't help being polite to people. He felt his son's scorn weigh heavily upon him; Simon thought him too humble, too abject; Simon was completely at ease, and oh! how his father envied him!

"So this is our young man?" Champeaux-Bussier cut in, looking Simon over from head to toe.

The boy bore the examination without any annoyance, looking the boss right in the eye. His expression was alert, his mien lively, and his tongue facile; he knew that he had made a good impression. He also knew that the name Mykhanowitzki was a guarantee of honesty and loyalty—both salable commodities. In short, he felt he was in a strong position and couldn't understand why his father felt so humble and allowed Champeaux-Bussier to lead him about, instead of the other way round. He suspected some secret Mykhanowitzki reason but didn't care about uncovering it; he intended to line up with the mighty of this earth.

"How much is five-per-cent interest on 730 francs?" fired His Grossness, point-blank.

"Too little!" Simon fired back at him. "You ought to get ten per cent!"

"Simon, Simon! Don't be so bold!"

Yankel was honestly upset; he took the examination seriously.

Champeaux-Bussier leaned back. "Let him alone." He laughed. "He'll go far!"

The big man was in a good mood; business was fine, thanks to the war. Because, again thanks to the war, labor was in short supply, he had from the first decided to employ Simon. Moreover, he had his own theories about Jews. Jews are either all good or all bad, no middle ground; either you run them or they run you. And you can take it for granted, a Mykhanowitzki is all good.

And so it was that Simon, age fourteen, began to enjoy life, working in a haberdashery near the Place de la République.

At first his salary was a joke; his father hadn't questioned the boss's offer and had even overwhelmed him with thanks. But Simon got a raise very quickly; he knew how to make use of his chances. With all the men at the front, the adolescents were kings. All you had to do was squeeze a little.

Just the same, one day he squeezed too hard. No matter; he was offered two other jobs. He took one, then a second, then a third; he changed jobs as often as he did shirts. His father tore his hair and predicted a final catastrophe.

"You'll end up in the gutter, I tell you! When I was young . . ."

When he was young? Poor Yankel, he had forgotten, it was so long ago. He too had changed his boss as often as he changed his shirt. True, under different circumstances; he didn't quit his boss, he tore himself loose, broke with the boss for good. Simon, on the other hand, moved lightly and tactfully. Joking, forthright and frank in business, he stayed on very good terms with his successive employers, who became a sort of family to him. Thus he made a tour of commercial France. He made use of it, he enriched his experience with various tricks of the trade. Before he was fifteen he was master of the art—more difficult than one might think—of rubbing the hands together at the decisive moment and saying, "Shall I have it wrapped for you?" He learned the art of the smile, too; not the commercial smile, but a happy warm, personal one. The art of discourse took him longer, since it was more complex. Nature had endowed him with poise and the gift of gab, but he soon realized that he had to cultivate those talents. First he rid himself of his slang, which sometimes produced a deplorable effect on his customers. Still something was lacking. What was it? Oh, if he only knew! Sometimes the sale would seem closed, then, at the last word, bang! the customer would suddenly change his mind, and the deal was off.

Simon finally realized that he had a tendency, as he put it, to lay it on with a trowel! After all, too much is too much. But where does "too much" begin? The critical point varies according to people, and no two persons are identical. Each time, before the blades engage, you must feel out your opponent, discover his weaknesses, and make your attack at those points; these preliminaries are essential. After all, the art of selling is custom-made, not ready-to-wear. Little by little, Simon's errors in psychology grew fewer and minor; he learned to feel them as soon as they were made and to repair them as soon as he could. What helped him most was that he enjoyed it immensely. He didn't care what he was selling; most of the time it was hats, because he had got into that line, but it didn't really matter.

Of course, Papa couldn't understand this impassioned preoccupation; to him a tradesman was nothing but a parasite.

"Oh, you're like Moishe, a real businessman!"

"So? Has Uncle Moishe done so badly?"

And the older man would turn his back and grumble.

"Look, Papa, I work, I pay my board, and I'm banking some money. What more do you want?"

What more *did* Yankel want? Well . . . well, there it was, what? The father realized that his complaints were unfair, and he even blamed himself for attacking his son in such an ugly manner. For, really, the only thing shared by Simon and the Moishe of long ago, outside of their business sense, was their carefree gaiety. But Simon, thank God, was no good-for-nothing; he led a very well-ordered life, never slept out, saved his money, and never threw out the dirty water till he had clean. So? What do you want from him, Yankel? What does this mean, this constant search for a quarrel with your son? Isn't he happy now? So?

Oh, yes, Simon was happy. His face was radiant. Always good-natured, always joking, playing tricks, always crooning snatches of the latest song hits—off key, but what of that? The tantrums were over; if a remark displeased him, he simply turned away silently, with a little smile. Well, he had found his way! All right, go ahead, my son, and God bless you. Very quickly, so quickly that Simon noticed it and was hurt, Yankel lost interest in his son's activities. Sometimes, stricken with remorse, he would try to find out what was going on; he was politely sent back to his capmaking. Is it the usual fate of fathers to see their sons become strangers? Or was Simon a special case?

Yankel even lost interest in asking himself that question and shut himself up more and more in his shell. So many hopes placed in Simon! And all to end in—what? Another businessman! Anti-Semites pretend that the Jews, those parasites of the human race, have business in their blood. Well, there it was, instead of flinging the lie in

their teeth, Yankel, because he had begotten such a son, was further-
ing their propaganda. Well, so much the worse, so much the worse!
To avoid suffering, Yankel tried not to see Simon, not to listen to
him; at the family table, he would sit silently, turning over his dark
thoughts, while the young man declaimed, warmed by the adoration
of his mother and his elder sister, Rivka, that fool!

Yankel was so gloomy that he scarcely felt any pleasure in the
success of his second daughter, Clara. After she had brilliantly won
her Certificate of Primary Studies, he had sent her to the Lycée
Victor-Hugo. She did well there, and every morning, at the beginning, he would take her to school, even though it hurt Yankel,
during the war, to show himself in public. And then one day, with
that arrogant air which made her so unpleasant, his daughter let him
know that she was old enough to go to the lycée by herself. Vexed,
he let her go her way—still proud of her, but only when he thought
about it. It must be admitted that Clara had a nasty disposition; from
the height of her newly acquired learning, she looked down upon
her parents in scorn. Yankel frowned and said nothing, but her
mother countered it with violence. Hannah was really brutal to
Clara. It seemed that she had reserved all her love for Simon; Clara
was fourteen years old and Hannah still pulled her hair at the slightest excuse, and hard, let me tell you. And Yankel would intervene,
but he was so tired of all these scenes.

When Clara had finished her third year at the lycée, he realized
that she was fifteen years old, and therefore one or two years behind
the normal age of her class. It wasn't her fault, of course; she should
have been brought to the lycée when she was younger, but no one
had told her parents, and that's the way it was. So then, three years,
four years, or more, for the diploma? But at eighteen or nineteen
years, a girl is ready to marry, isn't she? School should have been
over for her for a long time before then; a girl isn't a boy! Besides,
Clara herself didn't know what she would do with the diploma if she
got it. Teacher, she said. Why a teacher? Words in the air! She probably wanted to imitate one of the teachers she had a crush on. Now
she's beginning to talk about studying Latin next year. Now, I ask
you, Latin! What good is that? Not to mention that sending her to
school costs a lot of money, and after the diploma, how much more
time will she have to go? Years? "You'll end up an old maid, my
poor child!" And without listening to Clara's protests, Yankel took
her out of the lycée and put her into a good domestic-science school,

where they also taught her shorthand and typing. That's useful in life, not like Latin; we aren't priests. Immediately, the girl became more bitter than ever, which dispelled her father's faint regrets. He began to understand how, long ago in Rakwomir, old Avrom had broken with his daughter Rachel.

The second son, Fernand, was so eclipsed by Simon's brilliance that he was almost forgotten. And yet, Yankel favored him secretly because of his calmness, his modesty, and his reserve. Yankel would have liked to get close to the boy, but, with age and life's disappointments, he had lost his zest and his longing had become all but hopeless. The boy, taciturn and withdrawn, was hard to reach; it would have required more patience and skill than Yankel possessed. In short, the father had almost no contact with his younger son and limited himself to ratifying the decisions, always carefully considered, that the boy submitted for his approval. So it was that one fine day Fernand announced that he wanted to prepare for the Boulle Technical School. Boulle Technical School? What's that? To be a cabinetmaker? Good, very good, my son. Yankel was a little sorry that Fernand hadn't chosen capmaking; but isn't cabinetmaking a good trade? Intelligent, and artistic; not like business, or priests' Latin. His heart somewhat soothed, Yankel gave his blessing and thought no more about it. And Fernand received his Certificate of Primary Studies and went through Boulle almost without his father being aware of it. There were a few legal documents to sign, and that was all.

At this time, Yankel was going through the darkest period of his life. The threshold of the fortieth year is unpleasant to cross; you stop climbing and catch a glimpse of the descent prepared for you. You review your failures and disillusionments, now irremediable; you know, and you can't pretend not to know, that you've renounced most of your hopes. Your children are this and that, but not what you wanted. You've been making caps for so many years that you know the trade by heart, and you tell yourself that this will go on until death, unchanging, and it isn't pleasant. You've always thought about death, but after the fortieth year you think about it in another way; it's real, you see it. . . . And then there's your wife, suddenly grown old, and full of queer habits and quirks because of her coming change of life, and you try not to notice them, but you notice them anyway. She calls on the Lord and wards off the Evil Eye every three sentences; she tries to make you go to the synagogue because she's becoming more and more religious, your poor old wife, and you have to humor her from time to time. And because you try not to look, you end by treating your wife like a piece of furniture.

And this war, this interminable war, whole nations butchering each other without regard for anything, not even the little children. Right at this moment, bombs and shells were falling in the heart of Paris, on the Église Saint-Gervais, on houses, night and day, blindly killing women, old men, babies. And why, why? Yankel was so revolted that he almost forgot to fear for his own children. After all, his children were almost adults, and danger was less horrible for them than for poor, innocent babies. Men are wicked and depraved!

And what had become of Itcha? For many months now, he had been reported missing. Missing—what does that mean? What is this new word they've invented? Is he alive or dead? A man doesn't get blotted off the face of the earth without any trace. Dead or alive, a man is sacred. Itcha had some comrades in his regiment. They should know; why don't they question them? There it is, day after day, nothing. You're left hanging in emptiness, you tremble every time you see the postman, and the passing of time gnaws, gnaws, gnaws until you don't know any more whether to suffer or not, whether to hope or not; you don't even know whether you know, and the wound won't close, but keeps running endlessly. . . .

From time to time, Yankel would take his cane and hat and, in the greatest secrecy, would go to pay a visit to Mlle. Renée Genty, his brother's "fiancée." He had spoken of her to no one but Hannah, and he had made his wife swear, on the heads of her children, to preserve an absolute silence. Well, here, too, something wasn't going right. Mlle. Renée Genty was behaving badly. She had brought a pretty little girl into the world, Itcha's daughter, Yankel's niece, a Mykhanowitzki; but, under the pretext that she had to earn a living, she had put the child out to board in the country, far off, and Yankel never saw the little one. He regularly sent money to the mother in his brother's name; she took it so naturally, as if it were due her, that he became annoyed by it. People say that Jews are swayed by money; well, I tell you, this one must be a Jew several times over. Furthermore, from a number of tiny incidents, he had the feeling that Mlle. Genty—tchch, women are so weak!—was not maintaining strict fidelity to poor Itcha, who was at the front, and perhaps dead; in fact, on several occasions, he felt that if he, Yankel—a sort of brother-in-law

—had wanted to take advantage of the situation, he could have . . .
Pfeh! The whole thing stinks! You can say it again, a Jewish girl
would have acted better. Yankel finally realized that Mlle. Genty
didn't take kindly to his visits and would have been satisfied with
money orders. Naturally, he turned a deaf ear and continued to
come, until the day when he found the door locked; Mlle. Genty had
gone without leaving any address. Should he try to find her? He tortured himself with the question for several weeks; the decision was
really up to Itcha, not him, but could he leave the little girl with that
wicked woman? Finally, convinced that his brother would never
return, he dropped the whole business.

The Russian Revolution brought him another kind of worry. On
the one hand, he rejoiced at the downfall of the autocracy; but, on
the other hand, the separate peace between Bolshevik Russia and Germany placed him in a delicate position with regard to the French.
Wasn't Lenin an agent of the Germans—I beg your pardon, Boches—
who had transported him from Switzerland to Russia in a sealed carriage? Now a Russian was almost an enemy, and the reactionary
press was demanding that all Russian nationals should be sent to in-
ternment camps. Yankel felt ill will creeping all about him. Every
time he met a Frenchman, he wondered whether he wasn't doing
business with one of those countless holders of Russian bonds, now
ruined and cursing Slavic treachery. What could he tell him? That
for years the revolutionaries had been claiming that the czarist loans
were used only for secret police and pogroms, and, consequently,
they, the revolutionaries, refused to honor these debts? A ruined
man doesn't care for such reasoning! You're better off to keep quiet
and hide.

Of course, Yankel didn't lack arguments to employ, if the occasion
arose. He could speak of his two brothers, both volunteers, one missing and the other seriously wounded. (For many months, Moishe
had been undergoing treatment in a hospital in the country.) He
could boast of his two sons, born in France, future Frenchmen, future soldiers, yes, sir! (But his heart hurt at the thought that the war
would last, perhaps, till they were of age.) He could even give his
word, and swear, that he was French from the bottom of his heart
(and it was no lie), a true patriot, although he hadn't been naturalized and hadn't poured out his blood for the country. He could . . .
oh, he could say what he wanted to; to the law he was a Russian and

nothing but a Russian, and the law laughed at his feelings; and politics, which he had so carefully avoided, was now clutching him by the throat.

Simon came in one day, laughing at a joke he had played on a M. Rabinovitch. He had called him on the telephone.

"Hello! Monsieur Rabinovitch?"

"Ya!" (Simon imitated the man's accent perfectly.)

"This is Police Headquarters." Yankel could imagine poor Rabinovitch beginning to tremble at the other end of the line. "We've been informed that you're a disloyal Frenchman. Is this true?"

Frantic denials in Yiddish-French. Simon had expressed doubt, declared that there were things that needed explaining and, in brief, tortured his victim. Finally:

"At least you know the *Marseillaise?*"

And poor Rabinovitch, to prove his patriotism, had sung the *Marseillaise* over the phone, in his most convincing manner, but with such an accent! Simon still laughed at the thought. Yankel saw nothing funny in it and grew very angry.

"*Zhlub!* Don't you understand anything?"

Unfortunately, Simon didn't understand and couldn't understand; he was a Frenchman, not an alien barely tolerated by his hosts and always a prey to fear.

Yankel felt so wretched that, for the first time in his life, he sought comfort in his family. Till now, he had always felt that they needed him; now he needed them. He wrote two or three very affectionate, encouraging, fraternal letters to Moishe. No reply. Of course, that playboy had never been very strong with the pen. Yankel wrote to his sister Rachel and his brother Peretz in America. No reply. Yes, there was; after six months, a short note from Peretz, apologizing for not being able to send him any money. The idiot thought that Yankel was having financial difficulties.

It was useless to write to his other sister, Sarah Feinschneider, in Rakwomir; since the outbreak of the war, they had been without news of the Russian branch of the family; the mail couldn't get through. And the Revolution hadn't straightened things out either. Yankel realized that the war had snapped his last links with his native land, with the "Old Country," as he used to say. Rakwomir was right in the war zone. The tides of battle had swept over the village, it had been taken, retaken and, no doubt, plundered; and probably the Germans, though enemies, had been less ferocious than the Russians to the local Jewish population. Where were the Feinschneiders now? And the Schmirzmanns, Hannah's parents, sisters, and brothers? And old Avrom's brothers and sisters, still Mykhanowitzkis, and the Meltchiks, Breina's family? Deported to Germany? Refugees in Siberia? Dead? Now there was a revolution, and Yankel didn't need to be there to know that when the Whites came there would be a pogrom, and when the Reds came there would be a pogrom; the Jews would be massacred for being Jews, or liquidated for being bourgeois, the important thing being that they would be wiped out. If, by chance, some of them managed to survive, they would be finished off by famine and poverty. From time to time, Yankel would raise his voice at the table to evoke the misfortunes of his people. But his children paid no attention to the misfortunes of the Jews; they were French, and what did they care about these stories of another world? Rivka, gaping as usual, lived on the moon; Simon thought about business or giggled stupidly; Clara thrust out some venomous remark; Fernand alone seemed to understand, but he was still so young . . . As for Hannah, whose whole family had stayed in the Old Country, she wept and begged her husband to change the subject.

Yankel also wanted to draw closer to his father, whom he had neglected since the outbreak of the war. He saw that Avrom was really an old man now. Outwardly, nothing had changed; still hale, lively, aggressive, he kept grumbling in his beard, calling on the Almighty, and ruling his grocery ferociously. But a spring seemed to have broken; his heart wasn't in it, he found no joy. No more laughter. Did Itcha's disappearance burden his spirit more than appeared? You couldn't find out; he never spoke of it. Moishe's wound? "Na, he had no business going," cried the old man. "That good-for-nothing was always looking for trouble, and now he's found it!" He spoke of his sons as if they were still children. In fact, none of the family (for Rose, Moishe's wife, didn't count) had seen Moishe since he was wounded. He was being nursed in a hospital near Limoges, and, seen from afar, there's nothing impressive about a leg wound. They hadn't cut off his leg, had they? So, at least, he won't be killed!

The old man showed more uneasiness, if he showed anything at all, over his wife's health. For some time now, Breina was always tired. She complained of pain in her abdomen. But everyone knows that after a certain age all women have pains in the abdomen. Yankel, gifted with an iron constitution, couldn't imagine sickness. Mama was working too hard and she ought to rest awhile. It could be that Papa, in his old age, had found a small fund of tenderness in himself that he had been saving for his wife. Could that be enough to explain his slight change in disposition?

Now old Avrom got another bee in his bonnet; he wanted to go to the Holy Land. Yes, that's where an old Jew should die. When he got on that subject, his eyes would light up. *Yerushalaim,* Jerusalem, that was the place where all human misery was healed, and the old man grew irritated at not being able to realize that dream, the crown of his life, just because the *goyim* had invented war. Yankel could hardly believe that he would carry out such a crackbrained project. What was the sense of that, going off to weep at the Wailing Wall when your whole family, or at least that part of your family that counted, your children and grandchildren, were living here in France and living well? He tried not to contradict the old man, but his mania for discussion dragged him into it. Scolded, bullied, insulted, he gave up trying to draw closer to his father and walled himself up for good. He felt at home and sheltered in his apartment in the Rue des Francs-Bourgeois; he left it as little as possible. He began to read a great deal, borrowing the books from the public library. He bought a fine phonograph and records, not cylinders, and feasted on music; Beethoven, especially, brought the tears to his eyes. The insulation about him grew ever thicker; it was so difficult to get through to him that people thought he had grown hard of hearing.

When the war ended, he shook off his torpor. Since men had stopped slaughtering each other, since the kings and militarists had been crushed, since the League of Nations, guarantor of universal peace, was being organized, since Russia, after so much suffering, was turning—who knows?—toward justice and happiness, since noble England was founding a Jewish homeland in Palestine, and therefore pogroms would be finished forever, he had to rejoice. He wondered how he could celebrate the arrival of the new era. In an outburst of enthusiasm, he announced at the table one fine evening that they were all going to take a vacation and were going to the seashore. That's right, the seashore! He wasn't going to die without seeing the sea, was he? You live only once! And he began to refute the countless objections which no one had raised, but which could have been raised.

A trip to the seashore isn't a trifle, it's a big event in life. You have to think about it a long time in advance, if only to enjoy the expectation before enjoying the thing itself. Besides, we can't leave now, it's still winter. We'll wait for next summer. We'll wait till the off season. We'll wait till the family finds itself closely knit, as it was before the war. How can you really enjoy life when poor Moishe is still in the hospital with a leg that simply won't heal, when there's no news from the Feinschneiders of Rakwomir? Pfeh, you mustn't be selfish. If you're going to give yourself a great pleasure, it should be pure. How can you be happy when all over the world so many people are still suffering? Clemenceau is surrounding Russia with a political quarantine, the Russians are fighting the Poles, the Whites are fighting the Reds, a real mishmash, Yankel would say, for lack of a better term. And then, at the end, at the very moment when, to hell with the mishmash, you live only once, and he had made up his mind to go, a big customer in Lille starts yelling for caps, Champeaux-Bussier throws a new model into the market, an American sport style, and you'll see a little later about the trip, there's no fire! While you wait, there's always the pleasure of hoping. . . . The Mykhanowitzkis dreamed of the sea as others do of a prize in the sweepstakes.

One day, however, Simon left for Le Havre; he told his father about it the evening before.

"You're going to see the sea? Oh, Simon, you'll tell me about it, eh?" asked Yankel, his mouth watering.

Simon stayed away three days and, on his return, spoke only about surplus American stocks and portable sheds; he'd gone to Le Havre on business, not to have a good time. Or, if he had had a good time, it wasn't in contemplating the sea; but he was careful not to say it to dear Papa, who would have asked for the name of the "young lady," with a knowing smile, and then would have delivered a long, tedious sermon.

At last, Moishe came home. Or rather he had been home awhile when the news finally got to Yankel. He was hurt by his younger brother's rudeness. Was he supposed to take the first step? Stubbornly, he waited for the visit, which would be sure to come soon. But since it didn't come, since days and then weeks passed without any sign of Moishe, Yankel began to gnaw his fingernails. Finally he couldn't stand it any longer and wrote his brother a very dignified letter, not so much angry as hurt. But Moishe, disregarding his duty, didn't run immediately to the Rue des Francs-Bourgeois, and Yankel received only a note from Rose, his wife, a pretentious snob

whom he couldn't bear; in polite language she invited him to dinner
next Thursday "with his charming family." He hesitated and then
accepted; after all, a brother's a brother. And this one was just back
from the war and the hospital. But he came with only part of his
charming family; Simon and Clara had refused to come. So, accompanied by Hannah, Rivka, and Fernand, he entered the lobby, furnished with a rug and an elevator (he tipped his hat to the doorman),
abstained in humility from taking the elevator, and climbed the stairs.

He was struck dumb at the sight of his brother, whom he hardly
recognized; Moishe had shaved his beard and wore only a close-
clipped mustache. But Yankel soon realized that the disappearance
of the beard didn't account for the change; after the first shock he
soon recognized in the shaven face the features of the young boy of
long ago, graven deeper by twenty-five years of life. The change was
inside Moishe. All the while Rose was playing her role of great lady,
Yankel didn't take his eyes off his brother, trying to understand him.
White hairs in that mop whose red, once so bright, had become tarnished and dull? The wounded leg that scraped on the rug? The obvious fatigue of the massive body? Of course, of course. The voice
had lost its teasing nonchalance, it was clipped, almost gruff, and . . .
yes, impatient! His mannerisms were still there, his "Don't worry
about it, Yankel," his *Schmuck, go!*"; but he said them through
habit, mechanically, absent-mindedly. What had snapped inside Moishe? Slowly, Yankel felt himself grow uneasy, pitying. Moishe without his jauntiness, was it still Moishe? Moishe without his good
humor, without his jokes . . . What was left of him?

Carefully, Yankel tried to question him about the war, about his
exploits (Moishe wore many ribbons in his buttonhole), even his
health; his brother brushed him aside, without his old kindness. Just
the same, you can't always ask, "How's business?" With what, then,
could he keep the conversation alive, warm, intimate? The dinner
dragged along painfully. Hannah, as usual, was intimidated in her
sister-in-law's presence; the too-rich, too-modern furniture, the rugs,
the silverware, all froze her. As the well-bred mistress of the house,
Rose addressed a friendly word to one and to the other, with a fixed
smile which she erased when she rang for the maid. Moishe spoke
little, and when he did speak he grew angry over trifles; he even
roundly abused his wife (and Yankel didn't know where to hide)
because the roast was overdone.

It was only at the end of the meal that the old Moishe reappeared for an instant. He rose, winked at his brother. "Ah, leave the women to their gossip for a while, Yankele!" Dragging his leg, he led the way into the living room; once there, he sighed, let himself drop into an armchair, stuck a big cigar into his mouth, and asked in his old teasing manner, "So, Yankele, still at the caps? Go on, you old Yankele!"

And that was the end, he fell back into his morose mood. For lack of a better reason, Yankel blamed it on his fatigue.

The older brother tried to return the invitation of the younger, but he wasn't able. The Moishes always had a very good reason for not accepting. In the end, Yankel convinced himself that it was Rose who was keeping them apart. There was no quarrel between the two brothers, but their paths diverged too widely. Well, that's life! They saw each other only at important ceremonies, when the Mykhanowitzki family demonstrated its broken unity. Yes, broken indeed!

Long ago, Simon had made up his mind about his father; a fine man, yes, but really an ass with his phony idealism, his high-flown sentiments, and his scruples over nothing; a savage, that's all, who smelled of his native Russia a hundred yards away. On the other hand, he, Simon, knew himself and always wanted to be right up to date. As Papa says, you live only once—you might as well enjoy life. Simon meant to enjoy life bountifully and he sounded his gospel in his parents' ears, he even exaggerated his cynicism just for the pleasure of shocking them. Then Papa would groan in pained scorn:

"My poor child, you're no idealist!"

"I don't want to be! No one's going to play me for a sucker!"

One day, while he was still working for Champeaux-Bussier, Simon overheard the big boss say that Jews were good businessmen, of course, but, like the Greeks, the Armenians, and the other greasers, they were small-time; outside of one or two firms you couldn't expect any big deals from them—those were for Frenchmen! True or false, the remark hadn't fallen on deaf ears. Simon, who was aware that Champeaux-Bussier had built his fortune on the backs of little Jewish contractors like his father, swore to do things in a big way, like a Frenchman, not like a Jew. To be a Frenchman like everybody else—although never formulated, this principle nonetheless governed all of Simon's behavior. Even Yiddish, which had as much right as French to be his mother tongue, was relegated to the rank of an embarrassing dialect; he never made use of it except when absolutely necessary, as, for instance, to win the confidence of a customer. There were even times when he pretended not to know it. Sometimes, with his parents, he would amuse himself by stumbling over a word, as you do with a foreign language: "How do you people say that in Yiddish?" Then Papa would screw up his face and make his fly-swatting gesture. "Get out of here with your dirty tricks!"

No, Simon was certainly no idealist! In his eyes, idealism was identified with self-denial, humility, poverty, and defeat; he would very quickly have defined an idealist as a gentleman who, when he gets kicked in the rear, says thank you. For his part, Simon preferred to be thanked—without wanting, of course, to do the kicking. He was infuriated at the humbly grateful way his father spoke to anyone, even the meanest street sweeper. People were always doing Papa favors! Even when it was he who was doing the favors.

"What's wrong with you, treating him like that? Anyone would think you owed him money!"

To which Yankel would reply that politeness never hurt anyone, and that foreigners have to be twice as polite as anyone else in order to be approved. Foreigner, foreigner . . .

"But you've been living in France for a quarter of a century," Simon would cry. "It's just the same as if you were French, after all! You don't owe the French anything, you've given them as much as you've received and maybe more. Anyway, no one's asking you to act like a slave."

Simon wickedly threw the word "slave" into his father's face to hurt him, to get even for the humiliation that he himself felt; he hoped that the old man would revolt. But no; Papa put on his martyr's face and wagged his head.

"Tchch! My poor boy! You're lucky, you don't know what it is to be a foreigner."

"You're a foreigner because you want to be one!"

"Can you help it that you're a Jew?"

"Who cares about that? Do you think you're still in Russia?"

"My poor boy!"

And Papa would walk away, shaking his head—just an old stubborn Jew! Jew for Jew, Simon almost preferred his grandfather, a real savage but at least he knew how to run things!

Oh, to hell with the Jews, and kosher and *treif* food, and the Old Country, and all the rest of it! As if there were nothing else in life! One day Mama takes you aside and starts telling you interminable stories, each one more heart-rending and more boring than the other, about her relatives "whom you never met, my poor child," but Simon didn't give a damn about never having met them. The ones he knew were enough for him—all of them cut out of the same pattern. Or else Papa brings home a *landsman,* as he calls them, and during the whole evening the *landsman,* with a satisfied smile stretched across his face, discourses endlessly on human nature and sometimes calls Simon to witness, "since you're a cultured young man." They were all interchangeable, these dear *landsmen:* gentle, idealistic, sententious, and stupid, stupid—as stupid as Wolf himself.

Next to them, Papa ended by seeming intelligent. No, let's be fair; Papa is intelligent. What Simon wanted to say was that next to his savage *landsmen,* Papa acted like a slightly polished man; sometimes he even appeared in an unusual light. One day, for instance, without any warning, he began to talk about Nevers.

"Nevers? You know Nevers?" Simon exclaimed, astounded that his father hadn't always lived in the Rue des Francs-Bourgeois.

"And why shouldn't I know Nevers? It's forbidden?"

"No, but I didn't know—"

"You always think you know everything! The world began to exist before you, didn't it? Don't be so quick to take your father for an idiot. Yes, I did work at Nevers, and it was before you were even born . . ."

Whereupon he embarked on a confused account (he rarely spoke, but once he got started . . .) in which he mingled the beauty of the city, the idealism of the people, and this and that and bicycle trips.

"What? You rode on a bicycle?"

"And why shouldn't I ride on a bicycle?" Papa rejoined, offended. "I've even done weight lifting, and Greco-Roman wrestling. What do you think of that?"

After that whenever he was in a good mood, he would challenge his son to a little match; for instance to see who could force the other's arm down. He also won, very much to Simon's humiliation. After all, Simon didn't like games of contact. He only pretended in order to give his father some pleasure, and because moments of good humor had become so rare in that house that he had to make the most of every one. Everyday life at the Mykhanowitzkis' had become gloomy.

Even their gala occasions would very often become depressing. What can be gayer than a marriage? Well, Rivka's wedding took place in a most distressing atmosphere. The girl had fallen in love with a furrier with whom she worked, Chaim (Henri to the French) Rechnowitz. A Jew, of course, but Polish, which Papa didn't like— God knows why, for in Simon's eyes, Polish or Moldavian, it was all one. Troubles began before the ceremony. Papa wanted to do things simply— "We're plain people, aren't we?" But the fiancé insisted on a big splash, and he especially wanted a beautiful synagogue. So, discussions and bitter quarrels . . . Chaim alias Henri was firm under his apparent flabbiness; his side won.

The wedding was in a beautiful synagogue, but Papa looked as if he were burying someone. When the groom broke the ritual glass in front of the rabbi, Mama and Grandma burst into tears; they were joyful tears, usual under the circumstances, but tears nonetheless. Next was the wedding dinner, in a fine restaurant. There were fifty settings; but twice as many came, invited haphazardly by one or another of the guests or by themselves; when there's enough for two there's enough for three, and the Mykhanowitzkis are such fine people! This mob swooped down on the table without the slightest regard for the place cards; they pushed and elbowed and yelled to the frightened waiters for more chairs and place settings. . . . When the dust cleared, neither the newlyweds nor the close family had seats. It was found necessary to parley, negotiate, get angry, and some of the truly invited left, slamming the door, while the intruders played possum or screamed that Uncle Leib had asked them to come, and they wouldn't stand for such an insult, and they threatened to go— but they stayed. All this time the food grew cold and the waiters snickered louder and louder.

Finally it grew quieter. Everyone ate off his neighbor's stomach, but they ate, which was the important thing, and the mood brightened. Little fat Chaim alias Henri Rechnowitz ran around like a demon smoothing out quarrels and making people laugh. He was wearing a tail coat, his father-in-law a frock coat, Simon a dinner jacket, and most of the others business suits; "high style" dresses were side by side with ready-made cottons. Within ten minutes everyone was sweating big drops; it was mid-July and as if by order the ventilating fans of the restaurant weren't working; unless it was a trick of the waiters, who became more and more familiar.

All at once a violent and grotesque explosion occurred. On the service plates the letters B. G. were engraved, the initials of the Jewish caterer who had brought his own dishes so that the meal would be kosher. Suddenly old Avrom rose at his place and began to shriek in anger. What was wrong? Well, B. G. stands for Victor Hugo! That's right, Victor Hugo! For in Russian *V* is written *B*, and *H* doesn't exist so is transcribed by the letter *G*, pronounced *gay*, so that Hugo becomes *Gugo*. Mixing up his meager knowledge of Russian and French, old Avrom thanked God that he had been spared such a horrible sin; for the restaurant was on the Avenue Victor-Hugo, so the plates, the dishes bearing its initials were *treif*. Tumult, shouting, uproar. Already unnerved by the preceding incidents, Papa suddenly rose, white as the tablecloth, and, prey to one of his most terrible fits of anger, he lost all control of himself and began to insult his father in language of such unbridled violence, calling him a brute, a savage, and even (Simon wasn't sure of this but he thought he heard the French word in the torrent of Yiddish) a dirty slob. Rivka began to cry and Mama on one side and Grandma on the other also began to cry and were trying to calm the two men and Uncle Moishe quietly was trying to turn the whole thing into a joke and all over the place people were calling each other names. At last the old man walked out on the wedding and the restaurant with Grandma weeping, running behind him, trying to hold him back. . . . Oh, talk about your lovely weddings, that was a lovely wedding! Just savages. And yet, before the war, these people seemed less tense, less sad. When Simon recalled some of his childhood memories . . .

It was the Feast of the Passover. The family had gathered together around its head, old Avrom. Everyone was happy; the Lord wished it so, and old Avrom saw to it.

In the preceding days the women had swept out the house from top to bottom; the corners, crannies, and niches had been scrupulously cleaned. When they had finished the father had checked, poking his nose into the closet, under the furniture, into the drawers of the buffet. If by some misfortune he dug out a little crumb of bread, the heavens fell. He seized it between thumb and index finger and brandished it under his wife's eyes. Sometimes the crumb was so large that it would crack under his nails and fall to the floor; then for hours the family would be busy trying to find it. For the Lord has ordained that not a crumb of leavened bread shall remain in the house during the Passover, when only unleavened bread may be eaten; and old Avrom didn't play tricks on the Lord.

At last, all was orderly, neat, and proper, the house and the family, even the souls after the visit to the synagogue. You felt new, regenerated, as if time had been cut off or had stopped to take on a new spirit. Go, the past is finished and everything unclean is gone! We have erased it, we begin again, we start from zero, and this time with a clear conscience! Now there was nothing left to do but to sit down at the table and to laugh with your whole being; you could do it without the slightest hesitation gnawing at you, without any burden inherited from the past straining your shoulders. In those days Simon was surprised to see Papa and Uncle Moishe, so hostile to religion, yielding with such good grace to the innumerable little customs with a trace of an amused smile. Now he was beginning to understand.

And how many of these ritual customs there were! Thus at one fixed moment the father dipped his little finger ten times into a glass of wine and then shook it, while evoking in Hebrew the ten plagues of Egypt; after him the whole family, in hierarchical order, repeated the gesture. And you had to laugh with all your heart; you had to laugh because it was a sin to be sad; and because you laughed you were filled with true joy.

The children had to ask four questions of the head of the family; for example: "Grandpa, why is it permitted during the year to eat leavened or unleavened bread at the same time, but at the Passover only unleavened bread?" The four questions were always the same, of course, and after a while you knew the answers by heart, but that made no difference, Grandpa greeted you with an approval that was always new, leaned back in his armchair and replied nobly, slowly, as a patriarch who transmits the law, with solemnity and the requisite pedantry: "You wish to know, my child? Then listen well, my child. Once, long long ago, the Jews were . . ." The traditional story followed, but you had to listen religiously as it was told, of wicked Pharaoh and the Angel and the Flight from Egypt.

After the four required questions you had the right to ask any others you wanted to. Here was where the laughter really began. For Simon—and he was the one in the saddle as the heir of the eldest son —would mischievously invent embarrassing questions. Then Grandpa would knot his terrible eyebrows, all the while trying to hold on to his threatened good humor, and would cut him short: "Na, na, na, Simon, that's not a nice question to ask!" Papa and Uncle Moishe would laugh gently and the old man would be flattered in spite of his uneasiness because his grandson was so intelligent.

The most amusing game was the hunt for the hidden matzoth. During the meal, Grandpa would take a matzoth, bless it solemnly, and break it in two. He shared one of the halves among the diners; the second he kept for himself, hiding it under his cushion and guarding it jealously. Now it was up to the others to steal his half of the matzoth from him; and the happy thief would have the right to exact any forfeit, Grandpa would have to pay it. Only, old Avrom was cagey and tricky as a monkey; no one was ever able to steal his half of the matzoth.

Yes, wait a minute; once, only once, Simon had succeeded. He had planned it in advance with Papa and Uncle Moishe. While they were competing to see which one of them could tell the funniest story and while the old man, always an excellent audience, was laughing until the tears ran, Simon glided furtively behind him and hup! he had the matzoth. . . . "Simon! give me that immediately!" How very badly Grandpa took it! And uneasily; suppose the boy had decided to ask for a hundred thousand francs! To clear himself of that debt old Avrom would have sold his store without hesitation, right down to his last shirt. But of course he preferred to avoid that and he stretched a desperate hand toward his grandson. Finally Papa forced Simon to return the matzoth by paying him a hundred sous, and the old man, delighted at getting off so cheaply, went so far as to give him a louis.

Oh! Such good savages!

Old Avrom left for Palestine shortly after Rivka's marriage. Everyone tried to dissuade him but he refused to listen, cashed in all his goods, and there he was, a free man. Yankel had no choice but to become reconciled with him; when your old father is going away to die, you have to clean the slate of all the grievances you have against him. Besides, the old man, suddenly invigorated, was mixing his religion with a great many business projects. Nonsense, thought Yankel, who suddenly felt that he was old.

There was a farewell dinner in the small apartment on the Rue des Rosiers. The French section of the family were all there, the Yankels with their Rechnowitz, the Moishes with their swarm of brats; in addition, a stranger whom Simon didn't know and who seemed to count for two, a scraggly-bearded, solemn, aged man who, in a very high voice, gave the orders, made decisions, pronounced the blessings, and scolded everyone for everything, especially the head of the house.

"Who's he?" Simon whispered to his father, who was seated beside him.

"Nobody. A *schnorrer*."

A beggar! That's a good one! Softly Yankel explained to his son that Grandpa had taken this man under his wing quite a while ago—"Finkelbaum is his name, a *Chassid,* it seems"—and the old man had even given Finkelbaum large sums of money. Nothing for his own children, but he was showering gifts on the *schnorrer*. "He's beginning to do good deeds, you understand?"

In fact, Grandpa had always been very charitable, charitable to the point of stupidity. Thus, before the Finkelbaum era, there had been the era of the *gair*—a *gair* being a converted Christian. Yes, a man had shown up one day who said he had come from Palestine and was a converted Christian. Naturally all the good Jews of the neighborhood vied with one another to entertain him, Grandpa at their head. Think of it, a converted Christian, you don't meet one every day. The *gair* lived with one and then with another, well dressed, well fed, and with plenty of money in his pocket. This lasted for some months till they heard some news about him, that he had abandoned his wife and that he had swindled so-and-so and so-and-so—a convert, maybe, but a cheat, certainly. "Well, do you think that cured your grandfather? You don't know him!"

At this the *schnorrer* interrupted them sharply, scolded them for speaking in whispers, and explained how well-bred people behave. Simon wondered whether to laugh or be angry, but his father pulled his sleeve and said in French:

"Forget it! They're all ignorant!"

Simon remained with his mouth open at the sight of his father posing as a champion of modernism.

In spite of the intermingling of the guests and the injunctions of the *schnorrer* to rejoice, the banquet was only partly happy. Grandma seemed tired; Grandpa was in a rather ferocious mood and showed his teeth when he smiled, except when he addressed dear M. Finkelbaum, whereupon he became incredibly humble; Aunt Rose pursed her lips, humiliated at being in such company, and snubbed poor Hannah, who was trying to make her laugh. Only Moishe's youngsters and that fat tub of a Chaim alias Henri Rechnowitz were having a good time like morons, squealing and throwing wads of bread at each other across the table. Simon was withdrawn and thinking of his business. His trip to Le Havre had given him a really good lead which he intended to follow to the end; if it worked out he would be able to quit his job and go into business for himself. With that problem in mind he felt that he was the only adult among these babies, these old people, and these savages—outside of Uncle Moishe. His grandparents' leaving of course hurt a little if he wanted to think about it. On the other hand, they were going of their own free will. So? Everyone to his own taste. Anyway, what did he, Simon, have in common with these old people? They were related? But you didn't choose your relatives, they were forced on you. Of course he loved his grandmother and his grandfather because . . . just because! That didn't keep them from being strangers to him.

Beside him Papa was silent. Sad? Probably, in spite of everything. Papa was very sentimental. It was easy to understand why; his parents were leaving him, were going to a faraway country where it seemed every so often the Arabs began to massacre Jews with great gusto. It was true that with Papa you could never tell where his thoughts would lead him; he never stopped thinking. Right now there was a pensive, clouded look on his face as he sat there stuffing himself with gefilte fish. The gefilte fish, it must be admitted, was delicious and Simon liked it very much although he preferred French cooking. But you can't get that pensive over gefilte fish, no matter how good. No, there was something sad about this feast and not only because the grandparents were leaving. Simon didn't like to be alone with his thoughts, they bored him. He leaned toward his father and, in French, asked him why he was so sad. Yankel replied, with a nervous twitch of his face:

"Let me alone! You wouldn't understand."

No, Yankel thought, Simon can't understand. That boy is hard, selfish, and so French that a great many things go right past him. His grandparents are going away? What difference does it make to him? He doesn't know them. Yankel saw himself separated forever from his own parents, Mama sick, Papa changed, and without his ever having been able to restore their old intimacy. Only recently there had been that scene at Rivka's marriage, and he still felt heavy with remorse. With their going, a large portion of his life was being removed—his childhood, even his native land. All that was over! Already cut off from his brother Peretz and his sister Rachel in America, from his sister Sarah, from whom he never had any news any more so he didn't know whether she was dead or alive or begging in the streets, Yankel felt his roots cut away. Alone! Alone from now on. Of course there were the children, but they depended on him; he had no one for support.

A silent and secret ghost floated before his eyes—Itcha, disappeared, killed (how, God, how?); Itcha, whom you never heard, whom you hardly saw when he was alive, but who had become an obsession since his death; Itcha, whose only trace on earth, and Yankel alone knew the secret, was a little girl lost somewhere among the French people . . . Yankel felt that at that instant his father, too, was thinking of Itcha; perhaps the old man was nursing a vague sorrow at not having accompanied his son to the station when the boy had gone away forever.

Moishe. There was still Moishe, gaunt, sallow, and gray. Yankel felt a pang whenever he looked at his brother. Moishe admitted that he felt a little pain from his leg; to force that admission from him, the pain must have been keen and constant. Could this explain the new Moishe, with his dry quips? And why had he shaved his beard? Yankel had once asked him. "Yankele, you have to be in style, you have to be young. The older you get, the younger you have to look." All lightly. Yankel didn't believe in this lightness; he felt that there was some connection between the disappearance of the beard and the wound in the leg—but what connection?

Just then, Moishe seemed to wake up. Yankel tore himself out of his reverie; it's always painful to come back to the outside world, but for politeness' sake it has to be done. . . . Still the *schnorrer*. Who is his prey now? Moishe? Ho! Ho! Now we'll laugh, for over Moishe's eye there passed that veiled gleam which announced the resurrection of the old prankster.

"Hey! Hey! Monsieur Finkelbaum, why are you so hard on us?"

How gentle! Yankel elbowed Simon, but Simon had understood and was also prepared for what was coming, and the whole Mykhanowitzki family perked up its ears. Finkelbaum, however, didn't even do Moishe the honor of a direct attack; he took it out on old Avrom, who humbly tried to defend himself. What was all the uproar about? Oh! One of Moishe's sons had committed the crime of speaking in French, and that had unleashed the *schnorrer*'s thunderbolts. He screamed in fury:

"*Chassid!* The place is full of *goyim!* Haven't you anything but *goyim* in your family? They're all ashamed, instead of proud, of being Jews! Me, I . . ."

Patiently, Moishe waited, tracing circles on the tablecloth with his fingernail. When the other paused for breath, Moishe's peaceful, conciliating, and pained voice rose:

"Nu, nu, Monsieur Finkelbaum, no one on this earth is perfect. Everyone has his faults."

He stroked his clean-shaven chin, and old Avrom's eye sparkled under the bushy brow. The *schnorrer,* ready for battle, looked sideways at his adversary. But Moishe had time, plenty of time—there wasn't any fire, was there? Again he stroked his chin, as if the flamered beard were still there. At last, with that unchanging blandness:

"You, Monsieur Finkelbaum, for instance, are in the rag business . . ."

"So?" the other grumbled. He was waiting to be insulted about his business or the money with which he had bought his donkey cart, because old Avrom had given it to him. And you may be sure he had a reply all ready. But Moishe, after a new pause, finally said offhandedly:

"Hey, Monsieur Finkelbaum, on your donkey cart you've written, 'The Little Russian.' If you're such a patriot, why didn't you write 'The Big Jew'?"

The question was put so naïvely, and so amiably, that Finkelbaum was caught openmouthed and could only chew the air between his beard and his mustache. Then Moishe, without waiting this time, but as soothingly as possible, cooed in his tenderest voice:

"Nu, nu, nu, Monsieur Finkelbaum, now you see. You must get along with people in this life!"

Of all the Mykhanowitzkis, the one who laughed hardest was old Avrom, thus indirectly avenged for the persecutions by his *schnorrer.* He rapped on the table and dried his eyes and squealed with pleasure:

"Aie, aie, aie, still the same Moishe!"

M. Finkelbaum, having finally recovered his wind, rose furiously from his seat and hurled his napkin on the table; and it was Grandpa who caught it, as was fair:

"*Chassid!* Since everybody insults me in this house, and since you don't know how to make them respect your guest, I'm leaving, do you understand, and I'll never set foot in this house again!"

In his rage he had forgotten that old Avrom was leaving in a few days. Old Avrom had also forgotten, for he suddenly took on a terrified look.

"No, no, no," he groaned, "be nice, Monsieur Finkelbaum, and don't make any scenes today, it's a holiday! Moishele didn't want to hurt you; he's always playing tricks . . ."

The old man pleaded, begged, implored, and apologized over and over. Finkelbaum waited, wrapped in his dignity. And when he finally decided that there had been sufficient amends, he agreed to sit down again. At the same time, he had not dared to demand apologies from the real culprit.

"What characters!" thought Simon, looking over the members of his family. He felt full of scorn and yet strangely tender. Papa and Uncle Moishe were chuckling into their napkins; Grandpa was grumbling but was obviously holding back his laughter. Simon had the feeling that he had been initiated into one of the master secrets of the Mykhanowitzki clan.

Next, old Avrom, perhaps to appease his *schnorrer* completely, called for a little song.

"Moishe! You have such a fine voice, why don't you liven things up a little? Things are getting dull."

No, Moishe didn't want to sing. He shook his head with a gentle firmness.

"I'm too old to play the clown."

The old man spat. "Too old? Tchch! Me, I'm at least seventy, or seventy-two, what do I know? And . . ."

It was true; no one knew his age, not even he. On his French passport there was written: "Born, April 22, 1852." They had thrown this date as a bone to the clerk, who had insisted on precise information.

All at once, little Chaim alias Henri, who had been boiling in his corner, couldn't hold it in any longer; he leaped to his feet and, with a satisfied smile stretched across his moonface, declared:

"I'll sing you a song!"

Rivka pulled him by the sleeve, having seen her grandfather's frown at this breach of protocol; but her husband didn't understand and bounced around in his place until he got silence. Flabby, pot-bellied, and fat-bottomed, with the color of a turnip and thinning hair, little Rechnowitz wasn't handsome; in the eyes of the Mykhanowitzkis he had an even greater fault—he was a foreigner, a Polish Jew. His wife, Rivka, topped him by a head. Once again, Simon wondered why that big pumpkin had married such a punchinello. Had she become so fed up with her home and her mother's constant scolding? Or had she really succumbed to the charm of that windbag, as Simon put it? Women are so foolish.

Chaim began to sing, and everyone knew the song by heart; Simon even remembered that years ago they used to sing it at family reunions, the men winking slyly and the women snickering behind their hands. It was actually slightly off-color, but so covertly that the children could never suspect it. It was the story of a *reb* who comes and goes, who withdraws and returns, all the movements punctuated by joyous *scha, scha,* and *aie, aie!* But this lout Rechnowitz sang it with such ecstatic faces, with such hypocritically modest gestures, with such tremulous puckerings of the lips, with such cooing reflections, with the squirmings of a timid virgin, and his disgusting Polack accent, that he emphasized all the hidden allusions. It became filthy. Simon didn't think he was prudish, but after all there were children present! The atmosphere froze; the Mykhanowitzki clan stiffened. Moishe drummed on the table, Yankel knitted his brows, the women tried to think of something else, the *schnorrer* looked disgusted; as for old Avrom, having chewed his mustache he interrupted the young man right in the middle of a sentence.

"Na! That's enough, you, that's not a good song!"

"But why not?" Chaim asked, dumfounded.

Rivka pulled him by the sleeve.

"Don't argue. Sit down and be quiet for once!"

Disconcerted, he looked about him; but old Avrom was already calling for other volunteers.

"Can't the children sing something?"

No, the children couldn't sing anything; they knew only French songs learned at school. That threatened to spoil everything; Yankel sacrificed himself. Seeing his oldest son rise, the old man beamed with pleasure.

"What are you going to sing for us? Do you remember how you used to imitate the drunken Polack?"

With a wink, he designated poor Rechnowitz, a ready-made victim. Yankel, who gabbled a few words of Polish, had a fine talent for making fun of Poles, Christians and Jews alike. This was a guaranteed success; the Mykhanowitzki clan had adopted the Russians' contempt for the effeminate Poles.

Yankel conscientiously imitated the drunken Pole, with the most grotesque intonations, and everyone choked with laughter, even the *schnorrer,* even little Chaim, who probably believed that only Christians were being mocked. Then Yankel sang something else, and something else again, casting desperate glances at Moishe, who re-

223

fused to come to his relief. When he had finished, he sat down with a last look at Moishe, who didn't move. Odd; since Moishe had no beard you could read his face like an open book. Had the war changed him so much?

Now everyone was pounding on the table, calling for a song from Moishe; but Moishe, with a smile, continued to refuse.

"Na, Moishele!" cried the old man, really displeased. "Are you going to let your father and mother go like that, without giving them a little pleasure?"

At this Moishe yielded:

"What do you want me to sing? I don't know anything."

He straightened up in his chair but didn't rise—maybe his leg hurt? Suddenly:

"Well, what if I sing you a French soldier's song?" And without waiting for leave, at the top of his lungs he swung into the marching song of the Foreign Legion.

His voice was drowned under a roar of protest. Yankel didn't take his eyes off his brother. What was wrong with Moishe? Why that evil in his voice, that bitterness, almost hate?

"Why don't you want that?" Moishe said. "You should know some soldiers' songs, Papa, since you're going to the Zionists . . ."

The old man spat. "The Zionists? Pfeh! *Goyim!* I'm going to the Holy Land, I'm not going with the Zionists!"

"Well," Moishe said, "then what do you want from me?"

Suave, yes; but his parents, his wife, his brother looked at him uneasily. What was going on in his head at that moment, behind that fixed, unchanging smile?

Suddenly, the song burst out, brutal, barbaric. A shiver ran down Simon's spine. God split the sea with a breath, opened twelve glass roads for the twelve tribes, and engulfed the horsemen and the horses of Pharaoh. Simon had heard it a hundred times, that song like all the other Jewish songs, vaguely whining, vaguely mystic, good for the synagogues, good to make the women and the men cry together, evoking past glories and Jehovah's miracles. But now it was . . . it was . . . Moishe's bass voice, resounding from that vast chest, sounded like a war trumpet, beating the march of a people over a conquered land, unleashing the clamors of an enemy who is going to be swallowed in the gulfs. Uplifted with pride, frenzied, the whole Mykhanowitzki clan sang its war song, the bronze voice of Moishe soaring and leading, blended with Yankel's steely voice and the piercing flutes of the women, while the patriarch imperiously pounded the rhythm with his clenched fist, and Clara's eyes flashed fire. Sometimes, for centuries of servitude cannot pass over a people without sapping its strength, the song would suddenly weaken and fade. Then the bronze voice would overwhelm the feminine chorus, but all at once, like a whiplash, it would become firm, would resume the beat of the military step. . . . Then began the final psalm to the glory of God . . . and now, with sword in hand, the Lord of Hosts was marching at the head of His people.

Finally, Moishe fell silent. The guests, transported to another world, were sighing, shaking hands, looking at each other with eyes full of light. Calmly, Moishe remarked that it was getting warm.

Outside, a fine rain was falling, and a blackish slime smeared the pavement; it was cold and sad. The two families stopped near Moishe's car—two families now, grouped behind their chiefs, two separate clans now that their ancestor was departing. Yankel and Moishe spoke in subdued voices, dispiritedly. What had they to say to each other from now on? Nothing. The evening had gone well. Mama didn't look too bad. What an idea, to go to Palestine! Bah! The old people, what do you want, if it makes them happy . . . Silence. And that *schnorrer!* Does he live there? By God, Papa would give him his own bed . . . Silence. Neither Moishe nor Yankel dared to say good-bye . . .

"Well, be seeing you," said little Rechnowitz.

Be seeing you, be seeing you . . . See you, Rivkele, see you, Uncle, Aunt . . . Good night, sleep well, be careful going home . . .

Murmurs, handshakes, hugs. Rivka and her husband went off into the night. The rest followed them with their eyes.

"I can't give you a lift," Moishe said. "There are too many of you."

"Oh, we don't live too far off," Yankel replied.

Silence.

"Does your leg hurt you when you drive?"

"Oh, you can't let things get you down!"

Moishe's brood piles into the car; the springs creak and bend. . . .

And there, they were gone. Silently, slowly, Yankel's family set out for the Rue des Francs-Bourgeois.

Yankel felt his shoulders grow heavy.

II

A GOLDEN opportunity! The chance of a lifetime, to be grabbed immediately!

But it was useless—Simon hadn't done his two years' conscription yet. Even if he obtained a deferment now, it would hurt even more later; one day he would still have to go. So? Get a business started, and then leave it flat? That would be a kick in the belly!

Wait? But life goes on, opportunity knocks only once, and the world is changing with prodigious speed. Considering everything, Simon decided to wager his bankroll on the one throw. He'd see later how it would work out.

For two years now the Great Wheel left from the Exposition had been in the process of demolition—very slow demolition. Now some shrewd operators realized that they could use its cars, instead of tossing them on the scrap heap. They set the cars on the vacant land near the fairgrounds, lined them up, more or less, and sold them to businessmen to turn into stalls, booths, or anything else they wanted; that was their affair. Of course all this gave rise to snarled and knotted dealings in which the law had no hand; I sell, buy, or rent a car, half a car, a lot, a crust of bread—but who's the owner? I have a complaint to make. To whom? Against whom? You've got no right to set your shop so close to mine. . . . I certainly do have the right, they told me, they promised me. . . . A lease? You're crazy! The whole setup is temporary, as soon as the demolition is finished, the city will take back the lots and . . .

In short, a cluster of booths sprang up near the Champ-de-Mars, officially named—God knows why—the Swiss Village; but its inhabitants had renamed it, with much better reason, Jewtown. Half fair, half rag market, it offered a vast field of action to enterprising gentlemen who hadn't lost sight, among other things, of the inexhaustible American surplus stocks. Temporary? It looked like a very permanent temporary situation. Simon made a deal with a friend to share a car. And there it was, he had a foot in the door.

Now he had the job of getting cash and merchandise to start with. What merchandise? First of all, naturally, caps; some of his old bosses sent him some on consignment. But caps, men's hats, didn't appeal to Simon. He wanted ladies' apparel, because with women you've got the job all done. Still, you've got to begin somewhere.

He also tapped his father, who threw his hands to heaven, advised him to work honestly, save his money, and set himself up on his own in a real shop. Yankel warned his son against human wickedness, reminded him of his waiting conscription, and ended by lending him money and sending some caps to the stall. What Simon didn't know was that those caps had been made with such loving care that their purchasers would keep them for the rest of their lives.

That still wasn't enough. Should Simon go to his brother-in-law Rechnowitz the furrier? Out of the question! First of all, you don't sell furs from a stall; and then Simon had no trust in that Polack, whom he considered quite capable of trying to sink a hook into him if the business worked out well.

There still was Uncle Moishe. Simon loved his uncle very much. He was somebody, he knew how to live, he looked at life from the right side, he didn't knock himself out over trifles. Rich, too, which doesn't hurt; rich as Simon wanted to be rich, not a pinchpenny, but liberal with his cash—a big man! And he'd been in the war, not a— yes, not a slacker, like some people I know. . . .

So, his heart beating a little more rapidly in spite of his aplomb, he entered the beautiful jewelry shop on the Madeleine. Aunt Rose eyed him sourly, as she did all the Mykhanowitzkis, but his uncle greeted him with open arms and asked him to stay for lunch. Uncle Moishe was dragging his foot badly, much worse than Simon had remembered.

He didn't ask for any explanation. "How much do you want? Do you want me to put some merchandise in, too? Some loud costume jewelry—that ought to sell well there!"

Aunt Rose, pursing her lips, reminded her husband that it was the end of the month and bills had to be paid. He shrugged his shoulders, disdaining to discuss it, but took advantage of the opportunity to show his nephew how to use creditors—the "cavalry," he called them.

And Simon set up shop in Jewtown. Headgear of all sorts—that was the major part of his stock. In a showcase he displayed Uncle

227

Moishe's loud costume jewelry, among which, oddly enough, there were ribbons for military decorations—the Legion of Honor, Croix de Guerre, etc.

All winter long he shivered with cold, in spite of the stove. Business was rather good, but a grave danger hung over Jewtown; the longer its "temporary" status lasted, the more temporary it became. The nearby shopkeepers of the Motte-Piquet, the Avenue Suffren, the Rue Dupleix, began to make loud complaints about unfair competition. The merchants of the Village thereupon formed an association and, to counter the threat of expulsion, trumpeted loudly about the sacred rights of free enterprise. Some of the stalls were put up on concrete foundations. It was really for health; you couldn't spend your life in cabins with unjointed boards, could you?

Among his friends and acquaintances, Simon Mykhanowitzki passed for a playboy. When he had some business to do with an out-of-towner they almost always wound up in a night club. He knew Montmartre like the palm of his hand, didn't spare the champagne, and knew where to find the pretty girls. The girls, for their part, adored him, not only for his generosity but because something was always happening when Simon was around. Easygoing, free-spending, easy to get along with, he was always ready for a bit of fun; and women like that, as everyone knows.

Soldiers do, too. When he left for his regiment, Simon had nothing to worry about; after taking certain precautions, he had entrusted his half of the stall to the friend who owned the other half, and there! the job was done. He donned his uniform with a light heart and set about winning over the rough soldiers as he had won over the pretty girls.

He was sent to Nantes, to the Sixty-fifth Infantry, at the Cambronne Barracks. He had some education, as his certificate of elementary studies proved; and since he still remembered the declension of *rosa* in Latin, he claimed that he had gone to the lycée for three years. He was immediately placed in a squad for training noncommissioned officers.

At the beginning, his circumcision embarrassed him considerably, because of his comrades; then he learned that in some backward regions of Brittany it was the custom to circumcise the first-born sons. So he no longer hesitated, and his superiors remarked his assiduity at Mass. You have to get along; and since that was what they wanted

. . . He was clean, neat (he lost no time in having his uniform made to order), obedient, respectful, well-bred (he let it be known, discreetly, that he was a descendant of a noble Polish family). When he became a master in the art of standing at attention, he was taken from the noncom training squad and promoted to the band, the aristocratic elite of the regiment. Not that he knew music; but, having learned to read notes at school, or God knows where, he said he did. Nor did it matter in the least; the bandmaster started everyone equally at zero, the Conservatory prize winner as well as the beginner. With his eagle eye he sized Simon up immediately, and Simon knew he was doomed to the saxophone.

Thus Private Mykhanowitzki, having escaped all the dirty jobs, had an easy time in that regiment, where Pernod and muscatel were as important as the manual of arms and more important than service in the field. He was promoted to private, first class, "the only rank in the Army level with Marshal of France," he would say. His father was proud of him and admired him greatly when he saw him for the first time in the horizon blue, like a true Frenchman, with his garrison cap rakishly slanted on his close-cropped head. He admired him even more when he saw the red chevron on his sleeve. Simon told him a lot of stories, how he had the officers in the palm of his hand and what outrageous tricks he played on his dolt of a sergeant, and the old man would grow uneasy and advise him to be careful.

Remarkably enough, Simon, who was liked by his superiors, was equally well liked by his fellow rankers. He didn't have to force himself in; whatever his surroundings, he always found himself immediately in harmony. He told dirty stories to his comrades, laughed at the practical jokes they played on him, and paid them back—the bucket over the door, the turned-down sheets, the itching powder in the shirt. In addition, he was always obliging, writing letters for his bunkmates to their girl friends, and paying for drinks more often than he had to—so much so that the heavy-footed hayseeds would say: "That fellow Mica, oh, he's all right!" They were ready to go through hell for him.

Going to Mass needn't keep you from going to the brothel; Simon didn't fail to go, along with his buddies. He was prudent, of course, because of the diseases, but resolute. On the other hand, he was almost timid in his relationship with good girls. On Sundays, of course, when the gang went to have some fun in the hangouts along the Erdre, it was his duty (one isn't a Parisian for nothing) to make a pickup, even to dance with some local working girl, and even to ask her to have a drink and take her home. But as soon as he escaped from his comrades' admiring gaze, he would become extraordinarily polite and respectful; it was Mademoiselle this and Mademoiselle that. He never went further than a few kisses and some halfhearted petting. Why this reserve? Well, each case had a different reason; the girl had a mole on her lip, or a rough skin, or bad breath, or she was stupid. Always something. The truth (although he didn't know it) was that a woman's virginity was sacred to him; and, in a way, he considered every good woman a sort of virgin, and therefore not to be touched. He had divided all women into two groups: the good, whom you respected like a mother or a sister, and the bad, to be taken by storm. He would have been greatly surprised if he had been told that this morality bore the stamp of his father and of Rakwomir; he thought he was a complete cynic.

Everything considered, his timidity before the girls of Nantes was akin to the awkwardness of his comrades, the simple peasants. If he enjoyed being with the peasants it wasn't because, as he thought, he found more chance to shine with them than he would have among the few Parisians in the Sixty-fifth, but because, in so many ways, he was just like them.

When he returned from the Army, he found that the Village had changed. A square was beginning to emerge amid the booths, the walks branching from it had been asphalt-paved and had become avenues, dropping other paths to an inferior rank. Formerly all the locations had been equal; now there were good and bad. Certain trades were thriving and others were shrinking away. With organization, inequality developed, and there were quarrels, almost riots. The Bureau of the Merchants' Association played a more and more important part, almost like that of a Municipal Council; it began to issue rules—officious, to be sure, since they were only temporary.

Simon had always had luck; his stall was very well placed. His friend had to have his ear pulled before he would return Simon's half; but Simon hadn't been born yesterday, and he ended by regaining what was rightfully his. His friend severed relations with him forever; for more than two months they stepped on each other's toes. But they were like Siamese twins, linked by the partition in the center of the booth; after a while they decided it would be better to make peace than to continue fighting.

Once that was settled, Simon hustled his business along. He was through with child's play; he felt that he had become adult.

First he dropped the caps, men's hats, even berets, which weren't selling too well; since going bareheaded was the fashion, only an idiot would try to swim against the current. Women's wear—that was the sure winner; even surer than groceries, because girls would rather go hungry than stop beautifying themselves. And then women's wear is fun, it's varied; there are hats and purses, pullovers, silk stockings, lacy lingerie, and costume jewelry. Following the whims of his clientele, and also his own, Simon would shift the center of gravity of his trade. First the shop would switch to leather goods, then it would overflow with those white blouses which project the female bosom so enticingly. The young man was always careful not to put all his eggs in one basket, and he maintained two solid bases: ladies' hats and costume jewelry. These were his preparation for the future; though he liked the Village, he had no intention of taking root there. He wanted to rise to Uncle Moishe's level.

He led a pleasant life while waiting. As his uncle had predicted, all the servant girls of the neighborhood and all the middle-class housewives were his customers, actual or potential. Every day he was surrounded by plump little pullets, their eyes lit by his treasures, and it was Monsieur Simon this, and Monsieur Simon that. "Oh, Monsieur Simon, this one is simply adorable! Do I look well in it?" Pivoting before the mirror that Simon had installed in a corner, the pullet would make faces, purse her lips, tilt her head. Simon would stand behind her appreciatively. "If you permit, madame, not like that. Allow me!" Then a little dance step to get her into position, face to face; respectful sleight-of-hand gestures, at arm's length—Simon would set the hat straight. "There! Yes! It's just your type! And the latest thing, I give you my word. Look at the magazines!" He always kept a supply of fashion magazines on the counter. But his customers, however often they had consulted them before, rarely consulted the magazines afterward; once the oracle had spoken, once they heard that everyone was wearing it, they were delighted and found it beautiful. "How much is it? . . . Oh, that's not expensive!" As far back as he could remember, Simon had never heard one of these girls say a hat was expensive. They would wince, sometimes, at the price of a handbag, but never at that of a hat. M. Simon's hats were never dear! And they really weren't, because Simon believed in selling at the lowest possible price, depending on volume and turning his stock over often. "Mustn't keep it for ages in a showcase, or it'll rust!"

He became cock of the walk to these ladies, who freely asked his advice on their most intimate affairs. Should they, for instance, bob their hair, to follow the style? "Oh, madame," he would exclaim despairingly when he saw one of them hesitate at the sacrifice, "with such beautiful hair, it would be a crime!" But he would add quickly: "Of course bobbed hair is so practical! So easy to wash—and it's right in style!" Then the woman would unburden herself; she would like nothing better, but her husband was against it, and . . . "Oh, madame," Simon would interrupt, in his most intimate manner, "you know you can always lead a man around by the nose, pretty as you are; he'll be happy after a few days, like all the others." In short, there was always some woman or other dawdling about the shop. He didn't mind; he liked company. That was what he really wanted out of trade—the company of people rather than wealth.

He had hung a sign above the counter: "We give no credit." But Simon Mykhanowitzki had a good heart and he couldn't bear the sight of a little pullet twisting and turning, tortured by her desire for a particular hat. Whether he knew her or not, he would place the hat in her hands. "Here, here, madame, I trust you; you'll pay me at the end of the month!" Rarely was his trust betrayed; servant girls and housewives never failed to pay their debt to such a friendly tradesman. As for great ladies, he knew them from experience to be less scrupulous; he saw few of them and wasn't sorry; they cheapened everything, were as disagreeable as possible, and paid badly.

Many times, one of the girls, anxious for a hat but broke, would offer to let him take it out in trade. Simon didn't like that; business is business and fun is fun. He would pretend not to understand; he knew that whether he refused or accepted the offer the customer was lost. Not to mention the trouble he might have with the husband. Only once did he allow himself to be tempted. She was a dainty little thing, a maid in the home of a magistrate. She managed matters so skillfully that for a while Simon thought she really loved him. Afterward she showed her true colors and began to pillage the shop. "Oh, Simon, what a lovely little necklace!" What could he say but "Do you want it?" She would pout protestingly. "Oh, no, no, you've given me so much already. What do you take me for?" And he would be obliged to give her the necklace, if only to prove that he didn't

232

take her for what she was. Finally he threw her out; she came back
to make a scene, shouted about impairing the morals of a minor, under the pretext that she wasn't yet eighteen; threatened him with
the magistrate, who was so good to her; and ended by slapping him
and calling him a dirty Jew. That was lesson enough; more than ever
Simon avoided "good" women and preferred to lose the customer before rather than after. At the same time, as an unexpected conse-
quence, he began to think that marriage had something to offer, after
all.

He hadn't lived with his parents since his return from his military
service; in spite of the housing shortage, he had found a furnished
room near the Village. One afternoon, when he was standing in the
doorway of his shop waiting for customers, he saw his father in the
distance coming toward him, looking neither right nor left, his hat
firmly settled on his head and his cane in hand: a respectable gentleman. Good old Papa! Simon thought as he hurried to meet him.
He felt a pang; he hadn't been to the house for more than a month.
I hope no one's ill! No, for Papa had his usual look, half asleep
while things were swarming within. The two men embraced; neither
of them liked it, but each felt the other would be hurt by a simple
handshake. Simon took his father's arm and led him toward the shop.

"Mama's all right? Clara? Fernand?"

"Yes, yes," Papa replied absently; to him, sickness did not exist.
He stopped and meditated. Simon waited, wondering what would
come from this meditation.

The Swiss Village had become a very tidy little community now,
especially in the sunshine. The old cars no longer looked like cars,
nor the stalls like stalls; many of the stores had awnings; the ground
was paved, and the walks swept clean.

"Hmm! It's changed since I last saw it!" Yankel remarked finally.

"Yes, indeed. What a hullabaloo we had to make! Just to get that
drinking fountain over there, well . . ."

Simon had to use his hands every time he spoke. He let go of his
father's arm, and Yankel immediately began to walk again. Men
shouldn't hold each other by the arm; at most a father could take his
son's arm protectively, but certainly not the other way around! Simon
hadn't noticed anything; he never noticed anything. He talks, talks
all the time like a woman, bending your ears, but he doesn't know
how to use his brains.

Before entering the shop, Yankel stopped and looked down the

streets. There weren't many people about; at two o'clock in the afternoon most women are either washing dishes or at work. Even so,
the tradesmen mounted guard before each door, neighbors chatting
across the street. The dog days were just beginning; the sun beat
down hard and a thin mist hovered just above the softened asphalt.

A woman appeared at the other end, walking with hurried steps on
the left side of the street. She was certainly not a customer. Nevertheless, before each shop the proprietor stepped out and, obsequiously
cajoling, with a smile and gestures that placed the world at her feet,
he would follow her at a respectable distance to the limit of his territory, where another would take over while the first, his duty done,
would return to his post, licking his lips. The woman crossed the
Village in that manner, with a wheedling murmur just behind her
left ear. Did she hope to escape it? She moved out to the center of
the street. She succeeded only in doubling the murmur, for now the
tradesmen on the right side felt that they had the authority to intervene. Yankel narrowed his lips, knotted his brows, and turned toward his son.

"Do you solicit them like that, too?" he asked critically.

"Of course. I have to!"

Already distracted, Simon was preparing to take his turn at the
prey. He rubbed his hands and tried to smile.

"Pfeh!" grumbled Yankel. "Aren't you ashamed?"

"Wait a minute, I'll be right back . . ."

"Will you stay here! You know she doesn't intend to stop!"

"You never know, you have to . . ."

The woman passed by them, accompanied only by the tradesman
across the way. Simon followed her with his eyes as if he were in
love, seemed about to yield to the attraction, and suddenly the current
was cut, he came to himself and sighed.

"Tchch!" Yankel spat with scorn. "You're like a pack of dirty
dogs who line up to pee on the same lamppost. All Jews here, aren't
you? Only Jews could be so . . . so . . ."

"Well, Papa, have you become an anti-Semite?" Simon laughed.
"Don't worry, we have some *goyim* here too, and they're worse than
everybody else. Look, that one across the street, he's a goy and . . ."

"And do you think a woman likes to be pestered without a stop?
If I were a woman . . ."

Good God, Simon thought, what a pumpkin head! He looked his
father in the eye. "Listen, Papa, they know very well what to expect

here! Let me tell you something: They come here to be pestered. If you saw all the bitches that parade by here, you'd begin to understand."

It was almost as hot in the store as outside. Simon offered one of the two chairs to his father and perched himself on a corner of the counter.

"Nu! So how's business?" Yankel began in his slow voice.

"Not bad, not bad!" Simon rejoined, and he rubbed his hands joyfully. What does he want? he wondered. He never sets foot in this place . . . Maybe he needs money?

He knew his father's longwindedness; after two minutes he could stand it no longer and interrupted the discourse in the middle of a sentence.

"Are you thirsty? Would you like a beer?"

Disregarding the protests, he vaulted from the counter and drew a bottle and two glasses from beneath it.

"It's warm, but things are bad all over, eh?"

"Oh stop it!" Yankel was annoyed, and the lines in his face deepened. "Did I come here to drink beer? What a goy you've turned out to be, Simon!"

"I'm what you made me!" Simon shot back, with a wide grin. "To you, Papa!"

"To you, to you," Yankel grumbled ungraciously.

He downed the glass in one gulp, shook his head mournfully, and dried his lips.

"A little more?"

"E-e-eh! If there is any," Yankel muttered.

Simon refilled the glass and perched himself anew on the corner of the counter.

"A cigarette?" Yankel offered it sadly.

Simon whistled in surprise. Papa offering a cigarette to his son! Inciting his son to vice! The old man smoked very little himself and constantly warned his children about the evils of tobacco. The young man jumped down from his perch to take the cigarette, looked right and left for matches while Yankel was despairingly offering his own, and sat down again on the counter.

"Stop bouncing around like that!" Yankel cried in exasperation. "You can't stay in one place; down, up, swing your leg . . . Stay quiet, will you! I want to talk to you seriously."

He paused and waved his hand.

235

"Don't get worked up," Simon soothed. With independence, he had acquired understanding. He waited patiently for what was coming.

"Do you know the Zyssenblatts?" Yankel asked, suddenly.

"The who?"

"Zyssenblatts. You know—the ones who . . ."

Yankel began to define the Zyssenblatt family, through all the branches of its genealogy and its connections with the brother of Samuel Feinschneiders' nephew's wife, who . . .

Simon interrupted. "You have a nephew named Samuel Feinschneider?" What's all this leading to, he wondered.

"Will you listen?" Yankel was annoyed. "You know very well that my sister Sarah, your aunt, who stayed in the Old Country, married a Feinschneider. You know that, at least?"

"Oh, yes," Simon hastened to say. He remembered something of the sort, vaguely.

"Good. Well, your aunt's oldest son, your cousin—your first cousin —is named Samuel. He's married."

"Oh? *Mazeltov!*"

Simon had interjected the Hebrew congratulation without thinking. That unleashed the tempest, and, at first, Simon could see no reason.

"Don't talk like a fool!" his father stormed. "Or are you making fun of me? He's been married five, maybe ten years, who knows? Already he was married when I received my brother-in-law's first letter after the war. At least do you remember that? We didn't know what had become of them, and . . ."

And Simon did remember. First because of the postage stamp on the envelope, from some strange Baltic country, which had aroused the curiosity of the erstwhile stamp collector. Then, because Papa, stirred by this voice from the Old Country and rejoicing at the news that his sister had survived the war, had broken his usual silence and poured out a stream of amusing reminiscences . . . Yes, it had been right after Grandpa had left for Palestine.

"So?" he asked.

"So nothing!" Yankel was irritated. "I was just telling you. This has nothing to do with Samuel, but with the Zyssenblatts."

"Are they cousins too?"

"No, of course not!" Yankel cried, infuriated. "Are you deliberately trying to misunderstand, or what? As soon as it comes to your family, you get stupid!"

"Well, will you get to the point?" Simon was beginning to lose his patience.

"If you let me speak, I will!"

"Talk, talk."

"Well, then, here it is. The Zyssenblatts . . . Stop with your leg!"

Simon yielded, dropped from his perch, and sat down on a chair behind the counter. But just at this moment, in came a customer, and he rose immediately. His father imitated him, even lifting his hat; then he replaced it exactly as before. There ensued a discussion, bargaining, smiles, bowing and scraping . . . Somberly Yankel observed his son in action. What a way to make a living! But, after all, a son is a son, and Yankel deemed it his duty to rush to Simon's aid and back up his sales talk with his own words. The young man withered him with a look, by way of thanks; he didn't like to be disturbed when he was at work.

After the customer had gone, Yankel stated, conversationally, that he didn't think it necessary to be such a *tokhas-lekker* just to sell a hat. Furious, Simon went back behind the counter, sat down, lit a cigarette, and drew a few quick puffs. Yankel fidgeted, ill at ease.

Finally he plunged straight in. "You know, the Zyssenblatts are very nice people!" He nodded energetically to strengthen his statement.

"Yes?"

"Really, don't you know them? The shoe store on the Rue Rambuteau, near the Rue du Temple? . . . No?"

He looked so forlorn that Simon, who had very little rancor in him, took pity and pretended to think.

"A shoe store, you say?"

"Yes!" Yankel cried, and his face lit up. "He has a pretty little daughter, a brunette, neat and attractive. You must have noticed her; she's always in the store . . ."

No, Simon hadn't noticed . . . Wait a minute, maybe . . . A butterball with curly hair?

"Butterball, butterball!" Yankel protested. "She's well rounded, that's all. A woman shouldn't be flat. You and your modern women, all skin and bone, pfeh!"

He completed the sentence with an accordion-squeezing gesture.

"Oho! So you're looking at the young girls now, Papa?" Simon laughed. "I'm going to tell Mama!"

"Oh, don't be a *schlemiel!*"

237

The old man wriggled on his chair and wagged his head, smiling from ear to ear. He looks more and more Jewish, Simon thought.

"She's a fine girl," Yankel, who had recovered his poise, assured him. He raised his index finger to his eye to underline the statement. "She's very intellectual, she has her diploma. Her name is Alice . . . and her parents make a v-v-very good living, I'm telling you. Hmm! By the way, they're having dinner with us this Thursday. You'll be there, eh?"

The old fox! Simon thought. He was at a loss. He didn't want to hurt his parents needlessly. Though he had begun to view marriage without displeasure, he still didn't intend to have his bride chosen for him in the classic manner. At the back of his consciousness old stories of the family began to rise; in the old days, people would marry without knowing each other, without seeing the spouse until the wedding night. No, that must have been before Papa's and Mama's time. How had they met each other? . . . Yankel was awaiting his decision anxiously.

"Thursday. You said Thursday?" Simon murmured, thinking. "I don't think I'm free that evening. Wait, I'll look."

He began to leaf through his engagement book.

"Oh!" Yankel was completely upset. "Listen Simon, just this once, come and have dinner with us."

He hesitated, then bravely took the plunge.

"If you don't like the girl, you know you're not committed to anything. You'll get out of it with an evening's conversation with enlightened, cultured people . . . Oh, don't play the fool!" he added angrily, for Simon was very effectively playing the fool. "You know very well what I mean."

Simon began to laugh. "But, Papa, who told you I want to get married?"

Yankel shook his head to chase off some flies.

"What will it cost you? You'll come, you'll have dinner with us, so? So it's a crime now to have dinner with your parents? Are you annoyed to find yourself at the same table with a pretty young girl? Who knows, maybe she won't like you?" He threw this in with a sly wink.

"Then it isn't worth the trouble of my coming!"

"But I didn't say she wouldn't like you, I said . . . Oh, you always mix me up with your tricks! Come on—what can it cost you?"

Simon was writhing in laughter. The old man spoke again, imploringly.

"Come, then, because it will make your mother happy!"

"Not you?"

Simon was using his cunning to trap the old man into another argument. But his father refused the bait; he suddenly drew himself to his full height and took on his most dignified and severe air.

"If she were a *goya* you wouldn't make such a fuss, would you? Oh, Simon, Simon, my poor boy!" he repeated, in a pitying tone, with a faint smile. He was aware that he had touched his son in a sensitive place and he wanted to take advantage of it. "Anything Jewish isn't worth a straw to you! There's the whole truth."

Irritated and embarrassed, Simon rose from behind the counter and began to pace back and forth.

"What are you going to think of next? Jewish or not Jewish, it's all the same to me! Do you think you're still in Rakwomir?"

That knack the old man had of always putting his finger on the sensitive spots! To hell with all this nonsense! he thought.

With that, he grew angry. "You're always thinking up tricks and traps!" he shouted. "I don't want to get married, and that's the whole story!"

A pause. Yankel's voice was very quiet, as if to underline his statement.

"You can do what you will, Simon; a Jew you are, and a Jew you'll be. Even your nose is a Jew's; it can be spotted ten yards off."

Simon reddened, paled, shrugged his shoulders, stammered something like "But I don't hide it, you have no right to . . ." finally caught hold of himself and marched up to his father.

"Let's get it over with. What do you want from me?"

"Nothing, nothing at all." Yankel sighed, as if at the end of his strength.

Simon made three turns around the shop. Is he going to get out of here or not? he wondered, glancing at his father out of the corner of his eye. But Yankel wasn't at all ready to go; he was waiting patiently for the ripe fruit to fall. Simon forced himself to speak calmly.

"I assure you I haven't the least intention of getting married. I'm too young . . ."

"At your age I was the father of a family."

"We're not in Rakwomir here!"

239

Then his father rose, gripped by real anger, and came toward him as if to strike him.

"Shut up!" he roared. "What you say is as stupid as you are! Men are men everywhere! What do you do? You go to a whore, don't you?"

The word struck Simon like a blow, and he recoiled. And Papa was usually such a prude!

But Yankel's tone had already changed; the customary wheedling had returned.

"That isn't any good, Simon. Jews are clean people, Simon, and you shouldn't. And have you thought about the diseases?"

Simon, racked, didn't know what to say. Yankel waited for a moment; then, in the voice of a man concluding a bargain:

"So you'll come, eh?"

When he gets a notion into his head! . . . Simon raised his arms to heaven. His father waited, hat on head, cane in hand, ready to go as soon as he had the Yes in his pocket. Simon had a bright idea.

"Suppose I come," he began.

A satisfied smile lit Yankel's face.

"I've told you it won't be any use. Then what will happen? The girl—"

"Her name is Alice." Yankel was specific. "Alice Zyssenblatt."

"Alice Zyssenwhatever, all right—have you considered what she's going to think when she gets home?"

Yankel spread his hands, palms up, tilted his head and frowned. "What do I know? Let her think what she likes, it's none of my business!"

"But you don't understand!" Simon exclaimed impatiently. "The poor girl will be waiting for the next move, and there won't be any. She'll be hurt and humiliated, she'll think I found her ugly. It's not a pleasant position for a girl to be in—thinking she's been turned down. Think of it!"

Simon had never worried so much over a young girl's feelings. He wondered whether his father, always so sensitive, could find an answer to that argument. It was very simple.

"Alice doesn't know why she's coming. She's just like you."

Simon whistled, "Wheeeew!" and hurried on to say, "All right, all right, I'll come!" He had already decided not to.

Being a good son, he came anyway. Alice Zyssenblatt was a pleasant girl. Neither ugly nor beautiful, she had a clear voice, a ready wit, and a great deal of assurance. To his surprise, Simon found himself thinking she would be a very efficient mistress of a shop. She spoke French as well as he did and, like him, didn't seem to know any Yiddish outside the usual expressions. They enjoyed flirting with each other while the four Yiddish-gabbling parents beamed approvingly. Simon came away delighted with her; if he had met Alice by chance, he might have pushed the affair further. But he begged off when the Zyssenblatts returned the Mykhanowitzki's invitation. His parents told him afterward that Alice hadn't been there either; M. Zyssenblatt had announced her absence at the very moment that M. Mykhanowitzki was going to tell him of Simon's. For a while Simon felt a bit put out. Then he forgot the whole matter.

After Alice Zyssenblatt, his parents arranged meetings with Leah Krugelstein, then Helen Levine, Arlette Rabinovitch, and many others. The manner of introduction would vary, but always as a result of a happy coincidence . . . Thanks to the *shadchans,* the marriage brokers, of the Rue des Rosiers, the Mykhanowitzkis even dug up some French Jews, whose Yiddish was less aggressive and whose names were less outlandish: Meyer, Cohen, Aron. In vain; Simon proved unyielding and ended by growing angry and threatening to make a scene.

Now he had good reasons for it.

For a long time he had felt cramped in his shop in the Village, a shop that he disdainfully called a stall. Oh, he made a good living there—nothing to complain about on that score. He even had some cash in reserve. Only he didn't like having cash in reserve. Money must work or be spent. And while he was having a very gay time he knew, being a sensible young man, that fun wasn't everything. He wanted a real store, if for nothing else than to keep the cash at work.

Naturally you just don't let go of a good business. Simon would keep his stall in the Village, just in case; but he would put a manager in charge.

The main question still was: What should he sell in his future real store? Women's wear, of course. But a respectable store isn't a flea market, and it demands some specialization. Simon still hesitated: ladies' hats or costume jewelry? If he obeyed his whims, he would have leaped into jewelry immediately, because it was pretty, shiny, and clean, and because Uncle Moishe also sold jewelry, while the thought of hats evoked poor old Papa. All the same, he was wary of

his whims; he knew himself. Hats are solid; costume jewelry has its
ups and downs, unforeseen styles, changes of mood; it's fun, but
risky. Simon liked change and danger, but he was no daredevil and
wasn't at all anxious to have his neck broken. Feeling that he wasn't
yet able to come to a decision, he told himself there was no hurry;
and he kept gathering information.

One evening in a night club he noticed, around the neck of a tart
he'd picked up, a necklace of little fragile iridescent spheres that he
thought very pretty. The longer he looked at them, the prettier they
became. They reminded him of the agates he had dreamed of in his
childhood, or of the soap bubbles he would blow out the window of
his father's workroom.

"That's pretty!" he exclaimed.

The girl smiled and ran the beads over the tip of her finger. He
leaned over to see better. In the harsh light the nacreous beads glittered prettily, so light, so appealing, so airy. He had never seen anything like them. They weren't in style.

"What are they made of?"

"How should I know?"

"Would you let me see them?"

It never took Simon long to become familiar with anyone, especially women; right to the point, that was his method.

"Can't you see them well enough like that? You've got your nose
in them!"

The girl was annoyed. She had thought he was using the necklace
as an excuse to look down her dress.

"Come on, show it to me!" Simon pleaded, childishly eager. She
refused. The more he asked, the more stubbornly she refused. This
aroused his curiosity even more.

"At least tell me where you got it!" he cried, with his usual heed-
lessness.

"It's a family heirloom!" she grumbled, probably just to get rid
of him. She unhooked the necklace and slid it into her purse. Only
then did Simon realize that he had a tasty morsel under his nose and
remember his duty.

He didn't like being stalled. Only because of the necklace he saw
the girl again, and more often than he would have liked. But he
never saw the necklace again; she had stopped wearing it. He tried
his cleverest stratagems. It was labor lost. He ended by wondering
whether the necklace wasn't truly an heirloom. So he asked the girl

where she came from. On different occasions he learned that her father was a French colonel, an English lord, a Danish baron, and that she had been born in Lille, Saragossa, and Milan. He let the whole thing drop.

Meanwhile he conducted a thorough inquiry among the costume-jewelry houses. No one in Paris seemed to know anything about it. He searched with even more zeal, convinced that he had a gold mine there; once the style was launched, the girls would flock to buy.

In the end, it was an old craftsman who put him on the trail. A pearl necklace that was iridescent this way and that? Oh, yes, he remembered, and his younger daughter Yvonne certainly remembered because she had a girl friend who . . .

"Oh, but that isn't in style any more, Monsieur Simon."

"Not in style? Then it has been in style?" Simon was taken aback. "Was it long ago?"

If recent, you couldn't bring it back so soon. But a very old style, forgotten long ago, could be something; camouflaged as a novelty, it might sweep the country. Too bad! The fashion for necklaces of iridescent glass was just past; it dated from the war, or a little before, but its greatest vogue had coincided with the coming of the Americans. At one time, in fact, such high wages were offered that Yvonne had thought of giving up the artificial flowers for the fish scales.

"Fish scales?" Simon was at a loss.

"Yes, they paste the scales on beads. It's strictly a job for girls. . . . Look, Yvonne, since Monsieur Simon's so interested, why don't you give him your girl friend's address? She would know all about it."

M. Simon was not very interested any longer; a business complicated by fish scales couldn't be very profitable. Still, since he didn't want to hurt anyone, he carefully made a note of the girl friend's address. Then he thought no more about it.

Rather, he thought he didn't. But it kept gnawing away in a corner of his mind. Why the big vogue? Why the sudden drop? With his bulldog stubbornness, Simon couldn't bear to lose sight of it so easily. He decided to settle the question; after that he would be at peace.

Mlle. Jacqueline Saulnier, Tartre-Épisse Road, Virelay (Seine-et-Oise). Probably an old maid gone to seed, like Yvonne. Simon thought there might be some fun ahead with these fish scales. And then, Seine-et-Oise was out in the country. Simon had just bought his first car, a secondhand Unic, and he ought to take it out for a ride. He took a sheet of business stationery with his letterhead (SIMON, WOMEN'S WEAR, A House You Can Trust) and in a flourishing handwriting wrote a flowery letter to Mlle. Saulnier:

MADEMOISELLE:

I have been informed that you possess an altogether exceptional skill in the manufacture of glass bead necklaces, a business in which my firm, specializing in costume jewelry, has, at this time, a very keen interest. Your esteemed friend, Mlle. Yvonne Chauvet, with whom I have had a close business relationship, has assured me that I could write to you in complete confidence.

In view of this recommendation, I should be greatly obliged to you if you would have the kindness to communicate to me, confidentially and for reasonable indemnification, whatever information you may have on hand. This is, of course, without any commitment on my part.

Despite the limited time at my disposal, I should not hesitate, if the matter seemed susceptible of further development, to go out of my way personally for more ample information.

In the expectation of a prompt reply and with anticipatory thanks, please accept, mademoiselle, my sincere salutations."

Simon reread the letter and, satisfied with its impressive yet courteous tone, signed it, his initials twisting a half-dozen times around his name and carrying a few extra flourishes to foil any would-be forgers. He added a stamp for the reply and, whistling, sealed the envelope.

Virelay, Virelay, where is that hole?

The reply he received a few days later was disappointing. In two or three sentences on a sheet of copybook paper Mlle. Saulnier explained that she had stopped blowing glass beads several years ago but that she could, if M. Simon so desired, put him in touch with several old countrywomen who still kept up that work. Sincere salutations.

The cool tone of her letter piqued Simon. Although the iridescent-bead business seemed less interesting than ever, he sent her, by return mail, "in reply to your gracious letter of the 18th inst.," a notice that he would be out to see her the following Sunday. Besides, the Unic was rotting away in the garage; it would be a place to drive to.

Simon couldn't drive without a destination. He liked riding, but the idea of driving for pleasure had never occurred to him. A goal, a destination that you reached as quickly as possible by the most direct route, and there you were! Usually it would be an inn in the suburbs, or a house for intimate parties, that a friend had described as sensational and not to be missed, it was absolutely necessary. There were also the famous places that every up-to-date person should "do." Simon "did" the Vaux de Cernay and feasted at Barbizon. For the rest, hardly would he have set out before he wanted to arrive; hardly arrived, before he was off again. He enjoyed good food but became itchy if the meal lasted longer than a half-hour. As for the famous places—you could see them just as well from the car, without stopping. The Unic rolled along merrily, always loaded with his friends of both sexes, since Simon could not bear being alone. Even when he took a tart along for a weekend, he couldn't stand being alone with her except in bed; the rest of the time there would be another couple, dragged along to keep the conversation lively.

This time he was going on a business trip. No friends, then. Should he take the family along to get some air? . . . Easy, easy! he cautioned himself. He still had a horrified memory of the only automobile trip he had offered his parents, and he didn't want to go through that again; he knew only too well what would happen. Papa wouldn't stop playing the philosopher about the wonders of nature and its possible Author and human ingenuity; then he would grow angry because Simon wouldn't admire the countryside and would think only about speed; then he would offer to pay for his share of the gasoline. All this in French. Mama, for her part, would be screaming in Yiddish, "Simon, you're going too fast, Simon, watch out for that car over there. Oh, may the Evil Eye be averted!" No, no, not his parents. He would go alone. After all, business is business.

It was summer. With the top down, Simon became intoxicated with the feel of the wind ruffling his hair (as a true sportsman, he always drove bareheaded). It was a clear fresh morning, the sun glittered in the blue sky, and the car breathed along the road with a gentle humming like a kiss. The trees whistled on either side as he fled past. With his left arm resting on the door, Simon drove like a king of the road. Forty-five, fifty, fifty-five on the speedometer! The speedometer was wrong, as he well knew, but he was moving, anyway. Once outside Paris, he filled his tank. Now he was his own master unless he had a flat or a breakdown. Really, he said to himself in surprise, it isn't so bad to be alone for once, and it impresses the people on the road. . . . At the same time he decided that the business of the beads wasn't worth a tinker's damn. Foolishness! The whole costume-jewelry game was foolishness; women's hats, that was the sure thing.

The connection between these various thoughts seemed so weak to him that he wondered for a moment whether he wasn't becoming a little odd. Luckily, just at that moment a flock of fowl appeared under his wheels. He gaily bumped a couple and tossed some joyous insults to the clodhoppers at the side of the road who were shaking their fists at him. . . . As soon as he was at the wheel, he was a changed man and treated every pedestrian like a drooling idiot, if not worse.

He had some trouble finding Virelay, took the wrong road several times, and had to ask his way of the yokels. One of them absolutely insisted on knowing where the traveler came from before he would tell him where to go. He seemed convinced that your future route depended on the past. All this made Simon very happy. Wasn't it amazing—a few miles from Paris and you were in the sticks? . . . Finally, after a stretch of rutted roads and even cross-country, he suddenly broke out into the open air, it seemed, at the edge of an abrupt precipice. Insensitive as he was to landscapes, he gasped at the sight and stopped the car. Beautiful, oh so beautiful! he said to himself. And so near Paris!

Before him, as vast and waving as the sea, a forest gamboled all the way to the hills on the horizon. At the base of the precipice, a leap away, it seemed, so sheer was the drop, the Seine stretched, lolling comfortably in its wide bed. It seemed happy to lounge in this countryside, and not at all in a hurry to leave. With a slothful, maternal indulgence, like the sensuality of a fat woman, it took those thickset stumpy barges and graceful little sailboats to its bosom. Above, in the immense emptiness, swallows swooped and cried, very high, level with Simon. This must be something like the mountains, the young man thought. He knew only the sea—or what he called the sea, the casinos of Trouville, Cabourg, and Tréport.

The Unic's motor purred gently. Good! Now where is this Virelay? Toward the left, 'way down, at the mouth of a dry valley which cut through the precipice perpendicular to the river, a village nestled; a church, a cluster of roofs with old mossy tiles, and, scattered here and there among the meadows, some farmhouses. If you wanted a quiet place in the country, this was it. Here and there a few summer homes were set at the edge of the plateau. Those fellows have a wonderful view! And land must be pretty cheap here . . . An idea began to trot around in Simon's skull: to buy some land, build a weekend house, a boat on the Seine, fishing . . . For Simon, the same restless Simon who couldn't stand still in one place, was mad about fishing and able to sit motionless for hours at a time watching the bobbing of a float. A businessman's plans were also buzzing in his bonnet: An unknown place, but with a future, once people get more cars. All it will need is for the roads to be improved and there'll be one of those real-estate booms.

Carefully, foot on the brake, he drove down the hill. It was steep, not so steep as it had seemed from above, but steep all the same. . . . With a sigh of relief, he finally found himself in the village. The car bumped along between scaly walls and hovels falling into ruin. You wouldn't have thought from above that so many houses had been abandoned. But here and there some people, mostly old, came to their doorsteps and watched the car with cowlike eyes. Simon stopped.

"The Tartre-Épisse Road, please?"

He addressed an old man who was sunning himself in front of his door. The old man reflected before answering. At last:

"Whose house are you going to?"

What business is it of yours, thought Simon; all the same, he replied amiably that he was looking for Mlle. Saulnier.

"Which one?" the old man grunted.

"Which one?" Simon echoed.

"Aye! Baptiste's daughter or Charles's sister?"

This was said with crushing scorn; how could anyone be so ignorant?

"I don't know!" Simon was at a loss. "The one who lives on Tartre-Épisse Road."

The old man shrugged his shoulders as if to close a futile discussion.

"Tartre-Épisse is over that way." He pointed toward the Seine.

"I want Mademoiselle Jacqueline Saulnier," Simon called. He had just remembered her first name. The old man reddened with anger.

"I understood, I'm not deaf! I already told you that way. Baptiste's daughter! You have to know what you want."

Simon hastened to thank him, excused himself, and left in a rush. Who would believe it?

From door to door and from limping dotard to crafty urchin, he finally arrived at a rather handsome building whose façade fronted

247

on the towpath. Along one side a narrow little alley attacked the cliff perpendicularly. Could that be Tartre-Épisse Road? There were no street signs on the walls. Simon stopped the motor and climbed out of the car. A thickset man was standing before the door of the house, his hands in his pockets and a pipe in his mouth. He was in shirt sleeves and vest but he wore a black felt hat, probably to protect his head from the sun. Simon donned his most charming smile and walked toward him; the man watched his approach without moving.

"Mademoiselle Jacqueline Saulnier, please?"

Taking his time, the man removed his pipe; he must have been about forty years old and was massively built. Next to him, Simon, in spite of his pose, felt very small and very young.

"Oh, so you're the costume jewelry!"

What a greeting! Simon was speechless.

"Come, then!" The man added, and without having taken his hat off or offered his hand he turned on his heel and went into his house. Before Simon's eyes, his vast back bulged, rippling with muscles. The young man followed mechanically, still upset by the greeting. A courtyard. A farm, he thought vaguely. A paved walk, a well, flowers along the wall, on the right a garden, a corner for vegetables, some trees, one of them covered with roses. A tree bearing roses? That's peculiar, Simon thought, in spite of his ignorance of horticulture. No, it can't be a farm, there aren't any cows around. . . . At the end of a chain, a large watchdog was strangling itself barking.

"Shut up!" the man scolded, but without any anger. The dog stopped barking immediately, dropped his ears, and went back into his kennel.

"He seems intelligent," Simon ventured, trying to be friendly.

The man didn't think it worth a reply and set off again toward the house. This fellow's not very obliging! thought Simon. Who could he be? He acted like the master of the place. Earlier the crotchety old man had said "Baptiste's daughter." This must be Baptiste. Simon was preparing to have a good laugh out of this adventure when he suddenly remembered the Unic was all alone outside. Do you suppose one of those stupid bumpkins would hurt it? Nothing could be easier than to let the air out of the tires or to put some sugar in the gas tank. You never know what these morons can dream up! He cast a glance behind; the car was still there, undisturbed in the shade.

"Don't worry, nobody's going to eat it!"

Simon started and turned just in time to catch the fleeting smile.

248

Baptiste had opened the door of the house and was standing aside—yes, even he!—waiting for the visitor to please to enter.

The house was dark and cool, in contrast to the court burning in the sunlight. Then Simon made out several people, two women and a man. The head of the house placed a chair at the long table in the middle of the room.

"Sit!"

The young man obeyed sheepishly. He had expected to have a good time, laughing at some more or less crackbrained old maid, and here he found himself face to face with a whole family whose silent stares were making him most uncomfortable. He forgot all his poise and his usual glibness. It was actually the first time that he had entered a French household. The only French people he had known up to now had been men out for a good time, loose women, and manufacturers at business lunches. Well, Simon, Simon Mykhanowitzki, son of Yankel, son of Avrom of Rakwomir, what do you think of the French?

The man seated himself, as head of the household, opposite Simon at the other side of the table.

"So you're the costume jewelry!" he repeated pensively. He obviously thought his visitor wouldn't understand his meaning, for in a moment he added, "The women's wear!"

Well, now, how long is this going to go on? Simon wondered. He grew warm under the collar. He had regained his wits now and his eyes had grown accustomed to the dimness. He had known plenty of these yokels in the regiment; he knew how to handle them.

"That's me!" he replied rudely. And then, exaggerating his Parisian accent, "That would make you the potato, eh?"

The man thought for a moment and then, without the shadow of a smile, "I grow potatoes for pig feed. You want some?"

This was followed by a guffaw. Simon wasn't proud, he laughed, too. Then the peasant said loudly:

"Jacqueline! Come quick, quick, quick, the gentleman is very, very busy! He said so in his letter, didn't he?"

The ox, Simon thought. When the younger of the two women came closer he rose and extended his hand; she took it after a moment's hesitation.

"Delighted, mademoiselle!" he cooed in his most engaging tone. He couldn't help putting on the charm in front of any woman.

She blushed, mumbled something, and quickly withdrew her hand, which he was holding too long. He noticed that her bodice was well filled; he liked healthy bosoms, even though current taste dictated that he go out with flat-chested women only.

"Sit down, daughter," grumbled her father. "Your mother will serve, since the gentleman came to see you. The gentleman is very, very busy," he repeated with his heavy irony, "but surely he'll take something with us?"

"As a matter of fact," Simon replied, ostentatiously, consulting his watch (he was trying to re-establish his prestige), "I have an appointment at six o'clock . . . But he'll wait!" he hastened to add with a smile, and, having regained his volubility, he began singing the praises of country living. He was directing his speech to the daughter, but her father spoke.

"Well? Mirabelle? Cerise? Cassis?"

Simon felt the scorn in his voice but knew no reason for it.

"Whatever you're having," he replied good-naturedly.

"Oh, me, I leave liqueurs to women and Parisians! I drink wine from my own vines."

"Well, I'll be happy to try some," said Simon, still the good fellow.

The trouble is that a male yokel in his forties and his young yokel daughter can't be handled with the same methods. At the same time rude as a game warden to the father and well-mannered as a man of the world to the daughter, Simon was engaged in complicated but useless acrobatics, for the two techniques canceled each other. Nevertheless, he was beginning to feel at ease now, and he might have been completely happy had it not been for the uneasiness he felt about the Unic. He had established the relationships between the Saulniers who were present: the father, Baptiste; the daughter Jacqueline; the mother, who was called Catherine; and last, the big dumb ox, who must be Jacqueline's younger brother. Sitting well back in his chair, Simon held forth, feeling that he was one of the family. Fine people, in spite of their crudeness. Hearts of gold! They're honest, open, not like those rotten characters who . . . Simon was given to quick enthusiasms. Besides, he had completely forgotten the reasons for his visit. Baptiste had assiduously filled the large tumblers of wine for the men while the women were sipping their little glasses.

"Well, what do you think of my wine?" Baptiste asked. "It's only home-grown wine . . ."

"Wonderful," Simon, who was no connoisseur, declared.

"It's a bit young yet—" Baptiste began.

"It's this year's, isn't it?" Simon interrupted.

Baptiste looked at him and at his son; the two men guffawed; it was July. Simon realized he had dropped a brick, but where? Things of the earth, you know . . . On the spot he changed his tactics. He had found out long ago from experience with simple people that there are only two things to do: master them or put yourself completely in their hands. So, without losing any of his good humor, he took refuge in ignorance.

"I'm a fool, eh? You know, we Parisians . . . Well, to your health!"

There it was—the peasant seemed to be conquered. Simon swam in happiness, he felt that he was the best friend of all the world, felt like exchanging congratulatory backslaps with his honest Baptiste who had become so friendly, who kept filling his empty glass.

"Hey! Gently, gently! I have to drive back to the city!"

"Don't be afraid, it's light. To your health!"

At the same time, Baptiste, seemingly unintentionally, out of ordinary politeness, kept dropping odd little sentences, vaguely questioning.

"So you're the boss . . . So young to be able . . ."

After each sentence the voice would be hanging, to call forth a reply.

"And so you're from Paris . . ."

"Oh, yes!" Simon was feeling very happy. "A dyed-in-the-wool Parisian, the real thing, born in the Fourth Arrondissement . . ."

He stopped dead. A dyed-in-the-wool son of Yankel of Rakwomir, that's what passed for a Parisian. Suddenly he began to envy these people who called themselves Saulnier, an ordinary name like everyone else's, who could speak of their father and their grandfather, could go to Mass or touch iron when meeting a priest, who had their own land, who . . .

Meanwhile, Baptiste was nodding respectfully; a Parisian isn't just anybody! And in his slow, rasping voice, he kept the conversation going, complaining about the hard times, especially for farmers, with the drought and all. "Oh, I can't buy a handsome car like yours; it's expensive, isn't it? . . . You Parisians roll in money, especially the businessmen, although the taxes . . . Oh, those bandits, it's a dirty shame!" Simon finally realized that this "stupid" peasant was pumping him dry and had a very lively interest in his financial affairs. What business is it of his? he thought. He tried to change the subject

251

but Baptiste forestalled him; either he knew enough about him or else he was a mind reader.

"We talk, we talk, and you so busy! After all, you didn't come to see me. Go ahead, I won't say another word."

He filled his pipe. As if it were a signal, the mother and son disappeared and Simon found himself face to face again with the girl. Her father turned his back but didn't leave. The young man tried to recall that wonderful business of the beads and felt at a loss for words. His embarrassment must have been obvious, for Baptiste took his pipe out and said dryly:

"Excuse my interrupting you again, but you can get on with Jacqueline. Between you and me," he lowered his voice for a man-to-man communication, "she studied bookkeeping at school and she's been a secretary to some big shots. Watch yourself, I'm telling you; when it comes to business she's worse than a Jew."

Bang! said Simon to himself, as the sentence struck him full in the face. It wasn't the first time that he had received such an insult. Unfortunately he wasn't obviously Jewish. His hair was straight, his nose only slightly hooked, his mouth not thick-lipped, he didn't walk toes out like a duck, and he wasn't any shorter than most Frenchmen. He couldn't walk around all the time carrying a sign: *Caution! Jew! Unpleasant remarks strictly prohibited!*

The whole Jewish business annoyed him immensely. He had only one desire, to be like everyone else, and usually he felt like everyone else; Jew or not, what did he care about all that? That was for Papa! Yes; but from time to time a barb would stick into his skin. It was verbal anti-Semitism in its kindest form that would remind him most often of his origins, that would keep him from being "like everyone else."

After a while, he had developed a technique of reply. When a goy, not knowing with whom he was dealing, would exclaim, "What a Jew that man is!" Simon would reply automatically, "Worse than a Jew, an Auvergnat. I paid plenty to find out . . ."

If the word "Jew" was replaced by the word "kike," then the situation became more delicate. Usually Simon would let a little time go by and then would slip into the conversation, "I'm of Jewish origin myself . . ." The remark would invariably elicit the response, "Oh, I know some very fine Hebrews! Take, for example . . ." As for the expression "Jew-bastard," he had never heard it but he would certainly have been greatly upset by it.

The stupidest thing about the whole business was that other Jews never mistook him. How many times had Simon been stopped on the street and questioned in Yiddish! This irritated him almost as much as the unintentional insults of the *goyim;* he didn't find it very pleasant walking around with his origin stamped on his face. People are stupid. What difference does it all make? You are what you are, and since there's nothing you can do about it . . .

In truth, for Simon, the Jewish problem was reduced to some questions that were as annoying as they were useless. The only one that interested him deeply was posed by circumcision; did women like it better when their lovers had foreskins or not? He had discussed it often with his friends and even with girls he had picked up. No decision.

What was he going to reply to old Saulnier? He had allowed himself to be taken by surprise, perhaps because of the young girl's overflowing bodice, and his usual reply would have come too late. Oh, the hell with it, I don't give a damn for these people! I'll never see them again! Let's get down to business.

"Mademoiselle has been a secretary?" he asked politely.

He had spoken to the girl; once again her father replied.

"And not for just anybody! Would you like to see her references?"

Simon didn't give a hoot for her references. But Baptiste was already running toward the buffet—what a hurry he's in! He seized a bundle of papers, and stuck them under Simon's nose with appropriate commentaries. He's bragging about his merchandise! thought the young man. This fellow's worse than a Jew! Satisfied with his silent revenge, he wondered what Baptiste was leading up to. Jacqueline here, Jacqueline there. Mlle. Saulnier was certainly something, at least to her father.

"So Mademoiselle isn't in farming?"

The father again. Wouldn't he ever shut up?

"In farming? With her diplomas? I'd hate to see her dragging around in the manure like her parents."

Simon couldn't understand this fellow. . . . First he gives me the coldest of greetings, and now he confides in me. It's true that in the interval there's been a little questioning on the visitor's financial position. What does he want from me anyway? Has he had too much to drink?

Oh, no, Baptiste hadn't had too much to drink, in spite of the glasses of wine. He knew very well what he wanted. He gazed straight into Simon's eyes and repeated, tapping the papers, that his Jacqueline was pure gold, and when he wanted he would find her a position in Paris. All at once Simon understood. Nothing for nothing! The information about the beads in exchange for a position in Paris for Jacqueline! Oh, you dirty kike! Simon didn't care about the pearls now, but he loved to do favors for people, he would go to no end of trouble for anyone. Fine! He had a friend who was looking for a salesgirl for a dress shop. He mentioned the fact to Papa Saulnier, who replied softly that he would have to see, there wasn't any hurry, thank you very much, only too kind, but he made a note of the address, asked for a note of recommendation, that's always of use, waited until Simon had written it, read it, slipped it into an envelope, slipped the envelope into his pocket, and only then turned to Jacqueline.

"Well, why don't you tell this man about the beads? How much time do you think he has to spend on us?"

After that he didn't open his mouth until he accompanied the young man to the door with ceremonious politeness and surprising courtesy.

Jacqueline didn't talk much. She didn't have to, for every word she said was directly to the point. After a half-sentence of stammering because of timidity, her voice grew firm and unhesitating. Simon, whose greatest faults were not listening, interrupting at any point, and throwing himself into the midst of the most closely knit reasoning, was struck dumb. People who speak only to say something and shut up when they finish are rare! Believe me, they're worth listening to. Simon listened, questioned, and replied intelligently and thoughtfully. He felt at peace, and it was a new feeling for him and a very agreeable one. He didn't even think of watching the girl's bodice. He watched only her lips, lips made for speech, not kissing. Oh, well, he thought, this is a young lady, not a tart!

He had had his fill, and more, of tarts. After a while they all grew tiring. The chattering, the way they paint their mouths, their cheeks, their eyes, and the way they look the next morning! As for Mlle. Saulnier, ah! She wasn't painted; the rose on her lips was her own. Simon felt so much respect for Mlle. Saulnier that he didn't even undress her in his mind, he who couldn't see a nubile girl without imagining her in bed. A real young lady, a pure young girl (and Simon didn't realize that he was using his father's exact language). If it happened that the young man's look strayed in the direction of

254

that well-rounded bodice, immediately a little pang of conscience would remind him of his duty. Before such a well-bred person, a man must behave as a gentleman should. For Mlle. Saulnier didn't try to arouse you, certainly not. She didn't force her beautiful bosom under your nose as so many others did. You would even have said that she was ashamed of it, because her pink dress came all the way up to her throat. Simon's enthusiasm, one of his habitual enthusiasms, which for a time deprived him of his critical sense, kept him from noticing other evidence: that Mlle. Saulnier, in spite of her modesty, had nevertheless made herself up in honor of the important gentleman who was paying her a visit; that her toilette wasn't of a very Parisian taste; that brilliantine, perfume, rice powder, and curling iron hadn't been forgotten; and that her lips, while not smeared with an aggressive red, were protected from chapping by a transparent layer of rosy pomade. If, in the company of his pals, Simon had run across the girl in the village street, when she was clothed in her pink dress and covered with her straw hat, he would have thought of her as a peasant in her Sunday best and might at best have added: "Boy, did you see the pair on that one!"

But here, in this cool, quiet intimacy, far from the harshness of the summer light, the true values forced themselves upon him. The stream of time flowed unhurriedly between the girl's calm words and the tick-tock of the clock. The wood of the table gleamed, warm and alive, old as the countryside. This was the earth, stable and strong, where human order reigned, where each object, each being, felt at home. At home, completely at home, Jacqueline Saulnier took its most profound riches from her earth. In offering hospitality to this stranger, she was revealing herself and revealing her earth.

In a confused way, Simon felt all this. He had seen very few Old Masters, but before such a portrait of a Madonna or of a housewife by an old French or Dutch master he would have cried out, "Look! It's Mademoiselle Saulnier." The resemblance was only in the light within.

Meanwhile, the low-voiced conversation went on. Questions, answers. The bead business? There had once been a little factory at Virelay; all the young girls worked there before their marriage to increase their dowries. What did they do? Well, they blew beads. Is it difficult? Yes, very. In fact, very delicate. Did it pay well? Not too well, girls' work, you know. Did the beads have a good sale? Oh, yes, until the crash. What crash? Well, when they came into style with the Americans, the boss wanted to expand and he built a big factory somewhere else. Then he went broke. As a result, many of the local girls turned bad.

"Let's see, first a boom and then a crash?"

"If you want to put it that way," the girl said. "Although actually there was more to it than that. You see, the quality of the beads had gone down because they were made on a large scale. Our pearls were never etched with acid and they didn't burn the skin . . ."

These technical details bored Simon.

"It's all over now?"

"No, I told you so in my letter. We're back to the old way, that's all. Many of the older women are still working on the beads in their homes. Would you like me to take you to Mother Bru's?"

She had already risen; Baptiste too. Displeased at being snatched so soon from his bliss, Simon protested, "Oh, no, it isn't worth the trouble!" But he soon caught hold of himself and, more voluble than ever, he explained that the bead business no longer seemed very "consequential" to him, but that was all right, he would go to see Madame Bru just the same, if only to please Mademoiselle Saulnier; and you're never too old to learn, eh? and rest easy, Monsieur Saulnier, what I say is so, the salesgirl's job is as good as hers; if you didn't take care of your friends, then . . .

Baptiste accompanied them to the street. Simon took leave of him absently; he was interested only in the effect the beautiful Unic would have on Mlle. Saulnier.

Mlle. Saulnier said nothing. She was satisfied with a sidelong glance at the car. Simon, vexed, began prattling all over the place. She walked beside him, murmuring only a word or two from time to time: "Not here . . . It's near. No, to the left . . ." He noticed that she was small, smaller than he had thought when he had seen her seated. She wore very high heels, thin as matchsticks, and once she turned her ankle because of them, even though her ankles were rather thick. An idea sprang into being in Simon's mind and sped across it at full speed: With us Jews the women are often tall and the men small; with the *goyim* it's just the opposite.

He, Simon, was five feet, six inches tall. Without her high heels, how tall would Mlle. Saulnier be?

The visit was over. He climbed back into the Unic and started it with a noble gesture of farewell to Mlle. Saulnier. Oh, what a good girl the Unic was; the motor caught at the first try.

256

He sang Mlle. Saulnier's praises all the way home. The closer he came to Paris, the more extravagant they became. He spent the night with one of his usual girl friends; as a result, by next morning Mlle. Saulnier ranked even higher in his mind. At nine o'clock in the morning he called his friend to back his written reference with a few personal words; he knew how fleeting his enthusiasms were, and he wanted to keep his word to the Saulniers before he forgot it.

This time, to his great surprise, he didn't forget. Of course, his enthusiasm cooled a little in the following days, and the picture of the matchstick heels and the thick ankles was annoyingly sharp in his memory. Nevertheless, for over two weeks he had no desire to see any of his girl friends; the last one had left a bad taste in his mouth.

It must be said that in the beginning, for many praiseworthy reasons, he gave quite a bit of his time, materially and mentally, to Mlle. Saulnier. First—could he do any less?—he sent her a telegram informing her that she had been accepted and urging her to take the opportunity without waiting. He followed this with a letter to clear up some important points, especially the promised salary—for Simon knew his friend well and he was capable of all sorts of dirty tricks. After he received a reply forty-eight hours later, Simon's role seemed at an end. The young man thought that the thanks he had received were rather cold and was convinced that he had blundered somewhere. He sent another letter—what you don't do for nice people! "Have you found a convenient place to live? Don't hesitate to call on me; I have a great many acquaintances who . . ." Simon really thought that the distance to Virelay was so great that the girl would be obliged to live in Paris. And a young girl in Paris is exposed to such terrible dangers. This time the reply took a week in coming and was plainly cold. "Thank you, there's a train. I go home every evening." Simon tore his hair. What's wrong with her, what has she got against me? The purity of his intentions kept him from realizing how suspect was his eagerness.

Then he decided to go see her. Wasn't he her protector? Didn't he have certain responsibilities toward her? He feared only that he wouldn't recognize her; his memory refused to bring back the girl's face. Her ankles, her bosom, her walk, her height, he remembered them all. But as for her features—nothing!

If he had gone to see the girl the next morning, perhaps his imagination, satisfied, would have sought someone else. But he put off his visit from day to day. As a result, for over two weeks he thought about nothing but Mlle. Saulnier. Every morning, while he was shaving, the idea would suddenly come to him; he would snap his fingers. Damn it! I must go see her today! He didn't know why he had to; he felt he did. Every night before falling asleep, he would suddenly start: Another day gone and I haven't seen her!

He really did have a great deal of work to do. Immediately after his trip to Virelay, he had made some important decisions that he felt had to be made. There was no connection with Virelay, of course; at least he thought so. It dawned on him that the Swiss Village stank in his nostrils. He was through with this flea market; he'd had enough of digging in that hole! He wasn't an Arab peddler—he wanted a real business. And no more nonsense with costume jewelry. Ladies' hats, that was sure and clean.

Without waiting any longer, he rented a store on which he had had his eye for quite a while, on the Boulevard Beaumarchais. He liked this section of the city; elegant and at the same time near his middle-class customers; in short, ideal for business. Even more, it was back-to-back with the Jewish quarter, which gave him a certain feeling of security. The deposit being a considerable sum, instead of installing a manager at his shop in the Village he sold it outright. And good riddance!

And now to work! No skimping on this score. You have to thrust yourself forward in full view of the customers. Money draws money. Painters, electricians, plumbers, and masons began working busily so that everything would be ready in time—by September 1, the opening of the fall season! They had plenty to do. The preceding store-keeper, an old artists'-supply merchant who had retired, had let the place fall into disrepair. The store dated from the Flood, with its flaking paint, its pillars which upheld nothing, its nooks and corners, and its back room. Out, out, throw it all out! Modern, modern! Air, gaiety, light, youth! What's the use, in the twentieth century, on a busy boulevard, of keeping a show window divided into rectangular panes? One large sheet of plate glass, that's what it needed!

The alterations were costly, the more so since Simon, to speed up the workers and keep them on their toes, didn't hesitate to slip them an extra bill or two, following a time-tested method. He tapped his friends, tapped Uncle Moishe, even tapped Papa, and signed notes to his brother-in-law Rechnowitz. As usual, Papa raised his arms to heaven, prophesied catastrophes, and advised him to sell the car before going into debt. Sell the beautiful Unic? First, its price would be only a spit in the ocean, and then a car shows that you're somebody, and besides, you live only once! Meanwhile the work went on, and a gay calico banner floated in front of the store: LADIES' HATS. OPENING SEPTEMBER 1. OUR PRICES CAN'T BE BEATEN!

The only remaining problem was to find these ladies' hats. The stock from the Village was not enough for this new store, and starting shabbily was out of the question. Simon went hunting. What could be simpler than buying on consignment? Didn't he have a good reputation in the Parisian market? He was turned down a few times and finally realized what was wrong; people were wary; they had seen too many of these brilliant openings which led only to profitable bankruptcies. He summoned all his resourcefulness in an effort to strengthen his credit. He showed himself all over town in his beautiful Unic, deliberately spent a little too much money, and plugged up one or two holes with a great deal of noise while digging others, larger and less visible. In short, with a great deal of trouble he finally succeeded in building up a stock. He knew that he was walking on a tightrope; he had to run fast to keep from breaking his neck. Now, if things went badly, so much the worse. Plenty of people have made their first big haul, thanks to a nice little failure. He didn't go so far as to wish for one, but he faced the possibility without too much distaste. In fact, he wasn't proud of himself; he felt that his eyes were bigger than his belly. He had gone too far to back down . . .

In all this hurly-burly, Mlle. Saulnier had slipped to the back of his mind. At the same time, she had become the symbol of those virtues of order, prudence, and honesty upon which, at the moment, he was trampling so blithely. Simon reserved his feelings of morality for her; he would keep his commitments to her to the letter. What those commitments were he didn't know; but when, one evening, he found himself in the neighborhood of his friend's dress shop, he turned aside and, with pounding pulses, entered the store.

His fears were vain; he recognized Mlle. Saulnier immediately. She had changed, though; for the better. Her white salesgirl's smock, against the black of her dress, set off her magnificent bust. A little rouge, a little powder; under the dazzling electric lights her hair had golden glints. She was busy with a customer, so she was smiling and the gleam of her healthy white teeth animated her face. Simon's heart was torn by jealousy. He realized that his friend had dressed her, taught her, made her over. She tossed him a quick smile without leaving her customer; he waved and turned away; you mustn't interrupt a business deal.

His friend was in his thirties, tall, soft-spoken, and so good-looking that the ladies wanted to swallow him. What if he's already had her! Simon was thunderstruck. He looked over at her, to find out. How can your eye pick out a virgin from one who isn't? Simon felt that a heavy responsibility had been placed on his shoulders. Poor old Papa Saulnier, what a blow it would be to him to learn of his daughter's dishonor! He'd have a heart attack. If that dirty dog has done it, he'll answer to me, Simon swore, growing angrier by the second.

The presumed dirty dog came over. He wasn't Jewish, but he had rubbed against so many Jews in his business that he had become more Jewish than the most Jewish Jew. Simon had to restrain himself in order to chat with him in a friendly manner. How's business? Are you satisfied with your new salesgirl? . . . After a few minutes his friend said, as if it were the most natural thing in the world:

"I suppose you've come to see Mademoiselle Jacqueline."

And immediately he called:

"Mademoiselle Denise! Would you take over for Mademoiselle Jacqueline? . . . He winked slyly at Simon, said "Good luck!" and went off without giving him time to protest.

The evil-minded dog! Simon felt his face grow red.

Mlle. Jacqueline didn't seem at all happy to leave her customer. Damn it! I forgot she's on commission, thought Simon. What of it? If it weren't for me . . . He went over to her as she was coming out from behind the counter, and he had time to admire the curve of her hips underlined by her white smock, but not time enough to lower his eyes to the too-heavy legs. Anyway, he suddenly remembered that he had always liked women with heavy legs; everyone knew they were better in bed. Immediately he called himself a dirty-minded dog, he too.

"Well, how have you been?" he asked warmly, in too loud a voice, to disarm the suspicions of the gallery, and he shook the young woman's hand in a friendly fashion.

Her reply was quick and her hand immediately withdrawn but it took more than that to unseat Simon when he had an audience. He took Jacqueline's arm and drew her into a corner.

"Well? Are you happy, little one?"

"Very happy, thank you," said Jacqueline calmly, and she disen-

260

gaged her arm. And you, monsieur," she added quickly, "how is the bead business?"

"The beads, ha, ha!" Simon laughed loudly. "That's an old story! Now . . ."

With a torrent of words, he explained, with appropriate gestures, what he was doing, poured forth all his hopes and fears—or only a part of his fears, the honorable ones. As he spoke a marvelous panorama of the future unfolded before him, took on colors and grew larger; he had a fertile and optimistic imagination. She listened politely. Inebriated though he was by his own eloquence, he noticed that she was glancing at every customer coming in. Oh, yes, the commission! Why, the peasant! After all I've done for you, is that the thanks I get? Furious and hurt, he interrupted himself and grumbled:

"I keep talking and boring you with my stories . . ."

"Not at all!"

She had replied unhesitatingly, firm and clear. That warmed poor Simon's heart, but what warmed it even more was that Mlle. Saulnier drew near (Simon felt the warmth of her breath) and whispered:

"Only you speak too loudly, people are listening."

"Oh," he cried, delighted. "I haven't any secrets. Well, I hope everything goes the way you want it to . . ."

She was already extending her hand. He took it, shook it, and held it.

"Can we dine together one of these days?"

"I'd like to."

She took her hand away calmly. Simon couldn't bear feeling that someone was holding out against him. Safeguarding his dignity, he forced a good-humored air.

"Then it's all set? Call me on the phone and we'll arrange a little something."

He was very proud of his newly installed telephone; he recited the number and then scribbled it on the flap of an envelope which he gave Jacqueline. She took the piece of paper and thrust it carelessly into the pocket of her smock.

"You won't lose it, will you?"

"Don't worry."

He waved his index finger in the air with a queerly supplicating look.

"Will you come to the opening?"

261

"I'll try. Or perhaps I'll phone."

He went out of the store irritated and entranced. The moving fold of the white smock between her breasts was in his mind's eye, but the coldness of her voice was still in his ear.

That same evening he went to a night club and picked up a tart. It disgusted him even more than the last time and he began to dream of kissing Mlle. Saulnier's neck, yes, her neck, she had a beautiful neck, white and firm and as straight as a column. In the store Simon hadn't paid any attention to it, but the image had remained fixed in his mind. Have I fallen in love? he wondered, surprised and uneasy.

As for the young girl's face, it remained blurred.

The first customer to present herself was one of the neighborhood streetwalkers. Simon couldn't have been happier: whores brought good luck. No, he wasn't superstitious, only he knew from experience that when you have one of them you have them all. Paulette sees Simone. "Oh, that's a charming little hat! Where did you get it? How much did it cost? Oh, that's not expensive!" And you see them pop up one after the other.

And this neighborhood was really crawling with them, not the cheap kind you found around the Bastille or the Halles. Not as high-toned, of course, as the Champs-Elysées variety, but they had style, a certain chic. They didn't drag themselves around with their pimps, and they were discreet in their soliciting. A good clientele; all their money went into clothes.

The girl came in swaying her hips. Just out of habit; she wasn't working. There's a time for everything. She stood in the middle of the handsome new store while Simon hurried about, darting to and fro, chattering, joking, trying this hat and then another . . . "A brunette like you, madame, this is what you need, just your type, madame, Spanish . . ." She hardly answered. And yet Simon flattered himself that he knew the species. Since he was absolutely determined to make the sale, he gave the girl a large discount, and off she went, carrying her hat. She seemed satisfied, but something was wrong somewhere. What was it? Simon reflected and then understood.

A real store in a good neighborhood isn't a stall in the Village. In the Village, the merchant finds himself, so to speak, on the same level as his customers; they come to gossip a bit with him and they're only looking for an excuse to open the tap of their secrets. Here, they're looking for something else: respectability! They want the tradesman to act like a gentleman and to treat them as ladies. Nothing in the world would make them pour out their little stories to him, all the things that are sticking in their gullets, the pervert who wants them to do this and that, so that they have to call M. André to throw him out. But Simon had his theory on this question: No secrets, no friendship; no friendship, no steady customers. What should he do?

I need a woman in the place, he decided. Yes, with a woman they'd thaw out quickly. Simon could see them already, pouring their stories into a feminine ear: "As one woman to another, men are such pigs . . . Oh, if you only knew . . ." Should he hire a salesgirl? A salesgirl he could trust? Little Saulnier, for example?

He thought for a moment. Let's say business goes well. Good. I hire a salesgirl. Let's agree that she's the most devoted in Paris. It's still only a day's work to her, and then good-bye. In the best of circumstances she'll agree to lend an ear to her customers' unsavory stories; but only one ear, not two, and certainly not her heart. What do you want? She's there to make sales, not to listen to a lot of filth. But what these ladies want is a heart, not an ear. (Without considering that it wouldn't be fitting for the pure Mlle. Saulnier to be on friendly terms with whores.) You need a woman who's been around. Now Simon realized why a tradesman worthy of the name couldn't remain a bachelor. Only the boss's wife can take the place of the boss.

He had never meditated with such intensity. Customers came in, he spoke, smiled, sold or didn't sell, they went out, and he picked up the thread of his meditations. There's plenty of slack time in a store and you have to fill it. In the Village, between customers you'd stand in the doorway, you'd solicit, you'd gossip with your neighbors; you were never alone. Here, soliciting was out of the question, as was gossiping with the neighbors. So?

So Simon, leaning against the door jamb, his hands behind his back, watched the parade on the boulevard. In the end, it soothed him and he plunged back into his reverie. He went back inside and read the paper, but a paper isn't inexhaustible, and the reverie began again. Simon found this very tiring, even more tiring since money worries stubbornly kept cropping up, and he had to drive them away and substitute more agreeable images. After a while, he noticed that all his thoughts, by whatever road he took, led to marriage. Marriage, marriage . . . He snorted unhappily. He was too young to put his neck in the noose. You live only once. I won't deny that later, in my thirties . . . To have children, like everybody else; children are fun . . . Oddly enough, he had never thought of marrying for money. And yet, what else had Uncle Moishe done?

Shortly after noon he became edgy. Mlle. Saulnier had promised to telephone. She was able to call only at that time of day because of her work; either then or in the evening. Twelve-five, twelve-ten . . . Was she coming to see him? Twelve-twenty, the phone rang! He threw himself at it with beating heart. A woman's voice . . . No, only that big pumpkin of a Rivka, looking for news. "So how's it going? Are you satisfied? Here's Chaim." (In private, she called her husband nothing but Chaim, never Henri.) Now it was Chaim's turn to ask, "So how's it going? Are you satisfied?" And Simon had to be friendly to this little fat Rechnowitz, who stank in his nostrils, because he had signed notes to him. Maybe Mlle. Saulnier was trying to call him right at that moment and was finding the line busy . . .

During the afternoon there were other phone calls, from Uncle Moishe and from friends. "So how's it going? Are you satisfied?" Simon awaited the evening impatiently. Toward evening, bang! In came Papa and Mama, in their Sunday clothes. "So how's it going? Are you satisfied?" Simon kept an ear cocked for the phone. If only she doesn't call now! . . . "What did you say, Papa? Clara's sorry she couldn't come? Yes, I understand . . ." For the next five minutes, he was swamped under his father's moral advice. But no telephone. Papa and Mama left and in came the sententious Fernand. "How's it going? Are you satisfied?" Simon tried his best to be friendly; a brother is still a brother. But he had nothing to say to him. Fernand was just a simple cabinetmaker. It wasn't worth the trouble of having passed through the Boulle Trade School. If I were in Fernand's place, with that diploma, what wouldn't I do? Without being especially moved, he learned that his younger brother was leaving for his military service in October. Well, so long, nice of you to have come. They had stopped embracing each other a while back; now they simply shook hands.

And that girl hadn't shown any sign of life! Furious, Simon realized he was dying of fatigue; he felt he had been running around in a cage all day. And this was only the beginning. Was all his life going to be like this? A shiver ran down his spine. There was no question about it, running a shop was a woman's job. To begin with, how would he ever get together with his jobbers? You had to go out once in a while, go shopping around, the telephone wasn't enough. And his beautiful Unic—should he have it stuffed?

All at once, he had a brilliant idea. Why shouldn't he make his hats himself, while the salesgirl, or rather, his wife, ran the shop? Direct from producer to consumer; no need to give any profit to the wholesalers. That at least was a man's work. Wonderful plans began to take shape in the young man's fertile mind. All he needed was money, and you can always scrape some money together. Somewhat comforted, despite Mlle. Saulnier's betrayal, he treated himself to a good meal in a neighborhood restaurant; at noon he had eaten in the back of the store—a can of sardines, two fried eggs, some canned peas warmed on an alcohol lamp. He surprised himself by thinking, Tomorrow I'll cook myself a little stew. Or should he have the restaurant send something over? But that would be expensive.

No question about it, he needed a wife.

Mlle. Saulnier did not appear the day after, nor the day after that. She's angry, thought Simon sadly, without knowing exactly why she was angry. He felt heavyhearted; such ingratitude . . . Well, back to profit and loss!

The next day, he was at grips with three customers at once (these women arranged it so that they came together and then he would be alone for hours), when the phone rang again. Damn it! he thought, it's too much. The telephonic toy had lost its appeal. It would have to come out.

"Yes? Who is it? Oh, it's you?"

It was she. He stammered for a few seconds. What a strange voice she had on the telephone! Not at all like her own; at once hesitant and coarse, and so shrill that he had to hold the receiver away from his ear. And with that, there were endless silences that he filled as best he could. "It was kind of you not to have forgotten me. What's become of you?" He couldn't visualize her through the instrument. What's wrong with her? he wondered.

Besides, he was annoyed. All the while he was discharging wide smiles into the telephone, all the while he was showing his happy heart to the blank wall, he had not lost sight of the three good women who were pawing through the hats with savage glee. He was furious. A hat can't be handled like a loaf of bread; you must use your fingertips, with professional delicacy. He would always arrange it so that, without annoying the customers— "Allow me, madame?"—

he never let them touch the merchandise themselves. So, although he felt extraordinary pleasure at Mlle. Saulnier's phone call, he broke it off abruptly.

However, as soon as he had hung up the receiver, he was sorry. All day long he dragged around a vague remorse. Since he didn't like feeling gloomy without a reason for it, he put the blame on the stew he had warmed for his lunch. But things were no better the next morning. What a life! he thought, as he raised the shutters of the store. The weather was gray and sticky, every one of the passers-by had a long face, and the Madeleine-Bastille bus rattled the windows on every trip. Can't they use pneumatic tires instead of solid ones? . . . Simon took refuge at the back of the store, feeling like a wretched prisoner caught in a trap.

The morning dragged on endlessly. At noon he forced himself to eat a slice of ham with some pickles; and he whimpered; Good God, can't I even close this stinking box for lunch? He hesitated to do it; sometimes there were customers at noon. But today, as if by agreement, customers stayed away. What then, was his whole life to be the shop, the shop, the shop (he no longer said the store), mornings, evenings, Sundays, holidays? To hell with it! He stuck a notice on the door, janitor-style: "Back in two hours," ran to the pastry shop, swallowed two giant napoleons full of cream, and afterward, at the bistro on the corner, threw down a coffee and rum. He came back, a little warmer, and it began all over again, not even a cat, an empty, empty life. At five o'clock, as much to give himself some courage as to attract the roaming dogs, he lit all the lamps. Some wretched reflections trembled on the blackish slime of the sidewalk, and that was all. Good God, when I think that it's only September! . . . At half past six, he held out no longer. So much the worse, I'll lock up the box, let it go to the devil, I'm going out for a walk!

At once he felt sprightly again. Wasn't the world wide! And there were girls everywhere!

Wide the world, no argument there; girls everywhere, certainly; who doubted it? And yet—the most willing girls couldn't twist a look from him, the groups of loafers threw him into a rage, and he rushed straight toward a very particular point in Paris, in anguish lest he arrive too late. In fact, he realized that he had to see *her,* in short, to clear up, with *her,* all the silly misunderstandings that were keeping them apart. Would he go into his friend's shop? He certainly would not! He couldn't bring himself to undergo the dirty innuendos of that boor, and the amused looks of the other saleswomen; his own appearance would displease *her,* when *she* saw him in front of everyone, joking and free and easy to the audience, all broken up inside. He would lie in wait for *her* at the exit (the shop closed at seven o'clock), he would feign surprise at such a happy meeting. And then they would see!

Because of all the weeks—an eternity to Simon—that Jacqueline Saulnier had filled his mind, he was no longer able to call her Mademoiselle; and out of respect for her he didn't dare to use her first name, even in his thoughts. So he didn't use her name. *She,* that was enough to define her.

He got there too early. More than ten minutes to wait; he spent them, tongue hanging out, in cruising through the area, very much interested in a window display, walking twenty yards away, returning, passing back and forth in front of the shop. He posted himself on the sidewalk opposite, to see the saleswomen leaving, and didn't dare to go too far away, not knowing which way *she* would go. Through the brilliantly lighted plate glass he saw white smocks moving about, and his heart leaped when he thought he recognized *her.* At two minutes after seven he began to curse that dog, that exploiter who kept his saleswomen past their time.

Across the street, a group of three or four girls emerged, chatting and prattling. Simon began to tremble, and then he recognized *her;* she was laughing, she dared to laugh, rosy and fresh, in the midst of her friends. He saw only her.

And yet, to tell the truth, even though he was looking at her, he didn't see her. He had always been unable to describe the slightest detail of her face exactly. He saw her actions only, a gesture, the swell of her bosom, the wave of her hair. He felt faint with happiness. Think of it; he knew a young lady! A young *lady,* note that; not a girl. And she was there, just opposite him. Who would believe it? What had he done to deserve such luck?

She hadn't seen him, she was walking away arm in arm with a friend. Light as a wolf, he stalked through the passers-by on the opposite sidewalk, without losing sight of her. The two girls were babbling gaily; yes, his too! As though they could have anything to talk about! he said to himself, rage in his heart; he felt betrayed. Some men were passing, sullying her with their hateful stares. A little more, and he would have leaped at their throats. He didn't think for a moment that she could receive their admiring glances without displeasure, even wanted them, perhaps; or quite simply that she could flirt with other young men, any young man. He felt that he had always known her; he was convinced that she knew him as well, and only him.

Ah! At last! Her friend had decided to leave. She quickened her step. Simon followed her; he wanted to get ahead of her, cross the street, and meet her coming toward him, so that their meeting would seem really accidental and unplanned. Just luck, that's all! And now, there he was!

"Oh! What a happy surprise! I wasn't quite sure . . ."

He was still panting, from the race and also, perhaps, with emotion. But he thought he had acted out the scene perfectly. He would have been greatly surprised if you had told him that he didn't know how to lie. *He* didn't know how to lie? Why, what did he do all day long in his business? And all those stories that he invented with such laughable ease? True, but this was something vital.

She blushed. With pleasure, completely! She extended her hand daintily and stammered in a low voice: "Why, Monsieur Simon, I never expected . . ."

He choked with happiness; with pleasure, too, for she had been so cold until now. Her sturdy hand was warm in his, and she didn't withdraw it. The passers-by jostled them. Simon, radiant, was stuttering; then he caught hold of himself. But he had already forgotten to play the part of an important businessman. He was no more than what he was, a young man face to face with a girl. Simon and Jacqueline, Jacqueline Saulnier and Simon—no, not Simon Mykhanowitzki. Not that barbarous, ridiculous name. Just Simon.

When, at Virelay, Simon had appeared to Jacqueline for the first time, he had dazzled her.

When she heard his car's motor from afar, she had hidden herself behind the blind of her bedroom window. She was expecting to see a dusty, fifty-year-old man, a little bald, a little paunchy, with a small beard and eyeglasses, one of those businessmen of whom she had met some samples in her lifetime. Instead a shining youth had appeared, Prince Charming in his carriage, Rudolph Valentino in his sports car; he soared from his car, and with a winged, aerial, dancing step he crossed the street. Happiness, wealth, youth, mirth, grace—he had all the gifts! King Solomon in all his glory. The sky was blue, the sun shone, the chrome of the car sparkled, and the poor country girl felt herself so unworthy. . . .

However, Monsieur Simon proved to be very friendly. There wasn't a trace of haughtiness in him. He sat in the dim living room, and, fallen from heaven, he chatted and joked with these coarse peasants, nice enough not to make them feel their awkwardness. Jacqueline suffered at seeing her father conduct himself so clumsily before this refined, delicate, handsome young man. Finally, Papa went outside and she found herself alone, her throat a little tight, before *him*.

She noticed immediately that M. Simon's eyes rarely held hers, but when they did they held them too long; and they seemed more willing to caress her mouth and her throat, especially her throat. Poor Jacqueline grew weak all over, and very flattered, for M. Simon must be quite a connoisseur of beautiful women! And he had the grace to find her pretty—an ordinary country girl, with neither elegance nor wit! After he left, she realized that she was bored to death in her village.

She had placed no stock in the promises that he had made her, nor in his word of recommendation. Papa was naïve if he thought that a piece of paper was worth more than a word. Jacqueline knew her Parisians; two or three jobs as secretary or typist had enlightened her. M. Simon is an important man; he has many irons in the fire. What do we mean to him? Oh, if that business with the pearls had worked out, of course, but obviously it wasn't going to work out. . . . Finally, to please Papa, she agreed to try the effect of the letter of recommendation. She was just going to take the train when she received M. Simon's telegram. She was stupefied by it and a little uneasy. Why was M. Simon showing so much interest in her? The next morning, a letter. Three days later, another letter, in which he offered to find a place for her to live. Aha, now I see what you're driving at, my good man. She was willing enough to allow herself to be dazzled by this Prince Charming, but not to the point of falling head over heels for him, of acting stupidly and of everything which would follow. Only in the movies did princes marry country girls, and bosses their typists; in reality, they made them pregnant, kicked them out, and the girls wound up on the streets. Jacqueline meant to keep her head until she was married.

This didn't keep her from liking to flirt with the boys. Naturally she had had some lovers, but never below the waist. When one of them would prove too enterprising she was quick to slap. To tell the truth, none of the boys she knew had pleased her enough so that she wanted to tell him, "If you want any more, arrange it with the mayor." She hoped that one day one would appear, but someone new, someone worthy. A Parisian, for instance; not too handsome—handsome men are dangerous!—but none of these Virelay oafs.

M. Simon was out of the question. He even frightened her a little; if she let him come near her, would she have the strength to defend herself? She wasn't made of wood, and M. Simon was so attractive. Well, it would be better to cut it short at once; good day and thanks. It was flattering enough that this gentleman had shown some interest in her. Thus she would preserve an agreeable secret in the corner of her mind, very comforting in those days when her husband, the children, the household drudgery, would all seem unbearable to her. Then something like: Oh, if I had wanted to, I could have . . .

As long as he was Prince Charming, she hoped for nothing at all. But one hateful evening she saw before her a fatuous character who had the gall to humiliate her in front of the whole shop, the customers, her fellow workers, her employer, by putting on airs as her protector, her proprietor. Oh, how she detested him that evening! She swore to be avenged. She was burning to meet him again, of course only to put him in his place; not in the shop, where she wouldn't feel at ease, but anywhere else, no matter where. In the street, for instance. And if he dared to answer back . . . ! And then she would imagine the scene.

She had plenty of time to imagine it; for a long while she heard no mention of him. But she guarded his phone number as if it were precious. The opening of his shop would be September 1. In any case, for courtesy's sake, she would be obliged to show herself; she had not forgotten the service he had rendered her.

The closer the appointed day approached, the more nervous she became. Yes, the telephone frightened her. She had never used that apparatus; the two jobs as "secretary" that she had held had not included its use, and she wasn't going to humiliate herself so far as to pay him a visit. On the first of September, she walked courageously toward the post office to telephone and then fled at the last second. She managed to convince herself that she was acting like that for the sake of her dignity and to punish him. It was only after three days that she agreed to lift the punishment, and she needed all her courage. Oh, how well she was repaid! He greeted her like a weasel in a hencoop, little as she deserved it. Good, I'm through with that one, she told herself later, at once furious and relieved.

This was the moment that he chose to surprise her on the street. She had thought she was well armored, but when they met she didn't even have time to realize what was happening before she felt herself overflowing with happiness. Her armor? What armor? And to protect herself from what? She was threatened by no danger; life was opening before her, simply, naturally. She didn't even think of asking herself whether she loved this gentleman. She was satisfied just to see him, and he was no longer merely "a gentleman."

Of course she knew that he had come only for her. He stood there before her, sheepish, embarrassed, timid, feverish, at her mercy. A child, she thought; and she forgot any idea of scolding him.

"May I accompany you for a while?" He begged for it as if it were a crust of bread. Where would she have found the courage to refuse him?

"And your new shop?" she asked. "How is it going? Are you satisfied?"

"Oh, yes."

She felt that he was uneasy. That reassured her. From the moment that he showed his embarrassment, he lost his loftiness and stopped being unattainable. And thus she was able to put him at his ease, quietly and gently. He shivered with pleasure and suddenly invited her to dinner. She refused because she was rushed enough, what with the trains . . .

"Oh, don't worry about the trains. I'll take you home in my car."

"In a car?" Jacqueline was shocked; what would people think? He, always very obliging, saw nothing shocking in it. He knew nothing of the sensation that his visit had caused in Virelay. "A Parisian, a car, and it is not for Baptiste that he has come, it is for Jacqueline, old man Bertault Onésime told me that Baptiste had told him . . ." Then a telegram from Paris, from the Parisian; the postmaster had gossiped, the Parisian was named Simon; and Jacqueline was now working in Paris. "Oh, there's something shady here, there's never any smoke without fire, those Baptistes, I've always said it, there's nobody in the world more proper, and their stories about pearls—Mother Bru told me that the Parisian had no use for the pearls, but he had use for Jacqueline, he was devouring her with his eyes . . . !" Naturally, in the Saulnier family they were used to this sort of gossip. "All this," Baptiste would say, "only comes from

271

jealousy; all you can do is wait for it to blow over." This did not keep her father from listening to it, and even making use of it from time to time. When Jacqueline told him of M. Simon's visit to her boss, he growled that he would drag that seducer away by the ears, if he kept coming back. Finally, little by little he subsided, but Jacqueline held off telling him about her own phone call. So now if she came home in M. Simon's car, with everyone watching, there would be a scene. No, no dinner tonight.

The face that the poor boy was making! Jacqueline couldn't resist him. "Some other day, if you like . . . No, no, not tonight!" But, after all, why not tonight? It would be wonderful to dine in a restaurant at least once, to be served, adored, instead of eating the eternal soup in the family dining room, with Papa-Mama-Ernest who either never said anything or else abused you. I'll tell them that I went to the movies with my girl friend. Besides, what of it! I'm grown up, I make my own living! What spice would there be in a rendezvous if your parents knew about it? . . . Tomorrow? No, not tomorrow! She clung grimly to her refusal. Then Sunday? All right, Sunday. Till Sunday!

Altogether, they had seen each other three times; but with letters, phone calls, quarrels and reconciliations, and daydreams, they felt that they had known each other for years.

Jacqueline came home with her heart singing. She was considerate to her mother and surprised her by humming while she was scrubbing the pots.

"What's his name?" Her father tossed out the question slyly.

"What?"

"Your lover, damn it! You're as happy as a thrush tonight!"

Before she had time to think, she answered: "Simon, of course! Whom did you want it to be?"

Her father jumped up and then understood; she was joking. So he played along—he liked to tease with his daughter.

"Go on, that's his family name, not his first name!"

True. What was M. Simon's first name?

"It's also his first name," she threw back. "His name is Simon Simon. What have you got to say about it?"

Baptiste hadn't expected that. Simon Simon, that was very good! He slapped his thigh and guffawed, using the time to search for a retort. Finally, he grew sarcastic about people who lack imagination in their choice of names. And so it went until her mother whistled and scolded: "Have you two finished talking nonsense?" Ernest had gone to bed; the bickering annoyed him.

When Baptiste caught hold of a subject for raillery, he didn't let go of it easily. It became a bore in the Saulnier household. Every time Jacqueline went out—and she went out more and more often—her father asked her to say hello for him to Simon Simon. Still, Baptiste began to worry. He was sure there was a lover somewhere—not *that* Simon, of course; that one was forgotten, set aside, buried. But who? Let's hope she isn't doing something stupid, he said to himself. Clumsily, he tried to warn her. Poor Papa! Jacqueline thought, remorsefully, when she had the time. And she continued to hide the true Simon beneath Simon Simon, only too happy to be able to lie by telling the truth.

"He must be a Parisian," Baptiste confided to his wife one evening. "Even so, I'd like to see his ugly face. The little one is sensible, as far as that goes. But this has gone on quite a while . . ."

And it really was going on. The time flew by; Jacqueline was light-headed, Simon felt he had grown wings. They saw each other every day now. Jacqueline, who had two hours for lunch, formed the habit of going to Simon's every noon; she would prepare a good dinner on the alcohol chafing dish. They also arranged to meet every evening, after work. As for Sundays—too bad, you lived only once, the creditors wouldn't die of it—Simon began to close the shop from one to five. Earlier would not have been good, because of people coming home from Mass; later, because of the idlers who would begin to grow tired and would finally decide to go into the shops instead of drooling over the window displays. But from one to five, let's live! From five to eight, Jacqueline wisely stayed at the back of the shop. Afterward they would go to a restaurant, then to a movie.

They were very chaste. Simon hadn't even dared to kiss Jacqueline on the neck, or anywhere else; for her part, Jacqueline, although flattered and troubled by such an excess of respect, nevertheless felt a sweet security in it. She felt her trust in him grow deeper, little by little, and she entrusted herself completely to her companion. In silent agreement, they had given up the horrible titles Monsieur and Mademoiselle; but since each of them was waiting for the other to invite the use of first names, they didn't use anything, which was a nuisance.

They risked their tenderest gesture in the movies; they held hands. One evening, Jacqueline's head seemed to grow heavy, as though sleepy, and came to rest on Simon's shoulder. Pleasantly disturbed, he murmured, "Jacqueline," almost to himself, and the step was taken. Three days later, he was cooing "Jacqueline" at every chance, and he asked himself uneasily why she never used his first name to him. He asked himself first and later asked her.

"But I don't know your first name," she replied. "You never told it to me."

"What? Don't you know that my name is Simon?"

"Isn't that your family name?"

"My family name?" He stuttered, stammered, blushed, paled. Good God, I can't call myself Dupont, the way everybody else does. Bravely, he took the plunge. Here was the final test! And, posturing, he threw it out:

"My family name is Mykhanowitzki!"

He didn't swallow any of the syllables; instead, he accented their strangeness. However, he didn't dare look at her; he heard her gasp of surprise.

Just as well to settle the whole thing at once. "That's the way it is, my little Jacqueline; I'm a foreigner! My-kha-no-wit-zki; there it is!" He spelled it out for her. "I was born in Paris. But my father was born at the back end of Russia . . ." No, no hiding! No Russia! If she was anti-Semitic, it would be better to know it now. "I'm really a Jew. Does that bother you?" He drew himself up to his full height and stared her right in the eye.

Did that bother her? No; yes; a little, in one way. More than that, it stunned her. Here is a young man whom she's been meeting for quite a while, who is pleasing to her, and who looks like everyone else—normal, and she thought he was, and with one blow, bang! the personality explodes—Russian, Jew, Somethingwitzki—and here before her is a total stranger, who doesn't resemble anyone. First, why had he waited so long to reveal his secret? Hadn't he trusted her until now? Or was it such a shameful defect that . . . Jacqueline didn't understand. Russian, Jewish, Somethingwitski, all right; he is what he is, he can't do anything about it. So? Why did he have such a look of suffering on his face? Jacqueline had heard talk about Jews, certainly; but she had never met one; to her eyes they had almost a mythical existence, that of jokes and clichés; if anyone had told her they were Negroes, she might have believed him. At bottom, she asked herself suddenly, what difference does it make to me? But she had scarcely put the question when her thought carried it, with one leap, very far forward. Oh, yes! It would make a great deal of difference to her! She knew very well that her relations with Simon would not stay very long in their present delightful balance, that soon . . . My future husband? The question flashed out like lightning.

The two of them were standing face to face in the dining corner; they had been ready to leave for the restaurant when the discussion had started, and since then they hadn't dared to move. Simon heaved an enormous sigh, and his nostrils quivered. Why does everyone dislike Jewish noses? thought Jacqueline. My Simon hasn't got a hooked nose, but a handsome, straight, and intelligent one, a little long, perhaps, but Papa also has a long nose, and even more hooked than this. My poor Simon! Jacqueline's heart filled with tenderness. With a quick gesture, she clasped the young man's hands.

"Simon, what's happened to you? Let's see a smile!"

He grinned oddly and seemed ready to burst into tears. Oh, no, no! Without letting go of his hands, she searched for something consoling to say. What a baby he really was!

"What difference does it make to me whether you're Jewish or Chinese? First of all—" (she had just vaguely remembered her catechism) "aren't Jews and Christians related?"

"Then you like me just the same?" he stammered, in a small voice. "Because, if you don't—"

"Oh, how stupid can you be?"

She pretended to be angry; and since, in the dining corner, they had to be close together, they didn't know how it came about, but they found themselves kissing. When they drew apart they stared at each other with shining eyes. "Madame Mykhanowitzki!" Simon growled, with a clownish salute. "Will it bother you too much when you're called that?"

In ordinary times, there was no human being more home-loving, more peaceful, more distrustful of novelty than an inhabitant of Virelay.

Nevertheless, now here, now there, a white blackbird would be born into the village, a strange one whose memory would remain ever green, surrounded by admiring terror. So it was that in the fifteenth century, a Saulnier had had endless quarrels with his overlord; in the eighteenth, a Bertault had been hanged with Cartouche's band; in the nineteenth, a Bru had fled to America, having got the police captain's daughter with child. No family had any monopoly of these crises; in proof, during the great Revolution the entire village had boiled collectively. Nevertheless, each family preferred to place the mystery on the backs of its neighbors, and the Brus accused the Saulniers, the Saulniers the Bertaults, and the Bertaults the Brus of having always had a queer streak.

Baptiste's father, old Joseph, was a remarkably quiet man; therefore he had been elected mayor. The only originality with which he could be reproached lay in his extreme propriety. His dooryard was always well swept, his animals well groomed, and he had had the front of his house replastered. He had also shown some initiative at the time of the Phylloxera crisis which had ruined all the winegrowers, the better part of the village; it was he who first had thought of developing market gardening up above on the Plateau. In short, everything about him was praiseworthy.

Why then did his eldest daughter, Eugénie, get the idea of becoming a nun? And not even a nun in France, but with the savages down in Madagascar! Did she have a queer streak? Suddenly people began to look sideways at Baptiste, in case the streak was contagious. And Baptiste, although a proud man, hewed to the line, tried to live like the others, and succeeded without too much trouble.

Only once had he been tempted to break loose. It was during his military service, when his regiment had been sent to the Midi. Fifty years later, Baptiste still remembered the shock that he had felt when he arrived there, and he never stopped talking when he got started on that subject. What a country, oh, what a country! Yes, the land is bad, I agree, and their wine is water. But there's the sun, and it's beautiful everywhere, and the people are friendly, and the women— ah, the women!

The women, and especially one woman. She was named Jeanne, and she was a postmistress. Jeanne Espontieu she was called, and when Baptiste pronounced her name (inside him, for he had never revealed it to anyone in the village) he always did it with a bit of southern accent. Oh, he would gladly have married her, his Jeanne! Only he was engaged to Catherine Vacquaire, and when, on his return to the village, he had told his story to his father, the old man had complained: "But the farms, Baptiste, the farms! They're adjoining, my boy, and when they're together with one owner . . ." In fact, Catherine did own some land on the Plateau which would round out the Saulniers' farms admirably. Nevertheless, Baptiste held back

276

a little, because the girl didn't please him. Then the old man had taken him aside. "Listen, boy, there's a time for everything. You can always have yourself a spree." And there it was. "One soul and one flesh," the priest had proclaimed; "and one big farm," Baptiste had added to himself, chuckling.

Afterward, he had followed his father's advice and had "broken loose." Not often, but often enough. The good thing about Virelay is that it isn't a village like others. Paris is a stone's throw away, and on the river you could see boats pass from all sorts of countries. Sometimes they would stop, and you could talk with the people on them; you could learn things. From time to time a foreigner would settle in the village. Oh, not the Parisians of the Plateau; they held themselves aloof, that was another city up there. No! but that family of sailors, the Van Truc de Trucs, Flemings, who have settled here at the edge of the Seine. That changes your ideas, eh? A beautiful woman, by God! Big, blond, buxom. Not Jeanne's sort, Jeanne was black like a Negro, and deceivingly slender, but you need variety. The blood has to be renewed or the race perishes. We aren't the only ones on earth. There are others, and no more foolish than we. Oh well, you can't always stay with your feet stuck in your own mud. If you do, you stop being a man and become an animal.

When Baptiste got started on this subject he didn't lack for arguments. Where had he got them? Doubtless from the newspapers of the time when he was meeting Jeanne; for Jeanne was educated, and he had tried to raise himself to her level. In any case these ideas were his very own and it was in their name that he buried the "stick-in-the-muds" with his scorn. These "stick-in-the-muds" with their noses always on their own church steeples. He, Baptiste, thanks to the market gardening, had some connections with Paris; he participated in the world's advances; in brief, he had a queer streak. Just enough so that he could assume the leadership of the villagers without disturbing them.

He had always dreamed of more. Not for him; he was finished. For his children. Unfortunately, nothing could be done with Ernest, that mother's son, but Baptiste had found an echo in Jacqueline. She had gone to school, and now she was working in Paris. No stick-in-the-mud for her. What he hadn't had the courage to accomplish she was going to accomplish for him.

Jacqueline would have been very surprised to learn that her Simon was a substitute for a Fleming or a southerner. Actually it was by chance that she loved him. If she had known from the beginning what he was, perhaps she would have distrusted him more. Anyway, once the shock of the revelation had passed, she began to paint her lover in all the colors of far-off romance; he became again her Prince Charming, come from the other end of the world to choose her, a poor girl among so many others. He, on the other hand, found in her that stability, that peace, that reconciliation with the world for which his whole being clamored. The human plant needs to root itself firmly in the soil to reach its full development; but when it has remained there too long, it feels its degeneration approaching and tears itself loose to move away, to renew itself. Jacqueline's and Simon's love was based on these two opposing needs; they loved each other for what each represented as much as for themselves.

Jacqueline wondered how she was going to make her Russian, her Jew, her Mykhanowitzki, acceptable to her family. Oh, she had plenty of time, there was no rush! But she saw storms ahead, especially the vexing questions: "Where does he come from? Not a Frenchman? They're never any good, they're rolling stones—people who run from their homeland, who haven't any homeland . . ." Luckily, Simon had served out his conscription; she'd find some support in that. "Just the same, he's a foreigner! Can you tell what's going through their heads? They don't think the way we do! And what does he hide behind his beautiful shop? Maybe your Machinski's a swindler, or a thief. Did the wind bring him his money?"

Yes, Jacqueline asked herself uneasily, where did he get his money? Sometimes, Simon, all innocence, would tell her of his money troubles and, with a laugh that she disliked, would speak of mysterious ways of getting out of them. She ventured to murmur a few words of advice, of common sense; timidly, of course, for she had a boundless admiration for her lover's business ability. He laughed in her face, politely. "Little Jaconde, you don't understand any of this!" and he kissed her (he spent a good deal of time doing that, and they had become very familiar). Still, she noticed that without saying anything, perhaps without knowing it, he would sometimes take the advice that she whispered to him. Thus he dropped a risky idea of buying in bulk that he had told her about. She didn't exult, but she noted it; her Simon was more malleable than he seemed. In the restaurant, she tried to keep down his spending. "Look here, you aren't the Jew," he would toss at her laughingly; but he stopped ordering lobster.

One day, incidentally, but by design, she spoke of a certain piece of land left her by her great-aunt, which made up the greater part of her dowry.

"The devil with your dowry!" cried Simon. "What do you want me to do with it? I'm marrying a woman, not a field!"

"But Simon," she sighed, inwardly delighted, "you can't—"

He closed her lips by kissing her again; then, in a surprised tone—since he had admitted being Jewish, he was always saying this—"Sweetheart, you're more of a Jew than I am."

This, too, she noted; if her father stressed the question of money, she would shut his mouth with Simon's disinterest.

She blossomed and ripened so rapidly it amazed her, at first. Simon's brilliant assurance no longer fascinated her; she knew too well what was hidden beneath. "What a child!" she would think when she saw him strutting about; but she loved him even more tenderly for it, in another way. She felt that she was so much more sensible, so much older than he! Every day she came up against new thoughts, new worries; when she didn't dare to face them, she would pretend that they were some of the objections her father would raise against her marriage. Was she, for instance, disturbed by Simon's irresponsibility? That would become, in her father's mouth:

"After all, what do you know about him? Nothing! He respects you, all right; especially since you know how to take care of yourself. But what kind of marriage can it be with foreigners who have neither religion nor law? He'll marry you, give you some kids, and then, when he's had enough, pouf! he's gone, to America or to the devil! Do you even know his parents? Why hasn't he ever introduced you to them?"

It's true that Simon, although a very ardent lover, always stopped himself in time. It's also true that he never spoke of his parents. She questioned him. He seemed annoyed, almost ashamed; he answered evasively. Then, as she felt uneasiness growing, in a moment of folly she made Simon go beyond their usual limits. Afterward, solaced, freed from herself, she gave herself up to happiness with almost indecent joy. Now she was sure that he loved her worthily and honorably.

He, on the contrary, seemed tortured; with a vehemence that surprised her, he begged her to forgive him and swore that he was going to marry her immediately, immediately; he seemed to think he was guilty of a crime.

"What's the matter with you?" she asked languidly. "Aren't you happy?"

Oh, yes, of course he was happy, but how could he express feelings whose true nature he didn't understand? He had sullied his fiancée. He, a Jew, had acted like a blackguard toward his French fiancée, such a pure, fresh, honorable young girl! Through cowardice he hadn't been able to restrain himself until marriage and had torn the glory from it irreparably. "I've made a mistress of the woman who will be my wife. How will I be able to respect her again?" There were still strong vestiges of Rakwomirian morality in Simon's conscience.

All the same, this event forced him to face the major obstacle before which he had quailed for such a long time: his parents. He feared a whole mass of objections: "What? A *goya?*" He would have to get angry, pound on the table; in short, he would provoke one of those family scenes on which he usually turned his back.

Then, too, the stupid thing about marriage wasn't that one becomes two; everything multiplies by two, including worries. Not only would he have to show Jacqueline to his parents, but he would also have to show his parents to Jacqueline. Simon grew cold thinking of it. Papa would still pass in spite of his accent and his sermons, but Mama, oh Mama! she would begin to ramble in Yiddish, to ward off the Evil Eye, and all that sort of thing. To avoid this catastrophe he thought it would be a good idea to prepare the girl for it so that she wouldn't be too surprised.

"You know," he would say, "these are very simple people. You have to put yourself in their place. You mustn't make fun of their accent, you must be indulgent. Try to win them over . . ."

He talked about it so much that Jacqueline began to be afraid. Until then, seeing how independently the young man acted, she had thought his parents were negligible; she had even thought they would be only too happy to have her for a daughter-in-law; Simon's humility had resulted in inspiring a sort of pride in her, and now here was Simon raising an obstacle. Panic seized her; would these extraordinary people want her?

She became so nervous that Simon in his turn grew afraid and persuaded himself that she was hiding something. The whole thing wasn't natural! Was it, by chance, that the Saulnier family would oppose the marriage? He had hardly thought of them at the beginning. He had thought that he and Papa Baptiste were friends and that

that would be enough. He began to tell himself that after all they were Catholics, perhaps anti-Semites. How were they going to receive him, a foreigner, a Jew? At that his beaten-down pride sprang back. He was a man like anybody else. Why should he blush at his origins? Who was honoring whom in this business? Evil thoughts came to him, one of which he could hardly rid himself of; he had slept with their Jacqueline, hadn't he? This was no time to play games. Jew or not, they should be only too happy . . .

Nevertheless, he wasn't proud of himself. With a detached air, he asked Jacqueline one day if her parents were very devout.

"Papa? He jokes at religion," Jacqueline replied quickly. Simon noticed that she didn't speak about her mother, but she was already bouncing the ball back. "How do your father and you . . . ?"

"Papa? Oh, if you knew him you'd know that to him, religion . . ."

Jacqueline didn't protest; but she thought of it nonetheless. One day an allusion Simon made in a carefully disinterested tone told her that he was circumcised. Then wouldn't his father be hostile to her religion?

Thus, little by little, they reached the bursting point. At last the day came when they had had enough of it to frighten them and they were prepared to tell their parents that it was they and not the parents who were getting married, and if they didn't like it they would do without them and that's how it would be. They were grown up!

Now they threw themselves into the assault. Simon began; Jacqueline was expecting questions at home on the "young man's family" and she wanted to overcome them with her knowledge. So one fine evening, Simon, having gathered his courage, climbed the three flights of stairs on the Rue des Francs-Bourgeois, and rang.

A dragging step . . . Even before the door was opened, Simon saw his father in his shirt sleeves and his black vest, with his flat, turned-out feet, his back slightly bent, the eternal *yarmulke* on his graying hair. It was exactly so. No; a new detail, steel-rimmed eyeglasses. Simon, who hadn't seen his parents for a long time, didn't know that his father now wore glasses to read the newspaper. He's getting old, the poor old man!

"Nu? Simon, it's you? *Mazeltov* on us!" Yankel's melancholy face lit up. "He's becoming more and more Jewish!" Simon thought when he heard the Hebrew formula that greets the slightest joy.

"Hannele!" Yankel called happily. "We have a visitor and guess who?"

"Oooy, Simon, my treasure!" The old woman burst out of the kitchen with surprising speed for her size and threw herself at him, hugging her adored son convulsively. It begins, thought Simon, kissing his mother's cheek.

"You dine with us?" Papa's tone anticipated a refusal.

"Of course, if you really want me to."

A curious feeling, to find yourself back home with your parents, when your own life has been overturned by an extraordinary happening, when you've become a sensible adult. Everything seems too old, and at the same time childish. Everything is withered, stunted, wrinkled. Small talk: "So how's your health? business? the family? . . . Oh? Clara isn't here?"

The old man tightened his mouth, shook his head, heartbroken. "I don't know what's wrong with that girl. She's all upset. She can't hold a job, she comes to eat at impossible hours, or else she doesn't eat at all . . ."

"Maybe she has a boy friend," Simon thrust in with a wink.

But old Yankel shook his head. "If it were only that, I would understand. I know how girls are. But, tchch, there's something else. That girl never talks except to complain, to grumble, to find fault. She's all closed up. She has no confidence in her parents. If you saw how she treats your poor mother! Clara isn't happy, I'm telling you. A young girl like that, beautiful, healthy, she should laugh from morning to night, she should love life, sing. Oh Simon, Simon, there's something wrong with Clara. You should speak to her. Perhaps she'll trust you more." The old man now stopped his complaining and held his son's eyes for a minute. Being French, his two children would understand each other, no?

"Maybe she doesn't like her work," Simon ventured carefully. With his own affairs so confused he didn't care to mix into those of his sister. But the old man, with his habitual fly-swatting gesture, only groaned.

"Ach! Her work, her work . . ."

"What is she doing now?" For her brother-in-law, Rechnowitz, had taken Clara into his fur shop; but it hadn't worked out.

"Do I know what she's doing?" cried the old man. "She never tells us anything. Clara will come to no good, and I'm the one who's telling you so," he continued in an undertone. "Sometimes she reminds me of your Uncle Moishe when he was young." He shook his

282

head as if to drive away some distasteful images. "She also doesn't know how to hold a job."

"Well, it hasn't worked out too badly for Uncle Moishe!" remarked Simon maliciously. Yankel threw him a quick glance.

"Yes, yes! I know what I'm saying. Someday maybe I'll tell you about your Uncle Moishe. Right now I think she's working in the factories making what do they call them, bathtubs, sinks, all that. I wonder what she can know about that. Oy, let's not talk about Clara. You didn't come about her, did you?"

Once again Simon felt his father's look rest heavily on him and he stirred a little on his chair. Clever, the old man, a great deal cleverer than he seemed. Simon suddenly acquired true respect for his father.

The three of them were alone at the table. Rivka had her own life now, her own home, her business, Fernand was with his regiment, and Clara somewhere. If I hadn't come this evening, thought Simon, they would have been all alone. For the first time he contemplated his parents with the indulgent eye of an adult and was astounded to find them so pitiful, so sweet, so gently turned inward on themselves and on their own little ways, a couple of old Jews, without a history. Caps and the family, the family and caps, that was their whole life. There must have been an earthquake to have made them leave Russia. . . . A quarter of a century in this rut, never a vacation, never any change . . . Impulsively, Simon decided that at the first chance he would load his parents in the Unic and show them the sea. For all the time that they spoke of the sea it had become a myth for them; well, he, Simon, would bring the myth to life like a good son, a good son who was beginning to understand things because he was going to get married.

Yes. This didn't make the subject of the marriage any easier to broach, and Simon would perhaps not have known how to start it if Papa had not attacked it himself.

"Nu, nu, Simon, what's wrong with you that you twist around like a dog that can't find a place to lie down?" He smiled widely and continued, "You want to tell me something? Perhaps you want to bring a young lady here?" And Mama also smiled widely and clucked and began to shake her head.

"Nu, Simon, you don't have to blush like that!" the old man said teasingly. "That's life!"

"Of course, of course," the young man ground out. "There's nothing to make a fuss about! A girl friend, that's all! You know . . ."

"Do I know? Of course I know!" echoed the old man. "I know what young people are, I was young myself, me too, isn't it true, Hannele? Hannele, Hannele! Why don't you bring us some schnapps?"

And when the schnapps had been poured, Yankel lifted his glass, and Hannah and Simon imitated him.

"Well," the father spoke solemnly, "well, *mazeltov* to you, Simon!" He drank, and his wife and son after him; then he put down the glass, and leaned forward, and again the smile stretched his lips—hungrily, this time.

"So what's the young lady's name?"

"Jacqueline Saulnier," Simon answered abruptly. He expected a start of surprise, protestations; he was prepared for battle.

There was no apparent reaction; even the smile was not wiped off his father's face, instead it seemed to be fixed there even more firmly.

"Aha? Then she's a *goya?*" was all that Yankel said, in a tone of surprise. Simon, shriveled, caught a rapid exchange of looks between his father and his mother. Then his father continued soothingly.

"Well, good, good, my son, I hope you haven't made a mistake, that you've considered it well, and that you'll be happy. To your fiancée's health!"

The last words were in French and he raised his glass again. Simon, his throat constricted, could find nothing to say but "We're not engaged, I told you."

"Yes, yes, yes."

A plaintive and meaningful tone, but a congratulatory smile. No point for quarreling.

When they had drunk again, Yankel leaned toward his son as if to turn to more ordinary affairs.

"Do you remember your poor Uncle Itcha who was killed in the war? He too was engaged to a *goya.*"

"Uncle Itcha was engaged?" Simon sang out in surprise.

"No one knew. You, of course, were too small. And then, if your grandfather, my father, had known that—my father, you know, is not me—a *goya,* you understand? It would have been terrible."

A pause. How could Simon guess that deep in the penumbra of his consciousness, Yankel felt a stirring of old, old memories of his own youth, Nevers, a girl . . .

"Terrible," he repeated, mechanically. And suddenly: "She knows you're a Jew, no?"

"Of course, Papa."

"And, naturally, it doesn't bother her? Good, good. So you're sure she isn't anti-Semitic? And her family? Is she religious? What's her parents' business?"

In precise phrases, Yankel questioned his son; with such gentleness, such delicate precautions that Simon could do nothing but answer. Meanwhile a dull, irritating uneasiness wormed itself into Simon. Of course, Jacqueline loved him now; but who knew, later . . .

"You understand, Simon, I have no prejudices. But in every household, sooner or later, there's a quarrel, no? So you'll see, in one year or ten, your wife will get angry over something and she'll throw it in your face—dirty Jew!"

The insult cracked brutally across the quiet dining room; Simon almost believed it had happened.

"Of course, afterward she'll be sorry, if she's a good wife. But what's said is said! So you understand, Simon, you've got to consider everything beforehand. Because after, it's too late."

"You . . . You'll be polite to her, anyway?"

Yankel groaned under the insult, and his face took on such a grief-stricken dignity that Simon was ashamed of his question.

"What do you take me for, Simon?" his father asked softly.

"Excuse me, I . . ."

Yankel tossed his head. "My poor boy! You're getting married, not I. You're big enough to know what you're doing. Me, I wish nothing but your happiness. But don't come around later and tell me that I didn't warn you." He reflected for a moment before he concluded: "After you're married, wait a while before you have any children. You never know."

Hannah wept most of the night. Yankel consoled her as best he could. "How do you know she isn't a good girl? After all, Jew, goy, what can you do when you love somebody?" He spoke prudently. He wasn't sure that he really understood his wife's distress. Hannah was half devout; half or nine tenths, he didn't know. Did she consider her son's marriage to a Christian as a sin? He didn't think that her faith would go that far. So? Afraid of the unknown? Hannah had always been timid before anything out of the ordinary. In vain he tried to question her. He drew nothing from her but lamenta-

285

tions. They had introduced Simon to so many nice young Jewish girls. Why did it have to be a Christian?

Yankel thought that his own reasons for uneasiness were sensible. He knew his Simon and was afraid that he had been harpooned by one of those flighty and self-seeking women so numerous among the *goyim*. A Jewish girl, of course, is already a guarantee; Jews are honest, proper, simple people. Naturally, among the *goyim* there are also honest people; but after all, you never know. Then, even setting aside the wicked women, in every goy the old anti-Semitism is sleeping, and you have to have at least the minimum of intelligence to keep it from showing itself. Marriage itself raises plenty of delicate problems; there's no need to complicate it further by mixing in social, racial, and other conflicts. . . . And Yankel turned and turned again and chewed over these ideas without being aware that they were feeding on old taboos and old fears of which he had naïvely thought himself liberated.

Simon had told him that Jacqueline was of peasant stock; but Babylon takes these weak women over so quickly . . . Yankel expected a frivolous Parisienne to appear, too pretty, and with a tongue too facile. He was agreeably surprised; the young lady was neither beautiful nor bold. She blushed and stammered modestly. Modesty, ah, modesty; to Yankel it was the cardinal virtue of young people. So, having greeted Mlle. Saulnier with solemn dignity and extreme courtesy, he quickly relaxed his reserve. Simon was watching his father fearfully. He began to chuckle when he saw him unbend and clumsily thrust one or two jokes at Jacqueline. On her side, Mama clucked, laughed, but kept herself from talking too much and even from weeping. Simon, who had expected torrents of joyful tears and a deluge of Yiddish, heaved a sigh of relief. Perhaps Papa had been schooling Mama.

"Well, what did you think of my father?" asked Simon when they found themselves on the sidewalk.

"He's charming!" And for ten minutes Jacqueline didn't stop praising Yankel, so gentle, so simple, so sympathetic. She avoided the subject of Hannah; that good woman had produced no other impression on her than that of an annoying presence.

In truth, although she wasn't going to tell this to Simon, it was he who had surprised her most. He acted so naturally in that so unFrench atmosphere. He dropped shreds of foreign phrases with such ease; he seemed so much at home among these people who were not of her sort! At bottom, he's a foreigner, Jacqueline thought to herself, almost uneasily. She had just begun to realize it.

The next morning, at the Saulniers', Jacqueline took the offensive, rudely; she knew the right tactics to use on her father. Chin forward, ready for battle, she fired her announcement point-blank: The famous Simon was coming.

"Good. And what's your Simon's name?" asked Baptiste, relieved of his recent worries.

He was so confounded at hearing that it was Simon, really Simon, that he forgot to discuss it. To tell the truth, he remembered the Unic better than its owner; of him, he retained only the image of an elegant, voluble Parisian.

"He—he's your . . . your . . . ?" he faltered.

"What of it?" Jacqueline fired back. "What have you got against him?"

"Nothing, but . . ."

Still aggressive, Jacqueline told him the parents also were coming.

Baptiste began to gain control of himself. However, he cast imploring looks at Catherine; girls' love affairs were not where he shone. But her mother, even surlier than usual, didn't let out a chirp. You wanted to make a Parisienne out of your Jacqueline? You wanted to belch champagne instead of beer? Well, get yourself out of it! And she went from the pots to the table, and from the table back to the pots, to show that she would have nothing to do with this business. She didn't pay any attention when Jacqueline, embarrassed, undertook to describe the Mykhanowitzkis.

"What kind of name is that?"

"So? They haven't the right to call themselves that?"

"But what are they? Turks?"

And Baptiste prepared to curse these foreigners who come here to guzzle our food and steal our daughters, when Jacqueline cried out that it was true that they came from Russia, but Simon had done his military service in France, and . . .

Military service—that was Baptiste's password. As soon as he learned that Simon had been in the Army, Baptiste felt better about him. He immediately perceived that the word "Russia" sounded very acceptable to his ear; a Russian *émigré,* a Russian prince, a Colonel of the Guard turned taxi driver because of hard times . . .

"All right," he grumbled. "Since it's like that, we have to see him, eh? There are good men in every country." Secretly he was flattered that a Russian prince had come from the end of the world to fall madly in love with his Jacqueline.

Just then the mother interrupted with her habitual snarl. Poor Catherine hadn't had a pleasant life; her jovial husband, on whom she doted, cared nothing for her. The fact had made her permanently bitter.

"Are they good Christians?" she interjected.

Behind her Baptiste began to slap his thigh and laugh. He had no use for priests and he spent his life shooting sarcasms at poor Catherine and her curé.

Loudly, with beating heart, Jacqueline announced, "They are Jews."

"Jews?"

Father and mother had cried the word together; and Baptiste no longer laughed.

"So what? They're people like everybody else."

Arrogantly, Jacqueline defied the stares of her father, her mother, and her brother. Her father, shaken, kept repeating, "Jews! A hell of a note!" Her mother pinched her narrow mouth. Her brother Ernest put his enormous fists on the table. Jacqueline, her chin thrust forward, offered, "That's the way it is," after which there was a good five minutes of silence.

Baptiste rose and paced back and forth; at last he grumbled, "That's the way it is, that's the way it is. That's what you say. Me, I say, be careful. You mustn't get involved until . . ."

The result was that they asked themselves, "What are Jews?" Once the first distaste had passed, they tried to gather their knowledge on the subject, and, as they loved their little Jacqueline, they sought favorable factors energetically. Unfortunately, only the unfavorable factors came running to their minds. The little grasping, sly Jew, with his hooked nose, clutching fingers, bearded chin; a race of parasites, all usurers, who love only money! Although, as far as that goes, it isn't bad to love money. It's better than depending on charity. . . . Baptiste searched his memory to find if he had ever met any Jews.

"Am I not a fool!" he burst out suddenly. "I've seen him, Simon; he was a gentleman. And she's marrying him, I'm not."

Then he remembered that there had been a Jew in the second squad during the war. What did he look like? Forgotten. Anyway, nobody said anything good or bad about him, and when a shell burst and took away his shoulder they simply said, "The Jew in the Second got it!" All right, well . . . *The cut tail!* Baptiste almost groaned. Why do they do such a thing? Are they savages? He glanced at his daughter and grimaced. Poor thing, I can't let her waste her life on a character with a cut tail. And at this moment a phrase heard many years earlier rose from the depths of his memory—right to the point: "Jews are good husbands." Who had said that? . . . Oh, yes! Jeanne, by God! Baptiste reddened with pleasure; Jeanne's voice (with her southern accent) was sounding in his ear just as before. "They say the Jews make good husbands!" Word for word. Where was it? They had gone for a walk at Carpentras. And they had passed in front of a Jewish church—how are they called, Jewish churches?—in short, Baptiste thought that it was a church except that it had no cross, and Jeanne had explained it to him. Lost in his reverie, he was far away from his daughter; now he was at Carpentras, at Avignon. What a good life, youth, before the war, the sun, the free trips for soldiers, and Jeanne, so dainty . . .

Her mother took up the argument in a bitter voice: "How is your Jew going to make out with the Church?"

"My Jew, my Jew . . ." Jacqueline grew angry with the expression to avoid replying. She was completely unprepared; up to now she had never faced that aspect of the problem. To tell the truth, she was no more pious than her father; the only difference was that Baptiste made it a point of honor never to go into a church, while she, one Sunday out of three, would accompany her mother to Mass. As far as religious ceremonies were concerned—baptism, catechism, first communion, and the rest—the Saulniers, father and daughter, went along without attaching any importance thereto. It doesn't mean anything but it doesn't hurt anyone, does it? Like eating fish on Friday . . . A marriage is as much the priest's business as it is the mayor's. Only for Simon, the whole thing depended on whether it meant anything to him. Would he accept the Church? Jacqueline saw a world of customs, beliefs, and habits rise before her to separate her from Simon. There were so many obstacles to overcome. . . .

"And your children? They'll be baptized, naturally?"

In spite of herself, Jacqueline felt overwhelmed by troubles. Wouldn't Simon demand that their sons, if they had any, be circumcised? Would she, for love of him, agree to that? Then why should he yield to her rather than she to him? Baptism, after all, was nothing but a symbolic gesture, it didn't keep the child from doing as he pleased when he grew older; while circumcision stamped the body

289

in an irrevocable manner. We'll have to talk about it, she decided to herself. She had the feeling of being very little in an immense hostile world which would wipe her out—which would wipe them both out, Simon and her.

Her mother guessed that she was thinking of these things. Catherine couldn't hold herself back.

"If you don't get married in church," she cried, "you won't have a mother any more. There are no whores in my family!"

At this blow, Baptiste leaped forward. Someone had dared to insult his Jacqueline. He began to yell at his wife and she screamed back—there was a fight every week in the Saulnier home, almost every time Catherine opened her mouth, and the cries could be heard from one end of the village to the other. After five minutes, the wife was accusing the husband of sniffing around the petticoats of the Fleming, and the husband blamed the wife for not taking more care of her own underwear. Jacqueline wept hot tears thinking of the obstacles separating her from her sweet Simon, and she swore she would become a Jew if he insisted.

Finally, Baptiste ended the argument. He overcame his wife with his powerful voice to affirm that he liked Simon, Jew or not; after which he went out to relieve himself in the garden. Catherine, her word factory closed down for a week, decided to consult the priest tomorrow.

She consulted him the next day and returned slightly reassured. Yes, it could be arranged. Even if the fiancé refused to be baptized, all was not lost. Without doubt, Rome would grant them a dispensation, on the condition that the young man contract to raise his children in the Catholic faith. Of course, the ceremony would differ a little . . .

"But will they really be married in the church?"

"In the sacristy."

"But we'll be able to go through the church?"

"Certainly!"

So it was Catherine herself who, a few days later, and in her most disagreeable voice, asked her daughter when she would decide to bring them, her—how did she say it?—Mi . . . Minovisqui?"

In the meantime, Jacqueline had talked with Simon. Religion? Simon hadn't thought much about it. "You know me, I don't care much for that sort of thing. Are you religious?" No, no, luckily Jacqueline felt inwardly as anticlerical as her father. "Well, then? We'll get married at the Town Hall and the deed is done!"

When Simon learned that the deed was not done because of her parents, he was aghast. "Oh, they want the church? They want it as badly as that?" He had the feeling that by giving in he would be humiliating himself, cheapening himself, just because those Saulniers attached so much importance to the matter.

"Perhaps your parents would prefer the synagogue?" Jacqueline interjected.

"Mine?" Simon laughed full-throatedly. "Oh, you don't know them!"

He didn't know them either. For if Yankel didn't observe, or thought he didn't observe, the religious ceremonies, he hadn't thought it shameful when Rivka married her Chaim, called Henri, in the synagogue. As for Hannah, who became more and more pious with age, she suffered silently watching her son living irreligiously, and, to turn the lightning of the Lord away from him, she blamed herself for having been a bad mother; sometimes she blamed Yankel also for having raised his children badly. But no one cared how the poor old woman felt. When she learned that the wedding would not take place in the synagogue, she wept alone in a corner. So much the worse for her. Since it would make Simon happy to have his *goya,* let him have his *goya,* and may God punish me!

On a beautiful December day the Unic, polished like new, carried an austere, Sunday-clothed, close-shaven Yankel, and a Hannah whom a powerful corset had rejuvenated, toward Virelay for lunch. Simon, completely at his ease, whistled as he drove; Papa Saulnier was an old pal of his! Clara had refused to come, Fernand was with his regiment, and Rivka, being a married woman, only partly belonged to the family.

High on the crest over Virelay, Simon stopped the car so that Papa and Mama could grow ecstatic over the countryside. He had seen it once; that was enough for him. He hardly noticed that the fields were redder in December than in August. He lit a cigarette, gave Mama time enough to repeat three times, in Yiddish, "How beautiful it is, may no Evil Eye take it!" and Papa to repeat three times, in French, that it reminded him of Nevers; after which, they plunged into the valley.

291

"Good morning, sir, Good morning, madame!"

"Goot morning, goot morning!"

What an accent they drag around, Simon thought of his parents, while the Saulniers, who had expected worse, thought exactly the opposite. Blushing, Jacqueline squirmed; Papa Saulnier held himself as stiff as a gendarme in his ceremonial clothes; Mother Saulnier creaked like a cricket in her black silk dress; M. Mykhanowitzki, grave as an undertaker, politely held his hat in his hand and refused to enter the house before his host; Mme. Mykhanowitzki clucked, tittered, smiled from ear to ear, guessing that the tall goy was addressing some compliments to her but taking care not to say a word. Simon, unable to stay in one place, went from the door to the dog, and from the dog to the hencoop, chewing his cigarette all the while.

"You can see he's your son!" said Yankel to Baptiste, pointing out Ernest, who, hands in pockets, kept himself a little to one side. "What a lively one! You resemble each other like two drops of water."

He thought that he was paying a compliment. Dryly, Baptiste replied that Ernest was the image of his mother and had the personality of a pig. Yankel, shocked, reproved him gently, "Oh, you mustn't say that, Monsieur Saulnier." Finally they were all crowded together in the living room. Time for an apéritif, a glass of white wine which the Mykhanowitzkis did not dare to refuse, which Yankel tossed down gaily while Hannah touched it to her lips, and they grew acquainted, the fathers on one side, the mothers on the other, and the children elsewhere.

For once Catherine tried to be polite and undertook a conversation with Mme. Mykhanowitzki. Labor lost; the other knew nothing but how to laugh like an idiot. Catherine soon had had enough of it; she shrugged her shoulders and, inwardly relieved, leaped to her casseroles.

"Excuse me, please? Between women, you know how it is."

"Yes, yes, go, go!"

Poor Hannah had finally managed to get out two words in French.

On the men's side, Yankel, seated gravely and wisely with his two hands on the edge of the table, was torturing himself: Where, when, and how would he formulate the marriage request? But this drama remained inside him; only his face expressed the seriousness and intensity of his thought. Nevertheless, he said enough so that Baptiste understood that there was only one thing left to talk about, and he, too, felt more at ease and spoke without too much formality.

"Well," he said, "that Simon of yours is an only child?"

"Oh, no," said Yankel, with a proud and happy smile. "I have four of them. Two boys, two girls."

"By God! Have you got rabbit blood?"

This statement went right to Yankel's heart, since it showed that its author was a man with advanced ideas; what was the use of bringing children into the world for the war to kill? Nevertheless, since he was proud of his family, he explained to Baptiste that his mother had done even better, she had had thirteen children, of whom five were still alive. To which Baptiste, who was thinking on his part that these Jews are as prolific as the devil, retorted that his mother had had only two children and both were still living. There followed a very confused discussion on repopulation, its connections with hygiene and social progress; in short, an exchange of views at once philosophical and on a high political plane, well interwoven with references to their respective cousins, Anatol and Samuel, which delighted Yankel and exhausted Baptiste. A shot of white wine to gather their strength, and they went back to it.

"Do you still have your parents?" asked Baptiste, and, a little ashamed, Yankel was forced to admit that they were in Palestine. "You know, these old people, full of religious prejudices . . ." Good! they were also agreed on the subject of religion. Moreover, each had a tremendous effect on the other, Yankel on Baptiste through his innocent allusions to Palestine, Russia, America, the four corners of the earth; Baptiste on Yankel by his proud proclamation that the Saulniers from father to son had always been natives of Virelay. He's educated! thought Baptiste to himself, stunned that M. Mykhanowitzki expressed himself in a choice French which didn't keep him from using a mass of other languages; as to his scientific and literary knowledge, they raised him almost to the rank of a lecturer. He's intelligent for a peasant! thought Yankel, not without surprise; for in his circle *goyim* were supposed to be stupider than Jews, and since the old capmaker had stopped living among the French he had forgotten their character.

Once or twice, Simon thought it necessary to intervene; but his salesman's manner clashed so strongly with the grave and ceremonious conversation of the two fathers that the younger man felt almost expelled.

Finally that subject that Yankel feared above all others arose: his war service. To the rich memories of Baptiste he replied, not without shame, by allusions to his brothers Itcha and Moishe, which assured him his host's respect. Actually Baptiste had hardly dreamed of reproaching him for having stayed behind; if he had been able, he, Baptiste, would also have dodged it.

". . . who is in military service . . ."

Eh? Baptiste sat up. The extended conversation with M. Trickski was tiring him out a great deal. Oh, they were talking about the second son now, Fernand.

"Fernand is tall," Yankel explained proudly. "Not quite as tall as you, but much taller than Simon. Five feet ten, the scale makes it."

What difference does that make to me? thought Baptiste. Big or small, what do I care? He was tall and so was his son; how could he understand that to Yankel a tall Jew was proof of the falsity of the anti-Semitic legend of the "little Jew"? And, anyway, it was Simon that Jacqueline was marrying, not Fernand.

"What does your Fernand do in civil life?" he asked politely to keep the conversation alive.

"He's a cabinetmaker," answered the father, glowing. "He graduated from the Boulle Technical Institute."

"You don't say! That's a good line!"

Good line, worker, manufacturer of furniture, of hats, the difficulties of agriculture; they had enough to talk about until the end of time. Surprised, Baptiste learned that Yankel scorned business. He, himself, on the contrary, very much preferred an occupation which brought in money, gave you a car to ride in, and left you with white hands. Well, every man to his taste.

The meal went off without any trouble. Although Jacqueline had assured them that the Mykhanowitzkis didn't practice their religion, Mother Saulnier had obviously avoided serving pork. M. Mykhanowitzki made a conquest of her by the warmth with which he complimented the cook after each dish, and sometimes before it.

"Have you been in France a long time?"

"Since 1898," Yankel stated proudly.

"You don't tell me! That's a long lease! Enough to make you feel at home here. Aren't you homesick?"

"Oh, no, no!" Yankel forced the note slightly, but so slightly that it wasn't worth the trouble to talk about it.

"Everyone says that France is a good country," Baptiste went on with a knowing air. "We're very hospitable. I suppose that's why all the foreigners envy us. Isn't it true?"

Yes, yes, yes. Of course, we mustn't exaggerate. But Yankel kept his reservations to himself. Besides, he was almost sincere when he went even further than his host.

Then he began to recall a mass of Russian memories; he told of his departure from Rakwomir, his secret crossing of the frontier, his arrival in France. Simon sat there with his mouth open; he had never thought that his father, so timid and so self-effacing, had lived through such adventures. At my age, he had lived through ten times more than I, he said to himself, and he surprised himself by being— yes, jealous! Jealous of the interest that Jacqueline was taking in the story. It was foolish, but that's the way it was; he felt like a beardless youth.

When Yankel grew silent, Baptiste remarked sadly that he, alas, had never budged from this place.

"Not that I didn't want to. But you know how it is; you get married and then what can you do . . ."

Oh, yes, Yankel knew how it was! "You get married and then what can you do . . ." Energetically, he forced back certain old French memories; but sometimes they reappeared in all their splendor. What had become of Marguerite? Involuntarily, Yankel superimposed on old Hannah the image of a blond Marguerite of long ago, preserved in her youth for over a quarter of a century. Thoughts came to him that he tried to drive away. A man is foolish when he's young. You shouldn't get married too early. You should stay unattached. If you don't, instead of plunging into the flesh of your new country, you have to transfer your hopes to your children. . . .

To marry for land, thought Baptiste; what stupidity! I should have married Jeanne down there and let all these stick-in-the-muds go to hell. . . .

"I was away only when I was doing my service," he said aloud. "And then during the war, of course, but that . . ."

They began to compare their impressions of the provinces. What! You were at Nevers? I had a friend who . . .

"Nevers is pretty!" Yankel asserted with so much conviction that his accent accused him. "Do you know it?"

No, Baptiste didn't know it. He turned toward Hannah, remembering that one of his duties as host was not to neglect the ladies; however, that one didn't seem especially bored.

"And you, madame, did you enjoy yourself at Nevers?"

Hannah showed a smile full of kindness while tilting her head sideways. What's wrong with her? thought Baptiste, but Yankel came quickly to the rescue.

"She was still in Russia then," he explained, and he continued immediately, "Nevers, Monsieur Saulnier, is almost as beautiful as here. It resembles it a little, you know."

What's this with him and his Nevers? Simon wondered. All the while he was chatting with Jacqueline, he kept one ear on his father's conversation. He had never heard so much Nevers, Nevers. Ah! Can it be that the transparent, scrupulous Papa had had an affair with a woman there? And while Mama was still in Russia? Up to then Simon had always believed that Papa and Mama had arrived together, in fact that all the family, Grandpa Avrom and Uncle Moishe included, had entered in one group under Grandpa's command. So, it was Papa who had taken the initiative, and all alone! Saintly Papa, who'd been hiding plenty of things behind his moral sermons.

All this time, Yankel was maneuvering to get away; he didn't like to stay too long at the table. This worked out well since just at this moment Baptiste wanted to relieve himself. The two fathers went out together into the courtyard. The sun was still warm, the sky a very pale blue; it felt good to breathe the dry cold air. Baptiste dragged Yankel into the garden.

"So you like Virelay?" he said. And when the other began to repeat his admiration, Baptiste affected a modest air. "Oh, a little village, nothing at all. It's old, it's dirty." But he took Yankel on a tour of the place. On the road, he gave him details about the farming, complained because the pearl factory had closed its doors, pointed with pride to a Parisian's beautiful villa, spoke well of Herriot and ill of Poincaré; finally, he pointed out with his finger the place where Jacqueline's piece of land lay on the Plateau above.

"Can we go up there?" asked Yankel timidly. Baptiste's refusal surprised him by its curtness. "It's too far." Baptiste obviously thought that the Jew was trying to check up on the value of the dowry. Poor Yankel was forced to be satisfied with viewing the Seine from the bank, and he didn't even have time for that because the stupid peasant didn't once stop talking. And what did he have to say? That those poplars were planted five years ago; that lilacs did well there. And other stupidities. In short, there was a slight chill between them when they came back into the court. Baptiste looked out of the corner of his eye at the little man who was trotting at his shoulder. I'll show you something, my friend! He grabbed hold of an enormous log that was lying there, raised it against his chest, taking care to hide the effort, and threw it carelessly under the shed.

"Hmmm! You're strong, Monsieur Saulnier," Yankel remarked. "How much would you say that weighed?"

"I don't know," boasted the other. "Ninety, a hundred."

Yankel's biceps began to tingle. I'm going to show him! I'm not so old! He handled the log, made sure of his grip, balanced himself on his legs. Not too comfortable. I'm going to give myself a hernia, he thought. Snatch-and-press, a little awkward, not a very orthodox movement—and there it was! He brandished the log, arms above his head. Baptiste whistled with admiration.

Yankel threw the log away, drew down his vest, and said modestly, "Oh, that's nothing at all, Monsieur Saulnier. I used to work out with dumbbells when I was younger, but then I couldn't get a grip on this . . ."

Piqued, Baptiste had to try it himself, but he couldn't do it.

"Not like that, Monsieur Saulnier; you have to know how!" Yankel said with a grin. He gave him some lessons on the grip, grab, and press according to the right principles. When they went back in, they were warm friends again.

In the dining room, Hannah, still mute, still laughing, still nodding, had tied an apron on her pretty dress and was helping Madame and Mademoiselle with the dishes; and for all her slow movements, her thick, stubby fingers, she was doing her part of the job. Mme. Saulnier was moved by this; she would never have believed that the good woman could be so obliging. As for Simon, a cigarette in his mouth and a dish towel tied around his middle, he was drying the dishes. Simon drying dishes! In his own house he would never have done it. Ernest had taken himself off in his usual fashion.

"Good-bye, Monsieur Saulnier."

"Good-bye, Monsieur Mi-cahewski."

"Will you lunch with us some day soon?"

"Of course! It's been a pleasure . . ."

". . . pleasure . . ."

The Unic moved slowly off. Baptiste was critical.

"He wasn't too bad," he grumbled, taking off his vest. "But she— what a dunce!"

"Didn't you see that she couldn't speak French?" Catherine retorted.

"What? She doesn't speak French?"

How was it possible not to speak French? Baptiste looked blank, mechanically snapping his elastic suspenders with his thumb.

"They're polite, but they're still peasants!" Yankel complained critically. "I don't like her much. He . . . well! They're not anti-Semites, are they? Then that's that!"

When, immediately after Christmas, the Mykhanowitzkis reciprocated with lunch for the Saulniers, Hannah stewed some good Jewish dishes, enriched, however, with a chicken, French style. The closeness of the holidays and the strangeness of the cooking naturally provoked the diners to compare their two religions.

"What? You also have a sort of Christmas, with lights and gift-giving? I never would have believed it! . . . Easter, too? But Easter is the resurrection of Christ, and for you, of course, Christ . . . Ah? With you, Easter commemorates the Exodus from Egypt? Queer, just the same! Well, it looks as if you took your holidays from us . . ." "Ah? Do you think so? It would rather be we who . . . ?" "By God, you must be right, your religion is older than ours; and in one sense we're in unfair competition. At bottom, there isn't much difference between us, except that for you the Messiah hasn't come yet, and when I see what's going on today, poison gas and everything else, I wonder if you aren't right."

While Baptiste and Yankel were coming to agreement on the stupidity of religion, Catherine was telling herself that the Jewish religion couldn't be one of barbarians since it so closely resembled Christianity. Perhaps there was even some way of understanding each other. Hannah, her perpetual smile stretched across her moonface, felt the sympathy, for she blushingly dared to stammer two or three words in French. After dessert, Yankel showed Baptiste his workshop, explained to him the working of the button presses and the curling iron, and took his head size to make him a cap. Baptiste, for his part, promised him some bottles of wine from his vineyard.

"Their cooking is good," Baptiste confided to Jacqueline when they had left, "but they don't know anything about wine. My God, their drinks are strong!"

The marriage was celebrated a short time afterward at Virelay. On the Saulnier side there were numerous relatives, devoured by curiosity and with their broods clutched by the hand. The Mykhanowitzki side also added up to a goodly number. Clara-the-Beautiful agreed to be moved from her place; with a princess' indifference, she bowled over all the male peasants, young and old, while the females gnawed themselves with jealousy. Ernest Saulnier, mouth agape, followed her like her shadow but said not a word. Jacqueline took Simon aside.

"You didn't tell me you had such a pretty sister."

"Pretty?" echoed Simon, astonished. He'd never thought about it. A sister isn't a woman.

Fernand had obtained leave. In his horizon-blue uniform he stood erect, grave, and silent. Yankel secretly admired his son's five feet ten, his dignity, and his uniform. The girls were also impressed by him; but the young man limited himself politely to dancing with all of them without causing any jealousy. Rivka and Chaim had also come in their Renault. Rivka was now a talkative, domineering woman whose age could not be guessed. Thirty? Forty? She was actually only twenty-seven. She had had no children and she seemed to be forever barren but perhaps it was deliberate. She wasn't embarrassed at having to scold her rogue of a husband, who conquered the honorable society with his liveliness, his risqué stories, his card tricks, and his bottomless store of games.

Moishe's branch arrived late and left early, but while it was there it wrought havoc enough for three times as many. Innumerable children were crammed into the big Berliet, as many girls as boys, as many teen-agers as babies, and each one more ill-bred than the next. There were still some missing, but no one noticed it, not even Yankel, who had given up counting. They arrived like a tornado, jostling one another, knocking over the dancers, punching each other and the other children, and throwing pieces of bread, orange peels, and water in one another's face.

Rose was severely criticized because she couldn't keep her children in hand and because she posed as a lady; but Moishe created a sensation with his Croix-de-Guerre, his Médaille Militaire, his dragging leg, and his powerful voice. Baptiste pulled him off to one side and they exchanged memories of the war. When he left, Moishe threw a thundering "*Mazeltov ov dir,* Simon!" at his nephew, across the heads of all the others, causing the young man no little discomfort.

Outside of that, the wedding was very French, as the Saulniers realized happily. Jacqueline was dressed in a white gown and crowned with orange blossoms, Simon and his father wore dinner jackets, and everybody spoke only French. Of course, there was still the old lady.

At a certain moment, without any warning, she burst into tears. This caused some uneasiness; everyone wondered if she didn't feel well. Thank you, she felt fine, these were only tears of joy; it seemed that was the custom in her homeland. Fortunately, Mme. Mykhanowitzki had the good taste to take refuge in a corner where she ceased to be visible.

Poor Hannah! Yankel said to himself. None of her family were at the wedding. She had wanted to invite her closest relatives, the Schmirzmann cousins. But they were impossible, they lived in the Rue des Blancs-Manteaux, they jabbered in Yiddish, and they were scrupulously obedient to the religious taboos. Ashamed of himself, Yankel tried to make his wife understand that the Schmirzmanns would be out of place at this marriage, that they would feel, how should he put it . . . ?

"But why?" she asked naïvely. "They're fine people, and since the Saulniers invite whomever they want to, why can't we?"

"Oh, that would annoy Simon."

"Perhaps I also annoy him?"

Yankel didn't know what to say. Simon, Simon, why did you have to choose a *goya* when there are so many nice young Jewish girls? Hannah fought back feebly like a wounded bird.

"You know, Yankel, the Schmirzmanns are going to be angry. And don't you think Simon will be surprised not to see them?"

Poor Hannah! Your Simon laughs at you and the Schmirzmanns; aside from Moishe, he has nothing but scorn for his whole Jewish family. Oh, what a grudge Yankel bore his son for shaking off his origins so lightly!

He would have borne him a bigger grudge, perhaps even cast him out, if he had known the whole truth. For Simon, to satisfy his mother-in-law, had agreed to be married in church, in the Church, yes! And the priest was good enough, understanding enough, to permit the young man's family to be kept in the dark, so that the ceremony thus assumed a painful, almost secret character; the important thing was that the young couple contracted to raise their children in the Catholic faith. And Simon indeed promised, although with a black heart, to raise his children in the Catholic faith; and when Jacqueline murmured in his ear a little later that she would never hold him to that promise, Simon was in no way comforted.

For his own part, Yankel lied to his parents. He wrote them that Simon had married a young girl named Saulmann, whose first name

300

was Yaska; the poor man tried to lie as little as possible. He added that it had taken place in a beautiful synagogue. What was the use of hurting people, especially old people?

From America, there came sumptuous wedding gifts for the young couple, accompanied by congratulatory cards printed in English; Rachel Silverstone and Peretz Mykhanowitzki had not lost all their familial feeling. An uncle in America! thought the Saulniers, over-flowing with enormous respect.

From the Feinschneiders of Rakwomir, nothing came. Humanly speaking, they were too far off. Or, if Papa received a letter from them, he never said a word about it.

Simon detested being bored. Life in his company did not flow steadily; there were rapids, cascades, unexpected bends, and some-times lakes with stagnant waters.

Some time before their marriage, at Jacqueline's insistence, he had given up his project for a splendid honeymoon trip. "Things are a little tight right now," said Jacqueline, "and besides, it's not the sea-son. It would be smarter to wait a while." Three days later when she came to the Boulevard Beaumarchais, she ran into painters, masons, and plumbers, and Simon gleefully announced that he had a great surprise for her.

The surprise was a change in the firm's name. The panel above the front now read, in beautiful gold italic letters:

S I J A C

Sijac: Simon plus Jacqueline. It was a delicate compliment, and she was fully aware of it.

"Wait, wait, you haven't seen everything!" her husband teased.

A little disturbed, she wormed his plans out of him; it wasn't too hard.

Till then, he had slept on a narrow cot at the back of the shop and kept his belongings in a little commode. Now, of course, this wouldn't do; they needed a double bed, and a wardrobe—

"I have one," Jacqueline interrupted.

"Yes, but it won't be big enough."

"It'll be big enough for this place!"

"Yes, but . . ."

Simon scratched his head, and finally the whole story came out. "You must have vision, no? Well, since we're about it, why not buy bed, wardrobe, dining furniture all at once? You've got to foresee

301

children, a guest room. You know, if we buy it all we'll save money, because they'll cut the price." Fernand's boss had promised him a fantastic discount . . .

At the thought of spending money—spending to save!—Simon couldn't hold back his joy. Jacqueline let him talk; but finally she cut in:

"Where are you going to put it all, dearest? This is silly!"

Simon's face lit up.

"Exactly!"

Exactly; he would rent a fine six-room apartment not far from the shop; it seemed the absolute minimum to house Simon and Jacqueline Mykhanowitzki, their future children, their furniture, and their friends. A ridiculous rental, he repeated, a crust of bread.

"How much?" asked Jacqueline coldly; she was beginning to know her husband.

When the figure was named, the crust of bread became a ton of caviar.

"Look, dear," Jacqueline said sweetly, as if she were scolding a child. "We can wait awhile."

Simon protested vainly, arguing that, since they had given up their honeymoon trip, they could reward themselves with a few things; Jacqueline remained unmoved. They talked it over for quite a while; then she discovered the right method and pretended to give in.

"After all, it's your money; spend it as you like."

"No, no!" he cried, distracted. "Now it's yours too!"

And he surrendered immediately. There was no real regret; the setting of his own life mattered little to him; he had been thinking only of her.

So they moved into the room at the back of the shop, enlarged somewhat to accommodate them, and equipped with a gas heater. The camp cot gave way to a slightly larger bed, Simon's commode to Jacqueline's wardrobe. An unpainted pine kitchen buffet and table, and two rush-bottomed chairs; these sufficed for the lovers. Immediately, Jacqueline began to tighten the purse strings. Simon rejoiced. With him, it was all or nothing; since they hadn't bought princely furniture, unpainted wood delighted him; it proved he had become a serious man. Yankel himself, having come to see the young couple, found that they were going too far. Young people have to live a little, no? Simon maintained that a penny saved is a penny earned, and his father kept his mouth shut and went away shaking his head.

What influence that young woman already had over that booby! Was she going to make a miser of him? Pfeh! You had to do what you had to, but within reasonable limits; and Yankel didn't like too-rapid conversions.

Nevertheless, Jacqueline piloted her ship skillfully. At the beginning of her marriage, distrusting her husband's prodigality, she had asked him to sign a paper authorizing her to have her own account at the bank. Simon had signed it enthusiastically, delighted that their household possessed two bank accounts, delighted also for other reasons that he didn't tell his wife at the time. With the paper in her pocket, Jacqueline gave free reign to her peasant thrift. The cash that she had saved up before her marriage she used to buy some gilt-edged securities which grew silently in the bank's vaults; to them she added the revenues of that famous piece of land, whose existence Simon had forgotten. Furthermore, since the young wife ran the shop's cash register, from time to time she would take out a note or two to increase the secret hoard without saying anything about it to her husband. He never noticed anything. On the contrary, he was amazed that she needed so little money for their regular household expenses. He had never kept a budget and had always mixed his pocket money with the shop's. Now he was confounded by the benefits of order; his shop's finances were neither more nor less straight than before, but his wallet was always full.

In fact, without suffering at all by it, he had stopped throwing money out the window. The two young people lived only for each other, petting, fondling and caressing in their little corner, and that didn't cost much.

At first, Jacqueline avoided putting her nose into the shop's account books. Then she got the subtle feeling that Simon wasn't aware that he was the sort of man who would incur two large debts to pay off a small one. At the end of every month, especially, she would see him pacing about nervously; when he began to grow pale she knew that things were going badly. She began to question him and was shocked when she understood; Simon's debts were out of all proportion to her little economies.

"But—how do you expect to get out of it?"

"Don't worry about it, Jacounette."

He would put on a sly smile that she didn't like; he would talk of horse trading, of accommodation notes, and of other mysterious, perhaps dangerous things. He would end by hinting that a "good little bankruptcy" would fix everything. Yes, that was the idea in the back of his head; at the right moment, he would transfer as much money as possible from his name to hers; after which, *allez-oop!* . . . Jacqueline didn't like this solution at all, but for the moment she preferred to leave to her father-in-law, Yankel, the job of unsuccessfully protesting in the name of morality. She attacked Simon by getting him into a corner.

"If you're bankrupt you won't be able to run your business."

"Yes, but I can in your name. And then you know it never goes as far as a real bankruptcy. That doesn't do the creditors any good. You sign an agreement, you make a settlement and you work your way out . . . That's the way everybody does it."

To make even more certain he joined the Freemasons; a friend who was in it assured him that they never let one of their brethren go to the bottom. After a while he found a number of good philosophical reasons for it in addition.

Nevertheless he began to be agitated again; he had ideas, he wanted to grow bigger. Grow bigger? thought Jacqueline. Already? She felt sure of her mastery over her husband now; the time had come to oppose head-on any bankruptcy, even a fraudulent one. He, ignorant of what she was planning, kept talking and threading phrases together. He himself would manufacture the hats that he was selling; from the producer to the consumer without a middleman. Do you realize the profits, Jacounette? . . . No, Jacounette didn't seem to realize. He wasn't discouraged; he kept up his arguments and paraded all his eloquence: the advantages of mass production, the advantages of retailing, wiping out the competition, then a place for the factory, so many square feet, machines, a workman, maybe two . . .

She let him talk until she felt him weakening. "And the money, Simon?"

"Don't worry about it," he whispered slyly, unknowingly using an expression familiar to his Uncle Moishe.

She waited without taking her eyes off him. He capered, smiled, played the fool, and chucked her under the chin. Passively she allowed herself to be kissed. Finally he used the expected formula.

"Money you can always wangle somehow. A nice little failure . . ."

She said nothing; simply, smiling, she moved her index finger from right to left in front of her nose.

"What's come over you?" he asked naïvely.

304

"I say, No. None of that."

That was all. Simon withdrew into his shell, pouted like a scolded child, shook his head, exactly as his Grandfather Avrom acted when his wife scolded him.

"But what do you want me to do?" he groaned. "We can't bury our whole lives in this hole!"

Jacqueline knew that she mustn't overdo her victory.

"How much do you owe, Simon?"

He raised his arms to heaven, overwhelmed at such a childish question.

"How do I know? I owe, I'm owed, that's the way the world turns!"

"Have you borrowed much since our marriage?"

He thought about it and then, surprised, calculated that he hadn't, that he hadn't gone any further into debt, that he'd even been able to plug a couple of holes.

"Do you know that I know a little bit about accounting?"

They agreed to sit down and draw up a trial balance. He held off, thinking that it weakened his virile prerogatives, but his young wife's competence as much as her velvety insistence prevailed; after a quarter of an hour, he became zealous and tried to omit nothing. Their position, everything considered, was very shaky. Certainly there were some solid parts, but . . .

They talked it over for a long time. Every five minutes Simon would say, "You know, Jacounette, I have good backing, credit in the Paris market . . ."

"Of course, dearest."

She was counting on the sale of hats rather than on credit; she had a restricted conception of business. Since his, however, was too large, they ended by establishing a very happy balance. After some months, they had silently divided their jobs. He was audacity, she prudence; he had the ideas and the drive, it was up to her to see if reality would allow it. There were quarrels, but when either of them felt sure of his footing that one held firm and the other gave in. So Jacqueline agreed to start a workshop; in exchange Simon agreed to rent only a small area at first.

Their chief difficulties came from the fact that they didn't think on the same lines; Jacqueline reasoned like a shopkeeper and Simon like a broker. When she wanted to set aside so much per month to pay off their debts, he refused flatly, without being able to make her understand that you couldn't pay off large debts in the same way as you did small ones. One day she advised him to lower the quality of his workmanship and to raise the price; she figured by addition and subtraction that this would increase their profits. He looked at her pityingly and upheld the opposite point of view. They argued, but Simon did not yield; he lowered the price and raised the quality. The outcome proved him right; not only did their own shop's sales increase, but the Maison Sijac began to sell hats to other retailers. That made her think; she realized that if she was going to be of any real use to her husband she would have to enlarge her own viewpoint. She had some trouble getting there; some balancing exercises on the financial tightrope made her break into cold sweats, but she got there just the same, on the strength of her love.

For instance, after she took over the bookkeeping she cheated the Tax Bureau with professional skill, but on a shopkeeper's scale. One day, light broke over her and she understood that on a higher level, legal frauds are more efficacious; the most efficacious being to spend the store's profits freely. Expanding and redecorating the store on one hand increased the expenditures, thus diminishing the taxable income; on the other hand, it increased the amount of business and, therefore, the intake of cash—a twofold advantage. Having completed this reasoning, Jacqueline pushed Simon to expand his workshop; she reined him in only when she saw he was planning projects that were too grandiose.

Actually, the Maison Sijac's master stroke was a lucky hit. Simon had just installed his factory in a huge loft building in the Marais quarter, when the street was taken over for widening. A solid indemnity for expropriation—the State is generous, especially if you know where to put a few good bottles of wine—put him firmly in the saddle; a nice big expropriation is worth even more than a nice little bankruptcy. He immediately exploited his luck and threw himself into a huge publicity campaign. Jacqueline, frightened, opposed it; she thought that advertising was money thrown away. He held firm; and the country soon learned that the winner of the Tour de France bicycle race owed his victory to the fact that his wife wore a Sijac hat, the hat all Paris was wearing. Suddenly, the store on the Boulevard Beaumarchais became too narrow and gave birth to little ones.

But before the time of solid splendor finally arrived, the household lived through some difficult periods. Simon didn't like to count; his periods of parsimony never lasted long. In fact, they never consisted of more than a refusal to have his shoes resoled because it was too dear, only to buy new made-to-measure shoes two weeks later. Poor Jacqueline fought back desperately, trying to cut down unproductive spending. She ran into curt formulas: "You live only once! When you're sixty years old, with ulcers, what's the use of being wealthy?" Every time she managed to get enough together to pay off a debt, she had to spread it among the creditors. She succeeded in making him sell the Unic. He was sick over it; she pitied him, but she didn't give in. After a month, just when she thought the matter was buried, he drove up in a Donnet-Zédel, which he had bought without telling her—something contrary to all his habits. He blustered about uneasily, but she didn't scold. She had learned that when he really wanted something he could be unyielding. She noticed, after the honeymoon was over, that he was beginning to attend his Masonic Lodge too assiduously. She tried to bury that too. She was the one who, from time to time, suggested a ride in the car, the movies, a night club, either the Bouffes-Parisiens or the Folies-Bergères. She hoped that a slow disenchantment would be more efficacious than shock treatment. She was disappointed; he wanted more all the time, she less . . . Well, the important thing was that they weren't bankrupt.

So they were really in a stew when he announced one day that he wanted a child. Why? He didn't know; but he wanted one, as if it were a new car.

"But this is crazy, Simon!" Jacqueline groaned. "Give us a chance to breathe. There's plenty of time."

Slightly ashamed, she caught herself thinking that Jews were not only good husbands but prolific fathers. Grumbling, he shrugged and put on his most appealing expression . . .

"Listen, Jacounette, you don't have to wait till you're fifty to have children."

Without much hope, Jacqueline tried to reason with him; but now she knew her husband and his tyrannical desires; when he wanted something, it had to be right away. She asked herself if he would have the patience to wait nine months for the baby to be born.

She pointed to the dim back of the shop where they were still living.

"Look, darling, we can't have a baby in this place."

"That's right!" he said stubbornly.

"What do you mean, 'That's right!' "

But she understood.

"Which do you want, a baby or an apartment?" she went on gently. "Oh, how stupid you can be sometimes!"

Furious, he went out, slamming the door. It was the first time that he had allowed himself such a gesture. Jacqueline grew frightened and reflected upon it. No, she didn't know her husband yet. First overcome by his brilliant appearance, she had afterward rated him too low; she had judged him weak, pliable, irresponsible. One was no truer than the other. After all, she thought, he didn't wait for me to have his shop and his Unic. Irresponsible? Yes and no. Come to think of it, there wasn't anything unreasonable about his desires—a decent home and children by the woman he loved. Isn't that better than doing as those peasants who think they're so shrewd? They spend their whole lives piling up money for living, without ever living; and their heirs and the state get the benefit of it. Papa would be on Simon's side, Jacqueline thought. Not Mama. Watch out, or you'll be just like Mama!

When he returned he found Jacqueline in tears. He was completely repentant, kissed his young wife over and over, swore never to start quarreling again and kept on until he burst into tears.

Since Jacqueline was a sturdy young woman, she was pregnant in a month; the two young people could almost date the moment of conception. Simon almost burst with pride and joy. He hugged Jacqueline vehemently and then held back his vehemence; you have to go easy with a pregnant woman. He wanted to dance with her, then thought better of it for the same reason and danced instead with one of the two chairs, then shot outside like a cannon ball. Softened, with tears in her eyes, she judged herself severely; he really did want a baby, not an apartment! He came home loaded with bottles, with cakes and foie gras, gorged his wife with food because of the baby, but, because of the baby, forbade her any alcohol and allowed only a finger of claret and a finger of champagne. She had become an extraordinarily precious receptacle and he an extraordinarily attentive husband. Delighted, she allowed herself to be coddled. Immediately he announced that there would be no more discussion, he would rent the apartment on the first floor, which—see the coincidence!—was about to be vacant. He had known about it for some weeks. Six rooms, kitchen, bathroom, and the rent was laughable, and she was forced to realize that he adored not only babies, but also nice apartments.

308

Three days later the world was informed that M. Simon was expecting a son. When would it be? In seven and a half months? And Jacqueline, very annoyed, received the senior Mykhanowitzkis, ceremoniously come to congratulate her. Her father-in-law kissed her warmly on both cheeks, slapped his son on the shoulder, while joyously repeating, *"Mazeltov!"* (Some time ago Jacqueline had learned the meaning of certain ritual formulas.) Simon strutted fatuously, and Jacqueline finally realized that for these two men—yes, even for Simon!—the birth of the first male heir (for, automatically, that's what they expected) represented a sort of religious event.

Her mother-in-law was very strongly moved; for the first time Jacqueline heard her talk, and even prattle, as volubly as Simon, in an impossible mishmash, four-fifth Yiddish and one-fifth broken French, all this in the midst of a brook of joyful tears.

After Simon's parents, there followed a mass of close relatives, all coming from the Rue des Rosiers; tall, short, fat, thin, first braying in Yiddish, and then scandalized because the young wife didn't understand that language and closely examining the *goya*, who, completely surprised, felt that she was the foreigner! In loud voices and with their hats on their heads, the men laid down definitive rulings— always in Yiddish, since the *goya* didn't matter to them. The women, laughing and with ready tears, gave intimate advice and discussed their own complications, always in French, so that she could understand. And one and all burdened her with heavy Jewish cakes, perfumed with cumin and ginger. Finally she groaned, "Have you so many relatives, Simon?" and Simon admitted that he didn't know how many, that he didn't even know how he was related to most of the visitors.

"Mama's very close to her family, you know, but I . . ." He limited himself to enumerating a round dozen names ending in -witz, -ski, -witzki, -ovitch, and -son. Jacqueline cried for mercy, threatened to make her own relatives come, that is to say the whole village of Virelay; and Simon put an end to the invasion under the pretext that his wife was fatigued. The only remaining visitors were several shy and very polite whores of the Boulevard, the foundation of his clientele, who when they heard of the "interesting situation" felt they had to come; especially when it was such a sweet woman as Mme. Sijac.

Meanwhile Simon bubbled and rejoiced. He had rented his apartment, and put the painters and decorators to work; the money soared away. Once the apartment was ready he cloistered poor Jacqueline in it, tyrannizing over her, treating her from the beginning as if she were in her eighth month and threatened with a miscarriage. She was allowed to leave the chaise longue only to get into bed. If she rose from the table to go to the kitchen, he would leap from his chair, frightened. "Watch out for the baby!" He would scream in anger, until he remembered that hysteria would hurt the baby; then he became wheedling and cajoling, stuffed his wife with delicacies and tore out his hair when she said she wasn't hungry. "Look, you have to eat twice as much for the baby!" She began to wonder if his solicitude wasn't more for the baby than for herself. He stopped going out evenings. And from the first month, he believed it his duty to practice complete chastity; he was slightly upset because she showed no desire except the forbidden one for exercise. In short, in trying to spare her any fatigue, he wore her out; Jacqueline's face, once so glowing, grew pale.

Now the doctors came in procession. "She's too careful of herself!" they said, one after the other; and they advised long walks. Simon ended by obeying; he went along with his wife, holding back the pace, vigilant, ready to protect that precious belly with his life. One of the doctors, bombarded with questions about the length of the walks, prescribed an hour and a half. Simon watched and made sure that his young wife was back on the chaise longue on the ninety-first minute. It was useless to argue with him. "Look, she's expecting a baby!" he would cry, as if it had never happened before in the history of mankind. The closer the time came, the more terrible his imagination painted the childbirth. A belly, a poor female belly, so soft, so tender, so sensitive, so fragile, swelled and tore itself open to expel that huge bleeding mass. Oh, it was horrible! In his imagination he gave birth ten times before his wife did. He didn't dare tell her of his fears, lest he frighten her. He was wrong; she would have been delighted at this proof that he was worried about her, and not only about the child.

Catherine Saulnier paid her daughter four or five visits. She took her by the shoulders and shook her firmly; what a rag! Simon reacted violently. Mother-in-law and son-in-law became hotly embroiled and resolved not to see each other again. In his absence, she brought up the question of baptism. Jacqueline turned a deaf ear. Catherine insisted: "He promised; he's got to keep his promise!" Jacqueline replied that *he* wasn't opposed to baptism, *she* was. In truth, Simon had forgotten his promise; if he had been reminded, he would have kept it, albeit grudgingly.

The two women quarreled violently, all their old warmed-over hatreds reappearing. Finally Jacqueline cried:

"If it's a boy and I want to baptize him, he'll have the right to have the child circumcised! Well?"

"These savages!"

To Mother Saulnier, there was only one religion on earth and, consequently, no problem. She went home furious and didn't set foot in her daughter's house until the child was born.

Hannah, on the other hand, increased her visits and never forgot to bring candy or flowers to the young wife. Simon was stunned by his mother's gifts of flowers. Why? Bah! Whenever he had to furnish an explanation that was too delicate, Simon would shrug his shoulders and turn his back, grumbling all the while. Jacqueline finally understood that gifts of flowers were not customary with the Mykhanowitzki tribe; she recalled that the vases were always empty in the apartment in the Rue des Francs-Bourgeois, except when she filled them. Simon himself, although so attentive to his wife, rarely thought of bringing her flowers. Then she's imitating me! Jacqueline said to herself. She began to understand the effort that her mother-in-law was making to give her pleasure. Poor woman! Jacqueline became interested in Hannah as something other than a piece of furniture, and little by little, helped along by her leisure, and perhaps by the feeling of well-being caused by her pregnancy, she began to grow fond of her mother-in-law.

When the old woman came into the apartment, she would grow busy (without saying a word) putting things in place, sweeping and washing, for Jacqueline still had no maid. Then she would sit near her daughter-in-law and sew. The two women spoke only when they had something to say; but Hannah's mere presence was soothing to Jacqueline. On several occasions, Jacqueline scolded Simon for treating his mother so casually. In her idleness, she began to look forward to the old lady's visits. She even wondered why they weren't more frequent. It took her a long time to realize that the old lady was afraid to go out alone in Paris; to her, the short trip from the Rue des Francs-Bourgeois to the Boulevard Beaumarchais meant a perilous voyage which required all her courage.

Yankel also came; less often than Hannah, because of his work, but much more often than before Jacqueline's pregnancy. She learned to know him, too. He had a modest courtesy, a sensitive delicacy; for instance, he never failed to take off his hat when he greeted her. This regard was keenly felt by the young woman, still scarred by the coarseness of Virelay. Thus, little by little, she entered into an intimacy with these strangers; and the better she understood them, the better she understood her husband, Simon, who was French skin deep, but whose inner qualities went back to his origins. Oddly enough, it was his faults—instability, rootlessness—that had first attracted her; the effects of the storm of emigration that still, only slightly weakened, shook him. But now she went beyond that, and even deeper; she began to penetrate her husband's true nature and to love him for what he was, not for what he seemed.

It was a boy. Simon was overjoyed and named the child Jean-Claude. Why Jean-Claude? He didn't know. It pleased him, that's all! Jacqueline insisted on adding the names Jacques and Baptiste, in honor of the two grandfathers; he didn't see why, one first name seemed enough to him. But since she insisted . . .

Then the maternal and paternal grandparents came running, all honey and smiles, and glared at each other across the cradle. Perfidious words, sweet animosity . . . Simon, who had eyes only for the baby, noticed nothing, but Jacqueline understood. Baptism or circumcision? A little Christian or a little Jew? She hesitated, wondering whether to satisfy everybody. She would have him baptized and circumcised at different times; then she saw it would have the opposite effect and displease everybody. She had had enough; she realized that the child was hers and not theirs, and she decided to neither baptize nor circumcise him. She thought she would find an ally in her father; she was wrong.

Baptiste grumbled, scolded, complained and ended by asking:

"You aren't going to make a Jew of him?"

In vain she protested that the absence of baptism didn't mean circumcision; he wasn't convinced. So much the worse! She felt that she was growing away from him; she had long since grown away from her mother, and Catherine stayed there like a piece of wood, her hands crossed on her bag, her lips pursed.

On his side, Simon was at grips with Papa and Mama.

"So, when is the *B'rith?*" Hannah asked with a happy smile. Since she was on good terms with her daughter-in-law, she thought they were allied, and she rejoiced at the thought of the ritual feast, one of the gayest in life. Simon rebelled and stormed; no circumcision, they weren't savages, he wouldn't have anyone butchering his son. When the old woman realized that he wasn't going to yield, she withdrew, leaving the father and son to settle matters between them. It didn't take long. Yankel began a sermon, Simon cut him short, Yankel stared at him silently for a moment, and then, with a pleasant smile:

"Maybe you're going to baptize him a Catholic?"

He was only half convinced by the denials of his son, who himself suddenly remembered, uneasily, the promises made to the priest at his marriage.

Then the two grandfathers had a long, apparently cordial, but extremely strained conversation; they spoke of religion, in the abstract.

"Religion is silly," Yankel said.

"Yes, you have to be an idiot," Baptiste agreed. Then:

"Baptism," Baptiste said, "isn't like circumcision; it doesn't show, and it does no harm."

"True," Yankel replied, "but morally, it's just as serious."

They parted coldly. As for the grandmothers, they ignored each other deliberately.

Baptiste forgot it quickly enough; Catherine didn't forget, and Hannah wept for a long while. Yankel affected a detached air; every time he visited, he would say casually, looking at the baby, "Don't you think he's a little pinched?" Or else: "They say circumcision is more hygienic." Remarks which regularly fell into the abyss.

Since Jean-Claude's birth, Simon had become very domestic. He, who at one time hadn't been able to sit still, now could spend hours playing with the baby, or just watching it, with the patience of a fisherman. He hadn't dreamed of manufacturing a little being at once so complicated and so delicate. When he said "My son," it seemed as though he had said everything. He would call the doctor at the first sign of the baby's discomfort, and if the doctor expressed skepticism, he would cry, "Don't you understand—it's my son!" No one had had a son before this one.

A year later, Jacqueline brought a second boy into the world. He was named Pierre and caused no commotion; the course had already been set. Simon wasn't very happy about it; he had wanted a daughter this time. He was satisfied on this point two years later. Unfortunately, he had to yield on the question of her first name. He dreamed of "Monique," but Jacqueline had set her heart on "Edwige," which seemed chic to her, and she won, even though her husband protested against this alien name.

Three children fill a Parisian apartment, even one of six rooms. Simon's paternal fears were also spread thin, especially since his business distracted him very much at this time. But he always kept his weakness for Jean-Claude, who remained his "son," while the others were only his "children." Yankel, too, preferred Jean-Claude, although he forced himself to be fair to all.

The bond that bound the young couple to the Saulniers was for various reasons very loose. First, Virelay was distant and hardly a pleasant place to stay in winter, the only time when Baptiste was free. And then there was Catherine, who was now always either bitter or locked in silence. Somehow she got the notion of showing that she was too refined, especially toward her son-in-law, to reproach him for being what he was, a Jew; instead she stuffed him with food. When Yankel heard these stories of the Saulniers from his son, he didn't fail to point out that French families were not as close as Jewish ones; personal animosities and quarrels over money ravaged them endlessly.

Catherine never came to Paris. Baptiste, however, often longed to see his daughter. Sometimes in winter he would show up, ugly and clumsy, in his Sunday clothes. He scarcely spoke, as if he were frightened, and he didn't dare to play with the children. They were painful evenings. The old peasant wasn't able to be himself except in his accustomed surroundings.

Relations between the young Mykhanowitzkis and himself didn't improve until much later, when Simon had had a house built on Jacqueline's piece of ground, and especially after Catherine's death. (She fell accidentally into the well—accidentally was the official story; actually no one knew what had happened.)

In the meantime, the Mykhanowitzki parents became the preferred side. Every two weeks, regularly, the younger ones went to dine with their elders. Jacqueline was a bit bored by it but didn't dare to admit it. She would help her mother-in-law to clean up, and then she would knit silently, while the children played noisily in the workroom; their grandfather had prudently locked up everything which would cut, slice, or stab. "They're terrible!" he would exclaim tenderly. He blamed that on their Saulnier blood; for Jewish blood in general and Mykhanowitzki blood in particular produced only sweet and wise children.

Simon would pass the afternoon in a sort of happy torpor, playing dominoes with anyone who wanted to and even with anyone who didn't want to. Whence came this amazing patience? Jacqueline would ask herself this, and, without understanding it very well, she sensed that it was absolutely necessary to leave Simon in peace. He was having serious business troubles. Undoubtedly he was drawing strength from the surroundings of his youth; he was so French the rest of the time that she felt well able to permit him an occasional Judaeo-Rakwomirian debauch. All the time he was playing dominoes, Simon would listen to the family chronicle. His mother spoke only Yiddish; he would translate for Jacqueline whether it was necessary or not. His father, on the other hand, spoke only French and did it almost ostentatiously. After a time, Jacqueline began to feel that she was a target; in their own fashions, Grandpa and Grandma were trying to turn their daughter-in-law into a Jew; as for Simon, he let them. So Jacqueline also let them, first because she hadn't any choice, and secondly because these attempts were at once so clumsy and so well meant that she could only smile at them.

Grandpa especially was amusing. He never skipped a chance to teach his daughter-in-law Yiddish, and she would graciously repeat the foreign words, with an accent which would make everybody laugh, including herself. And then he would tell her endless stories. Tales of pogroms which horrified her—she had never heard anyone speak of such things. And funny stories which unfailingly lost all their humor in French. But whatever the story was, invariably the moral went to prove that Jews were good, kind, courageous, hard-working, honest. That, of course, to beat a breach in the walls of anti-Semitism.

Generally, it was Simon who drew them both out of this business; he would break in just to say that there were worse things than hanging some Jews, and his father, grievously hurt, would take refuge in silence, shaking his head.

These Sunday reunions would last for varying lengths of time—that is, until Simon had had enough of them. Suddenly, without the slightest warning, he would seem to wake up; he would stand up, pull himself together, and shoot out: "Well, shall we go?"

And they had to grab the children, the coats, kiss the parents

315

swiftly, and get down the stairs. Usually it was at the moment the parents would choose to remember some very important things they had to tell their children. So much the worse, it would keep for next time! And the retreat would turn into a rout.

Jacqueline ended by feeling herself slowly being absorbed by the Mykhanowitzkian milieu. Instinctively she reacted by falling back on French society. She multiplied her visits to Virelay, with the excuse that she was taking the children out to get the air. She grew friendlier with her father. It was really impossible to do that with her mother. Simon saw nothing of this. She attacked him more directly. She began to evoke memories of her childhood, spoke of her parents, of her friends, and especially of the countryside. She told, for example, the story of the rosebush that her father had told her of once having grafted on . . . but these stories annoyed Simon. He didn't listen. Piqued, she insisted:

"Oh, if you had known Virelay then! It wasn't as it is today. There weren't all these lilacs—"

"The lilacs are beautiful," Simon retorted with his Parisian logic. "What have you got against them?"

"The farmers—"

"Oh, the farmers, the farmers . . . What do you want? Everything changes! That's life!"

He didn't recognize the bee in her bonnet, and neither did she. Clumsily, she was searching for other complaints—against whom? Against what?

"Look at the houses! When I was a little girl there were only two houses on the Plateau. Now . . ."

"Well? Are you sorry? That only proves the countryside is growing richer. It doesn't hurt your father to have some new houses up there instead of his old rats' nests. Don't you think so?"

Yes, of course, Jacqueline thought so! Which didn't keep her from being all mixed up. Somehow she felt there was a subtle analogy between her own transformation and that of her village.

"I don't know what's been bothering you all this time," Simon ventured one day humorously. "But you certainly can be reactionary when you set yourself to it! Your father was going under; the Parisians' houses made everything beautiful, with central heating, electricity, and all that. Bathrooms, progress, life! Am I wrong?"

No, Simon wasn't wrong when you really thought about it. Even the peasants of the vineyards gained from contact with the newcom-

316

ers; they improved their dwellings; they grew civilized, and so the village became prettier, a little town.

Did Simon sense what was going on in his wife's heart? Or was it simply an old dream, hugged secretly, that came into his mind?

"Incidentally," he said casually one day, "if the expropriation goes well"—the proceedings were just beginning—"what would you say to building a little weekend villa on your land? It wouldn't cost too much . . ."

What could Jacqueline say about it? To her great shame, it filled her with joy. She saw herself as mistress of an estate, parading in full view of her old friends. But for the record, she protested and advised her husband to pay his debts first. He kissed her warmly; he understood.

They understood each other better and better, without any need for explanation. Theirs was as happy and contented a household as could be.

III

POOR Yankel Mykhanowitzki! He really had no luck with his children! His oldest daughter Rivka? All she could find to marry was a little Polack who looked like an anti-Semitic caricature. Are you going to tell me that they were happy together? What's that! Money, money . . . Did they have any children? No, eh? So? And when Rivka finally decided to propagate, she brought forth a daughter! And another girl a few years later. What, no boy? No, no boy, and Rivka stopped there. Tchch!

And Simon? Eh, Simon? He married a *goya!* Are you going to tell me the *goya* is sweet, modest, honest, loyal, and a good housekeeper? Of course! But she's still a *goya,* no? And the boys aren't circumcised, and who knows if they haven't been baptized? So?

And now, Clara. Yes, Clara! What she's done to her poor mother! And today she announces she's going away. Yes, unmarried, and she's leaving her father's house, she's going out into the country. Oy, tchch, that smells bad! A beautiful girl, twenty-four years old, how will you make anyone believe she's still a virgin? Yankel knew, Yankel sensed long ago—he's not as simple as he looks!—that his youngest daughter had done some foolish things. Naturally, he hadn't breathed a word of his suspicions to poor Hannah, who would have died of shame—think of it, her daughter a trollop!

"And why do you want to go so far away from your parents?"

"They've offered me a good job."

"Oy, a good job! First, who's *they?*"

"The corporation! They're starting a branch at Nîmes, and . . ."

Yankel thought. Then, timidly, for he himself felt there was something ridiculous in the question:

"Is Nîmes far from Nevers?"

Clara's eyes widened.

"Far enough. Why?"

Silence, a deep sigh.

And then Clara left. Hannah didn't weep much, contrary to her usual custom. She only looked her daughter in the eye.

"Try to be wise, Clara," she said in an odd voice.

Thinking about it, Yankel wondered whether Hannah hadn't had more than suspicions.

Are you going to tell me that a year later Clara too got married? Yes, but to whom? A man nobody knew, a stranger, an Italian! Now I ask you! Giardinelli, what kind of a name is that? Not Jewish, not even French! Pfeh! Whatever that girl has in her head, it'll end badly, I'm telling you!

Luckily, Yankel was well satisfied with his youngest son, his dear Fernand. Fernand was a boy full of good qualities. He was serious, reflective, sensible; his father thought he saw himself again in him. Besides, he was trained in a good trade and was five feet, ten inches tall. After his military service, the young man—the young people have to test their wings, no?—had left his father's roof to live on his own. Good! Perfect! And his parents were waiting for their son to bring home a young woman one day; burned by Simon and Clara, they avoided consulting marriage brokers.

So what happens? Fernand, himself, comes to scold his parents for not taking proper care of him. Yes! He was now old enough to get married, he wanted to start a family; and he was surprised that his father and mother had failed in their duty. Was he to marry just anyone? He wanted to meet a nice girl, a good housekeeper, with some money if possible, so that he could set up in business for himself. Jewish, naturally, so there wouldn't be any trouble. Yankel and Hannah were delighted at having such a good son; and Yankel scolded himself severely the next day when he sensed that, in spite of his delight, he thought that his son Fernand was a bit of a fool. Tchch! Man is a perverse animal. Instead of admiring good attitudes, immediately he makes fun of them. After that, are you surprised that the world goes so badly!

His father and mother sifted the candidates for Fernand's hand. Their choice was difficult; they wanted a pretty young girl, but not too pretty; lively, but not too lively; intelligent, but not too intelligent; with some money, but not too much; Jewish, but French. They ended by digging out one Odile Bloch, who filled their bill and, consequently, Fernand's. The marriage took place "with only the immediate families present"; and another household was begun. That's life!

Yankel was just beginning to gather himself together from all these emotions, when a letter from his father informed him of his mother's death. He wept as was fitting, but with a lack of feeling that surprised and humiliated him. He had loved his mother very much. Then why didn't he feel a deeper pain? Because she had died far away and you believe in death only when you see it? Truly, he had twice suffered his mother's death, the two times when they had separated with the idea that their separation was final. Since her departure for Palestine, the old woman lived only in her son's memory; her actual death changed nothing.

Nevertheless, little by little Yankel was overcome by the thought that something was ended. He began to talk about his mother a great deal, recounting and amplifying her virtues and forgetting her faults. Breina Mykhanowitzki thus became a sort of saint, and he wasn't satisfied any more with Hannah alone as confidante. He needed the whole family in order to expand. He called together this one and that one under various pretexts, but the evening almost always ended up with the old lady. He didn't realize that, in pushing his mother back into legend, he himself was beginning to take on the shape of a patriarch when he was barely past his fiftieth birthday.

After a while, Simon, patient at first, grew tired of it. Of course he remembered his grandmother, but she was far off. She was old, she was dead; well, it happens to everybody. You feel pain, and then you let it drop. Yankel, hurt, turned to his daughter-in-law, who was forced to listen politely. Jacqueline hadn't known the old woman.

She tried to be obliging. "How old was she?"

Yankel thought awhile. "Oh, seventy, seventy-five."

Jacqueline was silently surprised that he wasn't surer of this fact. "Then your father must be very old?"

"He? Oh, perhaps eighty-five," Yankel replied.

She spoke of her surprise to Simon, who began to laugh. "How do you expect Papa to know his parents' age? They don't know it themselves! When they were born, there were no civil records in Russia, at least not for them."

In one instant she measured the chasm. Then she remembered that Simon never celebrated the birthday of his father or his mother. She asked him why, whether it was also because of the lack of any records. He laughed; of course his parents knew their birthdays, the Russians had ended up by keeping records. The only thing was, their calendar wasn't the same as the French, it was thirteen days ahead

320

or behind. To make a long story short, Papa had snarled himself up so completely that now he kept three birthdays: a true one according to the Russians, a true one according to the French, and a false one according to the French.

"You'll go insane over these wild stories," he ended. "I'll tell you something about these people, Jacounette; when they feel old, right away they say they're a hundred."

After this, Jacqueline stopped worrying; she limited herself to allowing her father-in-law to talk without questioning him or hearing him; she was saturated.

Now that his mother was dead and embalmed in his memory, Yankel realized that he had been worrying about his father and that he had been doing it for a long while.

Oh, the old man had apparently been full of life when he left for Palestine, and he had announced his wish to die in the Holy Land in a gay voice; but the idea of shedding torrents of tears on the soil of his fathers had held no joy for him. He had also been full of business ideas; since Palestine was the source of all religious commodities and holiday foods, why shouldn't he work in that field for export? Actually, all he had to do was pick up the Jerusalem end of the thread that he had known at the Paris end. Groceries and prayers, prayers and tears, tears and groceries; his whole life could be traced there, full of happiness up to a happy death.

But from the beginning, Yankel had felt that things weren't going well. Why? Well, it was difficult to be exact; the old man's letters consisted nine tenths of praises of the Lord and curses on the impious. Business? He didn't speak of it. Health? He didn't speak of that either. Was he, for some obscure reasons, unhappy? On the contrary, he never stopped swimming in joy, and his wife also, to believe him. So?

Well, you had the feeling that the elasticity had gone out of him. At one time, Yankel blamed the Palestinian environment. Jerusalem, and the Wailing Wall, the atmosphere of ancient defeats, the weight of centuries of sorrow, all that must be so unhealthy, so morbid. Then he thought of the Arabs. From time to time, he would read in the newspapers of a massacre. He questioned his father insistently. No reply. One would think that the Arabs didn't exist, that the massacres were made up by the newspapers. In revenge, the old man never stopped cursing the Zionists, those heretics who respected none of the Lord's Commandments, who wanted to use Hebrew, the Holy

Tongue, for everyday talk. Yankel didn't understand anything any more. His imagination painted a Palestine that he felt was erroneous, but he didn't know how to modify it; he pictured, under the desert sun, a sort of Rue des Rosiers, peopled by old, pious and peaceful Jews, surrounded by frowning Arabs with their scimitars ready. He tried to find out for himself; the different information, mostly contradictory, that he received here and there only increased his confusion without satisfying his curiosity.

After a while, the old man's letters became more and more complaining. The one that announced the death of Breina hardly differed from the others: "The Lord has called your poor mother to Him, praised be the Lord; she, she's the lucky one now, she's happy, but I'm all alone, and at my age life is hard." The whole letter was in this tone. He mentioned only incidentally that the old woman had suffered in her last days. On the other hand, the old man complained a great deal of his eyesight, which was growing weaker, "and who's going to take care of me now?" He seemed to be blaming his wife for having abandoned him. He's getting old, thought Yankel, who blamed it on senile egotism.

Then the letters came further apart. One day Yankel got a shock when he saw the envelope; the handwriting wasn't his father's. Dead? No; the signature was old Avrom's, but only the signature, for, in order to save his sight, he had dictated the letter to a kindly neighbor. After a while, Yankel saw a certain Mme. Zipovitch rise to the surface in each phrase. Who was she? The old man didn't say; besides, he never worried about being understood, he wrote what he wanted to, and work it out for yourself. Yankel came to the conclusion that his father was talking about a very pious neighbor who, to do a *mitzvah,* was taking care of the old man—probably the same one who was writing his letters. He grew uneasy, suspected an intriguing woman drawn by his father's money, and became upset about it—but what could he do?

It wasn't the inheritance that bothered him. Before going away, his father had announced that he would leave all his worldly goods to charity; and his son thought that this was natural, agreeing, with Tolstoy, that inheritance was immoral; only he would have preferred, instead of pious works, socialist, philanthropic or other causes. But, well, his father was free. What bothered him in this Zipovitch business was that this swindler would snatch all this money to which she had no right, and crime would be rewarded.

As if to add to his suspicions, his father, by the hand of Mme. Zipovitch, began to plead for money, with sordid details as to the need: Mme. Zipovitch had to buy him some slippers, or some dishes, or else they needed oil and oil had gone up again. What's going on, Yankel wondered, overwhelmed. He knew that old Avrom's commercial plans hadn't turned out well; but from that to needing money for oil was a long way; his father had been well off when he left.

While all this was going on, he received a visitor, a forty-year-old rabbi straight from Jerusalem. Arrogant, despotic, swollen with pride, his red beard bristling with indignation, the rabbi suddenly began to thunder, "Ungrateful son, the blows of the lord, your father, the saintly *Chassid*," and so on. At first Yankel thought of throwing him out, revolted that a man younger than he, rabbi or not, dared to speak to him in that tone. Then he overcame the impulse; the news of his father stupefied him. The poor old man, that saint, almost blind, who is so wretched, who lives on public charity while he has such rich children, a shame, and that holy Mme. Zipovitch who eats herself up for him . . . all this was thrown pell-mell into Yankel's face. When the rabbi paused for breath, Yankel tried to question him. But the rabbi evidently knew nothing of M. Mykhanowitzki's past splendor; to him, he was only a poor infirm old *Chassid*, a kind of mendicant saint, who still found a way to make gifts to the Jewish community, who deprived himself of necessities to help those he thought more unfortunate. "You should kiss the feet of a man like that!" the rabbi screamed. First Yankel tried to clear himself, and then to obtain more precise information, some details, for instance, of his mother's death. The rabbi paused for a moment to growl:

"Mme. Mykhanowitzki? I don't know her!"

And back again to curses, screams and insults. In a last attempt to make peace, Yankel invited this worthy to dinner. He was greeted with a haughty refusal. "You'd probably give me pork to eat!" Then it was Yankel's turn to grow angry; he cried out that he knew nothing of these stories. The rabbi screamed, "You're a liar!" and Yankel was about to thump him one when the rabbi left, slamming the door. And there they were; Hannah was weeping, and Yankel was as white as a sheet. What was he trying to get at like that? he repeated to himself, pacing about in the apartment. There was only one explanation: The old man, in a frenzy of devotion and charity, must have given all that he owned to the synagogue—all, down to the last cent. Finally, Yankel took his hat and umbrella and went straight off to Moishe's house.

In the shop he found only his sister-in-law, at grips with a customer. He waved to her and then, as a member of the family, seated himself in the darkest corner, waiting until she was finished.

Yankel watched his sister-in-law. He didn't like her, of course, but he had to admit that she had a certain dignity. She showed that she was the owner's wife by wearing a well-made black dress instead of the smock of the saleswoman. She heightened the effect by the discreet use of a few obviously expensive jewels. Condescendingly amiable, she had never adopted that commercial grin that so annoyed Yankel in his son's shop. On the contrary, she seemed to be doing her customers a favor, with a certain chill grace, showing that she had worldly manners. Yankel never could understand how she was able to keep her customers by treating them with such hauteur. It is true that people are foolish. If the shopkeeper doesn't lick their boots, they'll lick his; they'll drive a good, simple man out of business, and the next minute they'll beg a great lady to deign to sell them an article at twice its worth. "Anyway, it's work for her!" Yankel said to himself, admiring the beautiful jewelry shop. There was a salesman, two saleswomen, wall-to-wall carpeting, sparkling silverware, and elegant conversation; outside the sparkle of a fine neighborhood . . . What does Moishe do in all this? What good is he here?

He had rarely seen his brother in action. First, because he had rarely seen him at the shop; three times out of four Moishe was at the races. The fourth time—well, he stood there, observing everything, his hands behind his back and his decorations very visible in his buttonhole. When a customer came in, he went, dragging his lame foot, to receive her at the door; he greeted her courteously, found out what she wanted, and turned her over to the salesman. He took no further interest in the matter unless it was a very important sale. If he knew the visitor, he kissed her hand, conversed with her for a moment as a gallant man would, and stayed near the salesman, from time to time dropping a soothing word. If the customer was a man, Prince Moishe did not concern himself with him and let his wife take care of the sale.

At bottom, he's only decorative, Yankel thought. A parasite, that's all! Rose takes care of everything.

Poor Rose! She hadn't done well by marrying this good-for-nothing, even though she had gone so far as to forget her noble origins and his Polackishness. She should have foreseen it, Yankel thought. Her sad, worn-out face, dyed hair; her body, which grew cowlike in spite of the diets, girdles, corsets, and the beauty shop; and all for what? How many children? Six? Seven? Yankel had never known the exact number, he remembered only that there were about half a dozen, some before and some after the war; and that there was a René, a Guy, an Arlette or Josette or Claudette or something of that sort; another daughter had the name of a flower, or like it; and . . . oh, yes, Solomon. The last one was called Solomon; God knows why, this Jewish name among all those French ones. How had Rose been able to run the shop with all those children in arms? You had to admit she was a courageous woman.

At one time, just the same, she had been forced to withdraw; there had been three or four childbirths, one after the other. But that hadn't lasted long; worn out as she was, she had quickly resumed her place. Suddenly, Yankel understood. He remembered the time, a few years ago; during her absence Rose had been replaced by a chief saleswoman, a very pretty chief saleswoman . . . Pfeh! To betray his wife, the mother of his children, with a tramp! What a disgrace!

So, Moishe was a bad husband? Tchch! The good-for-nothing! If he had betrayed his wife once, he must have done it fifty times! What does that mean? If you want to lead a gay life, you shouldn't marry. You haven't the right to make another human being unhappy for your own selfish pleasure. You're a man, not an animal! Poor Rose . . .

"Hello, Yankel. How are you?"

Rose stood there, finished with her customer. Yankel, as confused as if she had been able to read his thoughts, began to babble. He wanted to say something friendly; he had so much pity for this poor woman. But already she was going on mechanically, "And how is the family?"

She never named Yankel's wife and children. She lumped them all together under that ridiculous appellation, "the family," in the tone of a patron lady. In the blink of an eye, Yankel's affectionate feelings were dissipated.

"How's yours?" he replied rudely.

Rose gestured vaguely and plastered an artificial smile on her face. "Thank God, everybody's fine."

Yankel's lips tightened; his sister-in-law was always stuffing her conversation with "Thank Gods." Yankel found this ridiculous; he forgot that his own wife, Hannah, often enough warded off the Evil Eye.

Obviously, Rose didn't know what to say to her Polack of a brother-in-law; she began to speak of her children. René, Guy, Odette ... Mentally, Yankel noted the names in passing, while orally he enthused as much as possible. Oh? René, philosophy, the Sorbonne? Really, he's an intellectual, like you, not like his father. Oh? Georges wants to go into the films? Hou-ou! And Odette, medicine? But, really, for a girl ...

"I suppose you've come to see Moïse?" (Rose had Gallicized her husband's first name.) "You should have telephoned."

"Not here? But will he be here tonight?"

Yankel had put the question in all innocence. In a lightning flash he saw his sister-in-law's face become disturbed, but almost immediately the smile was plastered back on. Pfeh! He's still hunting! Poor woman ...

"I don't think so, Yankel. Moïse is in the country on business. Perhaps I can help?"

Yankel cast a disturbed glance about him. With all these people around, how ... He was surprised; Rose had understood and he hadn't even opened his mouth.

"Mr. John," she called, "I'll be back soon."

The apartment was on the first floor. Yankel always went up by the stairway, but Rose meant to use the elevator, which was there to be used. The wrought iron of the first gate, the clanging panel of the second, the glazed cage as unstable as a chemist's balance, the button carelessly pushed, the light jar of the lift, and then they stopped. Yankel emerged from the elevator carefully. Moishe's sumptuous apartment, rugs everywhere, china closets, bric-a-brac, Oriental vases, massive furniture—oooy! All this must cost a lot of money! Yankel didn't dare to admit that he didn't like the apartment.

"Well, Yankel, what's up?"

That immediate attack, as if there were a fire in the house, that cold, businesswoman's voice! Yankel was so annoyed that he decided to make better use of an armchair, a comfortable tapestry shepherdess which he had sat on only to the beginning of his thighs. He moved at least two inches backward.

Suddenly a swarm of little Moishes, the postwar series, burst into the living room, screeching, hugging him, leaping on his knees, shouting in his ears . . . No, once the count was taken, there were only three, two boys and a girl, a redhead, a brunette, and one undecided between brown and chestnut; but all the eyes sparkling and full of life. At the end of five minutes, Yankel was out of breath, had twice called Georges Solomon, and Florence Odette, believed himself dishonored, and apologized for having forgotten to buy bonbons.

Abruptly Rose clapped her hands and the demons vanished. Yankel made his smile as pleasant as possible, nodded like a master, and finally asserted, "They are darling."

"Adorable," Rose, who knew what to say, confirmed, and she immediately returned to the subject, blaming her haste on the needs of the shop. Shop or not, still she could offer me a cup of tea, couldn't she? . . . Yankel began to discuss his business, introducing it with a hyperbolical eulogy of old Avrom, that holy man who—

She cut him short: Yes, yes, she had known her father-in-law well, she appreciated his real worth. "But what exactly do you want from Moïse?"

Pfeh! How dry, brutal, positive, commercial this woman is! She doesn't even give you time to prepare your argument, all of a sudden, tchip, tchip, you have to talk. Is there a fire in the house? . . . Yankel wanted to depict lengthily, in fitting terms, the wretchedness in which the poor old man was living. But this woman was hustling him in an indecent manner. He limited himself to putting on an expression of the deepest affliction and nodding two or three times.

"You know, Rose, he's really unhappy, the poor old man; ill, all alone, far from his children . . ."

"I always said that at his age it was madness to go. Well! You want to make him come back?"

"Oy! Rose, Rose, you ought to understand, since you're so devout! We must sympathize with others. Palestine is the Promised Land for him, he would rather die of hunger there than—"

"But I thought he was well off? All right! You want his children to send him a pension?"

"Heh!" said Yankel, and he spread his palms wide. She was going too fast for him.

Rose had already risen. Yankel rose also. She was as tall as he. He noted on her face the lines of the wrinkles, ill-covered by cream, powder, make-up. She had been beautiful once, but now, with those pouches under her eyes, that witchlike nose . . . What hurt Yankel especially were her eyes, hard and fixed in that desert of dry skin.

"You know, Yankel, life is hard for everybody today. Haven't you some brothers in America?"

"Yes, a brother and a sister, but—"

"Children, thank God, should devote themselves, body and soul, to their parents," she trumpeted, and her voice grew very nasal, as it did each time she laid down a peremptory aphorism. "Moïse will decide," she added in a less solemn tone, "but you can count on me. We will do our duty, thank God; we will do our part on the condition, it is understood, that the others do theirs. You'll meet with Moïse," she repeated, and she almost pushed her brother-in-law outside.

Yankel understood why Moishe was a rich man.

He began by doing the obvious thing, sending his father a small money order accompanied by a short letter. Then he notified the *mishpocha* all over the world. In case of misfortune they would all tighten their belts. What else was the *mishpocha* for?

He even wrote to the Feinschneiders of Rakwomir, although without any hope. They were so backward there! When they thought they were doing well, they were actually struggling in a wretchedness that the poorest French peasant wouldn't tolerate. It was another world, where letters got lost and only money orders got through. Just think, in the Soviet Union they didn't even have the right to write, they were like dead men there, no news, no signs of life, nothing.

He expected a little more from Peretz and from Rachel. America was the land of millionaires, the place where everybody was rich, with machines to do the work. Whatever quarrels Rachel might have had with her father were far off, old matters of thirty years past, and a father is always a father. Even a selfish man like Peretz must feel his heart beat once in a while. To them, twenty or thirty dollars was nothing; now one dollar makes a great many francs, but what's one franc next to a Palestinian pound?

Once the letters had been sent off to Russia and America, Moishe still being invisible (Yankel wasn't going to lower himself to plead with him), he waited. He hesitated to try to raise money from his own children. After all, they were his children, not his father's, and everyone has his own weight of cares to bear. He ended by deciding to call together a little family council of the three children who lived near him. So Rivka and her little Chaim, Simon and his *goya,* Fernand and Odile were reunited under his chairmanship.

It took a good half-hour to paint the situation. At the end of that time the husbands and wives consulted each other with looks, and then each couple considered the others hostilely. Yankel, himself casting an eye at Hannah, understood what she was thinking: When we're dead, they'll act like this over the inheritance. Finally, Simon began his "Listen, Papa . . ." Little Chaim interrupted him in a confused babbling, in Yiddish, was called back to French by his father-in-law out of respect for Jacqueline and Odile, arrived at some very generous conclusions surrounded with "if's," quarreled with Rivka, and ended by angrily throwing three hundred francs on the table. Simon imitated him, all the while calling his grandfather an idiot; then he thought better of it and added two hundred francs more. Yankel, heartbroken, stared at his children giving alms to their grandfather.

What hurt him most was Fernand's attitude. Rational and sententious as always, Fernand explained, with unassailable logic, that since his grandfather had given all his wealth to the Jewish community of Jerusalem, it was up to the Jewish community of Jerusalem to care for him now. Besides, if you sent money to Grandpa, it would run off immediately into strangers' hands, so it wasn't worth the trouble. Yankel thought he heard his brother Peretz talking and weakly tried to protest. Then Fernand proposed to make Grandpa come back to France, to put him into a good home for the aged where he would be coddled and watched, and each one would contribute to his support, but of course in proportion to his means, since it wouldn't be fair for the poor to give as much as the rich . . . At once, Simon passed his hand over his face and began to vilify his brother, calling him a little *schmuck* and promising him some good kicks in the backside, and little Chaim threw himself in, flanked by Rivka, without anyone knowing which side they were on. No one could understand anything in this row, and when it quieted down a bit, Fernand, who had never lost his calm, explained to his brother that it was very easy to insult people, but that the insults did no good, and that everyone was free to do as he pleased. Yankel was forced to realize that his cherished Fernand was a heartless being with a shriveled mind, that Rivka was a scatterbrained chatterer. As for Simon, today he was generous and tomorrow he would forget everything; he was sensitive to misery only when you shoved it under his nose.

It was then that Jacqueline got her word in. She was annoyed because she felt that she was a stranger here, barely tolerated, and all these problems were really no concern of hers, but it troubled her to see these people squabbling endlessly when the solution was so simple.

"Suppose each one of us," she said, "agrees to pay in only a hundred francs a month. It won't mean much to us, and it will be a great deal for Grandfather."

The Rechnowitzes approved it clamorously; Fernand looked down at her from his height but didn't dare to protest. Yankel never forgot this gesture of his "little girl," as he called her from that time on. He remembered it even more because it was she, not Simon, who punctually, every month, sent her hundred francs. From Fernand, Yankel could not extract a cent. Rivka, sulking and pretending to hide it from her husband, would sometimes give him a note or two. Rachel in America, when she thought of it, would send him a packet of dollars; it was almost too much. Peretz acted as if he were dead. As for Moishe, Yankel, for dignity's sake, refused to pursue him into his house; he contented himself with emptying Moishe's wallet whenever that worthy presented himself at the Rue des Francs-Bourgeois.

In fact, as long as old Avrom lived, Yankel consecrated his leisure hours to extorting money from one or the other, squeezing, complaining vocally or by letters. He himself couldn't do much, first because the economic crisis of the thirties was killing capmaking, and then because he had other expenses: Hannah's relatives to support, and Clara, who was in difficulties most of the time. She wasn't getting on at all well with her Italian and she had put her child out to nurse. In short, it was a mishmash.

On his side, old Avrom didn't make his son's task very agreeable. His letters, or rather Mme. Zipovitch's, invariably were weeping and invariably asked for money and cursed the impious sons who left him in need. He never wrote to Moishe or to the Americans; no, Yankel was his only correspondent, the only one he scolded although he was the only one to do anything. Never any thanks; the old man would charge him to thank Moishe when that one sent his contribution (Yankel, who forwarded all the gifts, scrupulously indicated who sent them), or else Rachel when a packet of dollars arrived at Jerusalem. And Yankel, glowering, would transmit the thanks.

The last straw was that as soon as old Avrom had a little money he immediately distributed it among the poor. He didn't hide it, in fact, he told it in all his letters, it was such a *mitzvah*. Did Yankel dare to scold him? By return mail he would receive three pages of curses.

330

Then the old man even remarried. Yes, of course, Mme. Zipovitch. She was very polite; she even wrote the news herself, at the old man's dictation. Yankel couldn't believe his eyes when he read the letter which announced the news. To marry at that age? Eighty, eighty-five? And she, seventy, perhaps? They were crazy! Still, it wasn't so bad. Moishe laughed at it like a young man; the children raised their arms to heaven in wondering pity. Just think of it—Grandpa! What a character!

During the war and the Occupation, Yankel lost touch with his father. He was sure the old man had died, of hunger if not of old age—until he was once again able to write to Jerusalem. Well, old Avrom had not died. He had even had time enough to bury his second wife. His letters hadn't changed, except that now he dictated them to a kindly neighbor—complaints about the harshness of life, the ingratitude of children, praises of the Lord, and that was all. He scarcely seemed to have noticed the war; in his mind, the battles in the Egyptian desert were intermingled with the punishment inflicted by God upon the Egyptians of Moses' time.

He was perhaps a hundred years old, when, just before the outbreak of the Palestinian War, he decided to join his fathers. As the rabbi who sent the news wrote, he was a true saint, and his like was no longer to be found. Today *goyim* who called themselves Jews dared to work, smoke and fight on the Sabbath, with the excuse that they were soldiers. Old Avrom would have let the Arabs cut his throat rather than fight on the Sabbath. He entrusted himself completely to the Lord's hands, praised be the Lord, Amen!

Yankel found no more tears to mourn his father; he himself by then had grown so old, so overwhelmed by immediate griefs.

In Yankel's mind, the universe began with old Avrom, the patriarch. All the Mykhanowitzkis, the Americans as well as the French and the Russians, Moishes as well as the Silverstones, Feinschneiders or Rechnowitzes, were Avrom's sons; main branches, then secondary branches, and finally boughs of the old tree firmly rooted in humanity. He didn't realize that he himself, to his children and grandchildren, was the patriarch from whom everything began; he always felt he was the Eldest Son, not the Father. He was irritated at seeing his children treat Moishes as though they were strangers, not to speak of the little Silverstones, whom they had the right to speak of with some detachment.

331

The family council he had called to help his father had opened his eyes; with deep sorrow he realized that the Mykhanowitzki tree had splintered; that the ax had lopped, pruned, and cut branches and boughs off at random and that now there were only little ends of the family isolated here and there. Even his own children didn't know him! Let's forget Clara and her Italian who lived down there in the South, at the other end of France, and whom he never saw; Yankel didn't even know his son-in-law. But the others, who lived in Paris— why couldn't they visit each other once in a while, say hello in friendship? Pfeh! I tell you, none of this is any good. When I was young . . .

Timidly, he tried to revive family affection among his children. He would visit first one and then another, speak to one of the other. It was useless. Each lived his own life, and what could Chaim say to Jacqueline, or Jacqueline to Odile? In their households, Yankel always had the feeling that it was the stranger, son-in-law or daughter-in-law, who set the tone, not *his* son or daughter. Well? What could he do?

Three different backgrounds. And in each one he, Yankel, felt a particular discomfort. Which? That was hard to say! He understood it better when he found himself with the friends of each family; as if the friends made the difference more precise.

At the Rechnowitz home, he met only Jews, all of them vulgar and speaking Yiddish by preference. Yankel didn't like that; it reminded him too much of the ghetto. He hadn't brought children into the world to perpetuate Rakwomir. And especially a Polish Rakwomir . . .

At Simon's and Fernand's, on the other hand, they spoke nothing but French, although some of their friends—few enough!—were Jews. But the resemblance between the two brothers stopped there.

At Simon's house there was an uninterrupted flow of people called "friends" who were really business acquaintances: jovial types who talked about the theater, good restaurants, night clubs, discussed the merits of this and that wine, dared to poke fun at the President and boasted of cheating the Internal Revenue. Naturally, this headlong, futile, immoral, and dangerous conversation tortured Yankel. Besides, he didn't understand. No, he didn't understand! It was useless to explain to him the witticisms at which the others laughed so hard; he didn't find them funny. Fair enough, the jokes he himself dared to tell always fell flat. At the Rechnowitzes', at least, he felt at home;

the guests savored his wit and he enjoyed theirs, vulgar as they were.

The Fernands rarely joked. Their friends were serious people, true friends, steady as the compass, less numerous, and always the same. Artisans, craftsmen, they belonged to the people—not to the swarming crowd, but to the educated people, who formed a union of the chosen, who wore glasses for reading, and who read a great deal. Calm, reserved, reasonable and reasoning, but each one convinced of the truth of his opinions; he could talk to them, even talk too much. Yankel liked them, he felt they were very near his heart, and yet . . .

And yet . . . Oy, Man is a stupid animal, always there is something! All these good honest people, in whom Yankel felt he recognized himself—at bottom they were all niggards! Always counting: mine, yours, I've invited you, it's your turn to invite me; you offer me a cigarette, I have to offer you the next one . . . Among friends there should be no counting! Or else what's the good of having friends? True friendship is generous, expansive, indiscreet, even tyrannical on occasion; but these people didn't seem to know how to open their arms. They made him feel shut in! Yankel choked among them; he longed for vast horizons, for winds sweeping grandly across steppes and seas. After all, he had been capable of leaving his native land, secretly passing the frontier at the risk of his life, and crossing all Europe to build his future. He had chosen his future! That was something, if you thought about it. Were you truly a man unless some hope lifted you above everyday mediocrity? But Fernand's friends, and Fernand most of all, lived almost touching the ground, without yearning for anything. Then what distinguished them from animals?

Without daring to admit it, Yankel still preferred Simon's grand gestures, his generous carelessness, or even that rabble of Moishe's, their audacity, their love of gambling, their quivering ardor for the unknown, their curiosity for the world. They had force, pith, they were alive, they weren't little old misers like those others. Finally, while preserving a secret predilection for Fernand, so reasonable, so balanced, Yankel rather felt that Simon alone bore in him the true Mykhanowitzki character. Fernand would never have left Rakwomir; he was a sedentary man. Simon, in his own way, kept the line going.

It was thus that Yankel, sighing for the Fernand whom he loved, drew nearer little by little, without realizing it, to the Simon whom he hardly liked. He dreamed of Fernand's calm when Simon's brusqueness exasperated him; of Fernand's taste for learning when Simon boasted about business and sharp dealing; of Fernand's modest simple life when Simon's luxury overwhelmed him. He thought of his daughters only once in a great while; since they were married, they were lost to him.

He would have been astounded if he had been told that he was unjust and cruel to Clara; Clara, the closest to him of all his children.

And never, not for a second, did he suspect that in all this he was behaving exactly like his own father.

One Sunday when they went to dine at the Rue des Francs-Bourgeois, Simon and Jacqueline found themselves in the presence of a red-haired young man, oddly dressed in a gray-black pea jacket, vaguely military in cut.

"A cousin of yours!" Yankel exclaimed, in French, an ecstatic expression on his face. "He comes from the Old Country!"

Immediately forgetting his son and daughter-in-law, he busied himself with the young man, pushing the olives and chopped herring to him, and forcing him to stuff himself with tidbits; Hannah burst out of the kitchen every other minute and joined her husband in pressing food on the cousin. The cousin, who babbled a word or two, tried to smile; he had risen half fearfully on Simon's and Jacqueline's arrival. He was short, but thickset and powerful. Simon puckered his brows and whispered to Jacqueline: "What sort of bird is this?" and rudely interrupted his father in French:

"Look, Papa, you could introduce us, at least!"

He was furious, and Jacqueline couldn't see why. For some time her father-in-law had been receiving strange people, each one of them shabbier than the last. After all, the man was in his own house! Simon, shrugging his shoulders, had explained that his parents were beginning to do *mitzvahs,* good deeds; they weren't believers, but old customs, elderly people, the habit had been ironed in . . . "Grandpa was like that; you should have seen the parade of *schnorrers* in his house. Poor Papa, he's really getting old!"

But today's young man was very different from the usual guests. Jacqueline found him rather appealing, with his brooding melancholy gaze which moved slowly over people and objects, and his sudden blushes when caught off guard. Was he a Jewish type? Perhaps his nose was a bit thick . . . I have it! she thought suddenly. He looks like Simon's father. Not in his features; his look. Simon's father must have looked like that when he was young.

Meanwhile Yankel, obedient to his son's request, had introduced him to the cousin; he was speaking Yiddish and kept on. He had his own peculiarity in making introductions; he began with the men. Simply a habit, his sort of manners. What exasperated Simon was that his father's introductions were all one-way—going, and not returning. For instance, with a pleasant smile:

"My son Simon . . ."

And he would stop there, satisfied, while his son Simon remained in ignorance of the other person's name, shook his hand vaguely, and tried to fill in the blank himself. And nine times out of ten, the other would reply in a shocked voice:

"My God, I'm your cousin! I knew you when you were so high!"

The people that you met at Yankel's now were all, even the professional spongers, some sort of cousin to you, and were immediately familiar under the pretext that they had known you when you were so high.

Ah! Now it's my turn! Jacqueline thought. Smiling from ear to ear, Yankel introduced his daughter-in-law to his cousin from Rakwomir; but, perhaps because of his emotion, he continued to speak Yiddish. Clicking his heels and stiffly at attention, the young man bowed three times to half his height; so deeply the third time that Jacqueline saw the red hairs on the nape of his neck. She wanted to laugh but held it back; she glanced at her father-in-law, waiting for whatever would come next; but he also seemed to be waiting. She murmured a greeting and extended her hand to the unknown. He hesitated almost imperceptibly, offered his hand, touched Jacqueline's, withdrew his hastily, and reddened right up to his red hair. Well, I've made an impression on him, at least! thought the young woman, flattered.

"I . . . am . . . very honored!" he finally articulated with a roll of his *r*'s. Once again he blushed, once again he bowed from the waist.

"You speak French?" asked Jacqueline, to show how friendly she was.

A wave of the hands, a confused smile, a moment's thought. Then:

"I . . . learn!"

The *r* rolled like thunder.

Yankel contemplated the scene, his hands folded on his belly, his face wrinkled by a most beatific smile, without the slightest thought in the world of intervening. The cousin from Rakwomir and the

335

Frenchwoman stayed there, opposite one another, unable to speak and therefore unable to separate. They stood thus, eye to eye, while Yankel seemed satisfied and Hannah emerged from the kitchen, smiled at everyone, warded off the Evil Eye in Hebrew and disappeared again.

Simon had made four circuits of the room; with the fifth, he had enough, dashed in upon the group, stopped dead and furiously berated his father in Yiddish. What's going on? Jacqueline wondered; she didn't understand one word of it all. She knew only that Simon was yelling, that his father looked stricken, that the young stranger didn't know where to hide; and she saw her mother-in-law emerge frightened from the kitchen. She placed her hand on her husband's arm.

"Simon, calm down. What's wrong?"

He interrupted the stream of Yiddish to toss her "None of your business!" and went off again. Damn it, she thought, they're annoying me with their jabber! I'll leave if I bother them! She waited for a pause; then, wickedly:

"Dearest, I didn't know you could speak Yiddish so fluently!"

Simon suddenly turned his head to her, gaped like a fish, gestured in exasperation, and went back to galloping around the room.

Oh, yes, that was one of Simon's weaknesses; he pretended to have forgotten his Yiddish. Jacqueline didn't know why; she would have liked to know a foreign language. But Simon seemed to be ashamed of Yiddish.

"Well done, Jacqueline!" Yankel said with satisfaction. "You know, your husband isn't always well-mannered. He treats his parents like—"

"Well, then, what happened?" Jacqueline cut in impatiently.

The old man threw her a look in which all his feelings lay bare; her curtness had hurt him.

"Na! He was scolding me for not having made the introductions according to etiquette, as they do in noblemen's houses."

"That's all?" Jacqueline cried, shrugging her shoulders.

"Simon, you hear what she said?"

With an avenging index finger Yankel drove his son from one end of the room to the other, scolding in French. With glittering eyes, hunched shoulders, and hands thrust forward, Simon thrust back at his father.

"It isn't that!" he cried. "You have to be polite, just the same! Here she is" (he waved at Jacqueline) "in your house, and you speak Yiddish, Yiddish, Yiddish, all the time Yiddish, without caring whether she understands or not!"

He was at the peak of his fury, showing the whites of his eyes. Such a fuss over nothing! Jacqueline said to herself, but without being too surprised. She understood what lay underneath all this trouble.

"You see how he is, Jacqueline?" Yankel murmured with a melancholy nod of his head. "Even when he was a boy . . ."

Is this going to last long? the young woman wondered. She also noticed the young cousin who, frightened and obviously lost in this gabble of French, was turning his head from one to the other, and her good humor came back. She flashed him a smile of complicity; he grasped at it like a drowning man.

They went to the table and the storm slowly died down. Yiddish was still spoken in honor of the cousin, but once in a while Hannah would look at her husband in a way which, Jacqueline had learned, meant "Tell her." Then Yankel would translate a fragment of the conversation, something always devoid of interest; about such and such an uncle or cousin who had done this or that. Jacqueline politely asked what was the young man's trade. Everyone listened to the question in silence. Then Yankel translated. The young man replied. Silence. Yankel's translation into French: "He's a shoemaker." Jacqueline's reply: "Oh, that's a good trade. Does he do well at it?" Silence. Yiddish translation. Yiddish reply. Silence. French translation: "Not so well; they have a depression there, that's why he came to France." "Does he like it here? What does he think of Paris?" Translation, reply, translation: "He says that France is a wonderful country, Voltaire, Victor Hugo, Zola, Anatole France . . ." Jacqueline thought, for her part, that he was a very learned shoemaker, and she asked whether he was married, and the question went out, and the reply came back. This was becoming fatiguing. Jacqueline let them dive back into their Yiddish. Simon was champing at the bit and hadn't opened his mouth. . . . They left early. Jacqueline had never learned the cousin's name, and it was all the same to her; but the boy seemed well-bred.

It was a gentle autumn evening; the mist danced in the halo of the street lamps; their shoes slid on the slick sidewalk. For once, Simon hadn't taken the car; a spring was broken. Jacqueline was glad of it; no car, no children, she was alone with her husband and she hung delicately on his arm, like a lover. Simon heaved a great sigh.

"Pooh! This evening was unbearable! I don't know what's wrong with Papa, but . . ."

He enumerated his griefs, which ultimately came down to the fact that Yankel was becoming more and more of an old Jew, lacking only piety, "but that will come, that will come!"

"I thought him very polite," said Jacqueline, thinking of the cousin.

"Who, the redhead? Of course, but . . . Oh, you don't understand. You don't know these people, they're animals, they're backward . . ."

What a squabble! Obviously, it wasn't the cousin that Simon was thinking about. This one or another one, he was making fun of them.

"Oh, how many of them I've seen parade past, all the same. Papa was probably just like them when he came here."

"So?" Jacqueline was a bit surprised. "Your father isn't bad. I like him."

"Yes, yes. But if you had known him, if you had been raised in that environment . . . Of course, to be fair, there are worse than he. It's not his fault that he's like that, but . . ."

A great gesture with his arms; he didn't know how to express what he felt, now that it was all coming out.

"It's the whole thing together," he went on vaguely. "Tolstoy and morality, idealism . . . They spent their lives examining everything under a microscope, they split hairs in fourths, they had no other way to live. Me, I thought I'd burst when I was a kid!"

He must have been greatly moved, for he, who for so many years had watched his speech, had unconsciously fallen into the thick accent of the ghetto.

"All garbage, I tell you! All right, shall we go to the movies?"

He was fretting, anxious to sweep all this out of his mind. Jacqueline made herself heavy on his arm.

"Oh, Simon, let's walk a little," she begged. "It's such a lovely evening."

He took a deep breath. "It is a beautiful night, you're right, Jacounette."

He disengaged his arm and impulsively slipped it around her waist.

"You smell good," he breathed into her ear. He held her close and kissed her neck. Without saying anything, she pressed against her husband; it had been a long time since Simon had shown himself so tender. She felt his hand climb the length of her torso and envelop her breast. With a light movement she made it easier for him. Six years already, an old married couple! But still lovers . . .

They walked together in silence and in step. Jacqueline almost held her breath, to lose none of these precious moments. Occasionally Simon would turn his head and kiss her temple, her ear, her neck; he ended by drawing her into a dim entry, and there, still without a word, he seized her with both arms, pressed her close, kissed her mouth lengthily, while his hands ran over her back and her sides as if taking new possession of a body become unknown and fresh. She gripped his body with all her strength. In that clandestine embrace their love was rekindled. Arms still entwined, they continued on their way; they hadn't exchanged a word.

Finally, their arms fell apart, the tired muscles relaxing. They came to the Boulevard Beaumarchais.

"Shall we go home?" Simon murmured regretfully.

They did not go home, but went to the right, toward the Bastille. Jacqueline avoided the cafés and their lights; skillfully she maneuvered her husband through the dimly lighted streets. He allowed himself to be led; perhaps he felt the same desires as she; in any case he was calm and silent, unusual for him. They came out on the Seine. Still holding each other, they leaned against the large stone parapet.

It had rained a great deal lately. The river was high, a black, gleaming mass, running smoothly between its banks. Gripped one against the other, Simon and Jacqueline felt the same vertigo conquer them, and they abandoned themselves to it dizzily. In the gray night the river seemed even blacker; the lights on the bank were reflected in it, stretched out into green, red, orange, and blue rays to which the water gave life when they fell across the striations of the current.

"What are you thinking of?" Jacqueline murmured.

"Me? Nothing!"

But he had fallen back into thinking. Oh, yes, he was thinking, like Papa; that unaccustomed state was causing him a vague uneasiness, almost shame. Bravely, he admitted it.

"I was thinking of Virelay."

Just like Papa! The river had drawn all sorts of images and dreams out of him, a mass of confused, flowing ideas, moving and melting one into the other.

Jacqueline showed her surprise.

"Virelay? Why?"

"I don't know. If we had a boat, we'd only have to let ourselves drift with the current, wouldn't we? And we'd be carried down there . . ."

Relieved, she began to laugh, although there was no reason for it.

"Once," she began soothingly, "there was steady traffic on the Seine between Virelay and Paris. They called it the water coach. It's been gone for a long time now, maybe a hundred years, or more, I don't know . . ."

But Simon was listening with only one ear; the past didn't interest him, he was turned toward the future. She grew silent. Then he began to discuss the house he wanted to build on her famous dowry land. That would be a good investment! He was already going into the details; he knew exactly what he wanted: a modern house, with a goldfish pond in the garden, and a wide flat-roofed terrace so that they could enjoy the view. He had even consulted an architect . . .

"Aren't you going to ask me what I'm thinking?" Her voice was lightly reproachful.

"Yes?"

"I went farther than you did in your boat. To the sea, and even . . ."

Her arm rose in the dimness and described a circle.

"You want to see the world?" Simon asked, smiling.

She took a moment to reply.

"Can we get to your home by sea?"

"My home?"

When he understood, he stiffened, dropped her arm and smacked the cold, sweating stone of the parapet with the flat of his hand.

"My home is here!" he almost screamed. "Here!" he repeated fiercely. "Back there, they're foreigners—half-breeds!"

Of course, he ignored the exact meaning of the word. But one day he had overheard a conversation: "Simon? He's a half-breed." And it had registered. He would have been astounded had anyone told him that no one had ever called his father a half-breed. A foreigner, yes, and perhaps a kike. But not a half-breed.

Jacqueline drew near him.

"Look, darling, I didn't want to hurt you. I'm sorry, I . . ."

He broke away.

"Good God, what do you all want of me? I was born in France, I did my military service in France, I would have fought in the French Army if I'd been old enough. What more do you want? Is it my fault my father was born somewhere else? For the last time, Jacqueline, I tell you that I'm French to the tips of my fingernails, and I forbid you to question it!"

He had never used that tone to her. She gave him time to calm down. Then—oh why should she ask that question? But she couldn't keep it back.

"Then you really haven't the least desire, even out of simple curiosity, to see the place where your parents were born, where they—"

"Not the least. Maybe you've got the itch to travel, but I'm not going to budge. I've arrived, understand? Of course, I'd like a trip to Italy or Spain, the interesting countries. But why Rakwomir, especially? I'm sick of hearing about that hole!"

"Does your father ever regret . . . ?"

She felt Simon stiffen, watchful.

"I'd like to see it, very much," she said conciliatingly. He shrugged his shoulders without replying. She let some time pass. Then:

"What's your cousin's name?" she asked.

"My cousin, my cousin . . . With them, you stay cousins for thirty generations!"

She waited. He tossed it out ungraciously:

"His name is Nathan."

"Nathan what? Mykhanowitzki?"

"No, not Mykhanowitzki. How should I know?"

Of course he knew! Jacqueline was pitiless.

"Simon," she reproached him gently, "why don't you want to tell me his name? Really, sometimes I don't understand . . ."

"And I don't know why you want so much to know his name! Why should it matter to you?"

Absurd! Absurd and dangerous. He was determined not to talk, and she was determined to make him talk. Why? Was it a simple question of self-respect, a test of strength, to find out which would yield to the other? No. Something even deeper was at stake. Jacqueline felt that if she allowed her husband to keep this hidden, to lock this mocking secret within him, there would always be a cleavage between them.

"Look, darling, I meet a gentleman whose name I don't know; you know his name; I ask you what it is, you refuse to tell me. What am I to think of all this?"

"There you go again . . . His name is Meltchik," he finally admitted. "Are you any better off? Are you satisfied?"

"Not satisfied, not dissatisfied, dear; this is ridiculous! Why shouldn't he be called Meltchik? Does it mean something obscene, perhaps?"

341

He laughed. "No, I don't think so. I don't know."

She was still not satisfied.

"What is his exact relationship to you?"

"My God, she wants to learn everything and pay nothing!"

Feeling himself weaken, he had chosen to treat the whole thing as a joke; but he was laughing on the wrong side of his mouth. He chucked his wife's chin.

"Then listen, little one. But this is the last time, eh? My paternal grandmother was called—I think, but I'm not sure!—well, let's say her maiden name was Meltchik. She had brothers, who had sons, who themselves had sons, and one of these, unless he's a grandson of one, is the redhead. If it isn't that, it's something else; after all, it's possible that it goes back to my grandmother's father, who had brothers, and so on. But let's not make life too complicated."

"In short, you're cousins descended from first cousins?"

"If you like! And I'm sick of it; to hell with the whole family!"

This in such a tone that Jacqueline decided to say nothing. It was he who took up the thread again, but now he had relaxed.

"You see, Jacounette—no, you don't see. I'm not even sure that the redhead's name is Meltchik. His legal name must be something or other like it. You wanted to know everything; well, you'll get your wish! Before the war, that country was part of Russia. So the people, the countryside, everything had names that were more or less Russian. Now they're independent; their first concern was to translate everything into their own jargon. Everything! Place names, the rivers, the names of the people, and the rest. Even the names of the dead on the tombstones! In school, you heard about Livonia, remember? All right; well, Livonia doesn't exist any more. It's called Latvia. Lithuania? Now it's Lietuva, unless it's Ukmergia—you know, I've seen it on the postage stamps, I collected them when I was a kid. Well, now people's names end in -is or -as, so that they'll seem more Ukmergian, or Lietuvian. If you were Nagel before the war, you're Nagelis now. It's fashionable, you understand? Now add the quarrels with the Poles and the Germans. Why, Rakwomir, where Papa comes from, has changed hands a dozen times! For Papa it's always Rakwomir, but for the Poles it must have a name with a cluster of consonants, for the Lithuanians a name ending in -is, for the Letts something else; and I'm ready to bet that the Germans and the Estonians also get a lick in. You understand, all these people have historic rights to that country, clear to the Black Sea! Madmen, I tell you, savages! Come, let's call a taxi before you fall asleep."

This time, Jacqueline agreed readily.

As soon as they were home, they made love furiously, feeling as if they were newlyweds for the second time. Jacqueline had never questioned her husband about his background; now she understood him better.

Cousin Nathan disappeared; but she saw a parade of other more or less strange beings at her father-in-law's house. One intellectual young lady, notably a true cousin, was Yankel's own niece. She lived first with Yankel, then with Moishe, then no one knew where.

Another day, an American named Ralph Silverstone appeared. He was a young man of seventeen or eighteen, tall, loose-jointed, gangling, bored. Simon's first cousin, it seemed. Simon broke his rule and invited the young man to dinner at his home; he probably considered this one a deluxe foreigner, not a savage.

The young man arrived, loaded with chewing gum and cigarettes. Conversation, however, was difficult; Ralph had learned French at school but didn't know how to use it. Once again Yiddish saved the day. Ralph knew a few words—yes, his father was a Jew, of course, what a question—after all, Silverstone! But his Yankee accent complicated matters. With the help of gestures, and after many misunderstandings and mistakes, they finally got through to one another. Simon and Jacqueline discovered his most heartfelt interests: Ralph played baseball very well, he had a "sweetheart," a "girl friend," whose photograph he exhibited forthwith. What was he doing in "Yourope"? Well, he didn't know exactly; to see the country, he supposed; it was "Mom's" idea, but he liked it! He was fond of travel and the gaiety of Paris; it was too bad he couldn't stay more than two months. He found out what had happened to "Grandpa" but wasn't very interested; "Mom" had wanted him to. Yes, he might go on to Palestine; "Mom" seemed to think he should. Simon and Jacqueline exchanged a glance. By God, this aunt must have plenty of money!

Then Ralph, seemingly embarrassed, asked Simon a question: Who was this Uncle Peretz that Uncle Yankel spoke of all the time, as if Ralph saw him every day, back home? The Silverstones had no ties with him, and Ralph didn't even know who he was, but he hadn't dared to ask Uncle Yankel. Simon pretended to think and suddenly remembered that the Peretz in question was Papa's brother.

"Then he's Mom's brother, too?" Ralph was surprised. After this, their conversation was bogged down in petty difficulties: There was the question of the proper pronunciation of Mykhanowitzki, which was very difficult in English. When they had emerged from this swamp Ralph was surprised, and almost shocked, to learn that Jacqueline wasn't Jewish. In America, apparently, people married within their own group—Jews with Jews, Protestants with Protestants, and so on; so there were no religious problems. Ralph's "sweetheart" was Jewish, of course. Did Ralph practice his religion? Well, naturally; atheists are very low people, sort of anarchists . . . "Are you atheists? Oh!" Ralph recoiled slightly and declared that the French always had these strange ideas.

He went off, leaving an almost-full pack of Camels on the table. They didn't see the young man again. Some months later a package of toys and candies for the children arrived from New York, accompanied by a typewritten letter in English. Ralph, or more likely "Mom," was showing gratitude for a pleasant evening.

That very welcome condemnation of the property came just at the right time, in the midst of the depression of the thirties, when failures were multiplying like rabbits. Simon pocketed the hoard, held a council of war with Jacqueline, and allowed himself to be persuaded to pay off all his past-due debts, including his taxes.

As far as the taxes were concerned, it was a saving. He had long been dragging his arrears, which, in spite of the payoffs to the right parties, kept increasing with the penalties, growing and multiplying with the interest. Usually, Simon would wait until served with a seizure notice; then he would throw the Internal Revenue a bone, to show his good will and to gain some time. The time gained was really time lost; they began all over again. Evidently this could go on for a long time, as long as Simon himself; but it was annoying.

With the money in his pocket, Simon, assured and unconstrained, went to the right person, concluded a liquidation agreement, paid cash, sent a royal gift to the right person to thank him for the politely granted remission, and felt free and powerful.

Now that his fortune was established on a solid basis, he gave free rein to his business ability. His affairs prospered on the corpses of his competitors. This was certainly a reward from God for his honesty, because he had paid so much, if not all, that he had owed. Thus it was that he soon realized his dream: to build.

344

What a marvelous day that was, when his new house was ready! For months Simon had spent all his free time hurrying the workmen. He was never so happy as when he heard hammering, sawing, nailing, and planing going on all around him. He had become almost as distracted by it as he had been by Jean-Claude's birth. He unveiled the new house almost like a Minister unveiling a monument *coram populo;* Simon called it a housewarming.

Fortunately, the weather was fine; for, vast as the house was, it couldn't hold all those who came. Nature lovers like Papa Yankel, big-chested men like Papa Baptiste, and all the young people under twenty-five spent the afternoon in the garden, which suffered sorely.

The visitors toured the house in groups, under Simon's guidance. He would choose a cluster of guests in the living room, dining room, vestibule, or billiard room, and "Follow the guide!" he would call. The guide missed nothing: central heating, here's the boiler, the coal cellar, the garage, the laundry; on the ground floor, here's the bathroom, the kitchen; on the first floor . . . After a dozen tours, Simon, slightly worn, omitted the bathroom and the drying room; but he did not omit the terrace; everyone, willy-nilly, had to climb 'way up there, on the roof.

For now he had his terraced roof. The architect, a dainty perfumed and goateed young man, had guaranteed it impermeable. "Concrete, concrete! What a material it is! Oh, la, la! A flood would run over it without dampening a blotter!"

The house was modern, ultramodern, a perfect cube. By the second winter, though, there would be vast damp stretches—not on the ceilings, admittedly; the architect hadn't lied, the roof was impermeable —but on the west walls, which received the full force of the winds. . . . In the years that followed, a number of new houses adopted these terraced roofs and fared ill with them. At the edge of the plateau, almost on the cliff's side, the white cubes sprouted, each resembling the other, as one cube does another. It was a strange thing that though each house, close up, was attractive, the countryside, from afar, was marred by this succession of little white chalk boxes. Instead of mellowing, they weathered an ugly gray. The fashion changed; some of the white cubes were painted yellow, green, rose. The result was the same. Finally ivy and flowering vines veiled and thus humanized them. . . .

While they waited, all the visitors admired the terrace and grouped together for a moment to contemplate the countryside. M. Touquet,

345

the new mayor, had come in person, to show his regard for his deputy, M. Saulnier. In the name of the commune, he congratulated Monsieur—uh—Miscanoviski (he had almost said Stavisky), drew his attention to the beauty of the site, voiced some saddened reflections on our ancestors who (he indicated the old village huddled at the bottom of the bluff) didn't know how to enjoy wholesome nature but hid themselves in the depths of the valleys, instead of living as a Frenchman should, in the open air.

Toward evening the mob went away, and only intimate friends remained. Bowed with fatigue, but still beaming, Simon rejoined his father, father-in-law, and Uncle Moishe in the garden. The women were in the kitchen; all was quiet.

"Well, *mazeltov* to you, Simon! Now you're a landowner!" Uncle Moishe tossed at him.

In spite of Baptiste's presence, he had used the Hebrew ritual formula of congratulation. His tone, as usual, was lightly ironic.

Simon took his arm. "Do you like the house?"

"Yes! Yes! Yes!" the sonorous bass voice assured him.

Simon had already noted that Uncle Moishe was in fine form. He still dragged his foot, but less noticeably than he used to; and his wit, instead of being poisoned by sarcasm, was colored by nonchalant benevolence. Out of the depths of his childhood, Simon recalled the Moishe of long ago, with his flaming beard and hair, his huge chest, and his eternal smile. He had almost forgotten that Moishe. Since the war his uncle, though still tall, held himself less erect; stripped of his beard, his face was wrinkled, bony, ashen, a sick man's face, crowned with a brush of thick gray hair tarnished and soiled with red. Was it Virelay's fine air that was reviving Moishe, coloring his cheeks? Simon always felt in sympathy with his uncle, even though they rarely met now.

"Is your leg better?" he asked mechanically; it was a ritual question in the family.

"Of course! It will always be fine now."

A large smile was stretched across his uncle's face, but something in his tone alerted Simon. They were walking in the garden; behind them Yankel and Baptiste were contemplating the countryside and chatting.

"Fine, fine," Simon said, carefully.

Moishe seemed greatly amused.

"Then you haven't noticed anything, Simon?"

Noticed what? That his uncle was in fine form?

"You understand," Moishe continued placidly, "the old leg was really bothering me. So I had it replaced with a new wooden one. This way, I'm comfortable."

"What? You mean to say . . . ?"

Simon knew his uncle's acid wit. But this seemed too much. Moishe stopped, twirled his cane like Charlie Chaplin—yes, since the war he had always carried a cane.

"Yes, yes, yes," he murmured gently. "You understand, Simon, we must be modern. A good wooden leg is better than a bad flesh-and-blood one."

Simon was thunderstruck. To have dragged a sick leg around for fifteen years and to have come to this . . .

"Is it cut off high up?"

"Oh, a little above the knee; that was enough!" Moishe sighed. "You can't be too generous, you know, with your legs!"

Desperate, Simon searched for something to say. He had a vivid imagination for physical suffering. At that moment he could almost feel the saw grinding on his own thigh bone. Happily, Moishe kept talking.

"You can see that I couldn't leave the hospital with my real leg under my arm, like a package? No one in the world could do that. Besides, the Boches didn't take my leg, the French did. We're all patriots in our family . . ."

He kept on for some time in this vein, and Simon, unable to stop him, felt shivers run down his spine. Finally, Moishe condescended to put an end to his pleasantries; he leaned toward his nephew, and said with an accomplice's wink:

"Don't say anything to your father! I want to see whether he'll notice it by himself."

All his desires seemed to be concentrated on this one object: to have his wooden leg pass as his true one.

They walked together for some time in silence. Jacqueline's piece of land, so small when it was nothing but a field, seemed much larger now that it had been transformed into a garden. Truly, the gardener had utilized the land remarkably well. He had broken it up with hedgerows, keeping one section for a vegetable garden, another for flower beds; there was even a tiny lawn. No goldfish pond; Simon had had to renounce the satisfaction of that desire.

"Is Aunt Rose feeling well?" her nephew asked, distrait.

"Oh, yes, she's always well; no way of changing her for a wooden Rose. Excuse her not coming"—Simon hadn't noticed her absence—"but there's a little coldness between us. You know, with my wife . . . Do you get along well with yours?"

Simon started and replied dryly that he did.

"Well, *mazeltov* to you!" Moishe slapped him on the back.

Simon made no answer. He knew that things didn't always run smoothly in his uncle's house, but he preferred to ignore the fact. Now Moishe, with placid immodesty, began to unveil his intimate problems before his nephew. He had never spoken to his own brother like this; there was no doubt he considered his nephew his equal. He was amazed when Simon, replying to a pointed question, admitted that he hadn't yet cheated his wife.

"Oh, that will come, that will come!" His uncle was most encouraging. He laid bare his philosophy, assuring Simon that Youth was Beauty and you had to keep your senses sharp. Simon had never heard him talk so much. Then at the end:

"Look, Simon, can you let me have a little money until next week?"

Simon gave it to him immediately without being able to hide his surprise. Was business so bad? Then, even while putting the notes in his pocket—his vest pocket, without looking, like a nobleman who doesn't count money:

"What can you expect, Simon—you'll find out later. At my age you have to pay the little girls. And since she holds the purse strings . . ."

He smiled disarmingly, walked a few minutes longer with his nephew out of politeness, then headed toward Yankel and Baptiste; he had his money, what more did he need?

Simon had lost all respect for his uncle. He didn't like moochers even though he was unable to resist them.

Yankel and Baptiste were no longer talking; one was admiring nature, the other was smoking his pipe. When they heard the crunch of the gravel behind them, Baptiste turned his head slowly, and Yankel started.

"Happy, Papa?" Simon asked, rubbing his hands.

It was a curious thing. Earlier, while walking with his uncle, he had felt calm, happy, relaxed; but he wasn't in his father's presence for more than two seconds before he felt his skin crawling.

Yankel raised his head, then pointed toward the landscape. They waited. Finally:

"Haah! There must be Someone who made that immensity!"

Baptiste withdrew his pipe; the skin on Simon's legs began to crawl frantically. As for Moishe, he smiled, murmured tenderly, *"Putz, go!"* with the same accent that he had used in his youth, and Yankel was taken aback. He stared at his brother, opened his mouth, then shut it as Moishe went on:

"Would you like me to send René here, Yankele? He'd know how to answer you; he's a specialist."

René? Oh, yes, one of Moishe's sons—the first or second? And specialist in what? Yankel had already forgotten his own words.

"Is he the one who wants to be a movie producer?" he asked imprudently.

Moishe laughed, then, pretending to be deeply hurt:

"Yankele, Yankele, what are you thinking of? Georges is the movie producer—because of the girls," he said in an aside to Baptiste, who grunted appreciatively. "What, Yankele, you don't know René? You know, you're not a good uncle. . . . No, he wasn't here tonight, you're confusing him with Guy! Do I have to explain everything to you? René is the serious one in the family, the philosopher—"

"The one who wants to be a professor?" Yankel interrupted, trying to remember.

"Right! But now that's finished. Now he's a minister."

"Minister?"

"Don't you know what a minister is?" Moishe asked softly.

"He's been converted?" Yankel stammered, shocked to the point of forgetting the goy beside him.

"Of course! What do you want—it's a free country."

"So he's a priest? You're the father of a priest?"

"Oh, Yankele, Yankele," Moishe groaned. "I said minister; I didn't say priest. Monsieur Saulnier, would you explain it to him? You know, when a thing isn't in Tolstoy, my brother is a little . . . lost, you understand?"

Baptiste drew the pipe from his mouth to laugh more heartily, while Moishe spread his hands in a gesture of frankness. Simon began to suffer. Poor old Papa! He was incapable of defending himself against these darts.

"You know, Uncle," he interjected brutally, "if you want to borrow money you're not going at it the right way."

He could have found no better counterattack. Moishe tilted his head at him gently, whistled in admiration and, speaking to the father but looking at the son, said:

"Hu-u-u-u, Yankele, *mazeltov* to you! At least you have a son who protects you! A good son, respectful and a landowner. Me, I've never had any luck with my children; they spit on their poor old papa. Well, human wickedness is infinite, eh, Yankele?"

And he began exchanging memories of the war with Baptiste.

Simon watched his father. Yankel didn't take his eyes off Moishe. Scorn, sadness? Also, wounded love . . . He was the older, but his brother seemed ten years older than he.

"You know about his leg?" Simon whispered.

Yankel tossed him a quick glance of agreement and pursed his lips.

"I didn't dare talk to him about it," he murmured. "You mustn't talk about these things, Simon." He thrust his head forward suddenly. "Did he borrow money from you, too?"

It was Simon's turn to nod agreement. The father and son stared at each other for a moment, then the father turned away and leaned again on the balustrade. After a moment, Simon heard him grumbling: "What a family! Madmen, madmen . . ."

"Don't exaggerate," Simon murmured.

"Pfeh! The father chases women, at his age, and borrows from his nephew, his brother, everybody. A son who becomes a minister—a minister!—and he was the most serious of the lot. Another one in the movies—Swindlers and Company. And now one of the little ones—Solomon, no?—well, Solomon or another one, I don't know, at eight years old he quits school. What's wrong with him? He plays the violin! A real prodigy, a Yehudi Menuhin. Only Yehudi Menuhin is Yehudi Menuhin, he isn't Solomon Mykhanowitzki; and Solomon Mykhanowitzki, you watch what I tell you, will wind up cracked. There it is! You must give your children a real profession, Simon, remember. Well!"

The fly-swatting gesture, desolate and resigned: *Nitchevo,* we'll all end by dying one day, won't we? So there's no need of making such a fuss.

Below, on the other side of the Seine, the forest swelled, filling the immense hollow clear to the horizon. Leaning on his elbows near his father, Simon heard him breathe deeply, as if he were sweeping his lungs clean. After a few minutes:

"You've seen the sea, Simon. It's a little like that, no?"

At fifty-seven, despite innumerable plans, Yankel had still never been to the sea.

asked the question like a schoolmaster scolding his pupils. "We've been waiting dinner for you."

"We're coming, we're coming!" Yankel replied joyfully, rubbing his hands. He didn't want to leave the place, however, without sharing his feelings about Virelay's landscape with his younger son. He continued feelingly:

"Have you seen how beautiful nature is here, Fernand? Oy! You feel—"

"Of course I saw it!" the nasal voice cut in. "Do you think I'm blind? Or stupid?"

Poor Yankel crawled back into his shell. He found his only solace in affectionately taking the arms of his two tall sons. So he appeared to everyone, proudly framed, in the dining-room lights.

"Ouf!" Simon sighed. "I was beginning to feel worked over!"

Once again he was leaning on the garden's balustrade, but this time Jacqueline was with him. The guests had gone, Fernand returning with Moishe, Papa and Mama pushed by main force into the guest room, and he could breathe at last, fully enjoying his new position of rural landowner. The night was cool, but beautiful. There was no moon; the stars, clear and twinkling, seemed infinitely more numerous here than in the Parisian sky; to tell the truth, it was probably the first time in his life that Simon had watched the stars.

"Are you all right, Jacounette?" he murmured. "Not cold?"

She pressed his arm without replying. Simon was a very thoughtful husband, but in Paris he hadn't had the time.

The silence was extraordinary. No trucks or buses to shake the houses and rattle the windows. It was difficult, even straining your ears, to hear the far-off growling of a motor—no, it was the rumbling of a train, but it didn't matter, the stillness seemed even deeper. Below, in the plain on the other bank of the river, lay the sleeping forest; a rich black, massive, luxuriant, without a single gleam. From the east, however, the flood of lights rolled away, while a rosy glow spread over the hills and valleys. Paris, distant and alive; here, the fields, the good earth.

A wailing groan, or a plaintive scream, rose from somewhere.

"What's that?" Simon was alarmed.

Jacqueline smiled in the shadows.

"An owl."

"Oh . . . well! You'll have to help me, Jacounette. You know I

353

don't know anything at all about birds, flowers, trees. It's just like the wines; I was so ignorant about them I passed for an idiot."

In a restaurant, he depended on the wine steward. Left to himself, he would have been likely to warm the champagne, ice the Châteauneuf-du-Pape, order red Burgundy with oysters and a sweet white Bordeaux with a saddle of venison. Actually, shameful though it might be, he preferred a good pint of light, cold, sparkling beer, or just water.

"Are you happy to be here, in your own home?" he went on affectionately.

"Very happy."

Her approval was plain, but it lacked warmth.

"I ask," Simon explained, "because you've always lived here, but it's all new to me, so—"

"Anything new is beautiful, eh?"

"Wicked! You know I know myself, Jacounette, with my airs . . ."

He struggled to express himself. Was it the night, the intimacy, the silence of the countryside that was driving him to such introspection? Finally, with laughable force:

"Now, I'm serious! Yes, I swear it to you! I . . . I . . ."

It required an enormous intellectual effort, he had to lift such a heavy weight from his spirit.

"I like it here, do you understand? I feel at home here."

And all at once his restlessness left him. He drew a cigarette from his pocket and lit it calmly.

A long moment went past. The cigarette gleamed redly in the dark. Jacqueline heard her husband's even breathing. Miraculous; he didn't stir, didn't fidget, didn't pace like a caged beast. Yes, he seemed to be at home here, for good. Still, they didn't have to spend their vacation at Virelay every year. The world's wide, thought Jacqueline, and she hoped to travel over it; she felt that she was too young to bury herself in a hole.

They decided to call the house Four Winds; they thought it a pretty name.

In the months that followed, a silent struggle raged between Simon and Jacqueline. Over Four Winds, of course. Simon always thought their visits at the house too short; Jacqueline felt they were too long. "You have a house to live in!" Simon would exclaim. "It's a weekend house!" Jacqueline would reply. They would claw at each other a bit; never too much at any one time, but often.

354

Then Jacqueline saw what he was driving at. One day Simon told her that the apartment on the Boulevard Beaumarchais would make a wonderful warehouse, just what he needed. "What will we do, sleep under the bridges?" Jacqueline asked, seemingly uninterested. So her husband explained that, by car, Four Winds was only a half-hour or so from Paris; besides, he was worried about the children's health, Paris had become so unsanitary, for the parents too, and then, what a saving! Only one home instead of two . . . Jacqueline wondered how the children would get to school, to which Simon replied heatedly that the trains weren't for dogs, a half-hour or three quarters of an hour wasn't so terrible, and what did M. Touquet's grandchildren do? Virelay's a suburb, not a wilderness! Suburb or wilderness, Jacqueline, who loved the liveliness of Paris, refused to spend her whole life in that hole. "But you silly thing," Simon retorted, "we'll go out in the car every evening, just as we do in Paris! And since we'll live all year round in Virelay, we can go to the seashore or take a trip for our vacations . . . Well?"

Simon ended by winning his case. The family moved into Four Winds, and Simon turned into a home-loving suburbanite. In the evening, as soon as he entered the house, the first thing he did was turn up the radio; then he would put on his slippers and lounging robe, pick up the evening paper or a detective story, plump himself into his armchair with his back turned to the beautiful library of fine bindings that he had bought as a unit, and fall asleep. Sometimes, when the weather permitted, he would walk into the garden and, depending on conditions, drowse in a hammock, or bowl with the children, or pull weeds. He entered into frequent conversations with the gardener and ended by growing geraniums; he even became an expert in the art of grafting fruit trees, and he would proudly show his masterpiece, a quince tree which bore peaches on one branch, apricots on another, plums on a third, but no quinces. He bought a rowboat; on summer Sundays he would fish in the Seine from morning to night. The last step was to join the Fish and Game Club, with his father-in-law as sponsor. When his father heard of it, he raised his arms to heaven.

"You're going hunting? You? A Jew? Pfeh! You're going to kill the poor little animals like that, just for fun? Oh, Simon, Simon, let them alone, they haven't done you any harm! Leave hunting to the *goyim*, Simon, Jews aren't killers."

Simon laughed and continued his hunting. He never confessed to

355

anyone that it hurt him deeply. The first time the dog brought him a little ball of bloody feathers he almost fainted. Fortunately the dog didn't know his business and Simon spent most of his time romping with him. Still, he was hunting, like everyone else; that was essential.

Jacqueline, no longer able to pry him loose from Virelay, grew disconsolate and reminded him of his promises. It was useless; one day, he was tired; the next, there wasn't anything worth seeing in Paris; they would see tomorrow, the next day. Or else he would suffer an attack; for two weeks he would cram Jacqueline with a surfeit of plays, films, and dining out; afterwards he would reappear as a provincial and would plump down into his armchair. Jacqueline was forced to yield to this; but she felt a deep resentment which made her bitter and shrill, a true peasant; she began to resemble her mother more and more. He noticed none of this; he had finally managed to shed his differences and become like everyone else. He cherished the hope of being named municipal councilman. He received and gave hat-tippings, and people listened when he talked of his geraniums. His bonds with his parents were loosened, naturally; those with Baptiste strengthened, without ever becoming very binding. Baptiste kept his independence and was too happy as a widower to put a leash on; besides, it was no small matter to scale the cliff.

The children were growing up. The most remarkable of the three, and the favorite, was the oldest, Jean-Claude. No one said anything against Pierre and Edwige, perhaps because there was nothing to say; at best they weren't completely smothered by Jean-Claude. At thirteen, he was already well on the way, a tall, devil-may-care boy, taciturn but sarcastic, headstrong and dreaming only of battles and automobiles. His pale-blue eyes in his dark face always caused a certain uneasiness, a vague disquiet, which was soon relieved by the movements of his lively mouth. He resembled neither his father nor his mother; he was himself, a new vigorous product. Yankel and Baptiste each claimed the honor for his height, Baptiste in his own right, Yankel through his brother Moishe; one bitterly stressed the father's low stature, the other, the mother's. In revenge, since Jean Claude lisped slightly, Yankel on one side and Baptiste on the other cunningly blamed the opposite family for this blemish.

One evening Jean-Claude—he must have been about ten years old —came home from school with a split lip and a black eye.

356

"You've been fighting again, you bad boy," said his angry mother. "You'll see, when your father comes home . . ."

The boy protested that he wasn't going to allow himself to be insulted without defending himself; after all he was a man. There followed a confused story of marbles and of catechism.

"I've already told you I'll never send you to catechism."

"I don't care about the catechism, but that Maréchal called me a Jew and said I stole his marbles . . ."

Yes, Jacqueline understood, very well, and she was glad that Simon wasn't there. She hesitated an instant, then made up her mind and spoke to her son as if he were a man. He heard her without saying a word and then made her repeat what he couldn't grasp.

"Then it's true, Papa is a Jew? What are Jews?"

She explained it at length; and while she was about it she also explained that Papa's parents were foreigners. "Is that why Grandma speaks French so badly? Now I see!" And off he went to wash.

His mother watched him for quite a while, but he didn't change in any way. She noticed only that in his conversations with his friends he openly boasted of being descended from Jews and foreigners. It was a way of getting back at the others, of throwing it right in their faces; not everybody in the world had his luck. He was very proud of his name, Mykhanowitzki, because of its rare consonants; he listened carefully to make sure that no one skimmed over it. He felt that he was exceptional.

His father, on the other hand, felt more and more like everybody else. He laughed pityingly when old Yankel, at the end of 1933, prophesied gloomily, with much morose head-shaking, about Hitler, anti-Semites, Fascists, predicting cataclysms and catastrophies. He didn't know that, as the pigeon has a sense of direction, and the sea gull the feeling for a coming storm, so his father had a foreboding of a pogrom. Simon had sloughed off that atavistic sense under the effect of France.

When you've been like everyone else, it isn't easy to become like no one else. Simon never succeeded completely. The Occupation? Those things don't exist! He always thought of racial persecutions as accidents; disagreeable, certainly, but momentary. You had to gain time, hold on, shake yourself loose, and run between the drops, and things would finally return to normal. It was impossible for such

357

stupidity to last long. When the first anti-Jewish laws were passed, Simon opened a parenthesis in his life and waited impatiently for the moment to close it.

As a former saxophonist of the Sixty-fifth, he should have fought the war as a stretcher-bearer; but his age and family were considered, and he was made a chauffeur to a general, in the east. Everything ran smoothly until the tenth of May, the day the bombs began to rain from the sky and the generals began to run like greyhounds across country. Faithfully and punctually, Simon drove his general where he was ordered to drive him; and he envied those flat-footed infantrymen who were dug in safely in their trenches and snug in their dugouts, while the general's chauffeur, the general's car and the general himself were machine-gunned and bombed incessantly, over hill and dale, as soon as they showed themselves—a dog's life, an upside-down world! The first time it happened he was scared stiff; but as his general, who claimed to have divine protection, affected an Olympian calm, he imitated him, saying that worrying never was worth while; and he became convinced that speed was his best protection. Inwardly he was delighted that his life had become so exciting. He who used to be sick at the sight of three drops of blood suddenly was surprised to discover that corpses didn't turn him hot or cold. What do you expect, that's war; you today and me tomorrow!

He even gave birth to a historic wisecrack. One day when he was driving at full speed across a plain as flat as your hand, a plane dived and let go a burst; a shell pierced the car from side to side. Simon, glancing in his rearview mirror, saw that his general was calmly putting his notes together, bareheaded. "General, put on your helmet!" he tossed back over his shoulder. The general was delighted; he got Simon a fine citation: "An elite chauffeur to the General Staff of the Tenth Corps, showed imperturbable calm in the most dangerous missions. . . ." As a result of their wanderings, the car, the general, and the chauffeur ended by driving right into the midst of a group of German soldiers. Simon, who was a good driver, stopped just in time and didn't hit anyone, but a machine-gun burst came from no one knew where, and Private Mykhanowitzki caught a bullet in the fat of his arm. After that the soldier and the general could do nothing but climb out of the car. The general was greeted courteously by his title as a prisoner of war; the soldier had his wound dressed at the field hospital, while an interpreter explained to him that he owed his misfortunes to the English and to the Jews. He nodded agreement, escaped captivity thanks to his wound, fled to Virelay, and found all his family there unharmed.

Then he established a sort of incoherent order. In the first place, Simon felt he was protected by the fact that he was a wounded, decorated veteran; in the second place, he didn't declare his return as he should have; in the third place, he transferred Maison Sijac to his wife's name. Then he waited for the war to end. He ran the business secretly and Jacqueline managed to avoid all "Aryan syndicates"; when that threat drew close, she screamed to high heaven, swearing that her husband had left her flat for a Negress and was living somewhere in Peru; besides, ladies' hats weren't selling well. Simon stayed at Virelay until 1943; first he had false papers which M. Touquet had procured for him; and then he had numerous friends who warned him of sweeps, so that he could disappear beforehand and come back after the danger was passed. The children weren't in much danger, since they were half Christian; when the need arose, Jacqueline hinted that he wasn't really their father.

When things became impossible, Simon slipped down into the Midi, leaving Jacqueline and the children at Virelay, where, according to the general opinion, they would be safe. Thanks to her relatives, he found a job as chauffeur near Cahors; he took advantage of it to start a trucking business, which flourished.

And yet the virus had seeped into him without his knowing it. When he cursed the Boches and the collaborators, he thought he was doing as everyone else did; actually his motives were not those of everyone else. He really had a personal quarrel with the Boches. What are all these fairy tales about Jews? If it's a bad winter, the Jews are to blame; if Goebbels has a clubfoot, the Jews are to blame; if I'm a Jew, the Jews are to blame. I'm a man like everyone else.

Even his relationship with his wife took an ambiguous turn, at least as long as he lived in Virelay. He was a Jew, he was marked for the slaughterhouse, and she wasn't; he was more or less doomed, and she was a free human being. Maison Sijac went under Jacqueline's name, he became her subordinate, his wife's employee, completely dependent on her. Naturally, neither she nor he put these thoughts into words; but society made sure of suggesting it to them. And since Jacqueline took care not to exploit the situation, he unconsciously avoided arguing with her; he weighed his words and restrained his outbursts. His tenderness was also more controlled; he felt he was his wife's debtor. He knew that she would never turn

359

him over to the Germans. God Almighty, he trusted her, he didn't even question it. It was still true that she had the power to do this; she didn't use it of her own free choice, over which he had no control. He owed her gratitude because of this; and it was unbearable because it was imposed on him. As a reaction to this, he began to recall all that she owed him. After all, he had picked her up out of a barnyard! So it was only fair to do him a favor . . . He tried to protect himself against these strange thoughts; he had always loved to give and forgotten to claim what was due him. But the thoughts kept recurring spontaneously, and that bothered him and put him in a bad mood; and since he held back his feelings, since he watched himself ceaselessly, his conversation took on a sweet, honeyed tone which stank of falsehood.

For her part, Jacqueline, just because she loved her husband and suffered because of the humiliations that he was undergoing, acted more sweetly than before. She, who was protecting him, pretended to be protected by him and sought his approval of the slightest details. Maternal and soothing, she held herself to good humor and unchanging gentleness. She took his rebuffs (and God knows that at that time he knew how to be disagreeable!) with an angelic smile —which also stank of falsehood.

What she hid from Simon were the laborious reflections of her father, old Baptiste. Baptiste, as was just, detested the Boches; but he read the newspapers and grew frightened at the number of Jews, real or supposed, whose positions at the posts of command of the Third Republic were denounced. "Just the same, those fellows grew too big!" he would say in his son-in-law's absence. "As soon as you give them your little finger, they take the whole arm. It wouldn't hurt them to be put in their places. Oh, gently, of course, French style, we're not the Boches . . ." To sum it up, if the French lost the war, it was because the soldiers of 1940 were yellowbellies; if they were yellowbellies, it was because the Jews had corrupted them. Baptiste felt no pain in transferring his hatred of the Parisian, the foreigner, to the Jew. Jacqueline argued with him but didn't dare to make him too angry; he had a pipeline into the mayor's office, and she depended on him almost as much as Simon depended on her. In short, they all lived under painful tension, a secret-police suspicion. The husband and wife, apparently never closer, actually both breathed easier, without admitting it, when Simon took refuge in the Midi.

On the other hand, as soon as they were separated they rediscovered their first love, stimulated by danger and the devices used to avoid censorship and the police. When, with the Allied Landing, the mailman became a sort of myth, Simon felt his impatience envelop him, and he eased his fever to the advantage of the local Resistance, taking bold risks with his trucks right in the teeth of the occupying forces. He felt no particular hatred; at the Liberation he even saved the lives of a few piteous Germans. He didn't like to see blood flow.

As soon as he could he ran to Virelay, a joyous lover, only to learn that Jean-Claude was dead. What? Dead? Shot? By the Boches? But what had he . . . ? He stared right and left, incapable of understanding. Here were Pierre, Edwige, grown tall, dressed in black, Jacqueline older, her face white and hard, dressed in black. But Jean-Claude?

"Where is he? I want to see him!"

"I wrote you!"

"I got nothing!"

Short, hateful replies. Oh, to knock someone down, that woman with her fixed stare . . .

"Couldn't you protect him? If I'd been here . . ."

Dead. Shot. The Boches. A boy! But . . . but, but . . . Simon fled to his room, locked himself in, and drove Jacqueline away when she attempted to join him. Little by little, the truth came home to him. Jean-Claude, my own Jean-Claude! He saw the boy, his clear eyes in his olive face, he heard that lisping voice. A boy, but you don't shoot a boy! Twelve men lined up for one boy, the black eyes of the muzzles, the flames shooting out . . . What the hell, he had gone playing in the Resistance in the woods down there like a Boy Scout—you don't shoot an eighteen-year-old boy for as little as that. Oh, those monsters! Why didn't I cut a few of their throats when I had a chance? . . . And now the body of his child lay decomposing underground . . . Perhaps they even tortured him?

As that intolerable thought hit him like a thunderbolt, he leaped to his feet, seized the gun that he had brought back from the Midi, and hurtled out of the room. Jacqueline was there, all dressed in black, her face ravaged.

"Where are you going? Simon! Simon, stay here and don't do anything foolish!"

"I'm going to kill one of them!" he bellowed. "Where have they put them?"

"You won't find any, they're in prison. Simon—"

"Let me alone!"

He threw this woman he hated against the wall, this unworthy mother who hadn't been able to protect her child, her own flesh and blood. Pierre and Edwige hung on him, crying, he shook himself free. Not them! I don't want them, only Jean-Claude! He ran outside, stopping people. "Where's a Boche around here?" They spoke soothing words to him that he didn't hear, they withdrew from him fearfully; he ran to right and left, brandishing his gun.

He awoke in a field, disheveled, covered with mud, soaked with rain or dew. He stood up painfully and looked about him. He didn't remember anything . . . Oh, yes! He had run out with his pistol in his hand, what had he done with it? Stupidly, he began to search around him. He had a swollen, split lip. He must have been fighting with someone, they must have disarmed him, or else . . . He had forgotten. Jean-Claude was dead, under the earth, those clear eyes, full of earth. Worms crawling on his eyes, under the earth. Oh! He collapsed and began to sob. Those monsters have shot him! But Simon no longer had the strength to hate; he straightened up again and went back to his house.

No one spoke to him. Pierre and Edwige watched him pass without daring to go near him. He didn't see them, or he didn't notice that he was seeing them. He was hungry. He took a crust of bread from the cupboard, then threw it away. He couldn't swallow. Heavily, in the empty house, in the empty, creaking, echoing house, he climbed the stairway, reached his room, and lay down. After a moment Jacqueline appeared and silently handed him a steaming hot drink. He drank greedily and let himself drop backward on the pillow, trying to smile. Jacqueline sat down near him on the edge of the bed, regarded him for a moment, and stroked his hair. Her lips began to tremble, tears gushed from her eyes, and, sobbing, she fell heavily on her husband's chest; with a tired hand, he began to stroke her hair.

It was only after the end of the war that the Mykhanowitzki-Saulnier family tomb in which Jean-Claude reposed was unveiled in the cemetery of Virelay. There were a great many people there. The mayor, M. Touquet, delivered a sincere and clumsy oration. M. Simon stood near him, very moved, too moved; some evil tongues even said that he was exploiting the death of his son. Mme. Simon hid herself under her black veils. People were surprised, when a puff of wind blew them aside, to see how withered her face had become.

After the ceremony, all the Mykhanowitzkis present grouped around Simon in the living room of Four Winds; they felt the need to count the wounds that the war had inflicted on them. No Aryans, but, besides Yankel and his old Hannah, all who remained of the Moishes, of the Fernands, and of the Rechnowitzes, plus a Jewish-American officer, a friend of the Silverstones, who represented the New York branch of the family by proxy. He had brought a pile of good things, as many to eat as to smoke. Since he didn't speak French, from time to time he had the right to a Yiddish translation; for a moment Yiddish would prevail, then French, clearly the preferred language, would rise above it.

There was little conversation. In successive monologues, each one, in the style of funeral laments, enumerated his own misfortunes. When the others decided that the recital had lasted long enough, an approving and afflicted murmur would rise, then a new voice would rise above the confusion: "It's just like my . . ."

Every fifteen minutes Jacqueline, who had forbidden the maid to go into the living room, appeared, circulated refreshments and petits fours, and, excusing herself, withdrew. She left them to themselves, she felt that she would have annoyed them.

Leaning back in an armchair, his legs crossed, smoking cigarette after cigarette, Simon didn't say a word. Was he listening or not? Yankel asked himself the question, watching his son's frozen face and far-off gaze. Simon had changed greatly. He had grown fat, but this time with a yellow, flabby, unhealthy fat. In a few months he had lost almost all his hair; he had kept only some black shining strands plastered to his skull. He looked a good fifty years old, although he was scarcely forty. Secretly, Yankel felt proud of being better preserved than his own son. God knew the trials he had borne, but he had come home lean, lean and rejuvenated; he felt pleasantly light in his clothes, which were floating all around him, and he still had all his hair, yes, at sixty-nine. Oh, if only Hannah didn't have such pains in her stomach! . . . My poor old woman, Yankel thought tenderly. It'll go better now, you'll see, the war is over. When you're a little rested . . .

With his iron constitution, Yankel couldn't conceive of illness. Hannah was tired, and what was surprising about that? They had undergone so many sufferings in these last years, and at their age, too. . . .

363

As soon as Hitler came to power in 1933, Yankel had felt something quiver in him, and he had opened his eyes wide. He, who till then had never discussed politics except in high philosophical terms, began to read the Socialist *L'Oeuvre* and keep himself abreast of current events. He commented on them to his intimate friends, invariably in a pessimistic tone. "You say, Simon, the French will never want a Hitler? Oy, keep quiet, you'll be better off. You talk like a fool. Of course, France is France and the French are not Boches." (The word German had disappeared from his speech.) "Yes, yes, you can laugh like an idiot, but get your tears ready; anti-Semitism is a real epidemic; when it starts anywhere, it spreads everywhere. I know what I'm talking about. Is there a crisis? Then wait, wait, soon it'll be our fault. And here's proof of what I say—Stavisky! All we needed was a Jew to make some mistakes. Tchch! Jews are stupid . . ."

He triumphed when fascist bands tried to raid the Jewish quarter. "You say it isn't like before, now the Jews know how to defend themselves? Yes, yes, the butcher boys, the porters, all the bucks of the Anti-Fascist League, Jews and *goyim* together, met the little fascists with clubs and iron bars and chased them away like rabbits. But they'll come back, they'll come back!" Sadly the old capmaker shook his head. "Believe me, my little Simon, as long as Hitler keeps up with his Boches, *heil Hitler, heil Hitler,* pfeh, those fanatics . . ."

"But, Papa, what do you want us to do?"

"I'm not the government! But I know that if they let Hitler get too strong, he'll end by wiping out France."

"Listen, Papa, you can't start a war to stop a war, that's idiotic!"

"Tchch! An idiot is standing in front of me!"

When Blum became Prime Minister, Yankel, in spite of his secret pride, went everywhere lamenting. A Jew to run the government, who needed that today! There was nothing like that to excite anti-Semitism, couldn't they find anybody else? In short, when the real troubles began, Yankel had the advantage over his children of being ready; the trouble was that, before suffering in fact, he had already suffered for years in anticipation.

At the first threats of invasion he packed his bags. But he didn't want to go alone; a family should pull itself together in a storm. His two sons were soldiers and God knew what was happening to them at that very moment. Moishe? No, not he. The Saulniers? No, no *goyim;* in such circumstances you never knew how they would react. Yankel went to find the Rechnowitzes and attempted to persuade them to leave with him. His son-in-law would gladly have agreed, but his daughter didn't want to; and when that idiot took something into her head it was useless to reason with her, she opposed you with the inertia of a mountain. Yankel pleaded, begged, implored, tried to paint the future for them, for all Jews, in the most tragic colors. It was labor lost; the more he talked, the more they were determined to stay. In despair, he left them. He found out later that little Rechnowitz had got along very well with the Germans. He had made a connection with an officer, whom he bombarded with gifts, and who, in turn, protected him. He did some trading in gold while he worked in furs for the Wehrmacht's account. He thought he was indispensable and shrugged his shoulders scornfully when he learned that Bloch or Levy had been "shipped off"; he was shrewd and they weren't; so much the worse for them. He was really stupefied one day when they came for him. He thought it was a mistake, argued about his connections, and was shipped off just the same—but politely!—and, with him, his wife and the younger of his two daughters; the older, luckily, was at a friend's house. Through various channels, Yankel later learned that father, mother, and daughter had been put through the gas chamber as soon as they had arrived in Germany. The little girl was nine years old.

Yankel and Hannah left Paris all alone, just in time to find seats on the train. Scarcely an hour after their departure, Jacqueline came to take them away in her car. She never understood why they hadn't at least telephoned. Sometimes old people are queer.

At first Yankel had thought of joining his daughter Clara in the Midi. Hannah wanted to, and it seemed the natural thing to do. But something held him back. Clara was too unstable, and her position too ambiguous. She was separated from her husband, the Italian whom Yankel had never known; and she had placed her little girl in a boarding school and was living first in one city and then another.

It was at Nevers that Yankel finally took refuge. Didn't he know people there from his youthful days? He found his old friend Louis, grown stout and imposing, who hugged Yankel to his bosom, explained that the Jews really deserved their troubles, and lodged him like a brother in his country home. Yankel had hardly had the time to be irked by his friend's anti-Semitic theories when the Germans arrived. He wanted to be off again, but Louis held him back. "You know, Yankel, if they're here, they're everywhere. So why go to the trouble? And then, let's admit it, the Germans are men like everyone else, there are good ones and bad . . ."

So Yankel stayed. But it was too much for him; every time he saw a green-clad soldier, he suffered new tortures, he wanted to save himself or to kill; not only because he had no news of his own children, but because he felt the memories of the old Russian pogroms rise up in him, still fresh and bleeding. Louis agreed to help him; from farm to farm, Yankel and Hannah were passed to the boundary line between occupied and unoccupied France and secretly slipped across. Forty-two years earlier Yankel had slipped across another frontier to escape czarist oppression. How happy he had been then! And how had it all ended? . . . Hannah sobbed, dragging her heavy, varicose-veined legs in the mud of the fields and the woods. Finally she collapsed. "Oh, leave me, Yankel!" she cried. "Go on alone, I'll die here, I'm old enough!" The guide was uneasy and grumbled at them to hurry up—not as coarsely as the Russian guide had, long ago—but Yankel could understand, the man was risking his neck. So Yankel bent over, his left arm stretched by the heavy valise that held everything he owned, and with his right arm encircled his wife's heavy body, raised her, drew her close, and half dragged her along. "Let's go, Hannele, a little courage, just a little more, it's almost over, we've arrived, we're saved . . ." And that poor innocent old woman went along, weeping and occasionally calling on God to curse those butchers. . . .

They settled in the Lyons area, where capmaking was flourishing. Yankel had some business acquaintances there, and he found work. At his age, after being his own master for so long, it was hard to become subordinate to someone else. But you have to live, no? His first task—he made it a duty—was to register as a Jew. He knew perfectly well what he was doing; he was well aware of the danger to which he was exposing himself; but he felt he was vindicating himself, insulting these people by obeying their laws, and, in a way, asserting his own dignity. He had plenty of good advice offered to him. "Why are you doing it, Monsieur Mica? You don't look like a Jew, and no one would know it. Why bring trouble on yourself?" He was determined, and even the thought of poor old Hannah, who understood nothing of what was going on, couldn't hold him back. So much the worse—he had had enough humiliations! He hadn't walked erect for forty-two years to bow down now; he decided that, at sixty-four, he had lived long enough to have lost the fear of death.

He even had to overcome administrative opposition.

"You are an . . . Israelite?" the clerk asked, staring at him.

"Yes."

"You don't look it. Mykhanowitzki? That isn't a very typical name. It's really Russian, isn't it? . . . Have you any children?"

"Yes. Two are soldiers. I've just learned that the younger is a prisoner of war in Germany."

"Do you insist on being registered?" The clerk's voice had sunk to a whisper.

Yankel smiled gratefully but did not flinch; he had to be registered.

The result was that when the Germans occupied all of France the two old people had to run again; they wandered here and there, six months in one hamlet, eight months in another. They had never traveled so much in their lives, and Yankel bitterly regretted his gallant gesture, not so much for himself as for Hannah. At each new flight, the old woman sobbed, groaned that she was so tired, that she'd had enough, always running, always hiding, "and in the end they'll catch me, so let them catch me and get it over." Now Yankel registered as a Protestant, to explain his ignorance of Catholic ritual; it didn't fool many, but it allowed the authorities to shut their eyes. In every way, Yankel felt the trap closing in on him; he wouldn't stay free much longer, although now a race was going on between the liberators and the hunters. Once he thought of taking refuge with Simon, who was doing well where he was and had appealed to him urgently. Had he been alone, he would have done it. But with poor Hannah, who could speak nothing but Yiddish, and who would have been denounced on sight? No. They would only drag Simon down with them. If he, at least, escaped, it would be something saved.

Shortly before the Liberation they underwent their severest test. They were in a remote village to which they had been driven by flight after flight. Abruptly they were warned that the Germans were coming. Dressed as they were, they climbed out the window and ran for the safety of the woods. It was cold, and raining; shivering, they hid in a thicket and Hannah, exhausted, huddled against her husband. Suddenly they heard the baying of a hound. An overpowering terror gripped them; the old woman called on her last strength and ran, heavily, stumbling over the brambly ground and sliding in the bogs; after fifty yards, she fell and could move no more. Yankel put his back against a tree, crossed his arms, and waited for the end. No, it was only their friends, come to tell them the peril had passed. They had used the dog to find them quicker.

They weren't able to get back to Paris until several weeks after the Liberation. They found their apartment in the Rue des Francs-Bourgeois completely emptied of its furniture, completely pillaged; all the capmaking tools and equipment had disappeared. Instead, some person was there with a bedframe and some soapboxes for furniture; he claimed to be a refugee and took a condescending tone toward the former occupant. The long persecution had deepened Yankel's natural humility. He went to the concierge, who sent him to the manager, who lifted his arms to heaven and said he could do nothing. "Oh, monsieur, if you only knew!" Yankel lived with Hannah at a hotel for a few days, trying some timid appeals to the authorities; he received several pleasant speeches and promises of an investigation; he ran from bureau to bureau, filling out forms. Finally, desperate, he fled to Virelay, to Simon, to whom he related his misfortunes. Simon said nothing and left immediately; in his absence Yankel learned of Jean-Claude's death. Simon returned after a few hours; he brutally refused to listen to anything about Jean-Claude (his father thought him very hard and insensitive) but told his parents they could go home, everything was settled, the apartment was empty. He handed them new keys.

Yankel was stupefied. "How did you do it?"

"None of your business!"

Only later Yankel learned from his neighbors that Simon had come with two or three friends, had seized the intruder by the back of his neck and thrown him down the stairs, his goods after him; then he had had a new set of locks installed. Yankel felt that his son had gone too far. The law is the law, no? Maybe he could have arranged something with the poor fellow; left him a room, perhaps, until he could find another place. You must be human, after all! Well, what's done is done. Yankel borrowed some money from Simon, bought a bed, a table, and two chairs, picked up material and tools, and went back to work. He insisted upon repaying Simon as soon as he could. Simon didn't want to hear of it; he thought it was idiotic, but he finally gave in. Papa took such pleasure in paying his debts!

Now the old man sat in the living room of Four Winds, and contemplated his son, who smoked cigarette after cigarette while he drummed with his foot. He's really hard, he thought. I don't know

368

where he gets it. . . . Before the war, Simon had been kindness itself, to the point of folly. Thus, in his workroom he had tolerated
the men's taking home "cuts" of material; he knew that the workmen had arranged matters so that they were making money on the
side. "Everybody has to live," he would say, when he was scolded
for his indulgence. "They do all right for me, let them make something for themselves." And then, one day, the "cuts" had become
robbery. He had grown angry and called in the police. They had
come and had caught one of the girls sneaking out a bolt of cloth.
The culprit wept, sobbed, pleaded; Simon began to cry, too, and in
spite of the police he withdrew his complaint and, even worse, gave
the girl money. Jacqueline had been furious. . . . Today's Simon?
No one was going to take any "cuts" in his place! A pitiless man
who ran his business with an iron hand, and anyone who didn't like
it could leave. Yankel disapproved of this hardheartedness. Look,
Jews must be especially gentle and polite; in every Aryan there's an
anti-Semite sleeping, and we mustn't wake him.

Like Clara. She's become a Communist! Pfeh! When a Jew is a
Communist, right away the *goyim* say that all Jews are destructive,
and that feeds anti-Semitism. But Clara's Communism is a real religion to her! That girl's a fanatic, a mystic, always ready to work for
the Cause and neglecting to take care of her own children. Oh, people are so stupid! If you knew Russia as I do, you would realize that
it's still a barbarous country. Yes, they've done a great deal for their
schools, but compared to France, tchch! They're still eight or ten
centuries behind!

Fernand, who had spent five years as a prisoner of war in Germany, had been liberated by the Russians. He seemed to be deeply
disturbed about the "Popovs." Oh! if only Clara had been there,
thought Yankel, perhaps she too would have understood? But Clara
was a believer, and who can talk to believers! Yankel eagerly listened to his son speak about the Russians. The Russians! The old
man knew that today's Russians were clean-shaven and even had
their hair cut, instead of being bearded and unkempt as in his day.
But had any change taken place in their souls? Could civilization
have penetrated very deep in fifty years, of which only twenty-five
had been under the new regime? What surprised him most was Fernand's tone. Fernand spoke like any other Frenchman, and the Popovs were foreigners like any others to him, without any special dis-
tinction. Yankel had never really stopped considering them as com-

369

patriots, well, no, not compatriots, but . . . Well, he had been born there, no?

"You . . . you weren't able to get to Rakwomir?" he asked timidly.

Fernand had been a prisoner in East Prussia; from there to Rakwomir wasn't far.

"And why should I want to go to Rakwomir?" replied his son sourly.

"Fernand, look, Fernand! It's the country of your ancestors. You still have family there, your aunt my sister, your cousins."

Poor Yankel was desolated. He didn't understand that his own son hadn't even thought of this pilgrimage to the place of his origin, had not even had the curiosity to see where his parents had played as children, had grown up, nor the loving consideration to bring back to his father a fresh picture of his native land. No, to Fernand, Rakwomir was a wilderness, like all other wildernesses of that exotic country. In Yankel's mind's eye, after a half-century, Rakwomir still displayed the same face, low houses, wooden sidewalks, animals wandering in the unpaved streets, and the simple people leading their simple lives . . . Oh! he would have given a great deal to see the Old Country again!

"Everything's been smashed flat. Can't you understand that?" asked Fernand in his schoolmaster's tone. "There's been fighting there, and not one stone is still on another, and the people—well, what do I know? And then the Popovs wouldn't let us go where we wanted to. You've got to remember that, too . . ."

And while Yankel recoiled beneath this blow—Rakwomir finished! its inhabitants dead, massacred, disappeared! two wars, one of systematic extermination—his son, unaware of the effect he was producing, went on with his stories of the brutal, thieving Russians, raping every German woman between twelve and seventy, stealing all the French prisoners' watches. Of his true captivity he said nothing; he had hidden the fact that he was Jewish and the Germans had never noticed the mark on him, and he hadn't had too bad a time as a farm laborer. Of course the Boches were filthy pigs, but the German people were neither better nor worse than anyone else, while the Russians, oh, the Russians!

"They're really savages!" Fernand repeated, and his nasal voice took on shocked, scandalized inflections; he had never dreamed that men could be so savage.

370

"Why, when I was liberated, I was on the road with my boss in the farm wagon. I have to admit those particular Popovs knew how to behave. They hugged me, they gave me cigarettes and then vodka, and then they kicked my boss's backside. He was sixty-six years old, remember that? . . . Afterward they told me to take the wagon and go east. We were three buddies in the wagon. Well, after twenty or thirty kilometers, we came to the Mongols. Oh! There wasn't any question of cigarettes and vodka with them. They took the wagon, our belts, and our watches. We looked like scarecrows. Let's admit they needed the wagon. I must say the Russian supply services weren't like those of the Boches in 1940 . . ."

A genuine admiration for Germanic order filled Fernand's voice. Simon's foot stopped tapping, a ripple of uneasiness passed over him; Fernand didn't notice and went on.

"But the watches? That was plain robbery, and of Allies, too! The Boches would never have stolen my watch. Even though we were enemies . . . Oh, I tried to protest, to explain. You know what that Popov did? He stuck his machine gun into my belly, and I thought my last moment had come. Luckily, a Russian officer was nearby, and they told him what was going on. Well, you can believe me or not, that officer didn't blink an eye; he pulled out his pistol and bang! my Popov was dead! Liquidated on the spot! We felt a little sick about it. After all, to shoot a man for a lousy watch? If I'd known, I wouldn't have said a word, I'd have let him have it. . . . Afterward they put us to work, and not easy work either. Ten, twelve, and fourteen hours a day, and the food! I swear it was worse than the Prussians'. The Prussians at least . . ."

Simon's glance was fixed on Agnes Rechnowitz, the niece who had escaped deportation. It grew soft and caressed the orphan for a moment. She was seventeen years old. Two years earlier, returning to her home, she had found all her neighbors turning her away. "Save yourself! They've taken your father, your mother, and your sister." She had fled to some friends in the neighborhood, not thinking, in her fright, of taking refuge at her Aunt Jacqueline's; then from asylum to asylum, until she had ended with some nuns who had kept her. As soon as Simon had come home he had taken her into his house, and he coddled her with surprising tenderness.

"Tell me, Fernand," he cut in, "have you heard about the concentration camps?"

Of course Fernand had heard of them, did Simon take him for an idiot?

"Well, shut your trap," Simon finished peaceably.

The American officer, having picked out the words "concentration camps" in his host's French, asked if the camps were really as terrible as they were supposed to be. Hadn't it been exaggerated a bit? He had seen photos, but he had the feeling that they had been fixed up for purposes of propaganda . . . A tumult arose, Yankel protested, Agnes cried, Moishe's children—there were three of them there—were furious, Fernand tried to start his stories all over again. Simon rose and said simply to everyone: "All right, I've seen enough of you!" That was his unfailing formula for leaving his friends or sending them home; he judged it pleasant and fitting. That evening it was more fitting than pleasant.

Yankel and Hannah spent the night in their son's home. They slept badly, Hannah because she was in pain, Yankel because he was haunted by the atrocities evoked during the afternoon. Jean-Claude under the stone, Rivka and her dainty little Solange gassed, Rakwomir effaced from the earth and all his family there blasted by the bombs, burned in the crematoria. Dead, dead, dead, all dead, and if any survived no one would ever know it, for the Russians had spread their shadow everywhere, and what fell into the Russian shadow disappeared forever, there was no news, finished, eternal night. Yes, savages, as Fernand had said, the same savages as fifty years ago, only today there was a thin veneer . . . And the other, the shaven, smug American, with his cigarettes and his chewing gum, who dared to doubt the existence of concentration camps, who even, pfeh, a Jew, had racial prejudices against Negroes . . .

In the silence of the night, he lay with his eyes open; he watched vague things move past the window, heard a far-off barking and the creaking of branches close by. He thought of his brother Moishe, dead too. Yankel couldn't quite believe it. And yet he felt a deep grief, deeper than he thought he would. Yes, Moishe had been his own flesh.

Rose had told the story badly, as if her husband had been a hero and she herself had worshiped him and their household had been the most united of all. In spite of his irritation, Yankel had seen, truly seen, what had happened.

At the time of the invasion, Moishe had said to Rose, "Don't worry about it, sweetheart." (Yes, that was what he always called her.)

372

And he had stayed in Paris. She had begged him, she had groveled on her knees. "Oh!" she repeated pathetically, "I knew what would happen!" She hadn't been able to convince him, and she had fled alone with Florence and Solomon—the other boys were mobilized, and Odette, who was a doctor, stayed in her hospital. So she had suffered a thousand deaths (no one, unfortunately, cared about Rose's deaths) and had finally found refuge with some relatives, a fine family, at Monaco. There she had trembled, without a stop, for her dear Moïse who had refused to leave Paris.

"And so?"

Well, some friends had told her how Moïse had borne himself at Paris. "One of our race's heroes!" she exclaimed and sobbed into her handkerchief.

Médaille Militaire, Croix de Guerre, and the rest, Moishe had spread them all on his coat; not ribbons or bars—no, the complete insignia. And thus decorated he promenaded in the streets, in the subway, in all the public places, with a yellow star—six cloth points— fixed just above his decorations, holding himself as erect as possible and carrying his chin high; he had replaced his artificial leg with a peg leg for greater effect. He wouldn't yield a foot to anyone, and even the Germans, yes, the officers, stepped out of the way to let him pass. In the subway, unknown gentlemen came to him, shook his hand, and begged his pardon in the name of France.

Of course they had placed an "Aryan manager" at the head of the jewelry shop, a sneaking, cruel little man who had undertaken to torture his Jew. He poked his nose in everywhere, inspected the accounts, assumed that every statement was false to begin with, and, meddling, fidgeting, insulting, he never failed to insinuate that M. Mykhanowitzki possessed some hidden wealth. Moreover, he pressed, he squeezed, he went so far as to control Moishe's pocket money. M. Mykhanowitzki, with the dignity and scorn of a nobleman, bore all this pettiness smilingly, surveyed his manager from above, warned him politely that he would be hanged at the Liberation, and took advantage of every occasion to throw his wallet, empty or full, at his nose, while asking him to verify the contents. And the manager checked, made whatever deductions he wanted to— "Oh, the fortune that he was able to put together during the Occupation!" Rose groaned.

"What did they do to him after the Liberation?" asked Simon calmly.

373

Rose shrugged her shoulders.

"Oh, nothing. He hid for a while, and now . . ."

"Now?"

"He's president or secretary, I don't know which, a big shot in any case, in the Jewelry Syndicate."

"Oh, yes?" Simon's voice was always cold now. "You have no sons, Aunt Rose?"

"No sons?"

The widow's look went automatically toward her children; she had only her two daughters here and the youngest of her sons, Solomon, a young man of eighteen. The violinist.

"Yes," Simon replied. "To go break your friend's neck."

The words went straight to Yankel's heart.

In the long run it had been the little sneak who won the duel between the two men. Without doubt, Moishe was hiding his anger under the smiles and sarcasms. One day, in any case, he hadn't been able to restrain himself; he had burst into a frightful rage and had broken his cane across the face of the manager, who had run away threatening the worst reprisals. Limping, a terrible expression on his face, Moishe had pursued him to the sidewalk. The neighbors said they had never seen him in such a state. He, ordinarily so gentle, so courteous, was roaring, shaking his fist, cursing. All at once he had collapsed, there in the street. Dead.

A beautiful death, Yankel thought enviously. To die like that, all at once! I would like it myself . . .

Beside him, Hannah whimpered in her sleep. Yankel contemplated her. Nu, my poor old woman, your wretchedness is over now; you're going to rest peacefully, for as long as you want.

Six months later Hannah was dead.

Epilogue

POOR Monsieur Saulnier! He seemed so strong! A colossus next to me. And seven years younger. No one who knew the two of us would have said that he would be the first to go. Yet look! He has gone, and I—I continue to take walks and admire nature. Tchch! Man is a wretched being. Hardly born, and there it is, he's finished, he's dead. The strongest just like the others. And those who seem to be the strongest aren't really the strongest. After all, what use is life? . . .

Yankel trots with little steps along the ridge road. Every day, except when the weather is too bad, he takes the same route, from Four Winds to the cemetery, from Simon's house to Jean-Claude's, Hannah's, and Baptiste's graves. Every day at the same time, after lunch. He has time; he has all the time in the world, so he stops whenever he sees anything interesting. With his hands behind his back, he stands and watches the masons working on a new house, a gardener trimming a hedge, a child playing in sand. He gives a fistful of grass to the Widow Déniché's goat; the beast knows him well and is well-mannered and intelligent, as goats usually are; she bleats as soon as she sees him coming, butts him gently, in fun. The 3:07 train files past down below, slowly and amid clouds of steam. Yankel has no trouble following it with his eyes. In the sky, the London plane drones by. Yankel lifts his head, and long after the plane has disappeared the old man's head is still raised, for he is dreaming profoundly of human ingenuity, and, at the same time, of the vastness of the world and the joys of travel. Then he starts off again. Far below the Seine flows, always the same and never the same. Motorboats skim over the water, with their staccato, hollow coughing. Yankel stops as soon as he sees one of them pop around the bend in the river, and he doesn't continue until it disappears around the next bend.

He has the whole immense landscape to admire as well. Spring,

375

summer, autumn, winter; the countryside is always changing. The forest goes from the delicate light green of the young leaves to the massive deep green of maturity, then to the golds and rich reds of its last splendors, before dying in the violet-brown of its frozen sleep. The air grows heavy and wet; the plain settles back and shrinks into itself, and nothing stirs. . . .

Yankel trots on the ridge road. Summer, winter, autumn, spring. Look, last night's snowfall hasn't melted yet!

"Morning, Monsieur Mica. You, at least, aren't frightened by the snow!"

"Oh, with this sun . . ." And Simon wanted to keep him indoors! Simon is hard; I don't know what's been wrong with him the last few years. . . .

Rain, wind; Yankel stays on the veranda. He surveys the drowned countryside, the gray sky, the trees whipped by the squalls. The rain is good for the farmers, but the wind might do some damage. Yankel is in his armchair, safe and warm, while the tempest rages beyond the windowpane. He is reading *Les Misérables*. Tchch! Victor Hugo —after all, that's something! Well, the sun has decided to show itself, nearly level with the horizon, has torn the clouds apart. Ha-ah! What beauty there is in nature! Someone must have made it, no? . . .

Yankel turns the radio on. He likes listening to Beethoven; the music speaks to him. He waits impatiently for the meal to be finished; why are they dragging it out like that—the play is going to start on television! Well may you say that with the television and the radio we're making progress; in my day we didn't have such distractions. . . .

Yankel trots along the ridge road. Now, three years after Edwige's marriage, Agnes gets married. That's life! A good marriage, let me tell you; Simon didn't care what it cost. Simon's hard; but for Agnes —he's crazier about her than about his own daughter. What's the groom's name, now? Chazeaux, Cheysan, something like that, a goy, naturally, the son of that brick house down there. It seems that he's some sort of cousin to Monsieur Touquet, and to Jacqueline, too. I don't understand any of their relationships; around here, they're all cousins. Edwige also married a Touquet, but his name is really Touquet, the mayor's grandnephew. Is this Monsieur Touquet everywhere?

"Good morning, Madame Déniché, where is the little nanny goat?

At the buck, you say? So, if it's like that, she'll soon have some fine little kids?"

"Tell me, Monsieur Mica, why does that interest you so much? You must be very sentimental. I suppose you're often bored, without a wife?"

"Oh, Madame Déniché, at my age, you know . . ."

"You? You're so lively, I wouldn't trust myself with you!"

"Oh, Madame Déniché, at seventy-seven?"

"Well, I'm sixty-three, and I often dream of my man!"

"Oh, Madame Déniché, how can you talk like that!"

"So? Old people like us can speak freely, can't we? If you started to play the young man with me, Monsieur Mica, I'm not sure what would happen!"

"Oh, Madame Déniché . . ."

Yankel, all stirred up, trots along the ridge road. Pfeh! At my age, it wouldn't be nice. Not nice? What's so ugly about it? Yes, of course, if Madame Déniché were a young woman! But she's almost my age! So? Papa also found a wife when he was old. Right now, I think it would be platonic, but who knows? . . .

"So, Papa, how's your flirtation going?"

"Pfeh, Simon, to talk like that to your old father . . ."

"Oh, go on, Papa!"

I don't know what's been wrong with Simon for the last few years; he's grown hard. Maybe it's his health? That boy isn't well, I tell you; one day it's sinusitis, the next day his liver, he hasn't a hair on his head, and he's as fat as a slug. Me, I've never set foot in a doctor's office; I still have my hair, and I don't look like an overstuffed sofa cushion. If he only took a little exercise; at his age, pfeh! always in the armchair, and the car if he has to go fifty yards. Even the garden; I'm the one who takes care of it now, he hasn't the time. . . .

And Yankel trots, trots, from Four Winds to the cemetery, and from the cemetery to Four Winds.

"Bang! Biff! Boff! Ch-ch-ch! I got yuh!"

How cute they are, these children playing soldiers among the graves! Of course, a cemetery is a cemetery; but a child is a child! You can't expect them to understand grownup affairs. Go, play as much as you want on the land of the dead, my dears!

"What do you want, sweetheart? Can Patrick come to play with you? I think so, but he must ask his mother, no?"

377

Patrick's mother is Edwige. Oh yes, time passes, I tell you, and the children, they push us old ones to the tomb . . . Patrick is five years old! Patrick Touquet—it's strange when you think of it; my great-grandson's name is Touquet, with Mykhanowitzki and Saulnier inside. And here am I, three times a great-grandfather, since Edwige has a dainty little Giselle and Agnes has just had her little Alain. Perhaps Pierre, too, will get married, now that he has his position as an agronomist. That's a real profession, agronomist; not like being in a business. Simon absolutely insisted that his son come into the business, it made him ill when the little one refused. Tchch! Simon is hard; I don't know what's been wrong with him the last few years. . . . Oh, of course I understand; he wonders who'll get the business after him. That's human! Only, the little one is free to arrange his life just as he wants to! Jacqueline quarreled with Simon over this, and she was right, although she's always on her son's side. Well, that's life.

I often wonder what my father would think if he saw us all today. So many children born of his loins and dispersed everywhere over the vast world. Peretz . . . All right, let's forget Peretz; I don't know what became of him. Maybe he has children and grandchildren, too. But Rachel, with all her Silverstones? She must be an old woman now. Sometimes she writes to me, talking about this one and that one, as though I knew them. I don't know her family! Are there any Feinschneiders left in the depths of that great Russian darkness? And what has become of Itcha's little girl? Ah, those are unpleasant questions! The true Mykhanowitzkis are here, in France; the ones I know. Moishe's and mine, and there you are! That's still a lot of people. The lady doctor, the violinist, the minister, the jeweler—yes, one of Moishe's sons took over the store. Now the violinist runs all over the world, and the minister lives in some hamlet in the Juras, and from time to time we receive announcements from one or the other, but we really don't know them. What do you want, it's far away! I'm beginning to lose track of my own children. Clara doesn't let me know that she's alive, and even Fernand . . . I don't know, he's a strange one; he had his children after he came home from Germany—couldn't he have had them sooner? All the same, he's no longer young. . . . Oh, I'm beginning to get tired of people! Stay in my corner and wait for death, that's all!

Sometimes the old man takes the telephone directory and peruses it carefully.

378

"Are you memorizing it?" Simon asks. "Do you want to call your girl friend?"

Simon is stupid; he doesn't understand anything. He only nows how to laugh like an idiot. But Yankel doesn't answer him. Yankel doesn't hear him. Yankel is reading . . .

MYKHANOWITZKI, GUY, jeweler

DR. MYKHANOWITZKI-DUBREUIL, senior resident in the Paris hospitals

MIKHANOWITZKI, JOSEPH, gabardines of all kinds . . .

Well, now, who's this one? Certainly a relative, in spite of the difference in spelling. Maybe one of Papa's nephews?

"Simon, do you know this one?"

No, Simon doesn't know him. All he knows is SIJAC, ladies' hats (three lines). . . . How many other Mykhanowitzkis are hidden in the telephone directory under their firm names? And the women under their husbands' names . . . I wonder, has Nathan Meltchik a telephone? No, he hasn't. Maybe he lives out of town. Yankel hasn't those directories at hand. If he had, he would consult the one for Doubs, to find

MYKHANOWITZKI, JENÉ, minister.

Yankel has the directories only for Paris and Seine-et-Oise. So he takes the one for Seine-et-Oise . . . VA . . . VE . . . VI . . . VIRELAY, there it is . . .

M AND MME MYKHANOWITZKI, Four Winds . . .

That's us! Number 505. Now we also have to find the TOUQUETS. No, not Paul Touquet, he's the mayor . . . and the CHEYSANS . . . What? There's a General Cheysan? Hu-uh! Yankel didn't know that his granddaughter had married into a general's family, and he is greatly moved by the discovery. . . . And the Saulniers? He has never thought of looking up the Saulniers. After all, they're cousins too, aren't they? He goes back to the Paris directory and recoils in surprise; there are almost as many Saulniers as there are Levys, and how can he find the ones he's looking for? He muses for a long time, a long time, on the two directories. Yes, we've been well stirred together! he thinks vaguely. . . .

With little steps, he trots along the ridge road. What are those workmen doing there? Yankel talks to them for a while. They're

379

Arabs, but he hasn't any prejudices; you can't blame all the Arabs for the war in Palestine, can you? And to them, he's a real Frenchman. . . . Oh? They're widening the road? *Oooy, veh iss mir,* now there'll be trucks using it, and I won't be able to walk in peace. . . .

"Good morning, Madame Déniché. Are you pruning your vines already? I haven't even started on mine . . ." For Yankel has become an adept agriculturist. Oh, yes, that's the way our Yankel is! Since he can't be a capmaker any more, he's busy with the garden. Sometimes he discusses technical questions with Simon, who knows a little about it; in fact, they have hardly any other subject for conversation. When, at times, Pierre comes to the house, the three of them talk horticulture. Often, while Yankel is out for his walk on the ridge road, he is assailed by frightful remorse: Shouldn't he be at work in the garden? Shouldn't he be doing his duty in the good sunlight, instead of strutting around like one of the idle rich? Pfeh, Yankel, you're growing lazy in your old age! Aren't you ashamed? He looks at his hands, the callused palms, the fingers grimy with encrusted soil. No, Yankel isn't ashamed. These are the hands of a worker, the hands of a peasant; Yankel feels that he is the brother of the *kibbutzniks,* down there in Israel. . . .

Well! Here is Mme. Déniché beginning her teasing again. And, since it's spring, since the sun is bright, since the air is soft, Yankel replies gallantly.

"Ah, Madame Déniché, watch out. You'll push me too far, and then, look out!"

Mme. Déniché is still an attractive woman, if you look closely.

She shrugs her shoulders. "You?" she cries. "Strong in the tongue, that's what you are, but that's all; you couldn't hurt a fly!"

She's trying to ensnare him through his self-respect, of course; Yankel understands her perfectly. He's not stupid! Still, he feels humiliated—and tempted. After all, where would be the harm? He has known only one woman in his whole life. Should he die without having tasted another? And a *goya,* an Aryan—perhaps she's different from a Jewish woman? After all, he's free, adult, he owes nothing to anyone, not even to Simon. And you live only once. So?

"Tomorrow, tomorrow, you'll see, Madame Déniché, I'll take you at your word!" Jokingly, he threatens her with his finger, and he goes off with a smile and a heavy heart. Mme. Déniché still has many attractions, and she is very friendly. A little vulgar, of course, but who is without faults? So? Why shouldn't he give himself a good time before he dies? Is he afraid of others? Of himself? Of cheapening himself?

He trots along the ridge road. I don't know what's been wrong with Simon the last few years; I don't understand that boy any more; he's changed. He's just sold his Vedette and bought a Citroën. A Citroën, pfeh! Rrrrroum, rrrroum! Too much power! It starts with a jump, it stops dead, and grrr, the brake, and rrrron, the accelerator, and you're all shaken up inside. Me, I liked the Vedette better, you sat in it as if you were in an armchair, you rode smoothly, like a human being! So why did Simon change his car? I know what I'm talking about—that boy is a bit of a snob!

"Good morning, Madame Déniché . . ."

"Good morning, good morning . . ."

I don't know what's been wrong with Madame Déniché for these last few years; she sticks in my throat. Surely she doesn't take our joking seriously? Pfeh, at our age! Man is a stupid animal. . . . How much do you get from these cherry trees, Monsieur Maréchal? Houou, as much as that? I don't know what's been wrong with my cherry trees, these last few years . . .

"Here is the news. The Sultan of Morocco . . ."

Pfeh! Who cares about the news? I have my garden, music, books. . . . "What do you want, Patrick? You want me to hear you recite your lesson? Well, give me your book, boy . . ."

The sky, a lake of pale gold, . . .

Hmmm, that's beautiful! Yankel gazed through the bay window at the pale-gold sky above the plain. Ordinarily he didn't like verse, or rather he wasn't able to read it because the premature break in the lines annoyed him. But this evening the child's clear voice separated the meaning from the form, and the meaning corresponded so closely to Yankel's own feeling that the old man had tears in his eyes.

The empty, silent, new cleansed air . . .

The great sad soul of the night . . .

Why, oh why wasn't I able to go to school and become educated? Tchch! The world is unjust. . . . "Is that all you have to recite, Patrick?" The boy has been at Simon's for three days now; Edwige is expecting her third child. "Don't you want to recite a little La Fon-

381

taine for me?" Patrick does it on the run, grudgingly; he's finished his work, he's in a hurry to go out and play. Go play, little one, go play. . . . Yankel is beginning to like La Fontaine a great deal.

According to your condition—powerful or poor—
The court's decisions will turn you white or black.

Tchch! That's very strong, you know! That man must have known life. After all, Tolstoy is a great spirit, to be sure, but he's a little—how shall I put it? A little simple about the facts of life! Always idealistic; unfortunately, there are others besides idealists on this earth! While La Fontaine—there's a truly intelligent man. . . .

Yankel trots along the ridge road. Happily, there aren't many autos passing here, so it's safe for walking. I wonder what Simon is waiting for before he takes us to the sea this year. Is it beginning to rain? Tchch, I don't know what's been wrong with Simon these last few years. The weather is fine—let's go right away! I like the sea, it's grand, immense. I'd like to end my days beside the sea, although I like Virelay, naturally, because of the garden. . . .

Dramatic autumn skies, backgrounds of clouds of so furious a gray that they become blue, buffeted by hot and cold winds . . . Yankel trots beside Sister Eugénie. She isn't dead yet, not she, the old nun, although she is older than her brother Baptiste. Yankel likes her very much, and she likes him too; they have long discussions about God and man. Yankel blusters, defending his atheistic pantheism, and she promises him Paradise, since God saves all good people, whatever their faith, but it would be much better if he would become a convert; so he tries to convert her to Judaism. When they have enough of that, they evoke the distant lands they know, Rakwomir and Madagascar, and even the Virelay of long ago, which is as far off as Madagascar. What a pity Sister Eugénie doesn't come more often! She is the only human being with whom Yankel can talk from the bottom of his heart.

Mostly, however, he trots alone. Autumn skies, winter skies, springtime skies—the Wheel of Time turns, turns, and the old man follows his road; the same old man, the same road. Below the Seine flows, always peaceful in its perfect arc. The hills trace their unchanging line on the horizon. But the forest is wounded. They're putting up a new building right in its heart, red and white like an ancient temple, but a modern factory—a factory without smoke! All the same, it's a factory, whose presence is enough to reveal what lies be-

382

hind, a deep slash of railroad cutting the forest in two for its entire length.

The great ground swells of history roll over the countryside. The city grows, too powerful for a nation grown too small, a capital city great enough for a continent. At night, the paths of its lights encircle the dark forest; lights do sentry duty all along the periphery of the basin. They seed themselves little by little along the claws of the pincers, depending on the distance from the city; but, exactly at the opposite end, they are again brutally concentrated; an industrial center has sprouted there, grafted on an old hamlet. In the exact middle of the forest, splitting the heart of the night, the lights of the new factory are sparkling.

Men, men everywhere, men coming from everywhere, men whom the city stirs together, melts, and assimilates before hurling them forth on all the roads of the earth. These are new, regenerated people, who hear the call of tomorrow's world and aspire to greater equality; and, even now, under their thrust, the walls of the old nation are cracking.

Yankel Mykhanowitzki is trotting along the ridge road. He is of no age, he has passed the age of dying. One step, and another step, on the road. And another step. Why stop here, rather than there? Why die today rather than tomorrow? Life is good, no? So?